# HOME FROM THE MOVIES

For the first time Monica was able to see the man's face and immediately she recognized him as the kid from the theater.

"Lenny? What happened? Why am I here?"

"I brought you home."

Her eyes circled the room. "Home? This isn't my home. Why are my hands and feet tied?" She gestured to the ropes.

Monica tried desperately to figure out what was happening? She strained her mind to remember; she knew she must appease him. "Please untie me. I promise I won't do anything."

"That depends." His face swam before her eyes. She fought to keep it in focus.

"On what?" She swallowed twice and counted slowly to five, forcing herself to maintain some remnant of composure.

"On whether you earn it or not. . . ."

# MATINEE

*M.L. Salerno*

# MATINEE

## Sally Kemp

AN ONYX BOOK

ONYX
Published by the Penguin Group
Penguin Books USA Inc., 375 Hudson Street,
New York, New York 10014, U.S.A.
Penguin Books Ltd, 27 Wrights Lane,
London W8 5TZ, England
Penguin Books Australia Ltd, Ringwood,
Victoria, Australia
Penguin Books Canada Ltd, 10 Alcorn Avenue,
Toronto, Ontario, Canada M4V 3B2
Penguin Books (N.Z.) Ltd, 182–190 Wairau Road,
Auckland 10, New Zealand

Penguin Books Ltd, Registered Offices:
Harmondsworth, Middlesex, England

First published by Onyx, an imprint of Dutton Signet,
a division of Penguin Books USA Inc.

First Printing, March, 1997
10  9  8  7  6  5  4  3  2  1

PUBLISHER'S NOTE
This is a work of fiction. Names, characters, places, and incidents either are the
product of the author's imagination, or are used fictitiously, and any resemblance to
actual persons, living or dead, events, or locales is entirely coincidental.

To Don Harper
. . . for all the right reasons

# ACKNOWLEDGMENTS

My thanks to Tom Colgan and Barbara Wedgwood, two teachers and writers who nurtured my lifelong joy of writing; and to my writer's group, the Wedgwardians: Kate Bower, Don Harper, Jean Sudderth, Chris Molsen, Don Goldman, Barbara Miercort, Alice Shepperd, Sid Harris, and Margaret Richards, who offer constant support and encouragement, and who faithfully read and critiqued every chapter of the story. In addition, I'm indebted to Det. Randy Penn of the Dallas Police Department, and to Kevin Fox and Jim Curry for their time and technical assistance.

I'd also like to thank three incredibly talented people—Angela Rinaldi, my agent, for her unfailing support, and Hilary Ross and Jerry Gross for their editorial assistance.

Finally, my love and gratitude to Jim and our son, Jon David, who always believed I could write a book and get it published, even on the days when I never thought it would happen.

# chapter

# 1

Monica Foyles was naked except for a faded blue head-band and a pair of her husband's crew socks. Sweat poured from her body as she pumped and pushed herself through the last few minutes of her ten-mile ride aboard the bike in her bathroom. She picked up the cellular phone beside her, hoping its ring did not awaken the rest of her family.

"Sorry for calling so early, Monica, but how about sneaking over to Frenchie's and grabbing an almond croissant before the kids get up?"

"Nancy, I . . . I . . . can't," she said, panting heavily.

"What are you doing? You sound like an obscene phone call."

"I'm riding my exercise bike."

"At six-thirty in the morning?" Nancy could picture her trim friend, all red hair and long legs, pumping away on her bike. "You've probably put in five miles already."

"Yep."

"Did I ever tell you how much I hate regimented people?"

"No." Monica grinned.

"Well, I do, and the morning ones like you are the worst kind. Excuse me, but my cheese Danish is waiting."

"What happened to the almond croissant?"

"I'll probably have both, thanks to you."

"I love you, too, Nancy."

"Yeah, talk to you later, kid."

Monica laughed and hung up the phone. Nancy Crawford was her first Texas friend. They had met a year ago at a junior high school baseball game shortly after Monica and her husband, John, moved to Dallas. It had been a warm spring day, and the score was tied. In his excitement, Joey, the youngest of Nancy's five children, accidently knocked Monica's unzipped handbag off the bleachers and onto the ground beneath the stands.

Nancy left the guilty three-year-old in his older sister's care, and scrambled under the seats to help Monica retrieve her things. Seconds later, Nancy's purse met the same fate. A lasting friendship between the two women began as they sat laughing in the dirt, sorting through each other's credit cards, keys, and pocketbook paraphernalia.

The timer bell on her bike chimed, but Monica continued her exercise. Four mornings a week she pedaled alone, sweating, swearing, hating every second of it in order to earn her personal rewards: a size-eight body and a Wednesday matinee. That weekday afternoon was the oasis she carved out for herself amid juggling the needs of a husband, a home, three children, and a part-time job.

On this particular Wednesday morning, Monica slid off her bike, and threw the towel she had been sitting on to the terrazzo floor. Peach Pie, her golden retriever, lay in his favorite alcove beneath her built-in vanity. Sunshine streaming through the window and across his head failed to interrupt his slumber. With her husband gone on a business trip and her children asleep upstairs, Peach was her only companion this early morning.

Monica mopped up the puddles of sweat, working the sodden towel around his paws, shaking her tousled curls in amusement at the dog's sleepy indifference. She felt light-headed when she stood and leaned on the basin.

"Ohmigod," she said to the mirror, "you look like hell!

No, on second thought, you look worse, you look your age . . . every single minute of your forty-four years."

She grabbed a clean towel from the brass rack and blotted the perspiration from her face. Ignoring the rivulets of sweat running between her breasts, she tugged off the socks and headband while examining her reflection.

What was happening to her chin? She studied her neck. No sag yet, but there were four more new lines around her mouth.

"You should have gone to Frenchie's with Nancy," she told herself. "The croissant might have done you more good than the exercise."

She turned her backside to the mirror. "But look at those buns! What a tush—not an extra ounce of flab and tighter than a twenty-year-old's."

Giving her rump a smug smile, she wiggled her hips and stepped into the shower. She laughed at her foolishness, ignoring the tiny voice inside that asked that if she looked so good, why did her husband fail to find her bottom, or for that matter, any part of her anatomy, attractive anymore?

An hour later, dressed in navy blue linen shorts and a matching camp shirt, Monica passed out lunch boxes, double-checked that everyone had the necessary homework, and waved good-bye to the children as they left for school. She never worked on Wednesdays, the day her twelve-year-old son, Jeb, practiced baseball after school and her nine-year-old twins, Mia and Sarah, went to Girl Scouts until five-thirty. She never cooked dinner on Wednesdays either. John, a regional portfolio manager for a corporate insurance company, traveled Tuesdays through Thursdays. Because he strenuously watched his diet, she and the children went out for pizza, Mexican food, or burgers when he was traveling.

In the kitchen, she pulled the movie section from the morning paper. She scanned the eight choices at Town Park Eight, automatically rejecting the romantic films in favor of the thrillers, feeling a little guilty for loving the films she would never allow her children to see.

Her fascination with the unconventional had begun in grade school, when she spent hours reading children's mysteries. Later she graduated to horror and science fiction. Her campfire stories, although popular with the other kids, had always been bizarre. By the time she was twelve years old, she had seen more Alfred Hitchcock movies than she had seen cartoons. Halloween was still her favorite holiday.

Monica concentrated on the time listings for Town Park. After several minutes she narrowed her choices to two thrillers. By checking the schedules, she found that she could see both movies today if she skipped lunch.

The features were at eleven-thirty and two-thirty. She would even have a convenient break for a fresh box of popcorn. With a little luck in the traffic, she would be home at five o'clock, thirty minutes before the kids, in plenty of time to take Peach Pie for his daily walk. Perfect!

The voluptuous woman in the large movie poster laughed down at him, her green eyes enticing him to find her alluring, even as her cheek rested on another man's well-muscled bicep. Lenny Bruns hated green eyes and his first urge was to smash the protective glass and rip the poster from its case on the wall. He raised his fist, but before he landed the first blow, her eyes caught him again. Despite his abhorrence, there was a lingering attraction he could not ignore. Their depths held excitement, but they predicted death. His . . . ? Or someone else's? He glanced away, and then, compelled, he lowered his lips to hers. Expecting warmth, the chill of the glass shocked him and he straightened immediately. The seduction in her eyes turned to mockery. He picked up the glass cleaner he had dropped and soaked her image with its spray, turned sharply, and strode back to the concession stand.

"You, uh, you okay?"

Lenny focused on Kyle Williams, a recently hired employee at the theater, who had taken a break from filling the popper with corn. Lenny knew the kid's college classes allowed him to work odd hours, and so he was here on the matinee shifts as well as some evenings.

"Yeah. When you're done there, you can refill the ice bins." Lenny opened a lower cabinet and stowed the glass cleaner and rag on a shelf. He stood up and saw that Kyle was still watching him. Lenny ignored him. Instead his mind drifted back to the movie poster and the green-eyed woman.

His mother had had green eyes. She was dead now, but the memory of her cat's eyes remained. Those eyes had forced him to quit school and forfeit everything. For him there would be no high school diploma, no college, no career. She had asked him to work for his Uncle Phil, whom he hated, but he had acquiesced, as he had done all his life.

At home, she demanded obedience and adoration. He gave both without question. She made sure he had no friends and no skills; for was she not his salvation, his only defense against the world? She told him these things often enough, screaming at him when he was a child; later whispering in her husky voice when he awoke to find her lying beside him, petting him, stroking his arm or playing with the curve of his ear.

He was left alone one year ago, but his mother's eyes remained . . . to taunt, to laugh at him whenever the Devil took his hand and forced him to do unclean things to his body. So often since she left him, he had needed that release, but how he hated the green eyes that watched him writhe in the sweet spilling of his manhood.

A fender bender on the access road at Central and Park Lane had cost her ten minutes, but Monica pushed open the theater's glass double doors at eleven-twenty. The young man at the cashier's station was surprised by her request.

"You're seeing two movies today?"

"Yes, *Treacherous Dawn* and *Death by Invitation*."

"By yourself?"

"Is that unusual?" Monica handed him the money.

"You're a brave lady," he said, smiling. "Those are real scary shows."

"Then I'm sure I'll love them!"

She gave her tickets to the attendant and waited while he scrutinized them before tearing them in half. When she stepped onto the red carpet, the tantalizing aromas of buttered popcorn and grilling hot dogs welcomed her like old friends.

Since she was old enough to climb into the padded seats, Monica had loved going to the movies. Matinees had been a special part of her growing-up years. Still, she felt uneasy about her fascination with the afternoon shows. Were there more important things she should be doing with her time? Perhaps. For this reason, she never asked anyone to accompany her. Besides, most of her friends worked full-time.

John had his own ideas about the movies. Motion pictures were just one of several passions they did not share.

"Why should I sit in a theater with a bunch of strangers, paying good money for something I can watch for free from my living room couch in a few months?" he asked her.

She remembered one rainy Saturday afternoon when she had rediscovered the pleasure of going to a matinee. The children had been with friends, and she and John were at home. He was in his den, catching up on some desk work.

"John, it's a dreary day. Why don't we do something different for a change?"

"Like what?"

"How about a movie?" She tried to clear a corner of his

desk to perch on, but the open notebooks, and stacks of well-ordered papers stopped her.

"In the daytime? You're not serious." His eyes never left the column of figures he was double-checking against an identical list on his computer screen.

"It might be fun. When was the last time you spent the afternoon at the movies?"

She leaned over his back and wrapped her arms around him. He was wearing a fuzzy blue sweater, one that she especially liked, and she buried her face in its soft nap.

"Monica, matinees are an even bigger waste of time than evening shows."

"C'mon, John. You usually spend all your free time at the country club playing golf. If you don't want to go to the movies, how about we"—she turned his head and kissed him—"Let's take advantage of the empty house and . . ." She kissed him again.

"Monica, I need to finish this report." He stood up and put his hands on her shoulders. "Choose a nice restaurant and I'll take you out to dinner. Until then, why don't you go to the mall for a few hours? Buy yourself a new watch or something. God knows you don't have to keep that tacky Mickey Mouse watch anymore." He glanced at his own timepiece, an expensive gold watch he had bought himself, just after their move to Texas.

She had started to reply, but realized all further discussion was useless. Grabbing her coat and handbag, she had gone to the movies alone. It was more fun than she had expected, and she decided to go often. She never told John how she spent her Wednesday afternoons. Her matinee attendance highlighted a widening chasm in their marriage she was not yet able to acknowledge.

Shelving the self-reproach, reminding herself how she had earned this treat with her honest sweat, Monica walked to the refreshment stand. She loved its sounds almost as much as its scents: popping corn, ice cubes clattering down into plastic-coated cups before the whoosh of soda covered them, the sizzling grease spitting out of hot dogs as they rode their chrome-spoked Ferris wheel, even the delicious rattles inside the candy boxes that were slapped onto the counter and grabbed by eager hands.

She felt at home here, secure and happy, and more than a little daring because no one knew she had sneaked away for a while.

"May I help you, ma'am?"

Monica looked up from the Milk Duds she had been studying and smiled at the tall, good-looking boy behind the counter.

"Hi, Lenny," she said, not needing his nametag to remind her of his name. He was here on most Wednesdays. "You look great today! I bet the girls really go for you in that uniform." She gave him another smile as she looked him over.

The boy's cheeks reddened, and his fingers gripped the counter. "Thanks," he replied, staring at the heart-shaped locket she wore.

Unable to curb her playful flirtation, she placed her hand over his. "Lenny, be a sweetheart and get me a large popcorn and a medium diet cola."

Lenny stared at their hands and stammered, "N-no butter, right?"

"Hey, you remembered! Yeah, you can skip that. I'm seeing two shows today. I'll probably spend the extra calories later on some chocolate."

For a moment he leaned closer to her. "I'd recommend *Treacherous Dawn* in number four. I saw it yesterday."

"Good! I'm seeing that one first."

She watched him fill the large popcorn tub to over-flowing. He slid it toward her and at the same time pulled up a cup for her drink.

"Easy on the ice?"

"That's right! They should pay you extra for that great memory of yours!"

The boy blushed again, offering her a shy grin as he returned her change.

As she had before, Monica felt the boy was a little too intense and wondered for a moment what it was about him that made her a bit uneasy. The way he had leaned toward her? She had actually felt his breath on her face. She shrugged off the thought. After all he was just a kid. Maybe he was even a bit taken with her. Monica was glad, if a little guilty, and grateful that someone that young found her attractive. Giving him a saucy wink, she picked up her food and moved away from the counter. Only a few people were standing in the concession line, but she did not want Lenny to get into trouble for talking to her too much. Besides, it was show time.

She walked down the carpeted hallway, looking at signs overhead until she found the auditorium where the first of her choices was being shown. Dreamy instrumental music, the kind she and her boyfriends had necked to in high school, filled the large, dimly lit room. A movie star trivia game was flashing its questions across the wide screen.

She took a seat about halfway down on the left side. There were plenty to choose from. Rows and rows of deeply cushioned, gray velvet chairs stood empty.

*Looks like I have the place to myself again.*

She remembered the many matinees she had sat through alone, or with only one or two people in the auditorium. So much for Lenny's recommendation. . . .

Lenny took his lunch break at two. Finally he could escape the hideous smells of bursting corn and roasting tubes of pork and beef, the endless procession of fatuous, idle people, *hoi polloi* who had nothing better to do with their lives than to pay his uncle's exorbitant prices and waste several hours hunched down in the darkness. They were all frivolous people, especially the one who came every Wednesday, the one with the valentine locket and the evil green eyes. . . . No, . . . the beautiful green eyes like his mother's.

He had awaited this month with dread; the first anniversary of her death. He now called the day she left his Emerald Jubilee. Several weeks ago, he had seen a movie with that title, and he remembered it, knowing that it suited.

As he sat alone in the second-floor break room, unwrapping his sandwich, he thought about the day she went away, and the promise her eyes had extracted from him. Unlike this sunny day, that morning had pulsated with thunder and pounding rain.

He could still envision her body lying on the faded coverlet in the small room lit by a single lamp. Even the rosy warmth that came from the fringed scarf that she, in better days, had draped across the shade, could not soften the death mask creeping across her face. Only her green eyes remained alert, forcing him to bend closer to the twisted mouth, a reminder of the massive stroke that had ripped through her the evening before. How much time had passed? Sometimes it seemed as if she had left him a lifetime ago.

"Come with me," the lips had whispered harshly. "I need you. You won't be safe here. You must . . . obey."

She motioned with her eyes to the bedside table where she kept the gun. Somehow she must have perceived the shock and fear that rioted through him at her order. The eyes screamed their displeasure at his cowardice, and the feeble fingers he had been holding suddenly dug into his skin.

"Very well, for a while," the gnarled lips continued, "but you must come when I call you. You belong to me! Promise you'll come to me then. Kiss me now. Kiss me!"

And he had. When he lifted his head, he had promised. Moments later, she was gone.

"No. No, Mother. Come back! Come back to me!"

"Geez, Lenny. You knocked over your damned soda!

It's all over the table!" Kyle put down his box of popcorn and grabbed a stack of napkins from the dispenser. "Who were you talking to, anyway?"

Lenny stuffed the remains of his lunch into his sack and stood up. "Why are you up here? It's not time for you to be on break."

"Yes, it is. It's almost three." Kyle mopped up the worst of the spill since it appeared that Lenny wasn't going to and threw the soggy napkins in the trash. Lenny's back was to him. Kyle had to strain to hear Lenny's reply.

"Next time stay on the job until I relieve you." Without looking at Kyle, he left the room.

*Dammit! I never get any peace around here. I still have ten more minutes before my break is over. If Uncle Phil finds me in here he'll insist I get back to work.*

He felt he deserved his full break. Since early that morning he had been unpacking the new features and threading the platter trees, the three-tiered, stainless-steel, round trays that looked like giant lazy Susans which held the films during projection. The trees were much easier to handle than the reel-to-reel and carbon arc projectors his uncle used to have. He supposed he should be grateful his uncle had made him an assistant manager. The old man allowed only his assistants the plum job of working in the film room, but for him, the title just meant putting in more hours on every phase of the business with no raise in pay.

Two girls who worked the box office interrupted his thoughts as they passed him on the steps to the break room. Their chatter irritated him. Ignoring their friendly nods, he moved past them in silence. He still had time to check on the woman with the green eyes.

Downstairs, the theater's design reminded him of a large red spider, whose undulating carpet-covered legs sprawled out in ordered precision. He knew which of the legs the green eyes had followed. He always made a point of knowing exactly where she was. It was a game to him, but unlike the scenario of his own life, this was one in which he made all the rules.

He remembered the first time he had seen her. It had been raining and he had been morose, reliving the day Mother had left as he was wont to do on stormy days. He had been working the concessions, when suddenly he had seen Mother's eyes, a vision which appeared frequently, but this time they were smiling at him as they rarely had before. Since then he had waited for them. Wednesdays had become his favorite day of the week.

Monica gripped the velvet seat, watching in horror as the victim, lost his life to the assailant's knife. It was the final atrocity in her second matinee. Snow was falling gently, covering the man's contorted face as an achingly familiar Christmas hymn brought the bloody scene to a close. Beautifully scripted ending credits rolled up over the broken body that lay dying in the nameless back alley in Chicago.

Stunned, yet exhilarated by the ghastly show with its surprise ending, Monica was unable to move. Theater magic had woven itself through her psyche and held her fast. Once again she felt the mesmerizing power of the big screen.

Too quickly the house lights broke the spell. Time for reentry into the real world. She sighed and stood, rescued her handbag from the squashing folds of the seat beside hers, and started up the aisle, twisting an empty candy wrapper with her fingers. During the break between films, she had been unable to resist the chocolatey confection. She noticed that more people had attended the second show, but the group leaving the theater with her still numbered less than ten.

She nodded to the employee standing at the back and dutifully threw her trash into the large plastic can by his side. Avoiding the lobby and its crowds awaiting the popular five o'clock shows, she slipped down a side hallway and left the theater by an unmarked door that led to a rear parking lot. She had discovered this exit by accident a few weeks ago, and had used it ever since. The acrid smell from the Dumpsters was unpleasant as she walked past the parked cars, most of which were probably employee owned. Sliding into her new Volvo station wagon, she congratulated herself again on the secret way out. By taking this route, she avoided the crowds and easily cut five minutes off her time getting home.

Traffic moved quickly on the way home and Monica was inside her garage by five o'clock, just as she had planned. Peach Pie, well rested from his naps, met her at the back door, wiggling his large, furry body.

"Hi ya, Peach!" she said, rubbing his ears. "Did you have a nice day? Are you ready for your walk?"

Peach Pie wagged his tail harder when he heard his favorite word, "walk." Monica threw her handbag on the table and went for his leash.

The day had grown cooler, and she slipped a new gray cashmere sweater over her shirt. After a short tussle, she was able to hook the leash onto the big dog's collar before he pulled her out the front door and down the sidewalk. She laughed and let him have his way, disregarding her husband's continual admonitions to make the dog heel and mind.

Their exclusive neighborhood was less than five years old, and consisted mainly of large, expensive houses on small lots. Few trees softened the harshness of the broad concrete streets and matching white pavements. Monica missed the towering hardwood trees and more modest homes that she had grown up with in the Northeast. She and John had been high school sweethearts, and had lived in their Connecticut hometown for the first six years of their marriage.

How she cherished those early memories! Their initial closeness had spawned an extraordinary intimacy that they had never managed to regain after the babies' arrivals. They had wanted children badly, a natural completion to their union, but she had been sick for so long after Jeb's birth that the joy of his coming was often shadowed by weakness and pain.

By the time the twins were born three years later, John's career had charged into high gear and their days overflowed with blurring activity. Their nights, once heartily relished, became brief respites to relieve the numbing exhaustion that constantly dragged at their lives.

Moving to Texas had put further strain on the marriage. Financially, their situation had improved greatly. Monica was still not used to their sudden wealth, yet the promotion shook them apart for three days every week—John's travels widening the breach between them.

Monica stopped to wave to an elderly couple who were working in their front flower garden. Ray and Betty Gibson had recently celebrated their golden wedding anniversary. Their children had given them a party, and John and Monica had attended.

"Hi, Monica," Ray said, moving to scratch Peach Pie's ears. "Beautiful day!"

"Hello, dear," Betty added.

"Hi! Looks like the Gibson roses are on their way to another great season!"

"Oh, yes, Betty knows just what they like. They'll be prettier this year than ever!"

"How's your job, Monica? Still enjoying the folks at school?" Betty asked, referring to Monica's part-time work as an office and teacher's aide at her daughters' elementary school. "Are you ready to have your own classroom again?"

"It's fine, and no, I like what I'm doing. I work with the children without having the responsibilities of a full-time teacher. And it allows me an inside track on the twins' activities."

"Were you there today?"

"No, Wednesday's my day off."

"Seen any good movies lately?" asked Ray. He was an avid fan of murder mysteries.

"As a matter of fact, I have! Don't miss the new Erick Hartely film at Town Park Eight."

"That just came on today, didn't it? Don't tell me you've already seen it?"

Monica nodded and smiled. Ray turned to his wife.

"Mother, let's do up these roses quickly. Then, how about if I take my best girl to the show?"

"You've got a deal." Betty smiled and took her husband's hand, flirting with him like a young girl on her first date. "You know, Monica, Ray and I are taking a little holiday. We're driving to Florida this weekend."

"That sounds wonderful. How long will you be gone?"

"We're not sure," Ray replied. "Two, maybe three weeks. We'll come home when we feel like it."

"Well, I hope you have a great time." Monica hugged them both and added, "Peach and I must be on our way now. You two take care and don't get sunburned."

"Thanks, dear. I know we'll have fun." Betty laughed. Ray just chuckled and waved.

She walked on, touched by their togetherness but a little envious of it, too. What kind of glue held a couple together for fifty years? "What keeps my marriage together, Peach? A mucilage of things like friends and parents, favorite recipes, *Sixty Minutes,* and Grandmother Foyles' silver tea set?"

Some days it appeared as if only the children and the dog kept them together. Other days, especially when they had taken the time to make love, it seemed like much more, at least to her.

As they neared the house, Peach Pie saw the children first, unloading themselves and their gear from Nancy

Crawford's van. Nancy, too, got out of the van and waited for Monica. Double-checking for cars, Monica unclipped Peach Pie's leash and watched him run to greet her son and daughters as they piled through the front door of the house.

"Well, I'm sure they meant to thank you," Monica said as she gave her friend a quick hug. "How're you doing?"

"Great! I'm even planning parties. Next Wednesday, in addition to Billy's birthday party in the evening, I'm hosting my book club for lunch. I know it's your day off, so why don't you plan to come?"

"I went with you the last time. Isn't there a limit on how many times you can have the same guest?"

"Yeah, but, what can they say? The party's at my house."

"No, I'd feel funny going again so soon, and besides I have an appointment with the vet. Peach is overdue for his shots and I have to use my day off to do things like that."

"Well, I'd certainly skip the book club ladies any day if I could spend the time with that sexy vet. David Riley makes my toes tingle!"

"Nancy!" Monica feigned shock, but was used to her friend's bluntness.

"Just calling them like I see them, but he's still a great doctor."

Monica agreed. A year ago when she had asked some friends about a veterinarian, David had been the hands down choice. Since then she found that he more than lived up to his star billing.

"Thanks for the invitation, though."

"You're welcome. Guess I need to roll on now. We have piano lessons at six." Nancy smiled at her friend and then squeezed her arm. "You okay?"

Monica nodded and looked away. "Yeah, I'm all right. Thanks for asking."

"We'll talk soon. Take care of yourself."

Monica watched Nancy pull away and went into the house. By the time she caught up with the children, they were in the kitchen. Jeb and Mia were fighting over the last of the graham crackers and Sarah was sharing her apple juice with Peach.

He assumed that she was home now. With little effort he could recall vividly the moments he had stood at the back of the theater watching her. During the second movie today he had even walked down into the rows of chairs and had taken a seat behind, and to the right of her. No one noticed him, or if they had, they showed little interest. He was always quiet and careful when he watched her, and he left before she became aware of him.

Today he had been close enough to see the light from the screen jiggle and bounce off her gold earrings and the smooth plane of her cheek. He watched her long, graceful fingers tuck an errant strand of her fiery hair behind her ear. The soft sighs, the sudden gasps of excitement she emitted during a particularly gory part of the movie, reminded him of the sounds Mother had made when they touched, and then went on to do the other things naked men and women do to each other. And when she opened her lips, he caught a brief glimpse of her tongue as she bit into her chocolate bar, and he shivered.

Once, her eyes had looked briefly to the right, and he felt scorched by their green fire. Sudden flames embraced him, the heat forcing him to clutch his groin. He felt unbearable pain as he left her and hurried to one of the storage closets.

"Oh, Mother!" he cried, sliding down to lean against the metal shelves that held large boxes of unpopped corn, salt, and containers of oil. "Are you really here? Do I need to die after all? Or have you come back to me?

"Mother, am I safe? Are you here?" he sobbed over and over as his hand moved faster and faster on his erection. Thinking of the woman in the theater made him larger, more powerful, than he had ever been with Mother. Disloyalty rocketed through him. He whimpered his guilt until self-loathing flooded his body and he climaxed into shame and loneliness.

# chapter
# 2

On Thursday evening, Jeb Foyles paused at his sisters' bedroom door on his way downstairs. "Mom?" he called. "Dad's home. I just heard the garage door open." Jeb's rangy, twelve-year-old body held the promise of his father's tall, masculine grace, and his hazel eyes often revealed a seriousness well beyond his age.

"Thanks, Jeb. I'll be right there." Monica smiled at him and laid the stack of sweatshirts and jeans she had pulled from the dryer minutes before on the twins' dresser. A maid came in once a week to do the housecleaning and most of the laundry, but she often did in-between loads of the children's favorite things. Taking a quick look in the mirror, she tucked in her shirttail and ran down the steps to meet her husband.

"Hi, John!" she said, giving him a hug.

"God, the traffic coming in from the airport was just awful. I'm dead on my feet." He shrugged out of her embrace, and gave her a quick kiss on the cheek before handing her his briefcase and sorting through the mail that lay on the kitchen counter. His dark suit and pristine white shirt gave no indication he had worked all day or that he had spent the last three hours on a crowded plane. He looked as if he had just finished a cover shoot for *GQ*.

"I hope the rest of your trip was better," she said, moving out of his way.

"Hey, Dad," Jeb said, "Billy Crawford is getting a new bike for his birthday. A Schwinn Racer! His party's next Wednesday night."

John looked up from a bill he was reading. "Son, you can't go to parties during the week. You know the rules." To Monica he said, "I hope you didn't tell him he could go."

"The children don't have school next Thursday and Friday. The teachers have two days of district inservice."

"Again? It seems like they have a holiday every other week. I guess since you're a teacher's aide, you'll have the two days off, too." He laughed and shook his head. "I wish I had a soft job like that!"

"Well, we didn't make up the schedule, did we, Jeb?" Monica said.

"No, and I think we spend enough time in school. Too much, if you ask me!"

"Okay, Jeb, sorry I jumped on you," John said, squeezing his son's shoulders. "I need to get all the details first, don't I? Where are your sisters and old Peach?"

"Mom sent them down the street to the Gibsons' house. They'll be back soon."

"The Gibsons'? Is everything all right?" he asked Monica, as he started toward the bedroom.

"They're fine. I made an extra pan of gingerbread. I thought they'd enjoy it."

"Right. When's dinner?"

"In about ten minutes."

"Make it twenty so that I can get out of these clothes and have a quick shower."

Peach Pie was dragging the twins through the back door just as John walked into the kitchen, his hair still wet from his shower. He had changed into a golf shirt and denim shorts. Monica set the casserole of scalloped potatoes and the steaming platter of broiled chicken on the table. Green beans, fresh fruit salad, and hot rolls would complete the meal.

"Daddy! Daddy!" yelled the twins. So alike in their petiteness, they shared neither facial appearance nor temperament. Mia could be as fiery as her long, braided red hair; while Sarah had the dreamy quality of a fairy-tale maiden with her dark curls and translucent skin. Both of them had inherited their mother's clear green eyes.

"How are my beautiful girls?" John asked. "Come and give your old man a double hug."

Mia and Sarah laughed and launched themselves at John. Double hugs had been a shared joke for as long as they could remember. Not to be left out, Peach Pie pressed his furry body against John and the girls, almost pushing them all to the floor.

Monica loved the numerous, easy displays of affection between her husband and the children. They adored each other. The business trips that took him out of town seemed to strengthen his relationship with the children, but the nights away only added to the strain of their marriage.

Feeling excluded, she turned back to the dinner. Except for that small peck on the cheek, which she had initiated, John had not touched her since he had walked in the door. Now, even the dog had abandoned her, torn between the happy trio catching up on the week's activities, and the tantalizing odors coming from the table.

"Girls, call Jeb and wash your hands. Dinner's ready," she said.

"So," John said, alone with his wife for the first time since he got home, "what's new? Did you take Jeb to the orthodontist?"

"His appointment is tomorrow after school. I think he'll probably need braces on his bottom teeth." Monica filled three glasses with milk and set them by the children's dinner plates.

"Soup for supper then. He'll have a sore mouth."

"I guess so. Will you be here tomorrow at the usual time? I have a meeting after school, and we've been warned that it will run late. I'm hoping you can be here for the kids."

"No, uh . . . I won't be home until late. Several of the Atlanta people are flying in tomorrow and I'll be entertaining them. What kind of school meeting do you have on a Friday night?"

"It's the Parent-Faculty Communication Committee. The year-round school issue goes to the school board next Tuesday and so they had to call a last minute prep meeting. Tomorrow is the only day that everyone can attend."

He lifted a roll from the basket and popped half of it into his mouth. "Guess you'll have to get a sitter. Sorry I can't help you out."

Monica said nothing and finished filling the water glasses. John carried them to the table. He pulled out his chair and sat down. Soon the children, all talking at once, raced into the kitchen and dropped into their chairs, Mia nearly spilling her milk.

As usual, the dinner conversation centered around the children's experiences, John's latest accomplishments, and the weekend plans. Both girls had soccer games on Saturday morning, and Jeb had a baseball game on Saturday afternoon. Jeb wanted to ask his friend Billy to sleep over tomorrow night since the girls had been invited to a birthday party.

"We'll be home by nine-thirty, Jeb," Sarah reminded him. "It's not like we get to spend the whole night out."

"I still want Billy to come over. May I ask him, Mom?"

She smiled at him. "I don't mind as long as you promise to go to sleep at a decent hour. You'll have a sitter for the first part of the evening, so have him come over around seven-thirty. I'll be home from my meeting by then. Is it okay with you, John?"

"Sure, son. Monica, these potatoes taste greasy. You

know you really should watch the fat. Try boiling them or
something next time."

Monica stiffened at his words.

"Tastes great to me," said Jeb. "I get really tired of that
boring, healthy stuff and those weird vegetables."

"It's nice someone appreciates my efforts, Jeb."
Monica reached over the table and rubbed his arm.
"How'd you like a special dessert for being so sweet to
your mom?"

"No fair!" Mia and Sarah yelled.

Later that evening, Monica tucked the children in for
the night. Nine o'clock was lights out for the twins, but
Jeb was allowed to read until ten. Earlier, they had lined
up by their father's recliner for their nightly hugs, but
Monica enjoyed overseeing the bedtime rituals. In the
girls' room, she dispensed kisses, pulled polka-dot draperies shut, and heard prayers. Even though Jeb insisted on
saying his prayers by himself, she stopped by his room for
a hug and a few quiet words after she had settled the girls.

When all the good nights had been said, she collected
some sewing from her closet shelf and went downstairs to
join her husband. The den was her favorite room in the
house. Bookshelves and built-in cabinets lined two walls
of the large but cozy room. A huge, fieldstone fireplace
occupied most of the third wall, and a collage of hundreds
of framed family pictures she had assembled covered the
fourth. Several Oriental rugs that had belonged to her
grandmother lay on the hardwood floor.

On the wide-screen TV, the score at the top of the sixth
inning was two to zero in favor of the Texas Rangers, but
John was fast asleep. She went to the kitchen and made a
cup of tea before returning to the den. Peach Pie curled up
by her feet as she hemmed a skirt and a new pair of
church pants for Jeb.

*Here I am, the picture-perfect mother, just as John
wants me to be,* she thought. *The kids are asleep, the
house is beautiful and well cared for, even the dog is*

*flawlessly groomed. We could be in a damned magazine. God, I feel so empty sometimes. Why doesn't he love me anymore? Is there someone else in his life?*

By eleven o'clock, like most of the nights he was home, John still had not moved from his chair. Monica put away her sewing and got ready for bed. She padded through the darkened house in her short, lacey nightgown, and let Peach Pie out for his last run. After feeding him a dog biscuit, she locked the doors. Then she checked on the children before going back to the den.

She turned off the TV and gently rubbed her husband's hand until he awoke. He yawned and stretched his long arms and legs.

"Who won?" he asked.

"Chalk up another one for the hometown boys." She smiled at his huge yawn and sleepy grin, thinking what a good-looking guy he was. His large, muscular body always excited her. "Ready for bed?" she whispered, touching his cheek.

John rubbed his eyes and lowered his chair from its reclining position. "I have some papers to look at before I turn in. Early morning meeting with Harrison and Jones. You go on. I'll be up in a while."

"John, can't the papers wait? You've had a long day," she said. She caught his hand and rubbed her fingers back and forth across his palm. "Come to bed with me."

"No, I'm okay. I really do need to read over a few things. I'll be up later."

"Sure, John. Go do your old work! So sorry I bothered you." She turned and marched toward the doorway. His voice stopped her.

"Please, Monica. Give me a break, here. It's been a tough day."

She returned to his chair and lowered her head. She looked into his eyes, hoping to see a glimmer of desire. Slowly she kissed his mouth.

She was in bed with the covers pulled up before she

allowed herself to acknowledge that he had not returned her kiss.

The following evening, Monica and David Riley were leaving the Parent-Faculty Communications Committee meeting at the children's school. David closed the door and turned to smile at Monica.

Just over six feet in height, David's slim torso belied his muscular strength. He viewed the world through tortoise-shell glasses that enhanced the warmth of his brown eyes. Sandy blond hair fell across his forehead, giving him a boyish look even though he was well past his fortieth birthday. His unmistakable sex appeal was compelling and Monica had felt it the first time they had met.

Monica knew he was divorced, and he knew she was not. His son, Colin, was Jeb's age. The boys were good friends and were on all the same athletic teams. In the past six months, Monica and David had become acquainted not only with the various bleachers in town, but with each other, too.

"That session ran a lot longer than I thought it would. What time is it, anyway?" David had asked Monica as he walked her to her car.

"Almost six. It took a while to get through that agenda."

David shifted a manila folder from one arm to the other. Chairing the Parent-Faculty Communications Committee consumed more time than he had been led to believe, but it was time well spent.

"How do you really feel about students going to school year round?" he asked, referring to the meeting's main topic of discussion.

"There are lots of positives, but families could end up with children on two different schedules."

"Ah, another fence sitter." He winked at her and took her arm protectively as a car passed in front of them.

"David, that's not true. It's too broad an issue to make general comparisons."

"What we need here is a happy medium." David's coat blew open in the chilly March breeze. Monica grabbed his red scarf as it slipped from his coat collar.

"Now who's sitting on the fence?" she asked, twirling the scarf between her fingers.

"I'm supposed to straddle it. I'm the chairman."

"Pulling rank on me, huh?"

"That'll be the day! Give me your keys. I'll unlock your car." He watched as she rummaged in her handbag. "Who's sitting with your children tonight?"

"Megan Brightly."

"I thought you weren't using her again. You said the kids didn't like her."

"Only because she's a taskmaster, a mother's dream come true. She makes them do their homework, and then insists on checking to see that it's complete before she lets them watch TV. She even cleans up the kitchen."

"So how'd you talk the kids into her tonight?" he asked, leaning against her car, reluctant to let her go. They had become instant and easy friends shortly after she had moved to Dallas the year before.

"Since I knew the meeting would run late tonight, I told them they could order pizza for dinner."

"Ah, yes. Bribery. I find it particularly effective, myself."

"I let them choose when their dad's not home for dinner."

David pushed his body away from the car. "He travels a lot, doesn't he?"

Monica watched the last of the cars leave the parking lot before she answered, "Yes, he's gone more than ever before."

David watched the light fade from her eyes when she spoke of John. He knew she was slipping inside herself and closing the door.

"I'm sorry," he said. He wanted to take her hand, to tell her that he understood, that he cared, that he would help her if he could, but he only smiled at her and repeated, "I'm really sorry."

"Yeah, so am I." She took a deep breath and nodded her head.

"My ex-wife traveled a lot. I suppose some marriages thrive on separations, but ours didn't. She was away so much that it was a continual adjustment for Colin and me when she came home, only to leave again in a few days. Our lives were in a state of constant flux."

"I understand how that can happen." She looked up at him. The street light bouncing off her bright hair failed to lift the shadows from her eyes. "I shouldn't complain. John's a good man. He works hard."

David wondered if she realized how unhappy she looked at this moment. "Sometimes it's rough, huh?"

She lowered her head and nodded. "Yeah, sometimes it's rough." She moved to get into her station wagon, tossed her handbag and binder onto the passenger seat, and pulled her unbuttoned coat around her. David's hand on her arm stopped her.

"Since your kids are probably up to their ears in pizza by now, would you consider taking another thirty minutes and having some supper with me? It's no big deal . . . a club sandwich and a cup of soup at Harry's? It's just around the corner. We could be in and out in no time."

Monica studied her shoes. He had issued similar invitations before and she had always refused.

"It's no big deal, I promise," he reiterated. "Just a casual meal between two hard-working volunteers who also happen to be hungry."

Monica smiled and swallowed the polite refusal that had come automatically to her mind. "I'd love to. Thanks for asking. You've saved me from a supper of cold pepperoni pizza with holes where the meat should be."

David cocked his head in question.

"The twins love pepperoni and Mia picks it off any left-over pizza. Sarah yells at her, but only because she wishes she'd done it first."

"Doesn't Jeb mind?"

"No, by the time it comes to that on Fridays, he's long gone. He never wants to risk the possibility of being roped into kitchen chores on his night off."

"Makes sense to me. So, I'll see you at Harry's in a few minutes, or I'll drive you if you like. You could leave your car here and pick it up afterward."

Monica laughed and locked her car. "You got a date!"

"All clear on the home front?" David asked minutes later as she returned from the phone in Harry's.

"Couldn't be better. Megan let them off without doing homework since it's Friday night, and the pizza's on its way. I need to have late meetings more often." She dropped into the red vinyl booth opposite David.

He picked up the laminated menus and handed one to Monica, happy that she had accepted his invitation at last. He had not enjoyed a woman's company as much in a very long time.

"How's my favorite golden retriever?"

Monica laughed and related Peach Pie's latest antic. Between ear infections and upset stomachs caused by eating everything from bars of soap to paper napkins, gummy spiders, and banana peels, Peach was a frequent patient of David's.

They moved on to discuss children, schools, favorite books, and rap music. In no time their sandwiches appeared, disappeared, and they were having a final cup of coffee.

"I'm glad you finally relented, and decided to have supper with me, Monica."

"I'm glad, too. I've enjoyed it." She glanced at her watch and looked up quickly.

"Thank you. And I know you have to go."

They paid for their sandwiches and went out to David's car. They reached the deserted school parking lot in minutes. By mutual but unspoken agreement, they sat in the car listening to the final strains of a bluesy saxophone solo.

"I like that music. Kenny G. is one of my favorites," she told him.

He popped the cassette, put it in its case, and handed it to her.

"I can't take your tape."

"Consider it a loan. I've been yakking so much since we left Harry's, that you haven't had a decent chance to listen to it."

"I promise I'll return it."

They left the car and walked to the driver's side of Monica's car.

"Want to wear your coat?" David asked. The night had turned mild and she had not bothered with it after dinner.

"Yes, I'll put it on now."

David helped her with her coat. She reached into her collar and lifted out her hair, fanning it onto her shoulders.

It had been the simplest of feminine gestures, something she must have done a thousand times. David would always wonder how he managed to ignore the powerful urge to bury his face in her silky curls and whisper her name.

# chapter
# 3

"Hey, kid!"

"Uncle Phil?"

"What're you doing locked in the storage room? Stealing a candy bar? Let me in!"

"Sure. I was just straightening up the boxes and stuff." He watched his uncle come through the door and make a mental check of the contents of the room. Satisfied that all was in place, the older man turned angrily and moved close to his nephew.

"You're not off 'till eleven tonight. You owe me another couple of hours. It's time to start hauling those trash bags away before the next show starts!" The tall man's limp gray hair fluttered down over his high forehead as he shook his head at the boy.

"Always sneaking off into the corners, aren't you? If you weren't my brother's kid, I'd kick your butt out of here!" Phil Bruns reached out and squeezed the boy's shoulder until he winced with pain. Then the pressure changed and Phil's touch became almost tender, circling his nephew's shoulders and running his fingers down the boy's spine.

"What do you do all alone in that house now? Huh? It's been a year, pretty boy," Phil whispered. "Do you miss—"

"What's with the people downstairs?" Lenny tried to back away.

"They're moving out this weekend. They gave me their notice two weeks ago." Phil cupped Lenny's rear. "You're too weird for them, kid, killing their cat like that."

"You can't prove that. It's not because of me they're moving out. What'd you do? Raise the rent again?"

He threw off the old man's hand and stepped back against the shelves, hatred for his uncle churning his insides. He said nothing aloud, only stared at the floor until Phil turned and walked out into the hallway.

When he was certain his uncle had gone upstairs, he left the storage room and grabbed two large plastic sacks of garbage that were propped in the hallway. He hauled them to the back of the building, and out through a door to the dark blue Dumpsters in the employee parking area.

He worked steadily until eleven, helping customers, hauling garbage, filling the ice bins, sweeping auditoriums, and checking supplies in the restrooms. Promptly at 11:05 p.m. his shift ended and he slipped through the rear door. Hoping his uncle would not follow him, he ran past the Dumpsters, and unlocked his mother's black '81 Pontiac Bonneville. Putting the car in gear, he careened out of the parking lot, thinking that except for Wednesdays when the green eyes appeared, the other days of the week were hell.

His apartment was in a two-story house in an older neighborhood about a forty-minute drive from the theater. If its builder had once had grandiose plans for the house, he must have run out of cash and imagination long before its completion. Sand-colored brick covered the walls of the first floor; white weatherboard, now yellowed and peeling, was on the second. The ground-floor apartment had its entrance through an elaborately arched brick portico, originally intended as a porch but the concrete had never been poured to cover its dirt floor. Tan window shades, pulled down, hung in dingy unison throughout the house.

An open flight of wooden stairs, more suited to a beach house, ran up the left side of the house, the only entrance to his second-floor apartment. No fence encircled the house, so he was able to park his car at the base of those steps.

The street was deserted when he got out of his car. He ran up the stairway, unlocked the door and went inside without being seen or having to speak to anyone. He closed the door, threw the two bolts, and attached the security chain before glancing around. It was a small place: kitchen-dinette, living room, two bedrooms, a miniscule bath, and an attic.

The rooms were dank and airless from having been closed all day. His mother had insisted that the heavy shades always be drawn. She said open windows attracted nosy neighbors. Since her death, the windows and blinds had remained closed.

He pulled off his vest and shirt—how he despised that uniform—and tossed them in the direction of a kitchen stool. The room was old-fashioned without being quaint. Along one of the dingy walls, large sections of yellow paint peeled from the cheap metal cabinets that hovered around an ancient refrigerator. Those cupboard areas still covered by the sickly mustard color were mottled with fingerprints and grime.

A deep porcelain sink with green stains under the leaking taps, and dirty dishes piled to a precarious height, sat beneath the only window in the room. On the opposite wall, a large gas stove held a jumble of grease-spattered pots and pans.

He moved to the dinette set with its chrome legs and red plastic laminate tabletop, and sat down on the cracked remnants of a padded seat. After dumping the Burger Delight cheeseburger and fries onto the table, he wolfed them down, barely tasting the food. Like so many things in his life now, eating was just another motion, necessary to stay alive. It brought him no enjoyment, no satisfaction.

While his mother lived, he had derived pleasure in the simple act of getting a meal together. Sometimes even Uncle Phil's regular appearance at the dinner table had been tolerable. As much as he resented his uncle and his hold over their lives, sitting down together to eat was the closest he ever came to experiencing the family life he had seen on TV.

Even if he had objected, his mother would have permitted no interference with this nightly routine. After all, Uncle Phil brought his checkbook and paid the bills. It had not mattered why the older man supported them, only that he did.

The dirty linoleum snapped and popped under the weight of his body as he crossed to the sink. He stuffed his trash into an already overflowing can, ignoring the bits that fell to the floor, just as he ignored the state of the kitchen and the rest of the apartment. These days dusting and sweeping, and chores of any kind, seemed like too much trouble. He rarely cooked anything now. At Uncle Phil's insistence, he was always working extra hours at the theater. It was easier to buy fast food.

Angry voices from the apartment underneath shattered the stillness. The Elliots were having another argument. They had lived below him for as long as he could remember. He did not know either of their first names, and was fairly sure they could not recall his. Beyond an occasional grunt of recognition at the mailboxes, they had never communicated. He would not miss them when they moved out this weekend.

He wandered back through the living room, flicking the small black-and-white TV on, and then off. The sagging upholstery on the faded furniture emitted stale odors of cigarette smoke and sweat. The matching overstuffed chair and sofa appeared to be huddled together on the worn wooden floor as though embarrassed by their shabby appearance. He imagined that he could still see the imprint of his mother's body in the dark gray cushions. The idea depressed him, and he found that he could not stay in the room a moment longer.

He fled to the musty-smelling bathroom and pulled off the rest of his clothes. The apartment's two floor fans, plus a small window air conditioner in his bedroom, struggled to keep the air moving in July, but even in March the rooms were stuffy. He showered and tried to dry off, but the humidity made it impossible for him to feel refreshed.

By midnight he was in bed, attempting to sleep. For lack of anything better to do, he concentrated on his most treasured possessions, his sixty-three pairs of women's gloves, hidden away in the attic above him. Tonight, just thinking about their beauty and variety lulled him to sleep. Some days they were all he lived for.

Green eyes woke him. He shot up from the pillow when he heard her calling his name.

"Mother?" he whispered.

Silence, broken only by the faint sound of the living room clock chiming three, answered him.

"Mother? Is that you?"

He slipped out of bed and went next door to her room. Dim light from the street lamps slanted across the coverlet of the carefully made bed. He glanced down at her pillow, then over to her daybed in the corner of the room. A pale pink crocheted afghan lay across the foot of the bed, and her paisley housecoat still rested on the arm of her chair as though she would soon rise to don it.

He moved to her dressing table and fingered through her toilet articles: the jars of makeup and powders, and flasks of perfume. He stopped to dab a bit of her favorite scent across his cheek, under his arm, and behind his knee, just as she had done so often.

The lid on an old cedar box next to her hairbrush and comb creaked when he lifted it. She had bought the box a long time ago, during a childhood trip to the Ozark Moun-

tains. It was perfect for her jewelry, she always said.
Carefully he pulled out bead necklaces, bracelets, and
dangling earrings. His mother had pierced ears; his were
not, but the necklaces felt cool and welcome on the bare
skin of his neck and chest. He locked the bracelets around
his wrists. They brought him weighty delight as they rose
and fell, curled and twisted with the movement of his
arms. Anxious to see himself arrayed in her finery, he
turned on the small bedside light and stooped to gaze at
himself in the oval mirror above the vanity.

"Look at me, Mother. Look at your lover!"

Feeling quite satisfied with his reflection, he walked to
her closet and opened the door. The beads of perspiration
that formed on his nude body sparkled in the lamplight,
and lent richness to his jewelry. The closet where his
mother's clothing hung was small, barely four feet across,
but he stood among the dresses, the old shirts and skirts,
the well-worn sweaters, with his arms outstretched, as if
greeting a friend feared lost forever. He breathed deeply,
inhaling the pungent odor of the musky, unwashed gar-
ments, moving his body back and forth across their folds.

"Mother . . . Mother . . . Mother . . . ," he panted, as he
swayed against her clothing.

Stepping back, he pulled out a blue crepe dress, a
favorite of hers, and ran his hands up and down the fabric
before hugging it to his body. He dropped to his knees,
lay the dress beside him, and surveyed her few pairs of
scuffed shoes on the closet floor. One by one he picked
them up, rubbed them across his lips, and replaced them
in exactly the same spot. He sat back on his heels and
looked toward the ceiling.

"Everything is here, just waiting for you to return." He
stood up on his tiptoes and slowly circled the room,
hoping she might see him.

He hoped for some sign, some acknowledgment that
she was aware and grateful for his faithfulness. Suddenly,
he felt tired, her jewelry pulling like dead weights upon

his body. Assuming he had been ignored again, feelings of frustration mixed with his exhaustion.

"Oh, Mother, what do you want me to do?"

The green eyes summoned him out of the room and toward the steps of the attic. Long ago he had decided that the only saving grace of the apartment was its small, shadowy, low-ceilinged garret, concealed beneath the roof. Because of his collection, the attic had always been his secret refuge. Unfortunately, it had also provided an easy place for punishment when his mother decided he had misbehaved. Other kids lost the use of their bikes for a week; he had been tied to the metal bed in the attic.

Now, he walked up the steps and into the room. Years before, in one of her meaner moments, his mother had painted the dormered windows black, but he was used to the darkness and easily felt his way to the flat-topped lacquered trunk. Picking up a box of matches he knew was there, he lit the oil lamp and turned up the wick. The light from the long, smoke-encrusted globe threw dark shadows around the room. An iron bedstead stood in the corner, partially covered by a bug-ridden feather mattress in blue-and-white ticking. Its rumpled contents dipped at the corners and bulged around the missing buttons, a caricature of waves on a stormy sea.

No rugs softened the rough slatted floor. The monotony was broken only by a squeaky platform rocker, the trunk, and a few orange crates filled with long-outdated women's magazines and several cookbooks he had collected. For a while he had taken a real interest in learning to cook well, and had even hoped to become a chef one day. Of course, his mother had not allowed that to happen, and now it was too late. He had been bought and paid for by his Uncle Phil. Even after a year, his earnings barely made a dent in the repayment of the money he owed the man for the rent, food, and clothing he and his mother had needed over the years.

He lay down on the bed, allowing the memories of lost

days to well up in front of him. His mother had disliked his childhood use of this room for anything but his punishments, and upon finding him there, would scream at him to come downstairs. Once, when he refused, she had locked him up here for almost two days with only a thermos of water and a few rolls. Finally she had crept in, crying, and gathered him into her arms, begging his forgiveness, and blaming her rashness on his behavior.

He remembered that the first time his mother had come to him in the way a woman comes to a man had been here on this mattress. It was raining, and the dim solace of the attic was oddly comforting. He had been so scared, and then, so ashamed of the things he had done, of the way his body had roared out of control beneath the power of her clever hands and mouth. After a while, the intense pleasure he found with her during those intimacies far outweighed any feelings of guilt. He would try to recall those tender moments whenever he felt soiled and abused, knowing Mother was not to blame for those times. She protected him when she could, and usually he found peace in her comforting arms.

Pushing the memories away, and seeking respite from the green eyes that had tormented him all day, he yawned and fell into a fitful sleep, only to come face-to-face with an apparition of his mother's corpse. Her waxy, gray face was swollen and riddled with small holes. The folds of her neck and jaw had deepened to gullies that ran craterlike to her sunken chest. The lips he had kissed so often were pulled back into a snarl, exposing her large teeth and decaying gums. As before, only the eyes were alive.

"Come to me! Come to me!" they said. "I need you. You promised to come to me!"

It was the old dream, the dream he had had over and over again in the past months.

"You need me! I know what you like!" The voice deepened. "You'll always belong to me."

Terrified, he rolled over. The chains and beads gouged

his chest. He shifted again and the dream changed. The eyes were the same, but the rough voice and the rotted features had fled. Now a freckled face, surrounded by a nimbus of reddish curls, with a glimmer of gold at her ears and throat stood before him. It was the Wednesday face, and it was smiling at him, joking with him, handing him money, taking his advice on which picture to see, and complimenting him on his excellent memory.

"I am here," she said. Her lips bit into a chocolate bar, and the sensuous green eyes flashed. "I want to be with you."

Her lovely arms reached out to him.

"You know where I am. You need me," she said.

He awoke at dawn. Even through the blackened windows, he could sense the beginnings of a beautiful new day. He felt powerful and wise, no longer a victim. He was instead the architect of a miracle. He had gotten her to come to him. The new body was different—appealing, refreshing, yet the eyes and the necklace had assured him that it was she. How he loved seeing her wear the heart necklace he had given her so long ago. She hadn't thrown it away after all.

"You will be with me, Mother. You have come this far. Trust me to bring you the rest of the way."

Leaving the attic, he returned to her room. He reverently removed her jewelry from his body, and put it back into the cedar box. Like a musician fine-tuning his instrument to produce the most delicate note, he arranged each article on the dressing table with exacting care. He turned to the closet, hung up her favorite dress, checked the alignment of her shoes, and smoothed down her clothing before shutting the door.

"Mother will want everything to be perfect when she gets here," he said to himself.

He ran next door to his room and dropped onto the bed

they had so often shared. A pair of his favorite gloves lay on his nightstand and he pulled them onto his hands.

"The game is just beginning. Soon, soon, Mother, we will be together again. I will make the arrangements. . . ."

# chapter
## 4

They were returning from Jeb's baseball game on Saturday afternoon when Mia suggested they rent some movies for the evening.

"Yeah, Dad, let's!" said Jeb.

"Rangers play tonight, son. Channel nine."

"I know, but they play all the time. Let's watch a movie tonight. You and Mom aren't going out, are you?"

"No, no. I just thought you'd like to pick up a few pointers. Ryan is pitching. Of course, I know your mom will go along with your choice since she's the movie freak in the family."

Monica looked at him sharply, but said nothing.

"All right, you win. We'll stop for a film."

For once they agreed on two quick choices and were on their way home within twenty minutes. The children scattered, and John tended to Peach while Monica lit the gas grill and started dinner. She persuaded John to barbecue the chicken while she fixed the salad and rice.

"This reminds me of the old days when I used to do all the important cooking," he joked.

"I remember the first chicken you ever did on the grill. Do you?" she asked. It was a warm, breezy evening and her tulips and daffodils danced and bobbed along the fence.

"You must mean the time we invited my folks over for a picnic, just after we were married?" he asked.

"Yes, I couldn't believe you had cooked that chicken so fast. But when you brought it inside, it was brown and crispy. I thought you'd done a great job!"

"Until my mom cut into her piece and the blood poured out over her plate. If you hadn't stopped her, I really believe she would have eaten every bite." John chuckled at the recollection.

"To this day I keep ham and cheese on hand for sandwiches whenever we have a dinner party and you're cooking," she added.

"Very funny. Who baked and served a lasagna, complete with the sheets of paper between the slices of mozzarella, to my first boss? Huh? It's a wonder he didn't fire me on the spot!"

"He was laughing too hard! Oh my, we've made some meals, haven't we, John?"

"Yeah, babe, it's a wonder we didn't kill somebody."

Small flames licked the dripping grease and he stooped to adjust the heat as Monica went inside. Babe. He hadn't called her that in years. She used to love it. She still did! He probably did not even know it had slipped out. After what he said to her last night, she knew he could not mean it.

They had actually gotten into bed at the same time last evening, though John had fallen asleep almost immediately. Much later, she awoke to find his side of the bed empty. Afraid that he might be ill, she had gone to look for him. She found him on the screened porch, watching the clouds drift across the moon.

"John," she had called, "are you all right?"

"Yes. No. I don't know."

She moved to his side, but was suddenly afraid to touch him, afraid he might rebuff any gesture she might make.

"Sometimes I feel like a stranger in this house, as if I don't belong here anymore," he said. "I've changed. I'm so different from that guy you married. I don't even recognize myself. Sometimes I think I need to get out, start over. . . . I don't know. Do you ever feel that way? Do you ever hate your life?"

"No, I don't."

"Don't you ever ask yourself if this is as good as life gets? You're getting older. Don't you want something different, something more exciting for the second half of your life than just the same old routine?"

"No, I admit that these last few years haven't always been champagne and roses where you and I are concerned, but I think we can be happy." She clenched her hands so tightly she could have broken a finger and not even been aware of it.

"We have so little in common anymore."

"I disagree. We have three great children and an eighteen-year marriage in common. That's more than most people have. I think we're pretty lucky."

"Go to bed, Monica. You need your rest. I just need to think awhile."

This time she did touch him. She reached out and wrapped her arms around him and pulled him close to her.

"I love you, John. Don't throw us away. You can have all the time you need, but we're worth keeping."

He had stood there in her arms, and at last, when she had almost given up, she felt him soften, and he returned her hug.

Now, as she diced celery and carrots for the salad, added chicken stock and herbs to the rice, her mind tried to put together the mystery her husband had become. How could she match the agonized man she had heard last night on the porch with the teasing one just now? And then there was his newest side, the arrogant man who needed to hurt her for reasons known only to himself.

What had happened to their marriage, and why were there so many different personalities in this man where there used to be just one? How did he feel about her? Why didn't he need her? Was he needing someone else more? If she were suddenly gone, would he even miss her—except to run his errands and his house? Would he miss . . . her?"

"Oh, by the way, I forgot to tell you, but I'll be out of town three nights this week," John announced while he and Monica were folding and packing his clothes on Monday night. "Sales has set up a big meeting Friday morning and I really can't miss it."

"Then you'll be in Atlanta until Friday evening?" She tried to hide her disappointment. They had so little time together.

"Yes. No problem for you, is it? We don't have any plans for that night, do we?" John deliberated between five ties before discarding one. He threw it on the bed and then packed the rest.

"Not really. We owe the Crawfords a night of bridge. I was planning to mention something to Nancy this week about getting together on Friday, but nothing definite."

"I'll be here for the kids' games on Saturday, and I haven't forgotten the Father-Daughter Brunch at church on Sunday. I wouldn't miss that."

"The girls are looking forward to it, too."

"I'll try to think of something special to do with Jeb. Maybe we can go over to the batting cages after the brunch," he said. "Would you make us a reservation?"

"For the afternoon? About three?" She loved him for wanting to be such an attentive dad, but she could not help wondering why he seldom had special thoughts for her.

"Make the reservation for whenever it suits Jeb. You can handle the details, Monica. Now, would you hand me those shirts you just folded?"

She gave him the clothing and looked over the things he had piled on the bed. "Why are you taking your topsiders and the casual stuff? Don't you usually just take suits?"

"Yes, but one of the Dallas agents is hosting a picnic at Stone Mountain on Thursday night. I'd look pretty silly going in a shirt and tie."

"Oh, sure. Is it anyone I know?"

John hesitated. "I don't think so. She's only been with the company about eighteen months, but she's a real go-getter! She's bringing in tons of new business."

"What's her name?"

"Beth. Beth McKinnon. Yale graduate, tells great jokes . . . a real asset!"

"She must be. I've never heard you speak so glowingly about a new employee." Monica looked at her husband. When he didn't acknowledge her comment, she continued, "How about if you and I find some time next weekend to spend together, just the two of us?" She turned to him and put her arms around his neck. "Can you think of anything that might be fun?" She kissed his neck several times as she moved one hand to finger his belt buckle and slide downward.

"Monica, please, I have to get these things together." He pulled her hands from his body and placed them at her sides. She felt as if she were sixteen and had just been caught making a pass at a high school coach.

"Okay, John. Maybe we'd better talk about this. Is there something I've done to annoy you? I remember when you loved having me touch you. What's changed all that?"

"Nothing's changed, and you haven't done anything wrong. I'm just busy here and, well, I want to finish."

Monica moved closer. "This really isn't about the packing, John. We both know that."

"I guess it's more of what I said the other night. I'm just not sure where my life is headed right now." He backed away and picked up a stack of black socks.

"I'm willing to give you the time to figure out what you want, but it's tough living with you in the meantime." She took the socks from his hands and took a deep breath. "John, I have to ask. Is there somebody else in your life?"

"Monica, really." He took the socks and stuffed them into his bag. "I can't believe you'd even ask that."

Was that an answer? God, she hoped so. "What do you want me to do? How can I help you?"

"Just give me some space. I've been honest with you about how I feel. Go ahead and plan something for Saturday night. Just the two of us, if you like."

His reply caused a myriad of emotions to flutter inside her. Hope was close to the bottom of the list, but she chose to hang on to it and wait.

"You mean it?" she asked.

"Uh, sure," he said, counting his socks and underwear before putting them into his case. "But not a movie, okay? Would you get me some more socks? And did you remember to pick up my blue suit at the cleaners?"

Her earlier thought shot through her mind as she hung the blue suit in his hanging bag. If he didn't have me around, would I be missed . . . except to run his errands and his house? And just how good are Beth's jokes?

# chapter
# 5

On Wednesday, Monica moved through the early morning quiet of her big house as the antique clock in the living room chimed six times. Fitful sleep had pushed her out of her bed and so she had already ridden her bike, made coffee, and showered. Peach Pie dozed on the kitchen floor. She had noticed when she let him outside that he was limping again.

"Guess today's the day to have that toenail looked at, Peach," she told him. "Good thing we already have the appointment with David."

Monica poured herself a cup of coffee and sat down at the round oak table by the kitchen window, making certain that her slippered feet did not disturb the snoozing dog. She sipped her coffee and leaned back to enjoy the peacefulness of this rainy dawn, remembering how hectic yesterday morning had been. Everyone had been running late. The twins dawdled in the bathroom, having a screaming fight over hair ribbons. Jeb had misplaced his gym shoes.

Yesterday John had gotten up early to do some desk work, and had fallen twenty minutes behind his usual schedule. There had been no time for lengthy good-byes—only rushed hugs between him and the children as they all flew out the door.

Promptly at six-thirty, Monica's three children trooped

into the kitchen. Mia's braids were lopsided and Jeb was minus his shoes, but Monica responded to the excitement in their bright eyes with a grin.

"My goodness! Look at you! It's barely light outside and here you are, all dressed and ready for school! What are you up to?"

"Pancakes!" they yelled together, requesting their favorite fare usually reserved for Sundays and vacation days.

"With Jeb at Billy's birthday party, and Mia and me at Katie's for supper, can we have pancakes this morning since we won't be here for our usual Wednesday night out?" Sarah asked.

"We planned it last night. That's why we're up so early. We knew you wouldn't like the idea if we didn't get ready for school first," Jeb added.

"I'll mix the batter, and Jeb can set the table," Mia said.

"Geez! Thanks a lot, Squirt. Why do I get the grunt work? I'll make them and you get the plates and stuff!"

"Okay, Jeb, but I get to flip them on the griddle. Remember, Mom? It's my turn. You promised I could do it next time," Mia said.

"She's right, Mom, and I don't mind setting the table," said Sarah, the peacemaker.

Monica managed to pull all three children to her for a group hug. "I love you guys," she told them before they squirmed free. Breakfast would be a messy, six-handed affair, and she would be the sole member of the clean-up crew.

*So be it,* she thought, giving into them once again. *Wasn't this what memories were made of?*

As the children devoured the last of the pancakes, Monica sipped her coffee.

"Let's review everyone's plans for the day. Jeb, what time are you going to Billy's?"

"His mom's picking us up after school. We're going to try out his new bike before we go to Videorama for supper."

"What time should I pick you up tonight?"

"Mrs. Crawford said she'd bring me home early, about seven."

"Katie's asked Jennifer along with Mia and me to have supper with her tonight," Sarah said. "We'll walk to her house after Girl Scouts."

"And then we'll all be home together until Monday," Mia added, glancing around the breakfast table. "I sure like it when the teachers have school instead of us."

"Mom, since Katie's having us over there tonight, can we invite her and Jennifer for lunch tomorrow, to sort of say thank you?" Sarah asked.

"Well, I guess. . . ."

"Let's not have tomato soup, though. Jennifer says it reminds her of warm blood."

"Warm blood!" Jeb exclaimed. "Your friends are so weird! Mom, can I be excused?"

"Yes, you *may,* Jeb. Put your dishes in the sink, please. Girls, invite your friends for tomorrow. I'll make some brownies for dessert."

"Thanks, Mom. Let's go, Sarah! Last one in the bathroom loves Ronald Stokley, warts and all!"

"Oh, ick, Mia. You are so gross sometimes!"

"Hey, Mom," Jeb said, as he walked over to the dog, "Peach Pie's foot looks like it's been bleeding."

"Oh, dear. I was going to take him to the vet this afternoon, but I'll call and see if I can get him in sooner. Dr. Riley will probably want to remove his toenail."

"Will he have to stay overnight?" Jeb asked.

"Maybe just for the day."

"Poor Peach!"

"He'll be fine, Jeb. It's nothing serious. They'll fix him up and he'll probably be here to greet you when you come home from Billy's tonight."

Not totally convinced, Jeb slipped to the floor to fuss over the drowsing dog until the car pool came. Monica ignored the dishes and dropped down beside them.

She was still cleaning up the kitchen thirty minutes later when Nancy knocked on the door.

"I see I'm not the only party animal in the neighborhood," Nancy said, looking at the stack of newly washed dishes on Monica's counter.

"Pancake mania hit this morning and I was left with the aftershock. What are you doing here? I'm always glad to see you, but you have two parties today! How are Billy's birthday preparations coming along?" Monica offered Nancy the kitchen stool while she filled the tea kettle and set it on the stove. "Anything I can do to help?"

"Nope. Lunch is in the fridge, the house is reasonably clean, the presents are wrapped, and Videorama is making the pizza. They even threw in a cake! I farmed my kids out thinking I'd need the morning to get everything together, and now I find I've got hours to burn!"

"Well, I'm glad you dropped in to burn them with me," Monica said, setting two mugs of tea and a plate of ginger cookies on the bar.

"Yummy! Monica, your cookies are wonderful. I'm still trying to shake off the extra weight I put on over Christmas, but I can't resist these." Nancy picked up another two. Her brown eyes sparkled as she laughed. "Now, on to important matters. I stopped by to see if you and John can join us for some bridge."

"It's our turn to host, not yours," Monica protested.

"You're always telling me that friends don't keep score. Can we count on you?"

"I'm not sure. John is out of town until Friday this week."

"When does he usually get in? We won't start dealing the cards until eight."

"I know it will be a wonderful evening, but I just can't commit. John will be exhausted . . . and well, you know. . . ."

"Monica, is everything all right?"

"I guess I'm a little tired."

"Okay." Nancy paused. "Tell me to mind my own business if you want to, but I'm worried about you. You seem so sad lately."

"With your brood and all you have to do, how do you find the time to be such a good friend?"

"Maybe I should ask how you found the time to keep all five of my kids for a week when Tom and I flew to Pittsburgh a few months ago when my mom got sick?"

"I was glad to do it. We had a lot of fun."

"Or the time when my hot water heater broke an hour before my kid's Cub Scout party and you moved the whole business to your house . . . even ran the festivities until I could get things under control!"

"It was nothing, Nance. You'd have done the same thing for me." Monica picked up her tea and took a sip.

"I bet you still haven't gotten the bubble gum out of your draperies," said Nancy.

"It's almost gone, and besides, friends don't keep score."

"Well, friend, back to my question. Are you okay?"

No answer.

"What's wrong?" Nancy asked again.

"Nothing. It's . . . nothing." Monica glanced out the window and blinked back the tears that suddenly filled her eyes.

"Don't give me that crap. What is it?"

"Guess I need a friend to listen. John and I are . . . oh, God I can't believe I'm telling you this . . . that is, we're going through a rough patch right now."

"Temporary midlife insanity, or something serious?"

"The latter, I'm afraid."

"Want to talk about it?"

"He's there for the kids, but never for me. I don't understand what's going on in his mind. We spend so little time together. We hardly talk unless it concerns one of the children. Whenever I try to get close, he always has something else to do or somewhere he needs to go." The tears were flowing down her cheeks now. Monica grabbed a tissue from her pocket and wiped her eyes. "I'm sorry, Nancy. You don't need this today."

"Hey, it's okay. Let it go. Maybe it'll make you feel better. Have you thought of grabbing your black-lace nightie and whisking him off for a romantic getaway?"

"He'd probably take his briefcase and the latest marketing report. It's as though I don't exist for him anymore. I'm a mother, a gofer, a hostess, and an escort . . . but that's it."

"You're underestimating yourself. Look at you! You're the perfect wife, and you look great!"

"I'm far from perfect, but as a matter of fact, I have suggested a tryst for two, and just about everything else—including things that would make you blush."

"I doubt it. I didn't get five kids by doing laundry."

"I know, but the bottom line is he's just not interested in me, or in us!"

"I'm sorry." Nancy reached out and took Monica's hand.

"Some days I think if I didn't have the kids and my job at school, I'd go crazy. These should be the best years of our marriage, and instead they're the worst," said Monica.

Nancy hesitated, and then asked softly, "Could there be someone else in his life?"

"I wonder about that a lot, but I don't know. And he says there's no one."

"Is he happy with his job? Is he healthy?"

"He loves his job. It's the major force in his life. And, yes, as far as I know he's fine. He looks gorgeous!"

"I vote for midlife crazies. He seems to have all the signs. Unfortunately for you, there's not much you can do except wait it out and hope he makes the right choices. From what I've read, this may be something he has to handle himself."

"That's a rotten scenario, Nancy."

"Yeah, but the odds are on your side."

"Maybe I've become too predictable. Maybe I need to spice up my life so that I'll be more interesting, more fun to be around."

"I think you're great just the way you are. I'd like to knock some sense into that dumb ass husband of yours."

Monica leaned over and gave Nancy a big hug. "Thanks, friend. You're just what I needed today."

They talked until it was time for Nancy to go. Monica walked her to the front door.

"I enjoyed the tea and cookies," Nancy said. "We still need to sneak out for a croissant some morning."

"Thanks again for listening. I'll let you know about Friday night."

"No problem. You take care. I'll see you tonight when I bring Jeb home." Nancy dug her keys out of her purse. "Do something for yourself today. Something you enjoy. Okay?"

Monica nodded and watched her friend climb into her van. *Something for myself?* She returned to the kitchen and picked up the newspaper. After she took Peach to see David, would she have time for a matinee?

Monica was surprised at the lack of activity at David's veterinary office when she ushered a reluctant Peach Pie through the frosted-glass door. She took a seat by the window, next to a towering ficus tree, and persuaded her large dog to stop sniffing the brown Mexican tile and lie down at her feet. Only two other animals were ahead of them.

She nodded to a portly woman in her sixties holding a fat white poodle. The dog's jeweled collar was similar to the many rings that wrapped around the woman's pudgy fingers, and its pink hair bow exactly matched its mistress's silk dress. Monica, who was dressed in slim-cut jeans and a green turtleneck sweater, was amused by the glamorous pair.

"Chloe's got a little sniffle," the woman explained. Then looking at the poodle, she rubbed its ears and said in baby talk, "She's not eating, and Mommie's all worried."

Monica bit back a chuckle and looked at the second patient, a large, black feline whose mesmerizing eyes were watching Peach Pie through the wire mesh of its pet carrier. Peach whimpered, stared back for a few moments, then gave it up, preferring to spend the time relaxing, especially if Monica was rubbing his back.

At ten-minute intervals, the receptionist, Jolene Cooper, a thirtyish blonde who always wore her hair in two long ponytails, appeared in the doorway to summon the next patient. When she called Peach Pie, Monica shortened the leash and pulled him close, knowing Jolene was uncomfortable around large dogs.

"Good afternoon, Mrs. Foyles," said Jolene keeping her distance from Peach. "Dr. Riley will see you in room three, third door on your right."

"Thanks, Jolene. We can find it."

Monica started down the hall, but Peach had no interest in door number three. He plopped his hefty bulk in the middle of the hallway, and refused to heed Monica's pleas to enter the room. Jolene backed away. Neither woman was aware that David Riley had joined them until he spoke.

"Relax, Jolene. Peach is as gentle as they come. He's just an overgrown baby, aren't you, fellah? Come on, boy. That's a good boy."

The owner of the deep, masculine voice stooped to rub Peach's head and take his leash. The large dog lumbered to his feet, sniffed the man's shoes, and then ambled agreeably into the examining room.

"Here . . . here's his chart, Doctor," said Jolene. A telephone rang in the background, and she retreated into the hallway.

"Hi, Monica," he said, reaching across Peach to take her hand. "Great to see you again."

"Hi. Thanks," she said. "I like your tie." The brightly colored fabric he wore was a panoply of dog sounds spelled out in brilliant confusion.

"Yeah, so do I, but the cats I treat give me a lot of flak when I wear it."

"They want equal time," she said. "Maybe you could find some socks with catnip on them."

"And what about the hamsters and the ferrets?" he asked. He loved acting silly with her.

"Perhaps there's some aftershave they'd especially appreciate."

They both broke up laughing. Not for the first time, Monica marveled at how good he made her feel, and how much fun they always had together.

David stooped to rub Peach's stomach. The big dog had rolled on his back and was whimpering for attention. "You're a real terror, aren't you?" he said.

Monica winked at David. "Jolene thinks so."

"I bet you're still wondering why I keep her," David said.

"Because she's a master at handling angry felines?" Monica smiled. She knew exactly why he kept his dog-shy receptionist. Jolene was a single mom who needed a steady job. "David, you don't have to justify your employee choices to me. Besides, I already know what an old softie you are."

"What do you mean?" He looked at her with more than casual interest.

"You've got a reputation. You're a really nice guy!"

David smiled, enjoying the captivating green eyes, which matched her sweater. "I'm certain you have overestimated my popularity, but I thank you. Jolene's fears don't affect my practice. She's the best accountant and office manger I've ever had."

"You're still a nice guy, David."

"If you're hoping for a discount in exchange for your kind words, you're going to be disappointed."

"I take back everything complimentary I ever said about you. I can see my wiles won't work on you, Dr. Riley."

David looked at her steadily, but said nothing. Outside the door, dogs yipped, phones rang, conversations continued, but David was oblivious to everything but her.

"Don't bet the farm on that one," he said finally.

Monica blushed, but kept her eyes locked on his.

David looked away first, and turned his attention back to Peach. "Well, old boy, what brings you here to see me?" He rubbed the dog's ears, giving them both some time.

Monica spoke, surprising herself at the control in her voice. "He needs his annual shots, and he was outside with the children and somehow injured a toenail on his right front foot. We tried clipping it, but he wasn't too cooperative."

"Yeah, I see the problem." He examined it carefully. "It splits further every time he puts his weight on it. I really should remove it."

"I thought you might have to. Will he need to spend the day?"

"I'd prefer it. Is that a problem for you?" he asked, giving Peach's eyes and ears a quick check.

"No, Just as long as I can have him back by five. I'd like some company for dinner this evening. John's out of town, as usual, and the children all have plans."

David looked at her, deciding in a moment on the innocence of her remark. *She has no idea what she does to me. Let it go, Riley. She's married. Let it go.* But he found he couldn't.

"I'm sorry that you spend so much time alone, Monica."

"Yeah, so am I." Suddenly she was in tears. Embarrassed, she quickly looked away, but not before he had seen her face.

"It's okay. You haven't said anything that I haven't already guessed," he said softly.

"It's that evident, huh?" Monica turned back to him.

"No, it's not. Maybe where you're concerned, I have some extra radar." He pulled a tissue from a box on the counter and gently wiped the tears from her cheeks. "When the loneliness starts closing in on me, it's usually in the evening if Colin is with friends. I'm not much for shopping or the bar scene, and so I generally end up at the movies. The silver screen has lightened a lot of my solitary hours."

"Movies are fun for me, too. I like to go to matinees—"

Their conversation was interrupted by a loud knock on the door. David opened it to find a rattled Jolene standing in the hall.

"Doctor, there's a man in the waiting room. He says his dog just swallowed his wife's diamond earrings. He's ranting like a madman."

"Thanks, Jolene. I'll be right there."

"I think you'd better hurry."

"Get them into an examining room, and call Jeff up from the kennels. I might need his help. Monica, I'll talk with you later today. Don't worry about Peach Pie. He'll be fine."

"Thanks for everything. I'm sorry about the way I—"

"I'm not. I feel very privileged." He leaned toward her and covered his heart with his hands.

"As I said before, you're a nice guy."

"So are you," he replied.

She laughed a little and on impulse, reached out to give him a hug. Her chuckle was cut short when he pulled her tightly against him.

"So are you," he whispered once before letting her go. Then he took Peach's leash from her. " 'Bye, Monica. Take care." He smiled down at her, hesitated a second longer, and disappeared through the door.

# chapter
# 6

"One ticket for *Deathstalk*, please." Monica said, still feeling off balance. She couldn't forget the sparks she had felt in David's arms. She knew he cared about her; they were special friends, but . . .

She took her ticket to the concession stand, where it would be torn in half. She was used to this routine. So few people attended the matinees that the person behind the candy counter often took tickets, as well as sold food.

"Hello, Lenny. It must be Wednesday since we're both here." She nodded at the young, fair-haired man. His tall, strapping body seemed to her to be at odds with his elegant face. Long, silky eyelashes all but hid penetrating blue eyes that lay beneath a high forehead. His mouth was small, but beautifully shaped.

*He looks like an English poet . . . but one who plays soccer or lifts weights when he's not writing sonnets.*

Lenny returned her ticket stub after noting which film she was seeing. "I know you'll really like the show, ma'am. It got great reviews from everyone who works here. It's pretty scary, though."

"That's okay." She looked away.

"Uh, well . . . what can I get you to eat? Want some popcorn?" he asked, thinking how beautiful she looked today. He had never seen her in jeans before. How could he have forgotten how long her legs were?

"Yeah, the jumbo size. And a large diet cola." She pulled out her wallet and counted some money.

"You must be hungry. Skip lunch?" Why wasn't she wearing the locket today? She seemed more detached, more aloof, somehow.

"No, more like skipping dinner. The family's deserted me for the evening, and so your popcorn will be my supper."

"Sounds good to me! We just got a fresh supply of candy. I refilled the shelves right before you came. Why don't you check it out while I get your drink?"

"You're trying to fatten me up, aren't you? But, just so I won't hurt your feelings, I'll take a quick look."

Lenny relaxed. The old banter was back in her voice. He watched the green eyes lower to the candy selection at the same time as she slid her body a few feet along the counter. All the kids did that. It usually made him mad because he was the one who had to keep the top clean. But now, as he watched her breasts rub against the glass, he felt a tightening in his loins that had nothing to do with anger.

He pulled up a large cup and scooped in a little ice. Slipping his fingers into his pocket, he lifted out a small, plastic bag. Checking to see that she was still engrossed with the candy counter, he emptied the contents of the bag into her cup, then filled it with soda. He wiped his sweating hands on his pants after he set the drink and popcorn onto the counter.

"See anything you'd like in there?" He was proud of the calm way he was handling her. The plan was in place. It could not fail now.

"I guess not, but it sure is tempting. What do I owe you for my dinner?"

Lenny laughed with her and took her money. He watched as she picked up her drink in one hand and her popcorn in the other. Again, she reminded him of a child as she put her mouth directly on her popcorn and caught a few white kernels with her tongue. Then she stopped and took a big swallow of her soda before stepping away.

"My compliments to the chef!" she said.

He felt the world drop away as he looked into her eyes and returned her smile.

"Oh, Mother," he whispered, but she was gone.

"Hey, man. Is that your mother?" Kyle set down the cups he was stacking and walked closer to Lenny. "You okay?" he asked when he saw the color drop out of Lenny's face. "You don't look so good."

Lenny raised his shaking hands to his cheeks and looked at Kyle through his fingers. In a split second those fingers shoved Kyle aside, knocking him into the stack of cups, which clattered to the floor.

"Hey! What the fuck? Where're you going?" Kyle shook his head and stooped to pick up the cups. "Why do I always get to work Wednesdays with the weirdo?"

"Hey, mister! There's a lady in the movie in there, and she's sick or something!" a kid in blue jeans and a Dallas Cowboys' sweatshirt yelled as he and his companion ran to the concession stand.

"Yeah, she's all bent over and she's making funny noises. We couldn't see her face, but we think she's dying!" added his friend.

"Thanks, boys. I'll go see if I can help her. You say she's in *Deathstalk*, the movie in number seven?"

"Yeah, the bloody one! We'll show you. She's toward the back, on the left."

Lenny flipped up the sectioned counter between the hot dog machine and the wall, and followed the two boys down the hall.

"Hey, guys, this is an R-rated show. Only five people wanted to see this show and I checked everyone's ticket. I didn't let you two in. Why aren't you in school?"

"Well, uh, Mom kept us out of school for a doctor's appointment this morning. We only have PE and an assembly this afternoon, so she let us stay out for the rest of the day. We wanted to see *Deathstalk,* and Jeff here said, well—"

"I did not! It was your idea to sneak into the show, Davey. Don't blame it on me!"

"Where's your mom? What are your names?"

The bigger of the two told Lenny their names and then said, "She dropped us off to see *The Magic Frog,* but it was boring."

"I'm calling the cops. You two broke the law. How old are you anyhow?" he asked gruffly.

"N-nine. Please, mister. You help the lady and we'll go back to the frog movie. Honest! Don't call anybody, please?"

"Yeah, our mom will kill us!"

"Okay, if you forget everything about being in here, I'll let you go. But if you tell anyone, I'll find out and send the cops after you. Remember, I know your names. Now get the hell outta here. Scram!"

Lenny watched the terrified youngsters turn and run back into the G-rated movie before he entered the dark alcove leading into the auditorium. Bloodcurdling screams exploded from the gory movie. Scanning the audience was easy. An elderly couple sat on the far right aisle, eating popcorn, engrossed in the show. A middle-aged man snored softly in the middle of the theater beside a younger man dressed in a business suit and tie. At the back of the room on the left, a woman sat alone. She was hunched over, holding her stomach, and rocking her body.

He went to her and touched her shoulder. "Ma'am, are you all right? Is there anything I can do?"

Monica straightened slightly and whispered, "Oh, Lenny. I feel so lousy all of a sudden, dizzy, and sh-shaky all over, like I can't stand up or walk. It's . . . it's even dif-difficult to t-talk."

"Some kids came and got me. They told me you were sick."

"I'm s-so sorry to be this way."

"It's okay. Can you stand if I help you?"

"I think so."

"You're doing fine," he said as he led her out of the auditorium and down the hall. He loved having his hands on her at last. She was soft and wonderful. Feeling the warmth of her body through her lightweight sweater made him wish he had his gloves on, but he could never wear them in public. They were for secret times in secret places.

Something was different about her though. Her scent was lighter and sweeter smelling. He wanted to ask her when she had changed perfumes, but instead he said, "Where's your car?" even though he had watched her park the navy blue station wagon less than thirty minutes before.

"In the back, by the Dumpsters." Her head was pounding. She could not be sick. Not here. "I've got to get home," she told him.

Outside, he asked for her keys and unlocked the door. She threw her handbag on the floor in the front. The parking lot was deserted. A light rain was falling, and he watched as iridescent droplets gathered in her rusty curls. His stomach tightened when he saw a raindrop catch in her long eyelashes, and splash onto her cheek.

"T-thanks, Lenny. Go back now. Don't want you . . . to lose your j-job."

"It's okay. I'm on my break. No one will miss me for a half hour or so. You think you can drive?"

"What's wrong with me? Feel terrible. Can't th-think what to do." She put her hand to her forehead and moaned.

Needing to touch her again, Lenny put his hand on her arm.

"May I take you home? You could show me where you live."

She nodded once before slumping against his body. He

scooped her into his arms, and closed her car door with his hip. Then he crossed the lot to his Pontiac, and laid her down on the backseat. He wanted to kiss her, but he knew he had to wait.

"I'd forgotten how sleepy your medicine can make you, Mother."

Within moments, he was on the expressway, heading south to his apartment. His plan was foolproof. She would sleep for hours. There was more than enough time to get her into the attic, and return to take care of her car.

Suddenly an old Andy Williams song that had always been a favorite of his mother's sprang to his mind, and he found himself singing it softly as he drove her home.

Lenny heard the rusty springs of the old iron bed groan as he heaved the woman's weight upon them. After a moment they quieted, their burden leaden and unmoving. Except for the double sounds of breathing—one shallow and even, the other panting—silence reigned in the dark chamber at the top of the house.

He was breathless from having carried her up two flights of stairs, but he easily found the matches and lit the oil lamp on the lacquered trunk. Its wavering flame rose and fell, causing wraithlike shadows to bounce off the jumbled pile of clothing beside the light and crawl up the exposed timbers of the walls. He glanced at the heap, mentally reviewing its contents before turning his attention back to the unconscious woman.

"Welcome home, Mother," he whispered. "You're all mine now. We're together at last, just as I promised." He felt the perspiration that had dampened his shirt evaporating in the chilly attic air, but its coolness did nothing to suppress the rising heat in his groin.

"How beautiful you look in our bed! Your hair is wild and alluring and your eyes, if they could see me, would be dark and hungry. Do you think I've forgotten how they change when you're aroused? Let me see your eyes, Mother. I need to see how much you want me."

He lifted the lid of her left eye. Its drugged pupil was indeed large, allowing only a small rim of brilliant green to encircle it. He felt his body surge at such a bold indication of her lust. Often in the past she had teased him, belittled him, even tried to give fake responses to his lovemaking, but the dilation in her eyes never lied. He had always known the truth about the level of her arousal.

"Oh, Mother, I must have you soon! We've been apart too long."

He sat down on the bed, his weight on the mattress causing her to roll toward his body. Taking the involuntary movement as a sign of her acquiescence, he leaned against her and pulled on the black lace gloves that he had placed beside the lantern the night before. Then he allowed his hands to hover over her face like a hawk poised above his intended prey. He ached to touch her, to taste, to rub his tongue down her smooth cheeks and willowy neck.

As he watched her sleep, his mind filled with visions of what she had taught him to do to her, things that had pleased her so much. He longed to explore her new body to see if her desires were as he remembered them. Giving in to the impulse to touch, he ran his gloved fingers down her nose, under her chin, and across her breasts.

The thickness of the soft sweater hid any quickening in her nipples, but as he slowly caressed her he had no doubt she was responding to him as strongly as he was to her. The gloves worked their familiar magic as his fingers drew circles on her stomach, then traced the path of the zipper on her jeans before beginning the long journey down her legs. Her ankles were bare and even through the lace gloves, the heady contrast of smooth skin after rough denim was almost more than he could endure.

"Oh, God, how I want you, and how I need you to want me!" A physical ache engulfed him. He shook his head wildly and groaned. He pulled off her shoes and studied her feet. They were small and soft, and he was fascinated with their shape and the rosy tips of her toes. His intense concentration gave his body a much needed respite.

"Mother, what have you done? You never used to paint your toenails. They look so different, but I like them! Oh, yes, I like them!"

He knelt down and lifted her foot. Then he bent and kissed her heel, running his lips up the curve of the sole and ball before closing his mouth over her toes. They tasted of soap and leather, with a hint of saltiness, and he reveled in their texture and flavor as he suckled them hard, drawing them back toward his throat.

Her whimpers broke the mood and he dropped her foot. He stepped to the lamp, checked his watch in its dim light, and hurried to the pile of clothing.

"Damn it, I'm late," he said. "There'll be hell to pay if I'm not back soon. But I can't leave until I get you ready."

"What?" he asked. She murmured and tossed her head back and forth on the mattress.

"I'm sorry, Mother. I know you hate to hear me use curse words. Forgive me?" He reached for her hand, but she moaned again and rolled onto her side, giving him her back.

"Mother, please don't turn away ... not after all I've done to bring you here!"

She remained on her side, ignoring him and his outburst, just as she used to do when he had displeased her. He felt his hurt mix with anger as he threw some clothing on the bed. Then he roughly pulled her onto her back and picked up the wide adhesive tape he had bought. Leaning over her, he ground his lips against hers, feeling the imprint of her teeth.

"Don't start playing your games with me, Mother! Things are going to be different this time. You can't reject me anymore or force me to do anything I don't want to do. Soon you'll be begging me to kiss you, to love you, no matter what."

He pulled a strip of tape off the roll, cut it with the scissors he had brought from the kitchen, and slapped it across her mouth. She shifted slightly at his touch, but did not awaken.

Slightly embarrassed by his outburst and needing to make amends now that she understood he was in charge, Lenny smoothed her reddish curls and smiled sweetly.

"I've got all your favorite things here, Mother. I'm going to forgive your mood, and let you wear the blue dress and the pink mohair sweater you like so much. You'll be more than willing to be nice to me when you see how special I've made you look in your very own clothes. I've taken real good care of everything. They're exactly as you left them.

"Now, just relax and let me get you ready."

He reached around her waist and pulled her green sweater up and over her head. Desire pounded into him as he watched the rise and fall of her full breasts beneath the lacy, flowered bra. She had never worn such pretty things before. Instantly, he decided the bra must stay. He experienced a sudden weakness and wondered if his knees would collapse, as he unzipped her jeans and peeled them down her legs. The pants were tight, and it took a while to tug them over her hips and muscled thighs. He pulled his mother's ragged satin slip over the wispy, silk panties that covered the slim hips. The panties too would remain. He could not replace them with the ugly cotton ones she had worn in other days.

Next he picked up the blue crepe dress and opened the row of shiny black buttons that secured the bodice. Then shoving one of his arms under her shoulders, he raised them far enough off the bed so that he could drop the garment over her head. It fell loosely about her body. He worked her arms through the sleeves and buttoned it before pulling on the moth-eaten pink cardigan. He noted how much smaller she was than he remembered. He loved the changes in her: The fragility of her tiny frame made him feel large and powerful.

"You may test your wiles on me, Mother, but this time you will be easy to dominate. This time you will plead with me, the way you once made me beg for small favors."

He straightened her dress and turned her sleeping face toward him. A wide strip of adhesive tape pulled at the delicate corners of her mouth. White cotton rope stretched across her as he tied her arms and legs to the iron bars at the top and bottom of the bed. Once again he slid his hands over her body, rejoicing in the secrets beneath her dress, and moved his head to within inches of hers.

"You see, your green eyes are powerless against me now. You will have to earn your way out of these ropes. Even if you are more beautiful than ever, you must be deserving of your freedom—one limb at a time. Oh, I almost forgot. . . ."

He picked up a small cut-glass bottle. "You always said that no lady is completely dressed without her perfume."

He pulled the fancy stopper and dabbed stale, amber-colored liquid onto her wrists and ankles, just above the twisted ropes that were already beginning to mark her fair skin. He lifted her dress and patted the fragrance behind her knees, taking extra time to draw several capital "L"s on the inside of her thighs with his perfume-soaked finger. Just before he capped the bottle, he poured large droplets of her Attar of Rose perfume onto the bare mattress where she lay.

"I remember when you used to drench your bed with this stuff, Mother. You said it made you feel as if you were making love in a rose garden."

The thought of holding her, having her cry out for him made him weak, but he had his body under control now. Knowing she was completely his, he could wait to savor her later. His plan was running without a hitch.

For a moment he watched her sleep. In the dress that was much too large, and the old sweater that had seen better days, she looked sad and vulnerable. He knew she would be uncomfortable, perhaps hurting when she awoke. Remembering the bite and sting of cord against his own flesh, he stooped to loosen the knots at her ankles. Perhaps some soft cloth between the rope and her skin . . .

A sudden noise rattled the painted windows. He glanced up expecting to see an intruder, but saw himself, tied to this same bed, screaming, pleading with his mother to protect him, to save him, or at least to allow him a small light, confessing his fear of the dark. Shaken, he stepped away from the ropes and looked down at the woman on the bed. She had nearly bewitched him again. He must never underestimate her.

"You will heal, as I did," he told her. "Rest well, Mother, dear. I'll see you soon."

He turned off the lamp and moved swiftly through the darkness to the door. The sounds of his footsteps descending the uncarpeted stairwell mingled with remnants of his high-pitched laughter. Their echoes shattered the silence in the attic where Monica struggled toward consciousness.

# chapter
# 7

"So nice of you to drop in, kid," Phil Bruns said. "I was beginning to think you'd taken the rest of the day off, you worthless little shit. Where the hell have you been?"

"No problem. I had a little detour." Lenny giggled and playfully swatted Phil's arm. "I knew you could handle the dump without me for an hour or so."

"Like hell. We expected you this afternoon. Even with those sissy white hands of yours, you happen to be the only one around here today who can lift the syrup canisters for the sodas."

"I-I-I just needed a little, you know, personal time." Lenny giggled again and twisted his hair around his fingers.

Phil walked over to Lenny and slapped him hard across the face. "I don't know what you've been up to, but it sure as hell doesn't have anything to do with your job. Look at you! You're higher than a kite. You on something, kid? You doing drugs or some shit like that?"

Lenny reeled with the impact. What was he doing? He'd lost it! Five more minutes and he'd be spilling his guts to the old man.

"My car's acting up," he carefully answered. "I used my break time to run it by the garage."

"You tellin' me you needed an hour to drive two blocks?"

"The guy took his time checking it out. I'm sorry I'm late. You want me to stay extra tonight to make it up?"

Lenny put his hands in his pants pockets and reached for the gloves. This morning he had chosen the red kid ones from his mother's drawer. He seldom took any of the things from her room. Her things were too precious to carry around, but today, he had made an exception since she was coming home.

Caressing the soft, red leather between his fingers, he felt peaceful and safe from Uncle Phil's tirade.

*She's home, she's really home, and she's all mine. Nothing this old bastard can do will change that!*

"If you weren't my brother's kid, I'd—"

"Mr. Bruns, excuse me, but I'm gonna need some more change for the five o'clock rush."

Both men turned to look at the petite young woman with the cash drawer tucked beneath her arm. Susan Malone had worked at the theater about three weeks.

"Gee, I didn't mean to interrupt, or anything, Mr. Bruns." She looked at both men, wondering why these two were always yelling at each other. "Hi, Lenny," she added.

Susan moved closer to the boy, well aware that her dimpled smile was difficult to ignore. His aloofness bothered her. She knew guys found her attractive. Why was Lenny different? Maybe she had not given him the right signal. Shy guys took extra time, but this one was so cute that he might be worth the trouble.

"You coming, Susan? I said I'd get you the money from the office."

"Okay, Mr. Bruns." She moved between the men, making sure that her arm brushed Lenny's as she walked past.

Before Lenny could react, Uncle Phil was in his face. "You get back to work! I'd better not find you've slipped off again, or your ass is history in this place. Understand?"

Lenny nodded and found himself counting the number of times his uncle's whitish-pink tongue darted across his narrow mouth. The nervous habit had been a part of his uncle's demeanor for as long as Lenny could remember. Five, six, seven, eight times, Lenny counted.

Phil was disgusting, and his nails! God! They were always dirty, broken, and uneven. His hands were a mess, too—chapped, stained from those endless cigarettes he smoked, and made even more repulsive by the gray, curly hair that crawled all over the backs of his fingers.

Lenny hated knowing those hands had touched his mother. He remembered his banishment to the attic on several occasions so that Mother and Uncle Phil could be alone, but he was sure that his uncle knew nothing about the gloves. Mother would never have shared that special secret, would she?

The older man returned to his office. A chill shot through Lenny and his fingers rubbed harder against the soft leather gloves in his pockets.

*What if she asks about Phil? Oh, God, now that she is home, of course she will want to see him. I can't ever let that happen. I brought her home. She came to me. She needs to be with me! Uncle Phil must never know she's back. I don't want his ugly hands running over her naked body. I'd kill him first! I don't care what went on before between them. He's not getting near her!*

*I'll kill him! I'll kill him!* he repeated over and over under his breath.

Suddenly he needed more than just the touch of the leather gloves. He had to feel the soft fabric wrapped around his fingers, tightly sheathing the smooth skin of his palms. He raced across the lobby and in his haste to get to the storage room, bumped into two elderly women. He found the key and unlocked it. It was empty. He entered the dark recess with relief and bolted the door. Taking the gloves from his pockets, he rubbed them across his cheeks and mouth, thrusting his tongue into their openings before pulling them onto his hands, sighing as each one of his fingers slid into its tight leather womb.

"Oh, Mother, Mother!" he cried as the soft kid caressed him. "I am yours now, you are mine, only mine, and you won't share me with anyone, either. Mine, mine . . . ," he sobbed, as the gloves caressed his body and he fell to his knees in solitary ecstasy.

# chapter
# 8

Late Wednesday afternoon in Atlanta, John Foyles dropped the last few pages of the detailed report on his desk and smiled at Beth McKinnon perched on the corner of his desk. Her long blond hair was pulled into an elegant chignon, and even after putting in a ten-hour day, her makeup and tailored blue suit looked fresh.

"As usual, Beth, you've done your job well. This updated list of junk bonds is impressive. Your idea of perusing the less popular areas of the market for these hidden gems is right on target."

"Thanks, but the real fun comes when I can move in and out at just the right time. We all know the trick is to remember these babies were never intended to be long-term holdings." Pleased with herself, she leaned back on her hands and took a deep breath.

John smiled at her and glanced at the curve of her breast, which was accentuated by her movement. "I know our clients sleep better at night knowing you're looking after their investments."

"Well, speaking of sleeping," Beth said, sliding off his desk, "I'm going to wrap things up and get out of here. I'll be dead on my feet for those calls in the morning if I don't get something to eat and a few hours of sleep. We're meeting with the Jamison group at eight, right?"

John stood and faced her. He was used to petite

women: Monica barely reached his shoulder. The top of Beth's head came just below his eyes. He needed only to tilt his head to kiss her. For a moment he allowed himself to think about how well their bodies fit together—in and out of bed.

"John? Eight o'clock, tomorrow morning, the Jamison group?"

"What? Oh, yeah. We've managed their equity portfolio for years."

"Do you think they will buy into our changes?"

John forced himself to concentrate. Usually he had no trouble separating his personal life with Beth from his business life with her. She was so good at keeping the distance between them at the office, he sometimes thought she was two different people. With added resolve to be professional, he walked to the window and answered her.

"Given our performance this quarter, they can afford to get more aggressive," he said.

"Mr. Jamison seems pretty conservative. You might have a rough time convincing him to take more risk."

"Then we'll see how good a salesman I really am, won't we?"

"I guess so." Beth grinned at him, and opened the door that led to the outer offices. "If we're through for the day, can I interest you in a glass of wine and some dinner?"

"Sounds good. Just give me ten minutes to clean up my notes and call my kids. I want to check things on the home front and tell them good night."

"Fine. Stop by my desk when you're ready."

Later that evening, John Foyles and Beth McKinnon sat at a small table in the corner of their hotel lounge. John was accustomed to stopping off for a drink before dinner. It did not matter that it might be a different place every night. He thrived on change. Lately, he needed more and more of it in his life. He knew a lot of guys who really hated traveling and being away from home so much, but he loved discovering new places and meeting new people.

As regional manager, he was able to indulge his need by maintaining a heavy schedule of visits to the eighteen district offices under his charge. When his business life took precedence over his family, he reminded himself he had always been a caring father, and he was an excellent provider. He prided himself on his ability to give his family a wonderful life.

"So, how were things back home?" Beth asked. "Everybody all ready for dinner?"

"I really don't know. No one answered the phone," he said a little pensively.

"Is that a big deal?" She reached over and touched his hand. His fingers closed over hers.

"No, they usually eat out on Wednesdays. Monica's probably buying them cheeseburgers. I wish she wouldn't do that."

"Hey, John, lighten up!"

"That's easy for you to say."

"Yeah, I guess it is. I don't have much experience in feeding kids nutritional meals."

"Is my next line supposed to be, 'How come a pretty girl like you never married and had kids of her own?' "

"Aren't you glad I haven't?" She smiled and gazed at him for a few moments. "Oh, I've been close once or twice, but I was always more interested in my career, I guess. Besides, I'm only twenty-eight. I've got lots of time."

*Twenty-eight.* When he was that age, he had been married for five years. Maybe he should have waited, enjoyed his freedom for a few more years before getting tied down. He probably would be happier today if he had not done what everyone expected him to do back then. But it never seemed that he had much of a choice. Things just happened. Everyone he knew then had gotten married early, whether they were ready or not.

Misunderstanding the reason for his silence, Beth loosened her hand and patted his arm. "Relax, Dad, maybe they just went to a movie. Oh, but it's Wednesday. Guess good parents don't allow their kids out on weeknights."

"I'm not really worried. I'm sure they're fine. Now that I think about it, they don't have school tomorrow. Jeb was going to a friend's birthday party. Maybe the girls found something to do, too."

"What about your wife?"

"I don't know. Unless she's with the children, she's usually home, especially after dark."

"Maybe she went to see a friend."

"Could have, but Monica's afraid of her own shadow at night. She rarely leaves the house by herself after the sun goes down."

"If you want to try calling her again, there's a phone in the lobby. I'll save your seat."

"No, that's okay, Beth. I'll try later if I think about it." He leaned over and kissed her. "Now, what would you like for dinner? You must be starving!"

Lenny worked concessions for the five o'clock, five-fifteen, and five-thirty shows. He switched out the soda cannisters, popped corn, and swept the floor. Then he emptied the big plastic cans and hauled trash until six-thirty. Each time he took a bag to the Dumpster, he looked at the blue station wagon parked in the employee lot.

The afternoon sun had dipped below the surrounding buildings. Soon it would be dusk, then dark and time to move her car into the main part of the mall parking lot for the night. He hated to deviate from his plan, but he was running late, thanks to the old man, and so the mall would have to do. Tomorrow he would stash the car someplace safe. She wasn't going to need it. He could pull off the plates and ditch them, too. The plan, his perfect plan.

The minutes until his seven o'clock quitting time dragged by until he thought he would scream with pent-up emotion. Finally, his uncle allowed him to leave. He grabbed his jacket from the break room and hurried out the back door.

"Lenny, Lenny! Wait up!"

Lenny turned and saw the new girl who worked the box office running toward him.

"Hi there!" the girl chirped. "Remember me? Susan Malone? Tough day, huh? Thought you just might want to relax a little and have some fun. What do you say we go get a pizza or something?"

"I can't, thanks," said Lenny. He continued to walk across the lot.

"You sure? I think we could have a good time." She pursed her reddish lips and her heavily lashed, brown eyes issued an invitation a blind man could have seen in the dark.

"No, I gotta go."

"What's the matter? You already got a girlfriend?"

"Yeah, something like that," he mumbled, wondering why she did not get into her damn car and leave him alone. She was making him late!

Susan flipped back her long black hair and breathed deeply. Her maroon uniform vest accentuated her full breasts and nipped-in waist. She moved closer to him and tapped her finger on his chest. "Well, if you ever break up or anything, let me know. I think we'd have a lot in common. You like to watch movies?"

"Sometimes."

"So do I. Maybe we could sit together during the previews," she suggested, referring to the late-night showings of the new films Phil allowed the employees to see for free.

"Maybe. See you around, okay?"

Susan smiled and allowed her tongue to glide slowly across her upper lip. She felt that the gesture had always been one of her sexiest moves. Lenny recoiled as though she had slapped him. His reaction first surprised, then intrigued her.

"Yeah," she said, "see you around." She gave him a knowing wink and walked to her car, pulled open her door, and looked back at him. He had not moved. Why didn't he leave if he was in such a big hurry to get home? He was just standing there by the Dumpsters. What a strange guy. She would have her work cut out for her to snag that one, but then she loved a challenge!

"At last!" sighed Lenny as he watched Susan's car turn onto the highway. He felt his pockets for the car keys he had slipped into his jacket earlier in the day. Pulling them out, he looked at the ornate, silver ring with four keys swinging next to a small disc with a large "M" engraved in script.

"M," he said aloud. " 'M' for Mother. Were you afraid that I wouldn't recognize you? You must have carried this key ring just for me."

Ten minutes later, he parked her station wagon in the covered lot by Sears, then ran back to his own car, cursing the heavy crowds that were gathering for the evening shows. People and cars streamed in front of him seemingly intent on holding him up even more.

He hurried home with anxiety clutching his stomach, petrified of his mother's wrath. He should not be late. Not tonight. Not on her first night home.

Monica awoke in darkness to debilitating pain, so global she was unable to pinpoint its location or source. Her head pounded, churning up sounds and images that scattered across her mind's eye like dry leaves fluttering in a gusty, autumn wind. Jeb and the twins were flipping pancakes, and John's voice repeated, "I've changed; I don't belong here anymore." She smelled popcorn and wondered if it were someone's supper. A box of oversized popped kernels slid across a counter. Struggling to catch it, to stop it from spilling onto the floor, she tried to reach out, but her arms refused to obey. Peach Pie was limping. Were they at the vet? Where was David? He would help her. Was she at the hospital? It didn't smell like a hospital. Smelled more like rotting flowers. Was she in a funeral parlor? Had she died?

She shifted her aching head. A wave of nausea flooded over her senses, and so she lay still, willing the queasiness to pass. How could she be dead? She hurt too much. Oh, God, she hurt! Why couldn't she see? Her eyes were open. She tried to lift her hand to touch her face. One kind of pain snaked across her shoulder and another slithered up the tender underside of her arm. Her wrist burned, but she was unable to move her hand. What was wrong with her? She squinted her eyes and tried to see past the darkness.

Chilling ideas encircled her brain until finally, out of desperation, her mind fixed itself onto the only possible answer—an accident! She must have been in a car crash. Was she alone? Were the children with her? Peach? Was anyone else injured? Had she killed somebody and they were afraid to tell her?

Tears filled her eyes. Her stomach churned again, the twisting muscles producing a sharp cramp. Instinctively, she tried to ease the pain by drawing up her knees to curl into a ball, but found she could not do it. Something was holding her hands and feet. She formulated the words, "Help me!" in her mind, but was unable to open her mouth to say them aloud. Something was pulled taut across her lips, blocking her speech. The more she tried to cry out, the more she felt it tear at the skin around her mouth.

She reared up against the bindings, tossing and flailing her body from one side of the bed to the other. The mattress springs rattled beneath her, showering bits of rust onto the floor, but the iron bars held her fast. Finally exhausted, she tried to calm herself and gain some semblance of control by rocking herself back and forth within her confines. This had to be a dream. A nightmare. If she closed her eyes and tried to relax, things would improve. Someone will come and explain. . . .

Someone will come . . . someone will come. . . .

A fleeting touch on her face, a soft scratchiness that began on her cheek and feathered its way across her chin and down her neck was the first indication that something different was happening to her. Someone was with her. Someone was caressing her skin. It felt wonderful: warm and comforting, reminding her how her mother's soothing hand had felt when, as a child, she had been sick with fever. Sighing, she gave herself to the moment. She still could not move outside her confined space, nor see even dim shadows, but her fears had subsided. Someone had come at last. Someone was speaking to her.

"Mother, can you hear me? You've been sleeping for such a long time."

Had she heard the word "Mother?" Was Jeb here? If it were Jeb, then everything must be okay. If something awful had happened, they would not let him in here. A rush of happiness flowed over her.

*Oh, thank God, the children must be all right.*

"Mother, I want you to wake up now. Your medicine doesn't usually make you this sleepy. Maybe I gave you too much. I didn't realize how much weight you've lost."

The scratchy caress continued, but it no longer calmed her. Its insidious probing became annoying—like fingernails scratching across a chalkboard. This was not her son. This voice was too deep, and besides, Jeb never called her "Mother." What medicine? How had she lost weight?

She moved her head and tried to rise up to show that she was awake and listening. The pain had lessened, and the grogginess was dropping away, but she still could not understand what had happened to her.

*Sally Kemp*

"I've needed you so much, Mother. I know you missed me, too. That's why you came back, isn't it?"

"Mmm . . . mmmmuh . . ."

"Mother, are you awake? You want to tell me how glad you are to be home, don't you?"

Lenny left her to cross the room and pick up the lamp. He turned the burning wick higher, then put the light on the floor beside the bed. From its glow he could see the redness on her wrists and ankles where the ropes had bitten into her flesh. The skin around the tape on her mouth looked red and swollen. He knew he had done right to bind and gag her, though he could not say exactly why. He also knew that when she was fully awake, she would be furious with him for staking her out like a prisoner.

"Now, Mother, at least for a while, I need to keep your mouth taped . . . until I'm sure you won't cause a fuss. But I can take your blindfold off so that you can see me."

He moved close to her, lifting her head to untie the fabric covering her eyes. "I love what you've done to yourself. You are so beautiful, Mother. If it hadn't been for your green eyes and the locket, I might never have recognized you. But you knew me. I could tell that the first time I saw you at the theater."

The painful lump at the back of her head disappeared as Monica felt the knot loosen and the cloth pulled away from her face.

*It was only a blindfold. She really could see!* She stared up into the dimness, blinking her eyes to focus them. Exposed beams met at the center of the pitched roof and ran the length of the ceiling. She thought of the rafters in her attic, but the only house with an attic she had ever lived in was back east; and it had been a cheery apartment where her children loved to play. This place was dark and terrifying.

She became aware of a faint glow and forced her eyes to follow it down the wall and across the floor. Faded blue stripes ran the length of the mattress where she was lying.

Lifting her eyes, she saw a large form leaning against the iron bars at the foot of the bed. She could tell that it was a man, but his face was hidden in the shadows.

"Welcome home. Do you remember our special room?"

The voice sounded oddly familiar, although she had no idea who was speaking. She shook her head. The movement brought a painful remembrance of her restraints.

"Sorry about the ropes, Mother."

Only then did it hit her: The pain she felt was not from being injured; it was, in part, from being stretched out and tied to a bed! What was going on? Where was she? Monica squirmed and pulled at her bindings. The old bed rattled beneath her.

"Hey! Calm down. You'll hurt yourself. The ropes will only get tighter if you tug at them. Behave and I'll let you loose in a little while."

He shifted his weight and moved the lower part of his body into the light. She could not see his face, but she lay still and watched his hands stretch toward her.

"Ah, you recognize the gloves, I see. These were some of your favorites. I couldn't decide whether to surprise you with these or the red satin ones, but then I remembered how you especially liked the feel of these, the roughness of them, against your naked body, and so I chose the black lace. Just now you awoke to their touch on your face. That makes them even more precious to me, Mother."

Monica closed her eyes and tried to think, to remember how she had gotten here. Her arms and legs shook. Tears spilled from her eyes and trickled down the sides of her face. She began to sob and the jerky movements made it difficult for her to breathe. The adhesive across her mouth was suffocating her. Lifting her panic-stricken eyes to the figure at the foot of the bed, she tried to scream for help. She felt the tape being ripped from her face a moment before she slipped into unconsciousness.

# chapter
# 9

A chilly, night breeze held the promise of more rain when Nancy Crawford dropped Jeb at his house Wednesday night. He was the last birthday guest to be delivered, and Nancy looked forward to returning home to her husband and the cup of fresh coffee he had promised to have ready for her.

"Here you are, kiddo. Again, I'm sorry it's after nine, and we're an hour later than we thought we might be, but I called your mom about five and left a message on your recorder when she didn't answer."

"That's okay. She won't be mad or anything. She knew where I was." Jeb thanked Nancy and raced through the dark mist to the front door.

"Door's locked, but I have a key," Jeb yelled.

Nancy waited until the boy was inside, expecting to see Monica or Peach Pie pop out the door to say hello, but neither did. Just as she put the van in gear to move away, Jeb ran back.

"Mom's not home," he announced. "Maybe she went to get Peach since he's gone, too."

Not at this hour. David Riley did not have evening hours. Nancy hoped nothing had happened to Peach.

"I think I'd better come in with you. We'll leave your mom a note and you can come back home with Billy and me." They climbed out of the van and followed Jeb into the house.

Nancy had just flipped on the kitchen lights and looked around for a note or some indication of Monica's whereabouts when the front door opened. Mia and Sarah bounded down the hall and into the kitchen.

"Hi, Mrs. Crawford. Where's Mom?"

"She's not here," said Jeb.

"Hi, girls," Nancy said. "We're not sure where she is."

Jeb looked at his sisters. "Do you remember her saying anything about not being here tonight? I sure don't."

"She said she'd be here. She's always here when we get home." Sarah's eyes reddened. Nancy put her arm around the girl.

"I'm sure she's just a little late. Why don't you all go see what's on TV, and I'll hang around for a bit."

Nancy picked up the phone and called her husband, Peter. They decided that Nancy should stay with Monica's children until they located her. Ten minutes later, the phone rang. It was John, calling from Atlanta.

"What's up?" he asked. "I was just calling to tell the kids good night."

Nancy explained and waited for his reply.

"I'm sure Monica's fine. Probably got caught up in one of the stores. Maybe she drove out to the junk barns in Forney and got lost coming back."

"Well, maybe, but those places have been closed for hours. We're concerned about her, and the children—"

"Where are the kids? Are they all right?"

"They're fine, John. I just wish I had some answers for Jeb and the girls."

"Don't worry about them. They'll be okay. And thanks for looking after things. Why don't I call back in a couple of hours? I'm sure by then Monica will have appeared, loaded with packages and explanations. She'll really owe you after this one!"

"Don't you think her behavior is a little unusual? Has anything like this ever happened before?"

"Not that I remember, but I'm sure she has her reasons. I'm just sorry she's putting you out. Listen, Nancy, I really have to go. I'll check back with you and the kids in a couple of hours. Okay?"

"Sure, John. Call me."

Nancy slammed down the receiver. "Son of a bitch," she said under her breath. No wonder Monica's worried about her marriage. At least he could have pretended to be concerned.

She folded her arms on the desk and rested her head on top of them. The phone rang, startling her. She grabbed it on the first ring. It was David Riley. He had been trying to reach Monica since four that afternoon. She had wanted to know the minute Peach Pie was ready to come home.

"Monica's not here," Nancy replied to his first question. "The house was dark when I brought Jeb home. I'm really worried, David. It's just not like her to be five minutes off schedule and she's way overdue now."

David pulled off his glasses and rubbed his eyes. "Have you spoken with her husband?"

"Yes, he's in Atlanta. He says she's probably shopping."

"She might be."

"I doubt it. Not this long, with no word," said Nancy.

"I'll make a few calls, just to make sure she hasn't been in an accident, or something. Then I'll bring Peach over."

"Thanks, David. The kids would love to have him back, and I really appreciate your help."

"No thanks are needed. In the meantime, why don't you phone some of her friends and neighbors? I'm sure there's a logical explanation for all of this," he said, trying unsuccessfully to control the anxious feeling in his stomach.

"Isn't there someone on this list who knows you?" Nancy asked Jeb as they perused the neighborhood association roster after talking with David.

"Well, the Guthries nextdoor brought us a cake when we moved in, but they're hardly ever here. Same with the Housners across the street. They travel all over the country in their RV. Most of the people are older and don't have kids in school."

"Hmmm, how about the Pattersons who live on the other side of you?"

"They know us, but not well. They own a restaurant downtown and they're gone a lot. Oh, yeah, there is one couple, the Gibsons. They live at the end of the block. Mom really likes them. She's always taking them cookies and they bring her flowers from their garden."

"All right. I'll call them first," Nancy said, running her finger down the page to find the phone number.

"No answer," she said a few moments later. She called the other names listed on Monica's street. Jeb listened to a few of the conversations, then wandered back to Billy.

Nancy felt her frustration level soaring. No one was able to help her. She sat at the desk, rubbing her temples, deciding which homes on the surrounding streets she should try next when she heard a commotion at the door. Peach Pie was home. Nancy went out to greet the arrivals.

"Hi David," she said, extending her hand.

"Hi. How is it going? Any word?"

"Nothing, I'm sorry to say. How about you?" Nancy checked her watch. It was half past ten.

"Well," he began, glancing at Jeb.

"Go ahead," said Nancy. "Tell us what you've found." She lightly touched Jeb's hair.

David walked over to where Jeb was kneeling beside his dog. Peach had stretched out on the floor, content to have his young master's hand rubbing his ear. David knelt beside Jeb, put his hand on the boy's shoulder, and glanced at Nancy to include her in the conversation. She, too, knelt on the floor.

"I went to school with one of the detectives on the Dallas police force. He's a friend of mine," David said.

"When I phoned him tonight, he was real helpful. Between us, we contacted a lot of places . . . hospitals and the like . . . and your mom isn't in any of them."

*Thank God,* thought Nancy, realizing David meant he had checked the morgue. She watched David's hand deepen the pressure on Jeb's shoulder.

"Hey, that's good news, Jeb. We found out this evening that your mom hasn't been in any traffic accidents in the metroplex."

"Where . . . where is she then?" asked Jeb.

"I don't know, but we're going to find her. There may be some perfectly logical reason why she hasn't come home yet."

The boy slipped beyond David's reach to bury his face in Peach Pie's soft fur. After a moment, he lifted his head and looked at David and Nancy.

"Mom would be here if she could. Thanks for telling me this stuff, Dr. Riley."

"You're welcome. You know, I bet old Peach would really appreciate a dog biscuit and a drink of water. Why don't you take him out to the kitchen for a treat?"

"Is his foot okay? Can he hurt it by walking on it too much?" Jeb asked as he watched the dog roll to its feet.

"He'll favor it for a day or so, but he's fine. We'll take the bandage off at the end of the week. He'll be running like a pup in no time."

"Good. C'mon Peach, let's go get a cookie." Jeb rose to his feet, but kept his head lowered. He gripped the dog and led him slowly down the hall.

Nancy looked at David with apprehension. "You really believe something has happened to her, don't you?"

"Yes," David whispered.

"Let's go sit in the living room. Maybe we can start making a plan . . . or . . . or, I don't know. What do people do in a situation like this?"

"We start by remaining calm, as tough as that is going

to be." David took a deep breath. "First of all, where are
the twins? How much do they know?"

"They're getting ready for bed. Undoubtedly, they'll
have a lot of questions."

David nodded his head, wishing he had the answers.

They sat down on one of the large flowered sofas in
Monica's living room, surrounded by her books, plants,
and family pictures. A gardening book lay open on the
coffee table, a wooly afghan was tossed across an arm-
chair, and a dish of hard candy beckoned from the side
table. David reached over and picked one up, only to find
that it was an elegant, hand-blown piece of glass.

"Monica can't keep real candy in here because Peach
eats it," Nancy explained. "So she started a collection of
glass candies."

David ran his fingers over the piece of green-striped
candy. "They look good enough to eat," he murmured.

Then he took a moment to enjoy the welcoming aura
Monica had created. Despite everything that was here, the
real heart, the life of this room, this house was missing.
David thought about the paradox. For so long he had
wanted to see where and how she lived. Now that he was
here, surrounded at last by her things, Monica was gone.
Had he come too late?

He turned to the woman beside him. "What . . . what
have you found out?"

"Nothing. Absolutely nothing." Nancy shook her head
slowly. "I can't even find a neighbor who knows anything
about Monica, and she isn't with any of her friends. I
guess we were the last people she spoke with today."

"Do you remember her saying anything about her
plans, any errands she had to run?"

"No, only that she had taken Peach in to see you."

"Have you talked to the people she works with?"

"I called Mrs. Chester, the principal at Hyler Elementary, but she hasn't seen Monica since yesterday. You
know she never works on Wednesdays."

"When you spoke with Monica today, did you sense any uneasiness or unhappiness about her?" David asked. "Anything that indicated she might want to get away for a while, or that maybe she needed a change?"

"No, she was upset about a part of her life, and we talked about that, but I didn't get any feeling she wanted out. She wouldn't do that, David. Even if she wanted to, she'd never leave these kids."

"How about her husband?" David wondered why John had not caught the first plane to Dallas as soon as he heard his wife was missing.

"He said he'd call back in a couple of hours. He's in Atlanta."

"He has to come home. The children need him." *If John had been here all along to protect her, would we be worried sick about her now?* David's mind raced through the possibilities. *Was there something I should have seen or done today in the office?* He had forgotten Nancy's presence until she spoke.

"I hope he's figured that out by now," Nancy said. "My patience with John is wearing a little thin."

"Have you looked around her bedroom? Is anything missing?"

"Let's go have a look."

Nancy led the way to the master bedroom. David followed, somewhat hesitant to enter the intimate space. Flowers filled the room. A spring bouquet of tulips and hyacinths stood in a crystal vase on Monica's dressing table. The neatly made king-sized bed was covered with a floral bedspread that matched the fabric on the two high-backed wing chairs flanking a bay window.

David crossed the room and entered the adjoining bath. Was it real, or was he just dreaming that Monica's scent surrounded him? He ran his fingers across the towels and over the bristles of her toothbrush that stood upright in a flowered china holder. The shower sent his imagination spinning into high gear. A vision of her within the glass enclosure, rinsing shampoo from her hair, her eyes closed against the spray whirled in his mind. He felt the walls and tile floor. Everything was dry. He opened a drawer, not really knowing what he was looking for, and saw her collection of makeup. Another drawer held her brushes and combs, hair ribbons, a small handled mirror and several hand-made "I love you, Mom" cards from the children.

Nancy walked into the bathroom and opened a door to a closet. Men's suits, jackets, shirts, and slacks hung from the rods. The floor was littered with running shoes, three pairs of cowboy boots, and shoe-polishing equipment. Nancy closed that door and opened another. She and David peered into the pristine interior. All of Monica's things were in perfect order. Nancy recognized a few shirts and some of the shoes, but could not tell if anything was missing. They closed the door, and David leaned against the basin as Nancy returned to the bedroom.

"Her glasses are here on the table. She doesn't wear them to drive, but she can't read without them. She generally carries them with her if she knows she has to look at a menu or labels in the grocery store."

*Or a road map,* thought David, although he, too, believed that she would never leave the children without an explanation. "She left my office about one-forty-five this afternoon. We were talking ... we were interrupted. ... I had an emergency come in, and had to rush off. She was telling me something, but I don't remember what it was. It wasn't anything about leaving, though. She wasn't acting any differently." What he did remember was how lovely she had looked in her bright green sweater, how fresh and full of life she had seemed, how happy he had felt just being in the same room with her, and how his pulse had jumped when he touched her hand.

"What are we going to do? Should we call the police?"

"Officially, her husband will have to do that, but it's not against the law for adults to leave home unless there's a warrant out against them, or they're avoiding some type of court order."

Nancy's gaze flew to his. "What are you telling me? You mean because she's not wanted by the police, they won't help us find her?" She jumped to her feet. "Can people disappear, and the police won't do anything?"

"My friend at the station said they'll take John's statement, and write up an offense report for their computer. It'll be called a 'Want-to-locate' case. That report will stay in their files until she is found. But until they have concrete evidence of foul play, they must assume she is missing because she wants to be."

"But Monica wouldn't just go off somewhere!"

"I know. If children or juveniles are missing, they merit immediate action, but it's not that way with adults. I don't like it either, but they tell me it's the law."

The last time Nancy had felt this hopeless and lost was when her father had called to tell her that her mother had cancer. Monica had taken charge. Before nightfall, she had packed up Nancy's five children, moved them in with her own family, and put Nancy and Peter on a plane to her parents.

How could she help Monica now? She couldn't let her down, but Monica was the one who was great in emergencies, not her.

She and David returned to the living room. Before they had a chance to sit down, Mia and Sarah ran into the room at the same instant that the phone rang. Nancy took the call, and David took the girls to the kitchen.

The conversation with John was brief and cool. When Nancy went into the kitchen, everyone had a soda, and David was helping Mia open a bag of pretzels.

"Guess junk food's my cure for everything," he said sheepishly, aware that he was probably breaking house rules by offering carbonated drinks and snacks so close to bedtime.

Nancy smiled at him, thinking again what a very nice

man he was, and greeted the girls. Mia took charge of the pretzels, and Sarah blinked back tears. Nancy pulled her close.

"Your father is on his way home," she said.

One look at Nancy's face told David the phone conversation had been a tense one, but he said nothing. His handful of pretzels had lost their appeal and he lay them on the counter.

"When will Dad be here?" Sarah asked.

"Very late, sweetheart," Nancy answered. "His plane won't land until one-thirty tonight. You will have to wait and see him in the morning."

"Does he know about Mom? Is that why he's coming home?" asked Mia. "He's not supposed to be back 'til Friday."

"Yes, he knows, and, of course, he wants to be here with you."

"Are we going to have a sitter until he gets here?" Mia asked.

"No, Billy and I'll keep you company. My other kids will enjoy having their dad to themselves for the evening."

"Can you stay, too, Dr. Riley?"

"Wish I could, Jeb, but I've got to go home. How about if I bring some doughnuts over in the morning? I'll put them inside the front storm door if no one is up and about. Nancy, will you walk me to the door?"

"Night, Dr. Riley," Mia said.

"Night, kids. See you tomorrow."

"You going to wait up?" David asked as he and Nancy stood on the porch and watched the rain.

"Yeah, no way I could sleep."

"I know what you mean. If Monica comes in, no matter how late it is, will you call me?" He pulled a prescription pad from his shirt pocket, and scribbled his home phone number before tearing off the top sheet and handing it to her.

"Of course, David. And thanks again for all your help tonight."

David nodded and stepped off the porch. When he turned to wave good-bye, Nancy was surprised to see what she thought were tears glistening in his eyes. Maybe it was just the rain.

# chapter

# 10

On Wednesday evening, Lenny carried a bowl of hot soup up the attic steps. He hoped Mother had gotten over her little tantrum and was ready to be herself. Even during her loudest and most exasperating spells, she had never passed out on him before. What else about her had changed? He had seen real terror in her face right before she fainted.

What could she be so afraid of? She was home now, with someone who cared about her. Had he slipped too much of the clonidine into her drink at the theater? He had never been sure about the dosage. It was an old prescription he had found in the medicine cabinet. The next time he mixed her nightly dose, he would give her less.

Suddenly the thought hit him. Could her fainting spell have been a trick? Just an act to pull him back into the old days where she had been in charge? She was smart! She could manipulate any situation. He would have to be careful that she did not gain the upper hand this time.

At the top of the steps, he opened the door and left it ajar. The light from the stairwell pierced the darkness creating the shape of a large V, whose point ended on the woman lying on the low bed in the corner of the room. Since Lenny could detect no movement, he assumed she was still sleeping. He smiled and tiptoed over to her.

She lay in a tangle of red hair, arms and legs still

bound. He had not replaced the tape across her mouth. Her full lips were slightly open, and it seemed to him as though she were barely breathing. He set the supper tray on the floor and moved closer, leaning over her so that her soft breath caressed his cheek. Her eyelids were closed, hiding the remarkable green eyes that had bullied, teased, adored, invited, and protected him over the years. They were still exactly as he remembered.

What was different was the ripeness of her body, her scent, and the texture and feel of her skin. As he watched her sleeping, he congratulated himself on his good fortune. Not only had he brought her back, but she was more exciting than before. He lifted his hand, still encased in black lace, and touched her hair, twisting his fingers into the shiny curls.

She awoke with a start. It was only fast acting on Lenny's part that kept her from screaming.

"You're all right," he said, clapping his hand over her mouth. "You're safe as long as you don't holler. If you yell, I'll have to put the tape back on. Will you promise not to scream?"

Monica nodded to indicate she would comply with his wishes. Whatever else happened, she was still alive.

He removed his hand and sat back on his heels. For the first time she was able to see the man's face and immediately she recognized him as the kid from the theater.

"Lenny?"

"Yeah. It's me."

"What happened? Why am I here?"

"I brought you home."

Home? "This isn't my home. I live—"

"Here. This is your house."

"No, no, it's not." Her gaze circled the room. "I don't recognize anything. Why are my hands and feet . . . ?" She gestured to the ropes.

"I was afraid you might get hurt. I tied you down to

keep you safe." He remembered her rages. The ropes protected them both.

"They hurt. If I promise not to harm myself, will you untie me?" What was happening? She strained her mind to remember. This wasn't a dream, was it? "Will you untie me?"

"That depends."

His face swam before her eyes. She fought to keep it in focus. "On what?"

"On whether you earn it or not."

His words terrified her. She swallowed twice, and counted slowly to five, forcing herself to maintain some remnant of composure. Why was she here? Instinctively, she reasoned that her only way through this was to keep him talking. He held the key to this horrible place. Getting the ropes off had to be the first step.

"What do I have to do so that you will untie me?"

"Be nice to me."

"What do I have to do?" Her legs shook.

"For starters, I want you to stay with me and do what I say. If I unite you, you have to promise you won't run away or try to see Uncle Phil or anyone else. This is your home. You belong here, with me."

"Okay. I promise not to run away, and I promise not to go to see Uncle Phil," she said, having no idea who Uncle Phil was. "Will you untie me now?"

Lenny stood up.

"One more thing."

"Y-yes."

"Beg me."

"What . . . what did you say?"

"You heard me, Mother. I want to hear you beg me to untie you. Let me hear just how badly you want your freedom."

"Why are you calling me 'Mother'? I'm not your mother!" And why was he wearing those strange gloves?

Was he going to kill her . . . or worse? She knew he was in control and she was powerless to stop him.

*Calm down, calm down, and think, Monica,* an inner voice whispered. *Calm down and play his game.*

Monica mustered up her courage and looked at him. He was staring at her oddly. His head was cocked to the side, and he moved so close she could feel his breath on her face.

"Of course, you're my mother," he whispered. "Why else would you be here? You've come to protect me. You belong to me."

"Please, Lenny. Untie me. You've made a mistake. Don't make me lie here like this. I hurt and I have to use the bathroom. Please!"

Lenny laughed. "I know what you're up to, but your games won't work with me. Now you see what it feels like to lie there, staked out like an animal. How many times did you allow this to happen to me? When I was a kid, and when I got older? How often did you laugh at me, or scream, depending on your mood, before you walked away and left me tied to this bed? Too many times, Mother. Too many times."

His face twisted in remembrance of old injuries and his eyes reflected the countless indignities she had watched him suffer before she took pity on him and stopped his suffering. Feelings he thought he had hidden away forever tore through him. He could never allow her to hurt him again.

Beneath his anger and his harsh words, Monica could feel his pain, but was too scared for herself to reach out to him, even if she had been able. His feelings were more than she could deal with right now.

Lenny stood and checked the ropes on her ankles. Under the knots her skin was already bruised.

"Please untie me," she repeated. "Let me go to the bathroom." Tears, easily summoned, added to her desired effect by streaming off the sides of her face and rolling into her hair.

When he turned back to her, he saw her tears and stumbled over her tray, spilling her soup. His anger dissipated as he bent to push the crackers and the pear he had brought her away from the mess. How happy he had been just a few minutes ago when he lovingly fixed her food. He had even unearthed a cloth napkin from the cupboard instead of giving her one of the cheap paper ones he used.

She had to eat, he told himself, and use the bathroom. After all, he did not want her to die and leave him again—not after he had worked so hard to get her here. There were sweeter ways to make her pay . . . ways they would both enjoy. He went to her then, and without word, untied the knots that held her ankles.

Relief overrode pain as she flexed her knees and wiggled her toes. At least everything still worked. She had no thought of escape, no thought of running. She felt only the immense release of the moment. This small victory of limited freedom made the decision to beg, to play his game, acceptable. Even in her muddled state, she hoped she had somehow won the first round.

"Thank you, Lenny," she whispered. "Will you untie my hands?"

In moments she was free. She sighed and examined the angry red welts on her wrists before hugging her arms to her chest. When she sat up, the trembling began again. She knew it was fear causing the strange sensations she was experiencing, but it was something else, too. Her head felt as though it were stuffed with cotton balls. Her heart was racing.

"You ready to go to the bathroom? I'll take you downstairs. The chamber pot is still under the bed. You can use it when I'm not around."

As soon as he spoke, he forgot about her and paced back and forth across the floor, swinging his arms, then shaking his hands. His sweet grin and boyishness were gone now. He mumbled beneath his breath, angrily, and Monica wondered whom he was scolding in such fierce tones. Frightened that any movement she made might send him over the edge, she sat frozen. His eyes glittered, the intense stare threatened her, and his large torso looked superhuman in the dim light.

She forced herself to remember that he was just a boy. Eighteen, nineteen at most. He had always been nice to her. Her mind flashed back to the theater where they often shared a laugh over the candy counter. Once, when she dropped her entire carton of popcorn on the floor, he insisted on cleaning it up himself. Then he gave her a fresh box at no charge. "It'll be our secret," he had said.

She supposed there was goodness in him somewhere, but right now she did not know how to find it. Incapable of speaking, she rocked herself gently, too scared to do anything but listen while he talked.

"You'll be staying in the attic for a while. I think it's safer; besides, you never hesitated to let me rot up here, did you? But when I do take you downstairs, don't try to run away from me."

He tapped his finger on her chest. His touch jolted her as though he had used a hot poker. He was furious, ranting, but she sensed something else. Was it fear? Hurt? She stared at him as long as she could, forcing herself to concentrate, hoping to find some answer, some clue to this puzzle. Finally, she gave up, and looked away. She was near tears again, too exhausted to continue challenging him.

An abrupt change came over him. He relaxed his body, grinned, and tenderly patted her hair. Then he whispered into her ear.

"You'd never make it to the door, Mother. I couldn't let you go now. I love you. This is your home. Once you get used to it again, you'll want to be here . . . with me, forever."

Not allowing herself to think about what he had just told her, Monica slid her legs over the side of the bed, dangled them a minute, and stood up. Her movement forced him to step back. She looked down at her bare feet to see if they were really holding her, but her gaze caught on the row of ugly plastic buttons running down her dress.

*My God, what am I wearing?*

The blue garment, at one time merely gaudy, was now frightful. It fell to her ankles and was at least three sizes too big. Only a corner of the long lace collar was visible to her eye, but she could see that it was badly stained.

On top of her dress she was wearing a pink angora cardigan, riddled with moth holes. One particularly large rent in the sleeve had been poorly darned.

"These aren't my clothes, Lenny. Where are my things? I was wearing . . . I can't remember . . . but I know I don't own anything like this."

"That's your favorite dress, Mother. Your medicine must be confusing you. I'll cut back on the dosage tonight."

This, her favorite dress? What medicine? And why did he keep calling her "Mother?" What did he expect her to do? Cook for him? Clean his house and do his wash? What else? Monica shuddered at the thought.

"C'mon now," he said, "I'll take you downstairs and then get you more soup. Maybe you're just hungry."

He took her arm and led her down a narrow stairway. Monica wished for a hand railing, something to hold on to in her shaky state, but there was nothing. Twice she lost her footing and would have plunged down the steps except for Lenny's strong hands on her. He was right about one thing. She would never make it to the door alone.

They entered a dingy hallway and passed two closed doors. Lenny stopped at a third door that was slightly ajar. Monica assumed it was the bathroom.

"You can go in by yourself, but I'll be right here and the door stays open. Don't bother going through the cabinets or anything. I moved all your stuff to your room. If you need something, you'll have to ask me."

He put his hand on her face. The black lace glove he

wore felt scratchy on her cheek. She wanted to scream as he ran his fingers over her eyes, down her neck, and across her breasts. She tried not to flinch when his face came within inches of hers.

"What do you want?" she asked. His sweet grin and boyish airs fled. The odd light she had feared earlier, returned to his eyes as he popped a gloved finger into his mouth and made loud, sucking noises. She was shocked.

"Your green eyes have bewitched me, Mother," he said at last. "It's good we want the same thing."

"Why . . . why do you wear those gloves?"

"Oh, would you prefer a different pair? The gray silk? Or maybe the navy kid? It's too soon for you to choose the gloves. That is something else you'll have to earn. For now, I'm making those choices." He drew a large letter "L" on her cheek with his wet finger. "I did that once with perfume, there, on your thigh, but I guess you were still sleeping." Reaching down, he caressed her leg, then ran his fingers up the length of her body.

He laughed at her bewildered look, and kissed her on the mouth. She put her hands to his chest to push him away, but he caught them and laughed again. "No more for now. Why don't you try some cold water instead?"

His breathy, soundless laughter followed her into the dirty cubicle, unnerving her even more. For a few minutes, all she could do was hold on to the sink, forcing herself to take deep breaths to stave off nausea. If she got sick, she knew she would be completely defenseless. She had to keep a grip on herself and think. But how? She could barely stand.

Lenny was clearly psychotic, but somehow she had gotten him to untie her. She was not sure how. She fiddled with the plumbing fixtures, formulating outlandish escapes. Her mind cooperated to a point, then clouded up when the terror and confusion returned.

After using the toilet, she splashed her face several times with water. The cobwebs faded, and her brain started to function. She looked into the mirror that fronted the cheap metal cabinet above the sink, and noticed her eyes. Why were her pupils so dilated? Could the bastard have drugged her? Is that how he got her here?

"Are you finished in there yet, Mother? You always took too long in the john."

"Is there a comb I can use?" Monica asked, stalling for more time.

"I told you, I've moved all your stuff. You won't need your lipstick and war paint tonight. I like your hair the way it is."

Monica wiped her hands and face on a ragged blue towel and pushed back her hair. The pain in her head was almost gone: Only slight twinges remained when she moved it back and forth. She took a deep breath, and joined him in the narrow hallway.

Lenny lifted her chin with a gloved finger. He thought she was even more beautiful with her freshly scrubbed face. The contrast between her white skin and wild, reddish curls was overpowering. She flashed her eyes at him, and his body responded.

Lenny could not remember a time when he had wanted her as much as he did at this instant. He could take her right here in the hallway. She would love it, too. He would make her cry out with pleasure, just like in his dreams. But then what? Would she come hard and fast, then cast him aside, making him wait until she was ready for him again, or worse, force him to finish alone while she mocked him?

"Oh, you almost had me on my knees again, didn't you? You'd like to see me groveling at your feet."

"What are you talking about? I don't understand what you think I did," she said.

"I'm not that stupid kid I once was! I won't be used and hurt again. I'll see you back in hell first, even if I have to put you there myself!" He slapped her across the face and shook her until she cried out. Her head felt as though it were spinning off into space.

"Lenny, please don't!" she sobbed. "You're hur-hurting me. No, no . . ."

He stopped and removed his hands so quickly she nearly fell to the floor. His boyish grin returned.

"I'll get you that soup now. Because you've done everything I've asked, you can stay down here and eat in the kitchen."

Paralyzed by fear, unable to marshall any defense, she could not stop him when he took her arm and led her down the hall. She stumbled along, tears spilling from her eyes.

*I am not going to survive this. I will die in this horrible place.*

At the thought, a shred of defiance welled up inside her. She stopped walking and he turned to her.

"You're going to kill me, aren't you? Why don't you just do it and be done with it then?"

She stuck out her chin, holding her body rigid until her legs could no longer support her weight. Her knees buckled and she slipped out of his grasp. She felt herself falling as her bravado evaporated. His shirtfront was a blur of white as she passed it. In desperation, she grabbed at it, as if it were a life preserver and she was being swept overboard during a storm.

He pulled her up, tenderly enfolding her into his arms, and rocked her.

"Sh-sh-sh, it's okay, Mother," he whispered. "Everything is fine. You're in no danger. I'd never hurt you. You know I love you."

Moments passed, and still he held her. She felt almost comforted by the strong, steady beat of his heart, and the warmth of his arms. When she finally pulled away, Lenny gave her shoulders a last rub and turned her around. Behind her back, he slipped off his gloves and put them in his pocket.

"Soup time," he said, cheerfully steering her through an archway.

She looked around. They were in a living room that held a worn, gray corduroy sofa and matching chair pushed together in front of a small TV set. Piles of old newspapers, magazines, dirty dishes, and trash littered the dusty wooden floor. The room's two windows were heavily draped so that not even a flicker of light could slip through. She did not know if it was day or night.

Even more dismal was the small, airless kitchen they moved into next, with its cracking linoleum floor and peeling paint. A putrid smell of rotting garbage permeated the room. Lenny pointed to one of the padded, red vinyl chairs of the dinette set and told her to sit down.

"Hope you still like tomato soup. I don't keep much in the pantry anymore. Mostly I eat take-out stuff."

She sat down and clutched her hands together in her lap, trying to memorize every detail about his person. Her head ached, and all she wanted to do was lie down and sleep, but she forced herself to think, noting every nuance of his appearance—the eyebrow that assumed an "s" shape when he contemplated his next move, his lack of facial hair, his constant mumbling. Yet, in many ways he acted quite normal. He seemed bright enough. From what she could remember of him at the theater, he had a sub-servient, eager-to-please attitude. He had hidden his maniacal side well.

She surprised herself that she could catalogue these details about her captor. The drug he had given her was wearing off, taking with it her buffer against reality. She watched him turn on the burner and reheat whatever was in the saucepan before pouring it into a bowl. A few moments of his rummaging around a drawer produced a spoon. He picked out some crackers from the jumble of boxes on the counter. A half-empty bag of cookies fell on the floor. He looked at it, swore, and gave it a vicious kick. She cowered, expecting a violent reprisal, but he surprised her again by casually picking up the soup and carrying it to the table as if nothing had bothered him.

"I know you don't like using paper napkins, and I had a nice cloth one on the tray I took upstairs; but the soup spilled on it and I don't have another one. I'm sorry, Mother. I guess things aren't what they should be around here."

Unwilling to ask him anything and risk either of their fragile emotional states, she sat quietly while he served her dinner. It was tomato soup—warm blood.

The scene at her breakfast table flashed into her mind. Had it only been this morning that she was laughing with Mia over the menu for tomorrow's lunch? It seemed a thousand years ago.

# chapter

# 11

At midnight, Peter Crawford stopped by to check on his wife, Nancy, and Monica's children. He brought a thermos of hot coffee and a piece of Billy's birthday cake. He assured her things were fine at home. When Peter left a half hour later, he took a sleepy Billy with him.

John arrived home at two-fifteen, hassled and tired from the storm-delayed flight and his interrupted plans.

"You've heard nothing?" he asked when he and Nancy were in the kitchen.

"I've called everyone I can think of and no one knows anything. I believe you should call the police tonight and file a report."

"Police? Oh, my god." John put down his briefcase and walked around the kitchen. "How are the kids? They must be frantic."

"I think they just dropped from exhaustion. It's been terrible," replied Nancy. "John, what are we going to do? I can't believe this is happening. I just saw her this morning. We had some tea and we—"

"Hey, I'm lost here. This has been a shock for me, too." He came to her and touched her shoulder. "I'll get someone over here right away."

Nancy pulled herself together. The last thing John needed was for her to fall apart. That wouldn't help Monica either.

"If I understand the procedure, they'll probably take your statement over the phone and let it got at that," she said softly.

"But surely they'll send a detective, somebody out to investigate? It's possible Monica has been gone since before noon."

Nancy explained what David had told her earlier about how cases involving missing adults are handled. John pulled his suit jacket off in disgust.

"Bullshit! This is my wife we're talking about, not some vagrant from the streets!"

"David Riley says it's the law."

"I don't believe that, and besides, how does a vet know anything about police procedure? Shouldn't he be off vaccinating cows, or something?" Anger and frustration were taking their toll. John strode around the kitchen, emotions barely in check.

Nancy watched him. This was a different John. Quite unlike his usual cool, uninvolved self. Knowing he was upset, she ignored his rude remarks.

"I was just about to make some coffee. Would you like a cup?" she asked.

"What? Coffee? Yeah, sure."

She poured water and the ground beans into the machine, savoring the fine odor, wondering as she did, how many millions of times people had used this particular action to fill a void or keep themselves busy during tense moments. The simple action of preparing coffee calmed her, and when she turned back to John, she was able to do it with sympathy.

Her hands trembled as she poured the hot liquid into blue-and-white mugs and set them on the table. She cut a large slab of chocolate cake that she had found in the pantry, put it on a plate. "Long day," she said, giving him the cake.

"Unbelievable." John yanked out a chair and threw himself into it. Closing his eyes, he took a long swallow of coffee. He sat for a minute, loosening his tie with one hand, before he picked up his fork. Suddenly, he threw the fork down, stood up, and went to the phone that hung on the wall.

"Well?" he said. "Do I call 911, or what?"

"I think so," Nancy said. Even though she knew he would get minimal help, he needed to call.

The 911 dispatcher, upon hearing John's request, switched him to the sergeant on duty at the precinct. Nancy could hear only John's side of the conversation, but it was obvious he was being handled exactly as she had told him he would be. Even his outbursts of "But she's my wife, damn it!" fell on deaf ears as the sergeant took his statement and explained police procedures. John listened for several moments, then hung up and returned to the table.

"How can I help you?" she asked him. "Did they have any suggestions on where to begin?"

John lifted his shoulders and let them drop. Again she was struck by the helpless gesture, so out of sync for this man who was always in control.

"Until we can give them actual evidence of foul play, they can't do anything to help. They offered to check hospitals, etc., if it hadn't been done already," he replied.

"As of midnight, she wasn't in any of those places, nor had she been in an accident."

"Okay. They said they'd keep checking on that, and would let us know if she turned up."

"What else did they say?" Nancy topped off his coffee cup.

"They gave me a list of things to look for."

"Like what?"

"Things that would tell us if she had been planning to take off. Evidence of unusual long-distance phone calls, hotel or airline reservations, questionable charges on our credit cards, withdrawals from our bank accounts, road maps or transportation schedules lying around, or any unusual notations on her calendar."

John took a bite of the cake. He usually avoided heavy desserts, but in this case he felt he needed an extra shot of sugar. He wished Nancy would sit down, too. Her hovering was making him uncomfortable.

"Did the sergeant say anything else, John?"

"He told me to call her doctors in the morning to see if she's sick or something. They even told me to go through the trash!" John shook his head at the last suggestion and finished his cake.

Nancy took his plate and rinsed it in the sink before turning back to him. This time, she pulled out a chair and joined him at the table.

"I hope you won't mind, but I took a quick look through the bedroom and her things. I couldn't tell if anything was missing. Even her reading glasses were on the nightstand. You know she doesn't go far without them."

"That's her only pair, too. She told me last week Mia had sat on her other ones. You're right. She's lost without them." He looked out the window into the night and then abruptly stood up.

"I'll check the suitcases, but I won't be able to tell either if any of her personal things are gone. I don't keep track of that stuff."

Nancy nodded. "No one would expect you to."

"The police suggested we might distribute flyers with Monica's picture, description, etc., on them and offer a reward for information about her. A couple of the radio stations in town do missing persons' spots. So do the TV news programs. We could have a trace put on the phone line in case she calls home. Then we'd have a number to pinpoint her location."

"You'll be busy. I want to help any way I can." She knew David would, too, but decided against saying so at the moment. "Right now, I think you could use some time alone to think about all this. Can you handle things here if I go home?"

"What? Yes, you go on. We'll be fine," he said.

Nancy pulled on her raincoat and picked up the thermos her husband had dropped off earlier.

"Thanks for your help, Nancy," John said as they walked to the front door. "I'm sorry I'm such a bear."

"I was glad to help out and I'm in for the long haul. You aren't alone in this, John. I'll be here tomorrow. Until then, call me any time. Don't even think about it being too late or too early to phone." She leaned over and squeezed his arm. "Try to get some rest."

"Thanks, Nancy. Take care driving home." He watched until she was safely in her van before he closed the door.


After checking on his sleeping daughters, John looked in on Jeb. The boy was awake and sat up when John opened his door.

"Hi, son, how's it going?"

"She's not home yet, is she?"

"No, she isn't." John crossed the room to the bed.

Jeb drew his knees up and rested his arms on them. "Where can she be, Dad? People just don't disappear like this."

"I wish I could answer your question, Jeb, but I don't know where she is. I've called the police and they'll let us know if they find her. In the meantime, we cross our fingers and hope everything will be okay." John was so tired he was sure he was saying all the wrong things, but it was the best he could do at this hour.

"Mom's real smart and she's strong, too. She'll be able to figure something out," Jeb said with determination. "She's a fighter!" He sniffed and rubbed his eyes.

John wished he had thought to say something like that, but he was proud of Jeb for reacting that way. His kid was no sissy. "That's right, son, and we'll do everything we can to get her home fast."

Jeb slid down in his bed. He did not want his dad to see that he had his old teddy bear under his pillow. He knew he was too big for stuff like that. If Mom saw it, she would ignore it, but Dad might make a big deal out of it.

"I think we should both try to get some sleep now. It's real late," John said.

"Yeah, guess so. 'Night, Dad."

John reached out and patted Jeb's shoulder. " 'Night, son. See you in the morning."

Jeb turned over in bed and burrowed under his covers. John was unable to see the boy's face when he looked one last time before closing the door.

An hour later, John was still roaming the quiet house. He checked all the things the police sergeant had suggested, and found nothing out of the ordinary.

No unusual notes were scribbled on Monica's calendar, her drawers and closet were neatly organized as always, and the suitcases were all accounted for. The only things he was sure were missing were her handbag and the station wagon. And Monica. The thought was finally becoming real to him. Monica was missing.

The frustration caused by his abrupt departure from Atlanta, the cancellation of two important meetings in the morning, and the curtailing of his time with Beth, paled beside the realization that the world he had always been able to count on had changed irrevocably. The responsibilities of home and children had fallen on him. How would he ever be able to braid Mia's hair. And breakfast . . . what did the kids eat for breakfast? It had not been his job to notice. Suddenly, the specter of carpools, doctors' appointments, walking the dog, overseeing homework and chores, plus a thousand other things he probably had not thought of yet, loomed up and fell squarely onto his shoulders.

"Damn it!" He drove his fist into the door frame, sick and enraged by Monica's absence.

He wandered into their bedroom. The bedside lamp cast a subdued light on the flowered counterpane and its careless jumble of throw pillows, which were heaped onto the bed. The thought of removing them to the adjacent chair for the night was overwhelming. Monica always did that. He knew that if he pulled down the bedspread, he would be able to bounce a dime across the tightly drawn sheets she had placed there. He could not face it.

Several of her magazines and the Grisham novel she had been reading lay on the dresser where he put his wallet and keys. He went to his closet and saw her robe hanging behind the bathroom door, her perfume on the counter by the sink. Her presence permeated the entire area, and for the first time made him feel like an intruder in his own bedroom without understanding why.

Feelings of fright, rage, and frustration clamored inside him. Where the hell could she be? Had somebody picked her up? Why was this happening to him? He didn't deserve this. He was a self-made man, one who never asked anyone for anything. He was also a good husband, a loving father, and a damn fine executive. There was no time in his life for this crap. He had worked too hard to have something like this come along and destroy the life he had created.

For a moment, he allowed himself to think the unthinkable: *Maybe she's left me. Maybe's she with another man in some hotel somewhere.*

No, she would never do anything like that. "Absolutely not," he told himself as a twinge of guilt pricked him.

He walked back to the bed and grabbed the stack of pillows from the counterpane, and threw them against the wall. The colorful profusion rose into the air like a bride's bouquet and bounced to the floor.

*Damn it, Monica! I need you here, with me, in this house!* He waited, but heard nothing but the silence. Infuriated, he switched off the lamp, stomped to the den, and threw himself into his leather recliner. Within moments, he was asleep.

# chapter
# 12

An hour before dawn on Thursday, Lenny knelt by Monica's bed. "Mother . . . Moth-er, Moth-er-r-r. Wake up Moth-er-r-r."

Monica heard the whispered words before she was fully awake. She struggled to open her eyes, to shift the ten-pound weights that seemed to hang from each eyelash. When she swallowed, the acrid taste in her mouth made her feel sick. Her arms ached, her head throbbed as disjointed thoughts rambled through her mind.

*Am I getting the flu? What time is it?*

She had to make sure the children were awake. They would be late for school. Wait, there was no school today. Vet. Peach Pie was at the vet. With David. Brownies. She must make brownies for lunch and check the pantry for tomato soup.

"Time to wake up, Moth-er-r-r. Open your eyes and look at me, Moth-e-r-r."

"Cold," mumbled Monica as she felt the blankets being pulled from her body. She tried to turn over and curl her arms into her chest but found she could not. Whimpering with pain, she opened her eyes, and slowly focused on a face only inches from hers.

She cried out, and felt one smooth leather glove cover her mouth while another threaded its fingers into her hair. Lenny moved his face closer so that their noses touched.

His breath was moist and warm against her cheek, and with a faint hint of onion and mint. Even in the dim light from the oil lamp, she could see madness dancing in his eyes.

"What did I tell you about making loud noises, Mother? No one will hear you, and you know I don't like them."

He removed his hand from her mouth and traced circles on her cheeks with his gloved finger. She tried to pull away, but the hand in her hair tightened its grip as the leather-covered finger on her face increased its pressure, and then pushed into the skin beneath her chin and on her throat.

"How many times did you scold me when I screamed? When I needed your help? Remember when I begged you to come to me? You enjoyed seeing me suffer, didn't you?"

"I . . . I . . . what are you talking about? I've never hurt you. I've never been with you until now."

"Another memory lapse, Mother? How convenient. You always have an answer for everything."

"I'm not your mother, Lenny. I don't know why you think I am, but my name is Mon—"

"Shut up! I'm tired of this. I've only got time to take you to the bathroom before I leave. If you'd rather argue with me, I'll leave you here. Understand?"

She nodded her head, fearing that his powerful fingers might crack open her skull if she did not cooperate. A sob escaped her lips as he took his hands away.

"That's better. Now stand up," he said, briskly untying her and hauling her out of the bed. Monica pitched forward, her legs and feet tangling in the long dress. Lenny caught her by the shoulders and steadied her.

"If I hadn't put you to bed myself, I'd think you've been hitting the bottle again."

"I-I don't drink."

"Oh, sure, Mother. That memory loss again. You and

Uncle . . . you used to have your nips every day." He hustled her toward the stairs.

"Who? Uncle who?" Monica stumbled again.

"Never mind. Watch the steps. Hold your dress up."

"I feel sick." She put her hand to her temple and then moved it to cover her mouth. The steps before her undulated like waves.

"Must be the medicine," he said. "Guess I still don't have the dosage right. But you'll be okay. You'll have plenty of time today to sleep it off." He half carried, half dragged her down to the bathroom.

"What are you giving me?" And when? She did not remember taking anything. Was it in the soup, the milk? She struggled to recall what he had given her, but it was difficult to concentrate.

"Just let me handle that." He shoved her toward the basin.

Obviously, he was in a hurry this morning. Was it morning? Monica couldn't be sure. The house was as dark as it had been last night. She pulled the string that turned on the small light over the medicine cabinet, and stared at her face in the mirror.

"Hurry up in there," Lenny yelled from the hallway.

"I want to wash my face."

"Forget it. You've used the john, now let's go." He pushed the door open and grabbed her arm. He jerked her down the hall, up the stairs, and onto the bed. Whipping a pair of handcuffs from his back pocket, he snapped one cuff over her wrist and one to a bar at the head of the bed. Then he pulled a wooden crate within her reach and set a thermos bottle on top of the box.

"You never used to get up before noon, but just in case you get hungry, here's some water and an apple. Chamber pot's under the bed."

Monica stared at the fruit he put in her hand. Could this apple kill him if she threw it hard enough and hit him at just the right place on his body? Maybe she could force it down his throat and suffocate him. Or maybe she could smash it into his face. Could she poke his eye out or break his nose with it? If not the apple, how about the thermos? She needed to find something to stop him.

"I'll be back," he said, once again thrusting his hand through her hair. "And don't think you can sit up here and yell your head off. No one will hear you, and if they do, no one will care. The cuffs will come off when I can trust you."

His hand in her hair pulled her closer, his other played with the buttons on her dress. "Now, Mother, you want to kiss me good-bye?"

"Go to hell," she hissed.

He wrenched her closer. His eyes blazing, his sudden wrath exploding, he slammed his mouth down on her lips, grinding his lips against hers until she could taste blood. She beat at him with her free hand, but he only ground his mouth harder onto hers. She pulled at his clothing, twisted his ear, and yanked on his hair, but he remained pressed against her. Then, unable to breathe, her strength depleted, she gave up and went limp. Immediately, he lifted his head and grinned at her, catching her free hand as it fell, bringing it to his lips for a tender kiss.

"If that's hell, Mother, you can send me there anytime you wish."

He ogled her body. "You're a tempting witch. I've wanted you for . . ."

Monica shrank from his obvious state of arousal. She turned her face away and tried to break his hold on her. He yanked her back and kissed her again, while forcing one hand between her legs and squeezing her hard before shoving her down on the bed. She screamed and instantly he let her go. Cursing her, he stomped across the attic floor.

Had she hit a nerve? Was he angry with himself, or with her for rejecting him? She struggled to put the anger and fear from his attack on hold, and think about how he was acting. Propping herself up on one elbow, she watched him remove his gloves and lay them on the trunk at the far side of the attic. He handled them with great care, as though they were irreplaceable heirlooms.

Completely unaware of Monica, he chanted the words, "Love me, help me, save me," again and again in a squeaky falsetto voice. His actions both terrified and intrigued her. His emotions were a giant jigsaw puzzle with several key pieces missing. She would need all the pieces to escape from him.

For the first time, she noticed his clothing. How ordinary he looked in his tight chinos and maroon sweatshirt. His sneakered feet made hardly a sound when he walked.

His damp, curly hair gave him a look of boyish innocence. "You're just a kid," she said, unaware she had spoken the thought aloud until he stopped singing and turned abruptly to face her.

His eyes seemed to ignite from within as he looked at her. She swore she could feel them burning through her flesh, down to her muscles and bones. He blew out the lamp. Now he was only a shadow, a figment moving through the darkness. At the top of the steps, he paused and his voice floated across to her.

"No, Mother. Thanks to you, I'm much more than just a kid."

Pale fingers of light announcing the dawn streaked across the eastern sky as Lenny hopped off the crosstown bus that dropped him near the shopping mall where he worked. He needed to move Mother's car. Chill morning air crept beneath his loose sweatshirt, and he cursed himself for having forgotten his jacket. He had certainly been warm enough when he had left his mother.

Thoughts of their encounter teased his libido and he felt the familiar tug in his loins. It had taken a lot of strength on his part not to give into her this morning. She was already working her wiles on him. She had goaded him into kissing her and almost succeeded in seducing him. He must be more careful. She could not have him until he was ready. He wouldn't allow the old patterns to continue, even when she was so desirable. But she wanted him. She wanted him! That made his plan almost complete.

He broke into an easy jog and crossed the quarter mile of macadam to the covered parking area by Sears where he had parked the navy station wagon the evening before. Not for the first time he wondered why his mother now drove something as sedate as a wagon, when before she had always preferred sportier models.

He unlocked the door, and slid behind the wheel as he clipped the seat belt around him. He started the car, automatically checking the gas gauge, and drove it carefully around the perimeter of the large mall.

Despite the early hour, the area highways were thick with traffic, but Lenny enjoyed the thirty-five minute drive across town. The late model car drove like a dream and had all the amenities her old car lacked. Pleasure flowed through him as he sat in her seat, his hands on the steering wheel where her hands had been, listening to her tape pour smooth jazz from the speakers, as soft and silky as her skin. He preferred heavy metal and rap, but this music was an improvement over all those old ballads Mother used to like.

Lenny turned off the expressway and headed west on a six-lane street. After a few miles, the residential areas gave way to commercial establishments. He cruised by gas stations, convenience stores, and discount beer and wine stores advertising check cashing as a sideline. Laundromats, fast food places serving mostly Mexican food or fried chicken, and occasional retail businesses like photo imaging or medical supply houses were sandwiched between strip joints and men's clubs.

He had to hide the car where Mother could never find it. She might try to run away from him, to leave him alone and unprotected, as she had often done when he was a child. He turned off the highway and circled several of the men's clubs before he found one that might serve his purpose. She would never think to look for her car at a place like this.

Glancing up, he saw that the big neon sign advertising PONY TAILS' TOPLESS CLUB—BEAUTIFUL GIRLS, EXOTIC DANCING was dark. He noted the club's eleven A.M. opening and drove around the large prefab concrete building. The only windows were on the second-floor section that he guessed must be the office.

Lenny parked the station wagon behind the building, between an old Mercedes and a purple sports car. The lot, which Lenny knew would have over a hundred cars in it by noon, had only a dozen assorted vehicles parked there—a van, a few junkers, and surprisingly, two or three expensive, late-model cars. He hoped his mother's car wouldn't stand out too much. He turned off the ignition, popped the tape deck, and slid the cassette into his pocket, thinking Mother might enjoy making love to those soft jazzy sounds. He would surprise her with it, perhaps at a moment when she was particularly pleased with him. The thought of what would follow made him feel lusty and warm. He hurried to finish his business with her car.

Rummaging in his other pocket, he found the small screwdriver he had brought with him and quickly removed the license plates, taking care not to skin a knuckle or damage his hands on the tight screws. Now, even on the outside chance she might find the car, she would never get far without the plates. She would not run the risk of being picked up by the police.

He fingered the bumper sticker, wondering about the location of Hyler Elementary School, and who the honor student might be. Not him. She had never given him the chance. The sticker must have been on the car when she got it.

His rumbling stomach reminded him he had not eaten

and he needed a place to wash his hands after handling the grimy plates. He decided the Mexican place next door would do for both purposes, and he crossed the parking lot, tossed the license tags into the covered trash bin outside, and entered the restaurant. After washing down two scrambled-egg-and-bean burritos with a large soda, he walked east two miles to an intersection that led to his neighborhood.

Having lived all of his life within four blocks of the airport entrance, Lenny hardly noticed the passenger airplanes that regularly flew over the area. As a child, he had sometimes waved to the captains, or the passengers, wishing that he could be one of them instead of who he was. None of his dreams had ever come true. Until now. He still could not believe Mother was actually here, waiting for him to come home.

He picked up his pace and turned onto his street, walking along its grassy edge, dodging the puddles that remained after last night's rain. Nobody had ever called the neighborhood nice. Its small houses cried out for paint, new shingles, and sturdier porches. The yards, devoid of all but the meanest attempts at landscaping, were mostly enclosed, front and back, with rusted chain-link fences and littered with broken toys, trash, and old cars propped up on cement blocks.

A few scrub trees, live oak, and cedar had been awkwardly chopped off to accommodate heavy power lines. Thick bunches of parasitic mistletoe sucked out what little life remained in the small branches. Cheap apartments surrounded the area, their acres of concrete and crowded living conditions stealing any feeling of hominess from the small ill-kept homes in the neighborhood. He wondered if Mother would hate this place now as much as she had in the past.

They had moved to this house when he was five years old. In those early years, several families had come and gone in the downstairs apartment, but he had never been allowed to speak to any of them. Mother had always referred to them, collectively, as "trash."

She had never tolerated interference in their lives. "We have each other," she always told him when he asked why he could never have a friend. "And that is enough."

Except it had never been enough. For years he had tried to believe her strong attachment to Uncle Phil was because the older man paid the bills. Lenny now understood that their attraction had been based on something much stronger.

That part of her life was over. He climbed the board steps to the apartment, thinking that at last she was all his. She had no car, no money, and only the food and clothing he gave her. They had each other, and that was enough.

Suddenly, he heard noise from the apartment below. He ran down the steps.

"Who's there?" he yelled. "This is private property and you're trespassing!" He stood by the open front door of the bottom apartment and peered inside. Except for a few empty boxes and a pile of trash, the place seemed empty. He heard a shuffling noise from one of the back rooms.

"Get out of here, kid! This ain't none of your fuckin' business."

Lenny recognized his neighbor's voice. "I thought you moved out. What're you doing back here?" he said. The words came tumbling out. "Have you been upstairs? Have you heard anything?"

"Shit, no. Why in hell would I want to go up to your rat hole? You're slime, kid. I wouldn't be caught dead near any of your weird shit. You cat killer! All I want is to get the rest of my stuff and never see your ass again! You bastard!"

The neighbor picked up a tool box and a stack of magazines and pushed by Lenny to get to his truck. The pickup sat in the side yard. Lenny wondered how he had missed seeing it. He'd practically walked into it on his way to the steps. He must be more careful. He had to protect Mother.

# chapter
# 13

John awoke with a start. For a moment he thought he had fallen asleep for his usual evening nap in his chair. Except for the lighted lamp on the table beside him, the quiet house was dark. Was it time to go to bed? Then he remembered. Monica was gone. The room was warm, but he could not stop shivering.

He pried his body out of the soft leather folds of the recliner, and thought about how his life had been blown apart in less than twelve hours. Where would he begin to look for his wife, and how would he find words to reassure his kids?

He walked into the bedroom, entertaining a wisp of hope that somehow Monica might be curled up in bed, but all he found was Peach, sound asleep under Monica's vanity in the bathroom. Then, for reasons he could not explain, John went all over the house, into every room, looking for her. He even checked the garage and the front yard, picking up Thursday morning's newspaper, before he admitted to himself that she was still gone.

Where was she? The reality of Nancy's words came crashing down on him. Monica would not leave without letting someone know. She was much too responsible to run off with no thought for the children.

John sat down at her desk in the kitchen and covered his face with his hands. He and Monica had had some

problems lately. Maybe he had not been the easiest person
to live with, but she would never leave, or be gone this
long without contacting him. Either she had had an accident, or somebody had her. If that were true, would he ask
for ransom money? He had enemies. Everyone did. Could
a disgruntled employee have done this? An angry client?
Could her disappearance be tied to some nut case who lost
money in the junk bond market?

Kidnapping was bad enough, but what if someone hurt
her? Or worse? How could he ever make the kids understand if their mother never came home? Their lives would
be changed forever. They needed her. Whenever he had
considered leaving their marriage, he always knew that
Monica would be there to care for the children. That had
been the only option.

He decided the police had to get involved. He could not
handle this by himself. He was a money manager, for
God's sake! Didn't his tax money help support law
enforcement in this town? As soon as he got cleaned up,
he would call them again and demand that they launch a
full-scale investigation into Monica's disappearance.
After all, if they had been doing their job in the first
place, she would be here at home where she belonged.
Probably some convicted felon they had let out of prison
way too early had grabbed her. Everyone knew the streets
were unsafe.

John returned to the bathroom. Peach was snoring.
Realizing he knew as little of the dog's morning routine as he knew about practically everything else in the
house, he stripped off his clothes and stepped into the
shower, hoping the hot water would ease his anger and
frustration.

As he soaped and shampooed, he relaxed a little and
slipped into his habit of mentally reviewing his day's
activities. He had to call the police. And he would call
Beth to go over last-minute details on the Jamison group
meeting. They were much too important to offend. He had

to get to the office sometime today: He had a boatload of stuff that had to be done or delegated to someone else.

The kids would be in school . . . no, oh, shit, the kids were home today. He would have to find someone to take care of them for a few hours. Was Jeb old enough? No, better not leave him in charge. Monica would have a fit if he left the kids alone. What will they do all day?

He shaved, dressed in casual clothes, thinking perhaps they could make up a flyer about Monica's disappearance. He would have copies made of one of her photographs. Maybe he could copy it onto the flyer. Maybe he could get this terror that was inching its way beneath his skin under control. Where the hell could she be? He told himself to stay calm, stay collected. It helped to focus on things he had to do.

First thing this morning he would call the telephone people and have a tracer put on the line. The girls at the office could contact the TV and radio stations. He speculated about a reward. What amount was appropriate? He would ask the police for a suggestion. Who got to handle all the crank calls? Him, probably. How would he screen the calls? He was no detective. Did he need to hire one? He took a deep breath, trying to ignore the vulnerable feelings inside him. This whole mess could cost a fortune, and still, they might not find her.

He stooped to rouse the sleeping dog. Peach Pie pulled himself to his feet and walked over to sniff the exercise bike. After a few moments, he whimpered and followed John out of the room.

"Does she feed you in the morning, or just at night?" he asked Peach when they were in the kitchen. Thankfully, the dog made it clear he wanted something to eat and John gave him a few biscuits to hold him until he could ask the children about his feeding schedule.

He glanced at the clock. It was just past five. The kids would probably sleep another couple of hours. The coffee machine was half full of last night's coffee. He had never worried whether the machine was clean or the morning coffee made. It just always was. Until now Monica had never let him down.

It took him a few moments to clean the pot and longer to find the coffee and filter. While he waited for the coffee to brew, he rinsed the mugs and cake plate from last night, and opened the dishwasher to stack them inside, only to find the washer full of clean dishes. Another dilemma . . . where do all these belong? Maybe the kids would know, he decided, and closed the door.

With a cup of fresh coffee beside him, John opened the newspaper. He scanned the headlines on the front page and then pulled out the sports section, noting that the Rangers had won the night before. He folded that part of the paper and laid it by Jeb's place at the table, hoping the news of his favorite team might take his mind off his mom. John worried about what he could do to help his daughters. Sarah, especially, would be inconsolable.

He picked up the phone and dialed Beth McKinnon's number at their hotel room in Atlanta. On the fifth ring, she answered. It was obvious he had awakened her. He could envision her warm, naked limbs stretching like a sleepy cat after a nap in the sun. He felt that she, unlike most women, was truly beautiful first thing in the morning, soft and excitingly acquiescent.

"Morning, Beth."

"Hm-m-m."

"Hope I'm not calling too early."

Beth sat up and rubbed her eyes. "That depends on what you want."

John drummed his fingers on the counter. She was madder than he had thought she would be. "How about if I'm calling to apologize?"

"Why did you leave so abruptly? That was rude of you, John."

"I told you I had to get back to Dallas, that it was a

family matter." John wondered why women always needed to know every last detail.

"What was the emergency? I was miserable when you stormed out of here."

Watch it, John told himself. He did not need a fallout with Beth today. Life was going to be tough enough for him without her on his case, too.

"Believe me, if there had been any way around this, I'd be with you right now." John took a sip of his coffee. "Beth, Monica's gone."

"What do you mean gone? Where did she go?"

"I don't know. She hasn't been here since, maybe Wednesday afternoon. We don't have a clue where she could be."

"Oh, my God, John. Has she left you?"

"No, I don't think so. She wouldn't do that without telling me."

"Do you think she found out about us?"

John was surprised at the chilling arrow of fear streaking through his stomach. "No, I'm afraid she's in trouble."

"What kind of trouble?" Beth asked.

"I wish I knew. She's been gone all night!"

"That's awful! Have you called the police?"

"Yeah, but that's a long story I'll tell you later."

"Oh, John, I am so sorry. How can I help you?"

"Just take care of Jamison this morning," John said.

"Let me handle him. I'll explain the situation and I know he'll understand. If he doesn't feel comfortable with me, I'll make sure he knows you'll be in touch real soon."

John thanked her, and they spent the next fifteen minutes reviewing the account and the meeting agenda. Even though he felt he was the better man for this particular job, he was confident in her ability to keep Jamison happy.

"I don't want you to think about anything else but

finding your wife, John. I'll call the Dallas office twice a day with updates."

"Thanks, Beth." One of the things he liked best about Beth was her no-nonsense approach to solving problems.

John filled in the next two hours catching up on work at the kitchen table until a sleepy-eyed Jeb walked into the kitchen. He had pulled a Texas Rangers' sweatshirt over his pajamas, but his feet were bare.

"Hi, Dad. Did you hear from Mom?"

"Hey, son. No, I haven't. I'm sorry. Were you able to get any sleep last night?"

"A little, I guess. Peach? C'mere boy." Jeb sunk to the floor and hugged his dog, rubbing his face in the thick, blond fur.

"Heard anything from the girls?" John asked.

"Nope, guess they're still asleep."

"No, we're not," Mia announced as she and Sarah padded into the kitchen. Like Jeb, they still wore their pajamas, but theirs were covered with matching blue-and-white striped robes. Mia's long, shiny red hair hung straight down her back, while Sarah's halo of short black curls framed her delicate face.

"Hi, babies," John said as he turned to them. "How about a double hug for old Dad?"

The girls huddled close to John. He hugged them and rubbed Sarah's back when he felt her quiet sobs.

"Mom's not home yet, is she?" Mia asked, pulling back to look at him.

" 'Fraid not, honey."

The volume of Sarah's sobs increased and John pulled her tighter against him. Mia stood quietly within the circle of his other arm and studied his clothes. The fact that he was dressed in a casual shirt and sweater instead of his usual suit and tie terrified her. Her whole world was turning upside down.

"Sh-h-h, baby. It's all right. It's all right," John told Sarah.

"No, it's not all right, Dad. Nothing will be right until Mom comes home," Sarah said, shaking her head.

John looked at his three children, admitting to himself that he had no logical explanation for Monica's disappearance and no control over when she would return. The enormity of the situation was overwhelming, especially when he had to deal with his children's fears. Suddenly, all the money in the world could not buy the children the only thing they really wanted. He felt powerless and he despised the feeling.

"I think we should have some breakfast," he said at last. "What do you guys want to eat? Cereal? Juice?"

Pancakes had come first to Jeb's mind, but they were Mom's special treat. Memories of the breakfast pancakes he and the girls had helped her make yesterday brought tears to his eyes. He rubbed them away; he had already cried enough. Anyhow, could his dad even make pancakes? The only domestic thing he had ever seen him do, beside outdoor grilling, was opening wine bottles.

"We have cereal a lot," Jeb told his dad. "I think Dr. Riley may have left some doughnuts at the front door. He said last night he'd bring some by. I'll go check."

John wondered why the vet would be buying his children doughnuts, but said nothing as that announcement seemed to perk everyone up a little. "Okay, it'll be doughnuts and cereal. Mia, Sarah, get the bowls and spoons. I'll pour the milk and juice. And who knows when to feed Peach?"

During breakfast, John outlined his plans for the flyer. The children eagerly agreed to help. Sarah added that putting flyers around would be a good idea because Monica might see one and know how much they wanted her to come home, in case she left because she thought they were mad at her or something.

Once again John was at a loss for what to say. Sarah was the dreamer in the family, the most sensitive and the most vulnerable. The other two children had always been more aggressive and self-sufficient. His heart went out to this fragile, fairy child at his side, who took everything so seriously and so personally.

"Sarah, I don't think Mom is staying away because of anything you, or any of us have done," John said.

"Dr. Riley said she'd be here if she could," Jeb added.

John felt a momentary stiffening at yet another mention of the veterinarian's name.

"Dad, do you think somebody's kidnapped Mom? Maybe they're holding her for ransom, and we'll have to pay a pile of money to get her back, just like on TV," Mia said.

"I don't know, Mia, but if that's the case, we should hear from them today. That's why we're going to have a trace put on our telephone."

"What's a trace? Will they listen to all our phone conversations? Will they be able to hear Jeb when he gushy-mushes to his girlfriend?"

"Shut up, Mia," Jeb said.

"No, no one will listen to anyone's conversations. The phone company will record a phone number for each incoming call. We'll keep a list of calls, especially the times they come in. Then we'll compare it with the phone company's list. If we get a ransom call, or if Mom gets a chance to phone us, we'll be able to trace the phone number and find out where she is."

"How about if it's from a public phone?"

"I'm not sure, Jeb, but my guess is that would make it tougher, but not impossible. Those phones have numbers, too. But we'll still do the flyers. We want to know if anyone has seen her," John said.

"Will the police come to our house? Are they going to help find Mom?" Mia asked.

John explained what he had been told the night before. "I'll be phoning them today, and they'll call us if they have any news." He glanced at the children's full cereal bowls and the untouched stack of doughnuts that remained on the table. He urged them to drink their milk before they went upstairs to dress.

The phone rang. John jumped at its jarring sound, nearly dropping the dishes he was carrying to the sink.

"Morning, John. This is Nancy. How's everything going?"

John tried to keep the disappointment from his voice. He had hoped it was Monica. "Hi," he said. "We're okay, I guess. Survived the night, anyhow. The kids have just finished breakfast."

"So you've heard nothing?"

"No, not a word."

John heard Nancy take a deep breath. On second thought, maybe he wasn't okay. He wondered if things would ever be "okay" again.

"How can I help you?" Nancy asked. "I'm planning to bring lunch. Do you need to go out for a while? Peter's mom is here for my kids, so I'm free today."

"Well, I really should go into the office this morning. Just for a few hours to tie up some loose ends. I was going to get a sitter—"

"Oh, no. I'll come over. I can answer the phone and spend time with the children. I'd love to be with them today. Maybe I can help them with the flyer. When are you leaving?"

"How soon can you get here?"

"It's almost eight-thirty. I could be there by nine."

"That would be a big help. Thanks a lot."

While John waited for Nancy to relieve him, he called the phone company and ordered a trace. Then he called the police. After several tries, he was able to convince someone to pull the file on Monica. There was no information on her whereabouts. He was transferred to the Missing Persons' Department. A detective offered some suggestions and helped him to decide the amount of the reward. Ten thousand dollars seemed too high a price to pay for what could be a dribble of information, but appar-

ently, that was the going rate these days. When he pleaded
for additional help, he was politely but firmly reminded
that until they had concrete evidence of foul play, the
police could not be involved in the search.

John took the news better this time. In his rational
moments, he knew the police were only doing their jobs,
but this was his wife and he wanted immediate action.

Just as Nancy came through the door, the phone rang
again. He pounced on it, hoping it might be Monica.
Instead, David Riley introduced himself and asked if they
had heard anything more about Monica. John told him
that they had not.

"As a friend, I wanted you to know that I would be
available to help in any way that I can," David said.

"I think we've got things handled here. The only real
help we need, we can't get."

"What do you mean?"

"The police—they refuse to get involved. So unless
you can do anything to change their minds . . ."

"I do have a friend who's a detective on the force. He
can't help officially, but he might be able to add some
direction to our search. Shall I call him?"

John wondered why this guy was being so helpful. He
figured everybody had an angle these days, even veteri-
narians. But he could not pass up an opportunity to get
some free advice, especially from anyone who had an
inroad with the police department.

"I'd appreciate whatever your friend can do for us."

"Maybe he'll have some time to meet with you. I
assume you'll be home all day?"

"No, I'm on my way out to my office. Someone is
coming in to stay with the kids. I'll check back here early
to midafternoon."

"You're going to the office . . . this morning? How
about the children, the phone calls?"

"I've got that covered," John answered tersely.

"Right," said David. "My friend's name is Randy

Abbott. Could I give him a number where he can reach you today?"

John rattled off his office number, knowing he probably would not be at his desk to take the call, but his secretary could usually find him.

"Got to run. Thanks for your help, Riley."

"Forget it."

Nancy was braiding Mia's hair when John entered the kitchen. "I was wondering how I was going to get that done," he said, smiling at Mia. His daughter was dressed simply in blue jeans and a white cotton sweater, her thick, red hair brushed back over her shoulders. Freckles scattered across her nose and high forehead, giving her an elfin look that contrasted with the seriousness in her large, green eyes. John remembered falling in love with those eyes—Monica's eyes—twenty years ago. It was an uncomfortable thought. He shrugged it off and concentrated instead on listening to his daughter.

"Sarah can do them if Mom makes her, but she always gets the braids too tight."

"We could always get you a haircut like Jeb's."

"Oh, Dad, I'd look like a geek in short hair!"

"No, you wouldn't, but I'd miss those braids." John looked at his watch. He had to get to the office. "Mia, are you kids straight about what to do on the flyer?"

"I think so. We're using the computer."

"That's fine, just keep it simple. Mom's height is five feet, four inches, and she weighs about one hundred fifteen pounds, I guess. Green eyes, red hair . . ."

"Mom's hair is not red. It's auburn, like mine," said Mia.

"Sorry. Got that, Jeb?" John said to his son as he walked into the room. "Auburn hair. And don't forget our phone number and the reward."

"You leaving again?" Jeb asked, glancing at his dad's briefcase.

"I've got to go to the office for a while."

"What if Mom phones? Don't you even care? Aren't you worried about her?"

John winced. He started to say something, but changed his mind.

"I'll take those calls, Jeb," Nancy said quietly. She reached out and pulled him into a tight hug. For once he did not struggle free, allowing her to hold him close for several moments.

Neither said anything more to John. He shifted a bit, regripped his briefcase, and headed for the door, anxious to get away from the house and back to the familiarity of his office routine, if only for a few hours. He pulled his car keys from his pocket and turned to Nancy.

"Remember to record the time of any phone calls you get and, of course, write down who called if you can get the name," he said. "Let me know immediately if anything new comes up. I'll be back this afternoon. If you have the flyer done, we'll make copies then and start distributing them." John pondered Jeb's downcast face, and asked, "What's Sarah up to? I haven't seen her since breakfast."

"She was in your room, Dad, when I saw her last. Probably thinking about Mom, but she didn't want me around," Mia said.

Nancy looked at John. "I'll check on her," she told him.

# chapter
# 14

Lenny emptied a can of beef stew into a saucepan. It reminded him of dog food, but he knew Mother wouldn't care what she had to eat, just as long as she didn't have to cook it or clean up after the meal.

The cloudy morning made the kitchen look more dismal than usual. He turned on the single overhead light and pulled a jar of applesauce from the cupboard. He opened it and poured the fruit into two mismatched cereal bowls and set them on a table that was gritty with last night's cracker crumbs. He added a loaf of cheap white bread still in its plastic wrapper, and a half-empty jar of strawberry jam.

Since the napkin box was empty, he tore off two paper towels, folded them in half, and anchored the makeshift napkins to the table with two teaspoons he retrieved from the dish drainer in the sink. By the time he got his mother down here, the stew would be ready.

Monica heard him climb the steps and unlock the door. Her heartbeat quickened and she feigned sleep, hoping to gain a few more moments of peace. Surprisingly, she had slept most of the time he had been away. Whatever he was using to sedate her made her feel weighted down and listless, despite her determination to remain alert and ready to escape. She knew she must discover when and how he drugged her. On the other hand, the escape it offered, the hours of freedom from this hellish situation were a welcome release.

"Rise and shine, Mother," he said, pulling her to a sitting position before unsnapping the handcuff that bound her to the bed. "I have to be at work by two. That'll give you time to clean up a little and eat."

Monica had lost all concept of time. It was always dark in the attic. She had no watch, no way of counting the hours, even if she had managed to stay awake. She wondered how long she had been here. A few hours? A day, or longer? Day, night, it all looked the same in the attic. Her body, still clothed in the ragged navy dress and ancient sweater, felt stiff and sore as if she had lain on this smelly mattress for weeks. Her scalp hurt where her hair had been twisted into knots.

She shivered when he touched her hand. What would he do with her? Would she ever see her children again? Tears welled up in her eyes and she dashed them away.

"Come on, sleepyhead," he said, thinking how sweet she looked with her rumpled hair, her fists rubbing her eyes like a child. "We don't have all day."

"I'm not hungry. I just want to go home. Please let me go home."

Lenny rolled his eyes and reined in a flare of temper. What game she was playing this time? She sounded so sincere. He decided to play along, at least for a few minutes.

"You are home, Mother."

"This isn't my home. It's yours." She dabbed at her wet eyes with the sleeve of her sweater.

Lenny knelt down and patted her arm. He thought she looked a little pathetic this morning. Where had all her old fire gone? He had meant to subdue her, not turn her into a useless rag doll.

"You're just anxious to get downstairs to your room and all of your stuff. I kept everything—your magazines, your scrapbooks, even your old records are still down there."

"Lenny, this place isn't—"

"I know you don't like the attic, but you have a lesson to learn."

"No, no," she pleaded, moving out from under his touch. "I want to go home to my husband and children." She missed them so much. She missed braiding Mia's hair and sharing Sara's secrets. How was her Jeb? Even the thought of lovable, old Peach made her heart break.

Lenny looked at her smugly, wondering what she would come up with next: an invalid grandmother and a houseful of sick cats? He had not seen a performance this good since the last Sharon Stone flick.

Monica continued, desperate to make him understand. "I must go home to my family. My children need me. Can you imagine what it's like to be separated from someone you love?"

Anger darkened his features. He stood up and yanked her to her feet. "Yes, Mother. You always made sure I'd miss you when you went away, didn't you? Now what do you want from me? Do you need to hear how lost and miserable I was without you? What I had to endure after you left?" He started pawing her and kissing her. He tore open the bodice of her dress, and pulled at her bra, exposing the nipple on her left breast.

"Stop, Lenny, please!" She sobbed, pushing at his head, tearing his fingers from her body.

"Oh, come on. I don't have time for you to pitch a fit." He let her go and walked toward the steps. "Let's go. Watch your dress on the stairs. If you fall, I'm not picking you up."

Monica pulled her dress front together and stumbled after him.

He entered the bathroom with her and handed her a sliver of soap and a ragged excuse for a washcloth. She took them and waited for him to leave.

"Still protecting your privacy, I see. When are you going to remember that I've already seen everything you've got? Did you forget who put you into those clothes?"

Monica turned her back to him. When it was obvious she would not move until he left, he finally stormed out, reminding her he would be waiting for her in the hall. The door remained open.

She splashed cool water over her face and neck. Each pore of her skin seemed to open up to receive the refreshment. It was as if months, rather than hours, had gone by since she had washed. She watched the water spiral down the drain and envied the freedom of the droplets. If only she could escape that easily.

As she looked into the mirror, she asked herself what it was about her that made him think she was his mother. Was there a facial resemblance? Could they be the same age? Did they share certain mannerisms or similar temperaments? She might believe that similarities existed in all areas but the last. She had never set out to be as deliberately cruel to anyone as this young man's mother evidently had been to him.

What frightened her most was the sexual attraction he displayed for this person he called "Mother." Could "Mother" be a pet name for an old girlfriend? Or wife? Had he and this woman had a child? Is that why he called her Mother? That appellation was old-fashioned, but she supposed it could be possible. But where was the child?

She needed to learn so much about him. If she knew his motives, maybe she could understand why he had kidnapped her. Obviously, he had drugged her at the theater to bring her here.

Had her kidnapping been a random or a premeditated act? Was it part of some grand scheme whose dimensions and denouement lay solely within his sick mind? Had he tried to contact John? Did he want money? Somehow, Monica didn't think so. She had been around the block enough times to recognize the signs. What Lenny wanted was her—but why?

She picked up the soap and scrubbed her face. Maybe she should stop eating, allow herself to languish, to incite his pity so that he would release her, but Lenny's moods were anything but consistent. He might force more drugs on her. Without food, she would be incapable of refusing them. She would also feel worse: Any ability to think rationally would fade.

Could she overpower him? Hardly. He had her by at least eight inches in height and outweighed her by sixty or seventy pounds, not to mention his manic strength. He shifted her around easier than a child handles a baby doll.

What then? She peered into the crazed surface of the mirror and wondered how anyone could find her appealing in her present condition. Her hair was a disheveled mass of tangles. Her eyes were clear but their vivid color intensified the chalkiness of her skin. The area beneath her eyes was swollen and ringed by deep purple arcs. She looked like a green-eyed raccoon.

Lenny's face suddenly appeared in the mirror. She gasped her surprise but he acted as if he belonged there, staring at her with a fierce look she could feel in the pit of her stomach.

"You're beautiful, Mother. Your eyes torment me. You've always known how to use them against me."

"You frightened me. You said you'd wait for me in the hall."

He kept watching her. She doubted he'd even heard her speak. His mind seemed light-years away from the dingy bathroom. What was going on inside his head? He snatched her wrists, throwing the washcloth to the floor. He dragged her hands in front of her face, frowning at her as though she were an eight-year-old caught eating cake and ice cream five minutes before dinner time.

"You've been neglecting them."

"I . . . I have?"

"Why are your nails so short and why haven't you painted them?"

"I seldom wear nail polish on my fingernails. They're too short and it doesn't look good," she said, examining her hands as though they belonged to someone else. She could not imagine why they were discussing her fingernails.

"Even your cuticles are a mess. You always told me that there was no excuse for hangnails."

Monica hid her hands behind her back. Why was Lenny so interested in them?

"Show me yours," she said. She did not know why it suddenly seemed imperative for her to see them.

"How unfair of you! You know Thursday's our manicure night." He shyly held them out to her. "Hold them, Mother. Hold them." He swayed, keeping time to some music only he could hear. His hands moved gracefully back and forth in front of her eyes.

Their repelling beauty mesmerized her. The long slim fingers tapered to perfect almond-shaped nails that were identical in length. Not one hair, wrinkle, or rough spot marred the impeccable skin on his hands. The pores were invisible. Monica had never seen more exquisite hands on anyone, not even in magazine ads, and certainly never on a young man. She wondered if the high gloss on his nails came from strenuous buffing or a coat of polish.

Lenny preened, very pleased that Mother was still so impressed with his hands. She could be forgiven for not touching them as he had asked. It was obvious she was awestruck by their perfection.

"I've picked up several new colors of polish, Mother. You might like to try one of my Southwestern shades. Adobe Pink and Lush Terracotta are especially nice, though I like Sonora Sunset, too. It looks wonderful peeking out of the chocolate lace gloves."

The absurdity of the situation sickened her. Now that she thought about it, when had she seen his bare hands? Last night, maybe? Had he removed the gloves before dinner? She had not cared then. In the attic? It had been too dim to see clearly. She had never noticed his hands.

Nail polish and lace gloves: two more pieces to the terrifying puzzle. She had read about people having fetishes, but no one she had ever heard of had gone in for such bizarre behavior. Then again, why would she think that Lenny was like anyone else? A cool shiver washed over her, but she kept him talking, telling herself she needed to learn everything she could about him.

"After seeing yours, I can certainly understand why you think my hands and nails are a mess. Mine spend too much time in dishwater, I guess."

"Dishwater? Oh, right, Mother. You expect me to believe you've washed a dish in the last ten years?"

"I have three children. I do lots of dishes."

Instantly she knew she had said the wrong thing. His lazy insouciance vanished and the eerie, glinting anger reappeared in his eyes.

"If you're sticking to that ridiculous story, I can find lots of dishes for you to do. You can even scrub the floors if it will make you feel better."

"Right now the only thing I'd like to scrub is me. May I have some more time to wash?"

"Later. Lunch is ready."

"Before we eat could I have my own clothes, please? These things don't fit me. They're much too large. I remember I was wearing jeans and a green turtleneck sweater when I went to the matinee. What have you done with them?"

She did not understand why she felt so courageous. The soap and water? Another view of his flawed psyche? Whatever the reason, she had to take some kind of control over her life even if it was only about clothes.

Lenny had a different idea. He pointed one perfect finger in her face and shook his head. She knew she was pushing him, but at least she was showing some spirit.

"You'll wear what I give you. You really haven't

changed, have you? Despite your silly lies, you still think you can have everything your own way!"

"But I've slept in these. They're soiled, and the buttons are . . ." she said, refusing to back down.

Lenny led her out into the hallway. "You made me rip the dress, Mother. Oh, don't deny it." He sketched a circle over her breast. She pulled back, but he held her against him. "You wanted me to tear it off you, didn't you? And now, you have to earn other ones."

"H-how?"

"By pleasing me, of course."

Monica pulled the ragged edges of the pink cardigan across her breasts. He had said that before. She was terrified of what he might do to her, but she had to ask. "What do you want?"

They had reached the kitchen now. Still waiting for his answer, Monica took a deep breath and became aware of the combination of odors pervading the airless room. Suddenly, she could not decide which of the odors, the strong smell of must, the obnoxious reek of garbage overflowing the waste can in the corner, or the foul, tallowy smell of something greasy burning on the stove made her the sickest. Her empty stomach rebelled and she gagged. Unable to stand another minute, she sank into a chair by the table and laid her head on her arms.

"Mother?"

"I feel rotten. Can't you get some fresh air in here?" Her voice was muffled. She hid her face in the sleeves of the pink sweater, preferring its musty smell to that of the kitchen.

Lenny walked around the room. The kitchen was a pit, but he was used to it. She had never minded before. Why was she so touchy all of a sudden? He looked at her, huddled in apparent misery at the table. It did not look like another one of her tricks. He moved to the window above the sink.

"You want me to open it?"

"Yes, please," she begged. "I can't breathe in here."

Convinced she was ill, Lenny jerked on the brittle shade until it let go and rolled up with a clatter. Streaks of dirt and dust clouded the window beneath. After a few tries, he managed to lift it several inches. A damp, gusty spring breeze blew into the room.

Monica lifted her head and breathed in the fresh air. "Thank you," she whispered. "Lenny, why do you keep everything closed up? It's not healthy and it's so dark. Don't you like the sun?"

"Don't I like the sun? What about the nosy neighbors, Mother? You're the one who always complained if I touched a curtain!" As a child, he had had to hide in his bedroom to open a window and watch the airplanes in the sky.

"What was I afraid to let anyone see?" Monica asked, and then realized what she had just done. She had answered as if she really was the person he believed her to be.

"Oh, you know, Mother, when we . . ." He giggled and dished out the stew. "When we did . . . things, you wanted privacy. Not that you were ever what I would call modest."

What was he talking about? Did she even want to know?

"What things, Lenny? What exactly did we do?" She forced herself to pick up her fork and taste the meat and mushy vegetables he had put in front of her.

"We did good things and we did bad things. And we did bad things that were very, very good."

This time the pitch of his giggle rose an octave, and his strange, breathy laughter became loud. When he finally stopped, he leered at her from across the table and jammed two of his fingers into his mouth. The sucking noises he made, the suggestive way he drew his fingers in and out of his mouth before pausing to lick the saliva that dripped down onto his hand terrified her until she realized that he was testing her to get her reaction.

Instead of cowering in fright, she fixed him with a furious, green-eyed stare that had never failed to bring her children back into line. "Stop that! Stop that this instant!" she said. "I will not tolerate such disgusting behavior!"

She began to tremble. This guy was crazy, totally unbalanced, and she had just treated him like a rude child. He would probably kill her for it, or worse. Still, she watched him, refusing to let him think he had intimidated her.

Without saying a word, Lenny withdrew his fingers from his mouth and wiped them on a paper towel. Lowering his eyes, he picked up his spoon and began to eat his applesauce.

After the third spoonful, he spoke. "I'm working until eleven-thirty tonight. Don't worry, though. I get some time off around six. I'll come home and make you some supper."

"Is . . . is it a long drive?"

Lenny gave her a measured look. "Why?"

"I just meant, well, I thought if it was too long a drive, you could leave me some fruit and bread and eat at the theater. Don't you get all that concession food free?"

"Hell, I mean, heck no! We can have all the soda and corn we want, but the other stuff, the candy, hot dogs, and nachos we pay for. Besides, I want to come home. I want to be with you." He leaned across the table, captured her hand and slowly licked the back of her fingers.

"G-Guess they make a lot of money on the popcorn and drinks," she said, struggling with each word as he turned her palm up and licked the skin between her fingers.

"Uh-huh, most people like popcorn the best. A big box of it costs the theater about a nickel," he said, between sliding her fingers in and out of his mouth.

"Really, just f-five c-cents?" She was terrified. She tried to free her hand, but he snatched it back. He held her wrist tightly. All feeling left her fingers.

"Yeah, sodas cost the management about a dime, but they sell the drinks for two or three dollars."

"G-Going to the movies these days is expensive," she said.

"Yeah. Did you know that every third or fourth person who goes to the movies buys popcorn, and every other one buys a drink?" He scooted his chair around the table so that he was sitting beside her.

"No, no, I didn't." Her stomach was turning flips. Any moment she thought she would be sick.

"Going to a show can cost you. Most of our complaints come from people who think we charge too much for the tickets." His tongue left her palm and made wet circles around her wrist. "What they don't understand is that most of the time, like first runs, the theater manager only gets to keep about five cents of the six-dollar-ticket fee.

"The rest goes back to the distributor." His fingers replaced his tongue and lightly fluttered up her arm and across her breast. "It's only after a film's been out awhile that he might collect a couple dollars on each ticket."

"Then he-he makes m-most of his money from the concessions?" Monica thought her heart would surely stop. She felt as if a poisonous snake were sliding over her body as she followed his hand with her eyes.

"Yeah. It's a big deal. He locks it all up and we have to account for every hot dog and chocolate-covered raisin." He leaned closer to her and whispered into her ear, "I'd like to cover you in warm chocolate, Mother. Would you like that?"

"No-no, I wouldn't. Please may I have my arm back?" She pulled her arm back and held it against her body. It felt soiled, defiled, and she longed to wash his saliva from it. "You know a lot about the movie business, Lenny. Ever think you might want to manage your own place someday?" she said, thinking the likelihood of his moving up in the ranks was highly questionable, especially if anyone had the slightest clue about his behavior.

Lenny paused before answering her. His mood appeared to swing from actively romantic to pensive. His eyes narrowed and for a moment she thought he would not answer her.

"Who knows?" He shrugged. "All the managers do come from the ranks. There's no school where you can get a degree in threading projectors or selling corn. You learn by doing it. It's hard work."

"Sounds like you understand the job," she said.

"Yeah? Well, eat up. Uncle Phil punishes me when I'm late. He will make me . . . But you know what he will make me do. You stood there and watched him do it often enough while I screamed and cried and begged you to stop him. And sometimes you even helped him." He glared at her.

Monica froze, waiting for further explanation of his last comment, but Lenny said nothing and finally got up from the table and began piling dishes in the sink with a clatter. She picked at her stew and fruit. What had these people done to him? Was he making her pay for their actions? She felt light-headed and looked at her food. The greasy meat was lukewarm, but she supposed it was nourishing. Had she scored a few points over him today? She had gotten him to talk about something besides his fixation on her, but his actions told her the game of wits was far from being over.

Not only had the fat lady not sung, she wasn't even dressed.

# chapter
# 15

Sarah had been too upset to help Mia and Jeb with the flyer. After John left, Nancy found her sitting in Monica's closet, clutching her mother's robe, staring into space. Not knowing what else to do, Nancy sat down on the floor and pulled both robe and child onto her lap.

After a few moments, Sarah asked, "Mrs. Crawford, are they going to put Mom's picture on the milk cartons?"

"No, honey. I hope she'll be home long before that becomes necessary," Nancy said. She hugged the child closer, barely able to keep her own terror about Monica's disappearance in check.

"Where do you think she is? Why isn't she here?"

"I wish I could answer you, but I can't, Sarah. I do know we can make the time go faster if we keep busy. Will you help me make some cookies?"

Sarah stood up and hung her mother's robe on the hook inside the door. Nancy got to her feet and took Sarah's hand.

In the kitchen, Nancy mixed the dough while Sarah unloaded the dishwasher. The girl worked methodically, wiping the excess water off the glasses, stacking the plates in the cupboard, and emptying the silverware compartment. "Is it time to open the chocolate chips?" she asked when Nancy turned off the beaters.

Nancy squeezed the little girl's shoulders and handed

her the candies. Sarah dumped all but a few of them into the bowl.

"Mom always says it's part of the cookie maker's job to eat the last of the chips right out of the bag," she told Nancy. "Mom says if you don't, the cookies might not be an-any g-good." Her voice broke on the last words.

She gave a handful of the chocolate pieces to Nancy, who forced her lips into a half smile that never reached her eyes. Going along with the tradition, she solemnly popped the chips into her mouth. Sarah, too, ate some of the chocolate. Tears streamed down her face. She tried to hide them from Nancy, but they fell too fast for her to rub them all away.

Nancy stopped stirring the dough and put her hands on the girl's shoulders. "Sarah, I may not know where your mom is, but I've got lots of faith inside me that says she's coming home. I can't tell you when, or how, but I believe she'll walk in that door and give you a great big hug."

As she spoke, Nancy envisioned a hoard of child psychologists waiting to nail her hide to the wall for instilling what might be false hope in Monica's children, but that was all she could do. She had two choices: She could either assume the best or the worst.

Sarah moved away from Nancy to get a tissue and blow her nose. Nancy watched the child circle the kitchen, touching the cookbooks, Monica's calendar, a pot of violets, and a dish towel looped around the refrigerator handle. She wondered what was going through Sarah's mind. How much did a nine-year-old understand about what was happening?

Finally Sarah spoke. "Once I saw this show on TV where a lady hit her head and couldn't remember anything, not even her name, her family, or where she lived. Could that have happened to Mom?"

"It's a possibility. What happened to the lady on the show?"

"She got her memory back after a while."

"Did she come home?" asked Nancy.

Sarah shook her head "no." Nancy handed her the metal cookie sheets and Sarah put them on the counter. Then she stuck her finger into the cookie dough and lifted out a glob. Nancy watched her licking her finger, happy to see the quiet child lose herself for a moment in the impulsive gesture.

"No, uh, she remembered she hadn't been happy with her family, and so she stayed with the new people," said Sarah, dropping her eyes and carefully folding her hands in her lap.

"I bet she didn't have any kids," Nancy said, as she spooned the dough onto the cookie sheets. She was determined to keep the conversation going even as she felt Sarah slipping out of it.

"She wasn't even married. She had a real mean dad, though, and she was glad to get away from him."

"And I bet," Nancy added, "that the new guy was a real hunk, somebody like Tom Cruise. Did he ride a white horse?"

"No, he drove a convertible."

"Same thing. Would you put these cookies in the oven for me?"

Nancy smiled as Sarah slid the cookie sheet into the oven with practiced ease. "You must help your mom do this sort of thing a lot. You, Mia, and Jeb really know your way around the kitchen."

"It's fun with Mom," Sarah replied. As she turned to lean against the sink and gaze out the window, she appeared to grow older, and sadder as if she had leaped ahead in time, the child in her snatched away by unseen hands. Her shoulders seemed broader, her back beneath the white embroidered sweatshirt a little straighter, and her small chin jutted forward as she spoke.

"If Mom lost her memory . . . when she regains it, will she want to come home? Sometimes I hear her and Dad arguing and I know she's not happy. Maybe she wishes she were somewhere else. Do you think she wishes we were smarter in school?" Tears were running down Sarah's cheeks again, but this time she did nothing to hide them.

Nancy gasped at Sarah's feelings of responsibility about her mother's absence. "I think you know the answer to that," she managed to say.

Sarah rummaged under her sweatshirt and pulled out a heart-shaped locket she wore on a chain. She flipped open the clasp and looked at the pictures encased in the small sides of the locket.

"I borrowed this from Mom's jewelry box this morning. Jeb, Mia, and I bought it for her a long time ago. She has prettier stuff, but she still wears this a lot. If she weren't coming back, I guess she would have taken it with her."

"So . . ." Nancy prompted.

"Do you think she'll come home?"

"Yes, I do, honey. Until she does, will one of my hugs do?"

The aura of maturity fell away from Sarah and she ran into Nancy's arms. Nancy held her tightly, not sure which of them needed to be held more.


Monica pushed her lunch away and leaned back in her chair. Lenny had left the kitchen for a moment. She wondered where he had gone. It was so unusual that he left her alone. She looked at the door, but the series of locks and bolted hinges daunted her and she lay her head down on her folded arms. Rest, she told herself. Rest and think. Why was she here? How long would he keep her? What did he want? When would this hell end? The questions somersaulted across her brain. Unable to focus on anything right then, she stood up and added her dishes to the pile already in the sink.

A small mirror hung precariously from a nail on the wall by the sink. Its edges were corroded with rust and she had to twist her head to see herself in it. As before in the bathroom, she was appalled at her appearance. She fingered her hair. The curls were matted and dull. What was happening to her? Even her hair was changing.

"Primping again, I see. Mother, you never change, do you?" Lenny was suddenly behind her.

"Lenny, I wasn't . . . my hair. It just feels so awful."

"All you ever care about is how you look. You're the vainest person I know. You never cared how I looked. Never cared. Never cared." He pranced around her, pulling at her clothes and hair.

"Lenny, stop! You're making me dizzy. My head is hurting. Stop." She folded her arms across her chest, at the same time she tried to dodge his roving hands on her hair and body.

"Oh, no. It was always you. You came first. You and your clothes that had to be just right. You and your food. You and your makeup, your nails, and yes, you and that hair! God, how jealous I used to be of your hair." He moved faster and faster, circling her, and his movements became rougher. Twice he slapped her face, and when she tried to shield her eyes, he yanked hard on her hair until she cried out.

"Did you know I used to dream of you losing that hair? Maybe you'd get some disease, and survive, of course. I wouldn't want you to die, just lose all your hair. Maybe you'd be in an accident and it would get caught in some big machine and someone would have to cut it to get it free." He stopped circling and pulled her close. Bile rose in her throat and she gagged.

"Please, please let me go. Let me . . . go." Still in his arms she slid to the floor. Relief swept through her. Lenny let her go, but continued his dance around her. She paid no attention to him, but tried to get back her equilibrium.

"Is it where you get your power, Mother? Your strength? Like that man in the Bible? I believe that, Mother. I really believe that."

He grabbed her long hair, and ignoring her screams,

used it to pull her around in a circle. She grasped at his hands, digging her fingernails into his perfect skin until he too, yelled, not from pain, but from seeing the red welts and scratches she was causing to appear on the backs of his hands.

"You bitch! Look what you're doing!" He ran to the sink, turned on the tap and held his hands beneath its spray. She never moved, but lay curled in a ball on the floor.

"My hands, my hands," he whimpered. He dried them carefully and opened a drawer beside the sink. From it he withdrew a pair of white cotton gloves and a large can of salve. Gently he smeared the salve on his hands and donned the gloves.

He looked at her with hatred in his eyes. "You've always known how to hurt me, haven't you? Well, this time, Mother, maybe it's my turn."

Suddenly a large pair of scissors dangled from his gloved hands, inches from her eyes. She froze as he placed one knee across her chest, pinning her to the floor while he leaned over her.

"Say good-bye to these curls, Mother. Say good-bye to your strength."

Monica slipped into a trance, her lips repeating in silent litany, *It's just my hair, it will grow back. It's just my hair, it will grow back. It's just my hair. . . .* until her sobs overcame the words.

# chapter
# 16

"Is the flyer okay, Mrs. Crawford?" Jeb asked. It was Thursday afternoon. He and Mia had spent most of the day working on it.

"It looks like you've got everything here," Nancy said. "Name, reward, contact number, all the vital statistics." *God, has it been almost twenty-four hours since we heard from Monica?*

"You think Dad will be home soon? It's after four. We should get this out on the street today. If anyone has any information about Mom, we need to have it right away."

Jeb was trying hard to act brave and responsible in front of Nancy and his sisters, but Nancy recognized the terror in his eyes and the slight tremor of his hands when he handled the flyer. If the girls noticed his fear, they chose to ignore it. Even Mia, who seldom missed a nuance, was uncharacteristically quiet.

"He should be here any minute. I'm sure he—"

Nancy was interrupted by the doorbell. Jeb and the girls ran to answer it.

"It's Dr. Riley," Mia called when they opened the door.

"Hi, kids. Hello, Nancy." David made a point of smiling and touching each child, lightly squeezing the girls' shoulders, and play punching Jeb's upper arm before he introduced them to the man who accompanied him into the house.

Randy Abbott had been with the Dallas Police Department for the last twelve of his forty-three years, moving through the ranks to his present position of detective eight years ago. His conservative dark suit, white shirt, and navy blue tie covered a husky, five-foot, ten-inch body. He wore his black hair short, and complemented his swarthy face with a heavy mustache. His manner was friendly and low-key as he grinned at the children.

David introduced the detective to everyone. Nancy liked him immediately. That he was there as a favor was not evident in the professional way he moved his dark brown eyes over the children, the hallway, and in the direction of the living room, missing nothing. She was certain that if she asked him to turn around and close those eyes, he could describe every piece of furniture, every picture on the wall.

"Guess we're ahead of John," David said. "He asked us to meet him here about four-fifteen."

"I'm sure he's on his way. Why don't we all go into the living room and sit down? Would you care for some coffee? David? Mr. Abbott?" asked Nancy.

Both men declined, but followed Nancy and the children. Earlier clouds had fled, and now the late afternoon sunshine streamed through the living room window, bouncing off the brass picture frames arranged on the top of the baby grand piano. David saw a closeup shot of Monica, her coppery hair falling below her shoulders, a dreamy smile lighting her face and felt as if someone had just punched him in the stomach. He hoped his sharp intake of breath had not been noticed, and took a seat next to Randy on the flowered chintz sofa.

Nancy sat in the matching chair, with the children clustered about her; the twins perched on the wide arms of the chair, Jeb was at her feet. Once again she had the feeling that the detective, to put it mildly, was "casing the joint."

"Who's the gardener?" he asked, studying the large,

indoor planter of narcissus and hyacinths nestled beneath the window.

"Oh, that's Mom. She loves flowers," Mia said. "The house is full of them. We don't have a very big yard, so she keeps a lot of them inside."

"Did she force those bulbs?" he asked, being something of a gardener himself.

"I guess so. She planted them last fall in the garage," Jeb said. "And then we helped her bring them inside a couple of weeks ago."

"Spring flowers are her favorites, especially daffodils," Sarah whispered.

"Somebody's a collector here, too. Is that Wedgwood?"

"Yes," Mia said, hopping off the chair arm to point to the vases on the mantel. "Mom and Dad brought these back from England a few years ago. Mom says they are her most treasured possessions."

"What else does your mom like?" Randy asked Mia.

"Uh . . . she likes to cook. She makes great brownies."

"And sports," Jeb offered. "She goes to all our games—baseball, soccer, even football. Whenever we play, she's there to watch us."

"She loves animals, too," Sarah said. "Dad always says that if we left it up to Mom, the house would have more animals than people living here."

David and Nancy allowed the children to dominate the conversation. The detective was great with the kids. In no time at all, he had them talking about their interests, their school activities, and their dislikes. Even Sarah allowed herself to be included in the lively discussion. Randy's questions were never pushy or condescending. Nancy was thrilled by the attention he was giving the children. David had never seen a better, more subtle interview approach.

Eventually the conversation turned to favorites, especially food, books, movies, and cars. After a few minutes, Randy knew their mother drove a late-model, blue station wagon that had disappeared with her, allowed the children to choose most of the videos—as long as they were rated "G" or "PG"—and that she, and not John, watched the films with them. He learned that their dad's favorite snack food was pretzels, but Mom always went for the popcorn.

He now knew that Mia was terrified of spiders, Jeb was a computer whiz who had achieved Level Three of Super Mario Brothers, and that of the three kids, Sarah seemed the most affected by the mother's disappearance. He had not needed to ask any questions about that: He simply observed the interaction among the children.

By the time John breezed into the house fifteen minutes later, Randy had a fairly good picture of what life was like in the Foyles' household, at least from the children's point of view. If the woman had run off to escape marital difficulties or if she had been unhappy about the state of her life, she had hidden it from the children. It was obvious that they adored her, and were adored in return.

The men stood when John entered the living room. Randy noted a tall man who, even dressed casually in slacks and a sweater, carried an aura of power with him. Here was a guy who was used to calling the shots, who expected people to jump when he gave the word. He saw a tinge of dislike ripple across John's classic features when David extended his hand to him, and wondered why.

"John, this is Randy Abbott. Randy, meet John Foyles." David made the introductions and everyone sat down.

John nodded to Nancy, smiled at Jeb, and winked at the girls, his glance resting on Sarah's puffy eyes.

"I was just getting acquainted with your children, John," Randy said. "They're great kids. You're lucky to have them."

"Yes, I am. I appreciate your stopping by. We can use some direction in this mess. We've hit nothing but dead ends."

John sat back in his chair and rested the side of one spit-polished shoe over his knee. Randy thought it would be possible to slice open an apple on the crease in the man's pants. At first glance, John's pose may have appeared relaxed, but Randy understood that this man suffered no fools. Intimidation was his well-developed sixth sense. Randy wondered how many enemies John Foyles must have collected in his lifetime. Carefully, as if picking his way through a minefield, he continued.

"David has told me a little about your wife's disappearance, but why don't you fill me in on everything you've done so far?"

John repeated the things he'd been told to check: her personal items, their credit cards, financial statements, and phone bills, and how they had contacted the neighbors, Monica's friends, and coworkers, all to no avail. Frustration and barely controlled anger punctuated his words.

"None of Monica's treasures are missing. She hardly goes anywhere without her glasses or pictures of the kids. Her favorite perfume, her sentimental jewelry, her gifts from the children, even the running shoes she wears all the time are here in the house."

"Does anyone else ever care for the plants?" Randy asked.

John shrugged his shoulders and looked at the girls, wondering what the damned plants had to do with anything.

Sarah cleared her throat and answered. "Sometimes I help her water them, but she usually does everything herself when we're at school."

"Remember, Dad, when Grandma got sick and Mom went to Connecticut for a week, she left at least five pages of instructions, just for the plants?" Jeb said.

A smile flickered across John's face at the memory. "You're right, son." To Randy, he added, "The plants are strictly under my wife's care, as are most of the things connected with the house."

"And you've found no instructions?"

John's smile reappeared and fled so quickly that Randy wondered if he had imagined it.

"Nothing," he whispered.

Randy recognized the small but significant break in John's demeanor. "If you had to name Monica's five favorite places to go in town, where would they be?"

John dropped his foot to the floor and spent several moments chasing a piece of imaginary lint from his pants.

"I guess the mall," he said at last. "She's a shopper."

"Can you be more specific, John? Where in the mall would she go? Does she like the large department stores, or the small speciality shops?"

"I have no idea. Why is this important?"

"Bear with me. I'm trying to get a feel for a person I've never seen or spoken with. Only you and your family can help me with these answers."

"She likes the small stores," Mia said. "She only goes into the big stores if she absolutely has to."

"She doesn't spend a lot of time at the mall either. She doesn't like the crowds. She says sometimes they bother her," Sarah added.

*Ah,* thought Randy, *look to the children instead of the husband.*

"Mia, when your mother goes to the mall, where does she usually go?"

"Northpark. It's the closest."

"Okay, tell me, Sarah, if your mom had to spend some time at the mall, say, to kill a few hours while you're doing something like going to a movie with your friends, which store would she choose?"

"Probably the lingerie shop. She's always buying pretty underwear and stuff."

Nancy smiled at Sarah. The men seemed uncomfortable with that information . . . especially David, who dropped his gaze and studied his shoes.

"That's great, Sarah," Randy said. "Now let's say she's

been in one of those places and bought some things. Where would she go next?"

Sarah looked to her twin for help. As usual, Mia had an answer. "If she didn't have anything to buy for us, she'd probably go to the bookstore. Mom loves to read."

"What kinds of things does she like to read?" Randy asked.

"I can answer that one," John said. "Ever since I've known her, my wife has had an unquenchable desire for the supernatural, the more thrilling and bloodier, the better. Stephen King is her idol."

*So the lady has another side. An interesting combination: daffodils, popcorn, Wedgwood, and gore.* As long as Randy had been in this business, he had never stopped being amazed at the uniqueness of each person's interests and tastes.

"Let's get back to her favorite places," he said. "So far we have the mall, primarily for its lingerie and bookstores. Where else would she be likely to spend her time?"

"She's a teacher's aide, but she does library and computer stuff, too," Jeb said.

"Have you checked with the people there?" Randy asked John.

"Nancy called them yesterday. No one knows anything."

"Tomorrow, if I were you, I'd make a personal visit to her office there, John. Sit at her desk or wherever she has her base. Take some time and go through all of her things. Check her Rolodex if she has one. Look for anything unusual—a travel folder, ticket stubs, a personal letter. Talk to the people she sees every day. Find out what she tells them, what they know about her, what she likes best about her job, and why."

"How can that possibly help? We've already contacted them, and they've told us nothing," John said, questioning his wisdom in allowing David to drag the law officer into this.

"People often keep little things at work that they'd normally throw away at home. I don't know why," Randy explained.

"Are you saying she was hiding something from us?"

"Not necessarily. Look, John, no one here has any idea where your wife is, but somewhere there's a clue, and you've got to find it. It may be a return address on a discarded envelope you find on her desk, a receipt for something you didn't know she bought, or a flight schedule—"

"Mom didn't leave us! She would be here if she could," Jeb protested.

Randy turned his attention to the boy sitting Indian-style on the floor. The child's eyes were blazing.

*The father's not the only tiger here.*

"You're probably right," he told Jeb. "But in my business I have to consider everything. I know I'm upsetting you, but I'm just trying to help."

"Yeah, I know. Sorry." Jeb rubbed at his eyes and looked away.

Randy glanced at John. At first the man appeared to want to comfort his son without further adding to his embarrassment, but he just sat there, waiting for the conversation to continue.

"Why don't you get your flyer, Jeb?" Nancy said, her cheery voice cutting through the strained silence. "We know you have to make a few corrections, but your dad and Detective Abbott won't care."

"Of course, we won't, Jeb. Go get it," John said. His eyes followed his son's retreat to the kitchen.

"The flyer is a good idea," Randy said as Jeb handed him one. He read it quickly and passed it to John. "Are you including a picture of your mother?"

"We're putting it at the top. We're going to make lots of copies and pass them around."

Randy nodded his approval and turned to John. "Have you contacted the media?"

"Yes, several radio stations have agreed to run a short description, mention the reward and give our phone number. The newspaper's sending someone out tonight, if possible."

At John's announcement, a wave of nausea swept through David. Here was the reality he had fought against for the past twenty-four hours. Monica was truly missing, and although no one had mentioned the obvious, she was probably in serious danger.

Would they find her mutilated body in a ditch? He could not help imagining the worst, and the idea was ripping him apart. To never see her smile again, hear her soft voice, touch her, or laugh at her dumb jokes was more than he could bear.

Randy watched David with growing concern. His friend was clearly upset. But why? Had he a greater stake in this outcome than simple compassion for an acquaintance's absent wife? The ramifications of David's demeanor were endless, but he forced his mind back to John.

"Anything you can do might help in some way. You never know where the leads will come from," Randy told him.

"I just hope we can handle the calls," John said.

"Sometimes that can be a problem, sometimes not. It's hard to predict because each case is so different. Try to take notes on every phone call, but make no commitment about the reward. Be leery of anyone who won't leave a phone number for a call back. If they're legitimate, chances are they'll be more than helpful. Keep track of the hang-ups, too. If they happen often or follow a pattern, we'll need to consider them."

Randy paused. He had more to say, but was reluctant to continue. He looked to John for help, but received none. The man appeared to have moved into a world where others were forbidden to enter. His posture still indicated repose, but his attention was elsewhere. Randy caught

Nancy's eye. She understood immediately that he wanted to talk with John and David alone.

"Hey, kids," she said, "I think it's time we let the men have some private talk. Why don't we go out to the kitchen and sample those cookies?"

Nancy took the twins by the hands and pulled them off the chair. Jeb followed his sisters reluctantly, wondering how old you had to be before you were considered one of the men.

When the group had departed, Randy turned to John. "The questions I'm about to ask you are tough ones, but they are things I need to know before we continue."

John sat up straighter and wondered where this man could possibly go next. "What do you want to know?"

"Has your wife ever undergone treatment for mental problems? Severe depression? Bouts of nervousness? Does she take any medication like Valium, Elavil, or Prozac?"

"No, not that I'm aware of."

"Does she have any physical problems?"

"God, no! She's as healthy as a horse."

"Any alcohol dependency or drug problems?"

John shook his head in an emphatic "no."

"One more thing, and I know this is difficult. Could there be another man in her life? Someone with whom she might have left?"

John sucked in his breath. "You've got to be kidding. Monica has everything she needs here."

No one said anything. The silence was disturbing. Randy studied John while David took an in-depth inventory of the furniture in the room.

Finally, Randy sighed and continued, "If she doesn't turn up soon, and you truly believe she would never leave of her own accord, that leaves us two nasty choices: kidnapping or foul play. Unfortunately, the options diminish the longer she's gone.

"If it's kidnapping, you may be contacted for ransom.

If that happens, call me and we'll handle things from there. We get involved then, real quick!"

"Don't kidnappers warn you not to contact the police?" John asked.

"Usually only in the movies, but yes, they might. My advice to you would be to disregard that option and call me."

"How about if it's foul play?" David asked.

"Then we wait."

John wiped his hand across his eyes. "Do the police get involved then?"

"Officially, only if we have concrete evidence."

"Which is?" Both David and John spoke at the same time.

"You mentioned earlier that her car and her handbag are missing. Find either one of those and we may have a case."

John stood up and walked to the window. "Should I report my car stolen?" he asked, knowing he was grabbing at straws.

"Not if you know your wife was driving it. It isn't against the law for her to leave home, and it's not against the law for her to take the car. Texas is a community-property state, after all."

"You guys are blocking all the exits. I don't know what else to do," John said.

Randy could not figure him out. Sometimes the man seemed genuinely worried about his wife's disappearance. At other times, he appeared to view Monica's absence as a giant inconvenience. Was he indifferent to the fact that his wife might be dead, or was he a master at hiding his true feelings? David had shown much more emotion during the conversation about Monica's disappearance.

"One more thing I want you to consider, John. I'm not even sure it's a suggestion. Just call it a reflection of my experience, okay?"

"Sure, what is it?"

"When news of your wife's disappearance hits the

papers, TV, radio, whatever, all hell could break loose as far as your home life is concerned. TV stations have been known to set up shop in front of people's houses over things like this. Often a lot of good comes from the coverage: Folks come forth with information who might not have spoken up without it, your case gets attention, something shakes loose and your wife shows up. That's the upside."

"I'm sure there's a downside, too," John said.

"Yeah," Randy said, hating to add yet more weight to the burden, "there is. You'll be able to handle it. Sure, there'll be times when you'll want to tell the media people to take a hike, but you'll be okay. It's the kids. This stuff is really tough on them. Reporters aren't the most sensitive people around. They'll stick a microphone in anybody's face if they think they have something to say that the viewers want to hear. Unfortunately, it won't matter to them how young, or how emotionally involved the person is. Bottom line: Think about sending the kids away to Grandma's or something."

"Grandma doesn't know. I haven't told anyone." *Except Beth.*

"Jesus Christ, John, you mean you haven't called Monica's folks? What if they hear it on the TV?" David was furious. He jumped off the sofa and paced the room. The other two men watched him, concealing their thoughts about his outburst.

"You're right, of course, but it's so . . . so humiliating having to explain her absence," John said after a few moments' thought.

"How can you be so incredibly stupid?" David stopped pacing inches from John. "You make those calls, or dammit I will!"

"Okay, okay, I'll call both sets of parents tonight," said John. "I've had this misguided notion that I could spare them. Guess I wasn't thinking straight."

David returned to the sofa, slightly mollified by the

sight of John, who had dropped into a chair and was covering his face with his hands. "Maybe I was out of line, John," he said. "I apologize. I know these past two days haven't been easy."

Randy broke the tension. "I'm due back at the precinct," he said, figuring it was a good time to adjourn this meeting. He did not understand what was between these two men, or maybe he did, but he hoped they could set it aside for the time being. They needed to work together. One thing was obvious. Both had a big stake in finding Monica Foyles.

The seven-thirty radio news was winding down as Lenny backed onto the street. He nearly hit a blue Chevy parked by the curb when he heard the deejay say, ". . . reported missing from her home, Monica Foyles, aged forty-four, has green eyes and shoulder-length, auburn hair. She's five feet, four inches tall and weighs one hundred and fifteen pounds. She was last seen on Wednesday afternoon, that's yesterday, folks, wearing blue jeans, and a green turtleneck sweater. Anyone with informa—"

Lenny smashed his fist into the dashboard. The radio went dead. "No, Mother. Whatever you're up to, your plan won't work. You're all mine now! You can't escape again."

Anger surged through him and he drove like a maniac. He careened into a parking place at the theater, knocking out his left headlight on the corner of the Dumpster.

"Fuck it!" he screamed, jumping out of his car.

Cars from the Thursday matinee crowd at Town Park Eight filled the parking lot, reminding Lenny of what he could look forward to in June when kids were out of school and the temperature was too high to do much but sit in a cool theater. He hated these privileged crowds, and he hated the extra work they created. Today, especially, he was in no mood to handle any flak.

Inside, he went to the concession stand for a soda. As

he raised the cup to his mouth, he noticed his gloved hands and swore under his breath. He had not dared to be late today; and because of Mother and her hysterical behavior, he had not remembered to remove his gloves.

Tossing his cup into the nearest trash bin, he rounded the corner and punched in the security code that unlatched the door to the second floor. He bounded up the steps two at a time, and ran into the employees' bathroom, where he removed his gloves and applied more salve to his wounds. They looked better already, no thanks to Mother. Only then was he ready to unlock the door to the film room. He read the list of instructions posted by the first projector, and began to work. By the time Uncle Phil joined him an hour later, six of the platter trees were threaded, their timers set and ready for projection.

"Clean up the portals, kid," Phil snapped.

Lenny picked up a rag and a bottle of glass cleaner, and wiped down the small windows in front of each projector while Phil opened the metal shipping cabinets holding the newly arrived films. He stacked the five reels of the new Kevin Costner movie on the floor.

Lenny sighed, relieved that he could be home with Mother tonight while Phil and the new assistant manager built the Costner film, scheduled to open tomorrow. It would take at least three to four hours to set up and preview, assuming the trailers, or beginning ads, had already been chosen.

"Hey, kid. You're working tonight."

"Not me. I'm off at eleven. Mark's on deck to help you."

"Something wrong with your ears? I said you're working tonight. This Costner movie's real important. Only one other theater in town's got it, so I want our presentation to be perfect. You got the experience; I need you, so you're working."

"How about if I have important plans?"

"Then you break 'em, kid. I need you here. You can take an extra half hour for dinner tomorrow."

"I've built the last three shows, dammit!"

Phil stepped around the reels. "You owe me, kid. You owe me big time." He pushed Lenny back against the wall, knocking the bottle of blue window cleaner out of his hand. "And you watch your mouth, too. I've got better uses for it than to hear you swear at me." He laughed derisively at him and gave him another push for emphasis before returning to the cases.

Lenny left the room, and for the second time that day he felt overwhelming rage churn through his body, his heart pumping the hatred across his shoulders and down his arms until his fingers tingled from the need to hurt his uncle.

He skirted the break room and headed for the second floor storage closet to steal a couple of chocolate bars. As he looked at the metal shelves holding the neatly stacked boxes of candy, light bulbs, and paper goods, his hands tingled again with the urge to inflict more damage. These were his uncle's profits. He could destroy it all.

"Hey, Lenny." Kyle Williams stepped out from behind one of the high shelves. "I organized the napkins, cups, and other paper goods. Do you want me to keep it all up here, or should I carry some of it downstairs and put it behind the counter in some of those cupboards?"

Lenny turned to Kyle in a rage. "Don't bother me with that stuff now! I told you once what to do. How many times do you have to hear it?"

"But I was just asking where to . . . we never talked about where you wanted the stuff. Geez, Lenny. Calm down."

"You want to know where to put the shit? I'll tell you! Why don't you stick it up your ass?" He walked to where Kyle had put the cartons of nacho dishes and long tubes of different sized cups. With one powerful swipe of his hand, he pushed everything to the floor.

"What the . . . ? Why'd you do that? What's wrong with you, man?" Kyle gave Lenny one last hard look. "What's wrong with you?" He waited for a few moments, and receiving no answer, turned and stomped out of the room.

Lenny rifled through the cartons, wondering if Mother still preferred peanut butter cups. He stuffed fifteen packages of candy beneath his jacket before relocking the door. Cheating Uncle Phil, even a few dollars' worth, would have to be his revenge for now. The old man hated it when his inventory didn't balance.

# chapter

# 17

"I hope," Beth said as she watched the city lights of Atlanta from her window, "you'll be able to squeeze me into your schedule, John. You need a break. In the morning I'm catching the eight o'clock plane back to Dallas."

"There's nothing I'd like better than spending time with you, but I've got to devote the weekend to finding Monica. If some creep has picked her up and wants money, I've got to be here to handle it." He pushed the yellow legal pad away and threw down his pen.

"I understand, really, I do. I have no right to your time when you've already got so much going on, but I miss you, darling." She twisted the phone cord around a long red fingernail, imagining it was a lock of his hair.

"I miss you, too. Bear with me on this, okay? I have a responsibility here. I've told you about the police not being able to help."

"Yes, I know. It's not fair to you to have to handle this alone."

"Maybe we can have a drink, or something, late tomorrow afternoon?"

"Oh, I hope so, John. I have the Chamberlin meeting at four. How about after that?"

"I can't promise anything, Beth. Maybe later, after the

kids go to sleep, I can get a sitter and slip out for an hour or so."

Beth tried to hide an exasperated sigh. "Why don't you call me when you think you might have some time? If not tomorrow, maybe you can break away on Saturday."

"I'm sorry, hon. I really am. You have a nice evening and I'll check back with you tomorrow. If we can't see each other, at least we can talk." He remembered the phone trace. It wouldn't be wise to make too many calls to Beth's apartment from his house. Things were getting more complicated all the time. He wondered if he would ever get his normal life back.

"Sure, John. I'm trying to be patient, but you know that's not one of my virtues."

"I know. Sometimes your impatience is your most appealing asset." He chuckled, remembering the times when she could not wait for him to lock the hotel door. She was an exciting woman, one worth coddling. "I promise to let you know the moment I've got some time. All right?"

"That sounds like an offer I shouldn't refuse. I'll wait for your call, darling."

John replaced the receiver and stood up. Was it only twenty-four hours ago that he was having a few drinks and a nice dinner in Atlanta, with nothing more on his mind than making love to Beth and then getting a good night's sleep? Would life ever be that simple again? Wait a minute, he told himself. When had he ever considered that his life was simple? Not for a long time . . . not since he had started up with Beth. Life got real complicated after that. And now? Today? Today his life alternated between spiraling masses of terror when he thought of where Monica could be, rage at his inability to help her, and a sickening premonition that his children's lives were about to change forever in the most horrifying way—their mother might never return. The responsibility that that would entail overwhelmed him and he stood in the gathering darkness and quiet of his study, crying for his children and all they would miss.

"Dad? You ready to go to dinner?" Jeb appeared at the doorway. "You said we'd take the flyer to be copied. We're kind of hungry, too."

John hastily wiped his eyes, summoned a smile, and faced his son. "Just give me two minutes to wash up and I'll be right there, I promise."

"You okay, Dad? Why are you standing here in the dark?"

John heard the tremor of fear in Jeb's voice.

"I was just thinking and I guess I lost track of the time. I'm fine, but I am hungry, so get the girls together and we'll go."

He wished he was better at saying the right things to make his children feel better. Monica would have known exactly what to say to Jeb.

"They're all ready," Jeb said. "We'll wait for you in the garage, Dad."

Ten minutes later, John and the children dropped the flyer at the copy center and drove to the restaurant. The kids had chosen a noisy, trendy, hamburger place called "Burger Up!" where all the waiters sported funny baseball uniforms with an assortment of buttons with zany slogans pinned to their wide-brimmed hats. Bright lights, green AstroTurf and lots of baseball trivia on the walls further enhanced the restaurant's theme.

Sarah pulled menus out from between a bottle of ketchup and a napkin dispenser shaped like a catcher's mitt, and slid them across the tabletop that was painted to look like a baseball diamond. "They have salads here, too, Dad, but we usually eat hamburgers and cheese fries."

John swallowed his views on those particular choices. Now was not the time for a lesson in nutrition. Nancy had told him the children had eaten almost nothing all day.

He'd have bought them each two sundaes and a pile of French fries if he thought they'd eat them.

"Just wait until you kids have to count calories and watch your cholesterol. I'll be too old to care by then, and I'll be eating cheeseburgers and banana splits by the truckload while you're all eating rabbit food."

For a moment, they chuckled together. John was relieved to see, if only for a moment, a slight break in the tension that surrounded them. They ordered their food and discussed a strategy for distributing the flyers. Jeb was eager to get started.

"My soccer coach said he'd call some parents to help us if we need them," he said. "I can get the team to help since there's no school tomorrow."

"We can use all the help we can get," John said. "That reminds me of something else I think we should talk about."

"What's that, Dad?" asked Mia.

"I was wondering what you're telling your friends about all of this. Are you having a rough time explaining your mother's absence? I know it must be confusing to everyone." So far John had avoided telling anyone else about his wife's disappearance.

"Mom always says to tell the truth and that's what I'm doing," Mia said. "What else is there to say?"

"How about you, Jeb? Anybody giving you a hard time about it, or making you feel bad?"

"Heck no, Dad. The guys can handle it."

"Sarah?"

She shook her head and avoided his eyes.

"You told us about a newspaper man," said Jeb. "Is he coming tonight?"

"We had an initial interview over the phone. He has the information for a small article in tomorrow's paper. Later on, he said he may decide to do an in-depth story on us.

"As you heard a little while ago, the radio spots are already airing," John continued. It had been a chilling experience for all of them to hear about Monica on the car radio. "The TV stations will probably put something on the ten o'clock news tonight."

"Mom's going to be famous," said Mia.

Their conversation was interrupted by the arrival of their food. For the next ten minutes, they picked at their sandwiches in silence. Finally, John spoke.

"I don't think this stuff is any good warmed over. This isn't a doggy bag sort of place," he said.

Mia looked up and down. John saw the moisture glittering in her green eyes, and set down his iced tea.

"Look, kids, we can't just stop eating. I know this is really tough, but we have to continue with our lives, and that includes eating dinner," he said.

"Guess we're not as hungry as we thought we were," Jeb whispered. He wanted to get out of the restaurant before he broke down and bawled like a baby.

"Guess not, son," John said, signaling to the waiter for the check. He couldn't force them to eat. One look at their faces revealed how fruitless a gesture that would be. Besides he was exhausted. He doubted he was capable of doing much more right now than paying the bill.

They drove home in silence. The house they entered was uncharacteristically dark and quiet. Monica was the one who always remembered to leave some lights lit, and to leave the radio on for Peach.

"It keeps him company," she explained. The children would laugh as she lengthened the joke by trying to decide what kind of music he would enjoy listening to while they were gone. Once she had found a news talk show. "That'll keep Peach Pie up on world affairs," she said, while adjusting the dial to ensure the clearest reception. "He'll be able to impress his friends." The children had giggled all the way to the car.

How different the house was now, and how lonely.

John flipped on some lights, but the children, unable to stay in the empty rooms, escaped to the backyard for a few minutes with Peach.

"Anything on TV you want to watch?" he asked them when they returned.

No one answered. The children huddled around the dog, rubbing his back and playing with his ears.

John supposed he should stay with them, but he had to phone Monica's parents. That was one call he didn't want to make within earshot of the children.

"Well, I guess I'll go make some phone calls and read a couple of things from work," he told them. "If you want to play a game or choose a video to watch, I'll be free in about an hour."

Jeb stopped to get Peach's water dish. He carried it to the sink to rinse it out and refill it before placing it back on the floor by the refrigerator. "Sure, Dad," he said, without looking up.

The girls followed the dog to the dish and watched him drink. John was sure he'd witnessed some sadder things in his life, but the sight of his kids, in tears again, standing guard over the dog was more than he could handle.

"I think we need something better than a double hug here," he said as he walked toward them. "This calls for an all-out group hug, don't you think?"

In a moment, all three children were in his arms.

John decided to call his folks first, but no one was home. When he dialed Monica's parents, her father, William, answered the phone on the first ring from his den. As John asked all the preliminary health and well-being questions, he could picture his father-in-law sitting at his desk, fiddling with the checkbook, or whatever he had been working on prior to the call.

William was a man of great warmth but few words. He and John quickly ran out of small talk, and John sensed the older man's building anxiety. Although John considered himself to be on good terms with Monica's parents, in the past ten years he could remember calling them only twice: Once when the twins were born, and two years ago when Jeb broke his leg.

"William, have you heard from Monica?"

"Not since her usual call on Sunday."

"Then I'm afraid I have some upsetting news."

"Is it the children? What's happened?" William asked.

"No, the kids are okay. They're having a few days of vacation from school and are . . ." What could he say? That the kids are absolutely miserable, terrified beyond belief? "Uh . . . they're okay. This is about Monica."

"Should I put her mother on the line?" William's voice lowered and he cleared his throat.

"Yes, perhaps that would be best."

John could see Monica's father seeking out Grace, who was probably reading or knitting in the living room. She would have one of her handmade afghans thrown over her legs, tapping her feet to Glenn Miller's rendition of "String of Pearls" or some of the other Big Band music she loved. Connecticut evenings were chilly in March, and John knew they would have a fire in the fireplace—a real wood-burning fire—none of those gas logs for William and Grace. Was he about to shatter that peace, perhaps forever?

"Oh, John," Grace said, her voice sounding reedy and thin, quite unlike her normal tones, "what's happened?"

"I wish there were some way to break this gently, but there isn't."

"Please, just tell us what is wrong," said Grace.

"Monica has disappeared. Yesterday she dropped the dog off at the vet's about nine-thirty in the morning, had tea with a friend, and no one has seen her since."

William caught his breath and absorbed the anguish of John's words. His baby, his little girl . . . missing? He didn't want to believe it. "No, no, John," he said. "She must be . . ." Where?

"Where would she go?" Grace cried shrilly. "Where is she?"

William heard the rising panic in Grace's voice and his next thought was for his wife. "John, hold on a minute. I want to change phones. I . . . I need to be with Grace." He hung up the receiver at his desk and got the portable extension.

"All right, John," he said quietly. "Tell us all you know." He sat down with his wife, who was crying, and took her hand, his own heart breaking at what the terror in her eyes might mean.

Upon hearing the news, John's parents offered to catch the first plane to Dallas, but John assured them that for the time being they could remain in Connecticut.

"Monica's folks will be here tomorrow, Mom," he said.

"Of course, but you know we're here for you, too," Henry Foyles added.

"Thanks, Dad, but we've got things covered for now. Later, if it becomes necessary for the children to leave Dallas for a while, I'll send them home to Connecticut."

"Whatever you say, son. We'll be happy to have them nearby," Henry said. "I know William and Grace will be a great help to you."

As John bid his parents good-bye, a large feeling of relief swept over him. His in-laws would take over the house and the children, freeing him to run the search, man the phone, and keep up with things at work. With renewed energy, he picked up the phone and dialed the first number on his list of possible helpers for tomorrow.

Pleased he had enlisted fifty people to distribute flyers, it was ten-thirty before John looked up from his work. He dropped his pencil and pushed himself away from his desk. He found the kids in the family room, watching home videos he and Monica had taken over the years. Usually such screenings were punctuated with loud bursts of laughter. Tonight, however, the audience watched in silence.

A montage of Christmas Day celebrations, Easter egg hunts, sand castles at the seashore, birthday cakes, first days of school, and backyard picnics chronicled the Foyles' life together. Clothing and hairstyles were dated, some of the scenes silly, even campy and contrived, but the joy showing in their faces seemed lit from within. He had forgotten they had ever been so happy. It was as if those days belonged to another lifetime, one he could barely recall. The young couple with their twin toddlers and sturdy little boy looked like strangers to him. He turned his head away, uncomfortable with his feelings, unable to watch any longer.

"Time for bed now," he said, more gruffly than he had intended. "Anyone want anything to eat or drink?"

"No, thanks," was the reply.

"Sorry I didn't get back here sooner. I got busy laying out the distribution route for the flyers and lost track of time," John said.

"That's okay," Jeb said as he flipped off the VCR.

"Night, Dad," Mia said. "Come on Peach. Time for bed."

"Shouldn't he go out, or something?"

"We took him out and gave him his treat," Jeb added. The big dog followed the children up the stairs.

"I'll be up in a few minutes to tuck you into bed."

John watched them separate at the top of the steps and go into their rooms. He tried, but he could think of nothing more to say or do to alleviate his children's pain.

Where was Monica? No ransom note. No contact of any sort. Not even one lousy phone call.

"Look for a clue," the detective had said. "Somewhere there's a clue."

John threw the newspapers on the floor and turned off CNN. As he had the night before, he wandered through the house in search of her. When they were first married, he could walk into their apartment and know immediately if she was at home. Her presence, her aura, had been everywhere and he had felt overwhelming happiness in the simple knowledge that she was near. He wondered how he had lost those feelings, that ability to be so entwined in her psyche. When had it ceased to be important to him?

He had never felt that closeness with Beth. There was attraction, certainly, but it was mainly physical. Her youth, her tall, sylphlike body, and her blatant sexiness had captivated him from the beginning. She had been like a booster shot to his ego when he had needed it most. Did she want to marry him? He was not sure. Would he like to spend the rest of his life with her? Probably not. She lacked the qualities he wanted in a wife and mother, but she was a passionate side trip.

"What I need are two different lives. One here with Monica and the children, and one with a new and exciting creature like Beth," he said to himself, as he continued his search.

In their bathroom, he picked up a bottle of Monica's perfume. It was not a particular favorite of his, and he put it down. He opened a drawer and flicked through her underthings, wondering if most women chose to wear the lacy, feminine things Monica did. Beth did not. She preferred plain camisoles, undershirts, and cotton briefs. Her masculine undergarments were the one thing he would like to change about her.

He opened Monica's closet. If a clue was in here, he would never recognize it. The rows of neatly hung clothes, racks of shoes, and plastic boxes of sweaters offered no help. Feeling frustrated, he closed the door.

John went to her side of the bed and opened the top drawer of her nightstand. A paperback book and a half-written letter were inside. He pulled out the letter, deciding the need for answers outranked the right of privacy. "Dear Mother and Daddy," it began, followed by a page detailing the children's activities. The letter offered no clues. He replaced it, slamming the drawer.

The bed was even less inviting than it had been the night before. Although the numbness of fatigue clouded his feelings, he dreaded a return of the terror he had faced the night before. Certainly they would find something soon. A person could not disappear without a trace. That sort of thing only happened in the movies. He considered what his life would be like if Monica were never found. The answers that came to him were vague and surprisingly unsettling.

He moved away from the bed and kicked off his deck shoes. They landed somewhere across the room. It did not matter where. Who was there besides himself to care? He unbuttoned the sleeves of his plaid sport shirt and folded them back across the generous amount of black hair on his arms. Monica had always referred to it and the hair on his chest as his pelt. Why did that remembrance suddenly bother him? In the old days, he had loved the way she touched him, the way she delighted in his body as he had in hers. When had that feeling changed? Would it ever return, even if she came home?

He took off his watch and laid it on the dresser beside the crystal vase filled with fresh flowers. The colorful blooms were beginning to droop. He ran his fingers across the waxy petals of a pink tulip. Maybe they needed water. Or, maybe they, too, felt the desperation, the agonizing oppression that had fallen over this house. Looking around the room, he expected to see the flowers on the bedspread and matching chairs wilting as well. The cheerless thought made him impatient to leave the punishing gaiety of their bedroom.

For the second night in a row he sought haven in his study. He opened the top three buttons of his shirt. His tan khaki slacks were stylishly loose. He decided they would do well as pajamas. Turning off the desk light, he slid into his leather recliner. It was an acceptable alternative to the bed.

# chapter
# 18

Lenny made a quick stop at the all-night drugstore on the way home from work to pick up a special surprise for Mother. He had seen it in a magazine one of the girls had left in the break room. It was just the thing to pull Mother out of her current mood.

He unlocked the door to his house and thought about what he might take her to eat. Since she had not wanted any dinner, he knew she must be hungry. She loved sardines and crackers. If he allowed her to have a beer, it would show her that things were right between them again.

He grabbed the food, and a couple of beers, and took the attic steps two at a time. He should have felt tired—it was past one in the morning—but he could not wait to see Mother. They would have a picnic in bed, just like old times, and then he would give her the surprise.

After lighting the lamp, he kissed her on the cheek. She flailed about the bed, striking out at him with her free hand.

"Stop it, Mother! Stop it! You'll hurt yourself. Haven't you already done enough?" She opened her eyes, but continued to pant like a wild animal. He smiled at her and bent to rock her gently in his arms.

"There, there. To think I was worried that you'd lost

your spirit, Mother. Now you're acting normal. You must be feeling better."

"Get your hands off me. I can't breathe."

"Of course, Mother. Whatever you say." He released her immediately and reached for the food. "I've brought you some supper, and just to show you that all is forgiven, you can even have a beer tonight."

Monica shook her head and cried out, reaching for her hair. The scissors had nicked her scalp several places. It had bled while she lay here, and some of the blood had dried on her bruised face. She ached in so many different places, she could hardly concentrate on what he was saying. "What?" she asked him.

"I said I brought you a beer for your supper."

"I don't drink beer."

"You've changed, Mother," he said, not challenging her lie. "How about some crackers? I've got some sardines, too."

Monica wanted nothing from him, but she also understood that he did not care whether she ate or not. Maybe she would feel a little better if she had something in her stomach. All she could think of was her butchered hair.

"Just the crackers. I'm not very hungry."

"Whatever you say." But he wanted her acknowledgment of his thoughtfulness whether or not she chose to accept his offerings. He handed her a few saltines, popped the top off his beer and opened the can of sardines. They ate in silence for a few minutes. Lenny finished his beer and set the empty can on the floor.

"Know what night this is?" he asked.

Her eyes shifted to his and away again. "I'm not sure."

"It's Thursday!"

"Oh." Had she only been here a day? It seemed like forever.

"And what do we do on Thursday, Mother?"

"I don't know."

Lenny pulled the plastic drugstore sack from his pocket

and waved it in front of her nose. Movement that close to
her face made her nauseous. She closed her eyes, but that
only made her feel worse. Finally, she concentrated on
staring at a rafter above her head, and her queasiness
passed.

"Ask me! Ask me what's in the bag!" He juggled the
bag up and down like a kid at Christmas.

"What?"

"It's Revlon's new nail color from their upcoming
summer collection! Christie, Cindy, and all the models
will be wearing it. I can't wait to see what it looks like on
us!" He handled the small vial with the flourish of a magi-
cian and set it on her chest.

This time Monica opened her eyes to look at the bottle
of nail polish, then at him. Even exhausted and aching,
she could see he was ecstatic over something. Earlier,
when he had cuffed her to the bed, he had practically been
foaming at the mouth. Whatever had changed his demeanor was all right with her. She needed some peace.

"I know you're just playing with me, Mother, but tonight I'll go along with you. As you very well know,
Thursday is manicure day, and I bought us a new color to
celebrate. I want to see your nails grow back the way they
used to be—long and sexy! I want to feel them on my
back. I want to see their fresh color peeking out at me
through your lacy gloves."

As he spoke, he picked up her hand and caressed her
fingers. He smoothed her nails as if he could lengthen
them just by his touch.

"I wish we could give each other a manicure tonight,
but I know you're probably not in the mood."

She shook her head, completely lost. She was so tired.

"You're my sleepyhead tonight, aren't you? You're
going to make me do all the work."

Monica said nothing.

"Well, okay, but only because I want it to be this way.
You'll owe me, Mother. Remember that."

Just before she dropped off to sleep, she heard a light scraping noise and felt something wet on her cuticles. She never moved as he applied "Summer Roses" to her nails. When they were dry, he painted his own, but not before he kissed each of her fingers, and murmured, "Just like Christie and Cindy . . ."

Lenny watched her sleep. She was so beautiful. He crossed to the old steamer trunk by the wall. He opened its lid and lifted his collection of gloves from the velvet-lined shelves of the trunk. Tenderly, he kissed each glove before laying it across her still form on the iron bed. The oil lamp at his side created a pale oasis of light in the dark attic. In its smoky dimness, his graceful hands appeared ethereal as he pointed to each pair and counted them again. Sixty-three pairs.

To showcase his beloved treasures, he kept his hands in pristine condition. As a child he had watched his mother wash her hands with mild soap and lemon juice. To soften them, she coated them with an almond-paste mixture she prepared herself. During her more charitable moments, she would bathe his hands, slowly massaging his small knuckles and palms while he closed his eyes and rested his head against her abdomen. Later as he grew taller, his head rested against her breasts, and then her shoulder.

As far back as he could remember, she had set aside Thursday afternoons to do her hands and nails. He would rush home from school to be included in this weekly ritual. After the cleansing, she would shape her long nails with an emery board, buff them hard with a piece of soft chamois, and paint them. If she were in a generous mood, or if he had been especially good to her, he would be allowed to choose the nail color for the week. She loved the soft, old-fashioned colors, the pinks, mauves, and ashes of roses. Garish shades of red and purple cheapened a woman, she always said.

And then at last would come his favorite part, when she

would actually don the gloves, pulling them slowly over her flawless hands, fitting the material down between her knuckles. He loved to watch her flex her hands and place them across her face so that her green eyes flashed through the span of her fingers.

"Peekaboo, where are you?" she would say.

"Have you seen my beautiful mother?" he would ask.

"Come and find her, come and love her," she responded.

Those words were his signal to give his freshly painted nails a last shake to dry them, before putting on another pair of her gloves. Then he would go to her. Sometimes they played tea party and giggled and gossiped; other times she would hold him close as they sat together in the big rocking chair in the living room, watching a game show on TV, or paging through one of her magazines.

In her absence, Lenny continued the Thursday tradition. His hands still had to be as beautiful as his gloves. Even though he had built strength into his tall, lean frame through years of exercise and heavy work at the theater, his hands remained slender and smoothly feminine through regular applications of dipilatories to remove any offensive hair that might detract from their loveliness. The rounded tips of his fingernails fell just outside the limit of the acceptable length for men. Often after cleansing, filing, and buffing, he painted his nails, if only for the evening. He differed from his mother in choice of colors, though. He preferred the bolder hues—crimson, deep purple, and sienna, especially when he chose to wear gloves from his collection of see-through fabrics of net, eyelet, or lace.

He could still remember his eighth birthday when he had gotten his first pair of gloves. As a small child, he spent hours trying on his mother's shoes, dresses, and jewelry, but he thought the times when she allowed him to play in her glove drawer were the best moments of his young life. He loved feeling the soft material surround and enclose each of his fingers. Somehow he felt that wearing her gloves made him safe, and special.

He had begged her to give him a pair of her gloves for his very own. He did not want kids' mittens or gloves, but her fine lady's handwear. Finally, after months of pleading, he was thrilled to receive her oldest pair for his birthday. He still had them. Their black fabric had become threadbare and faded after countless wearings, but they remained his sentimental favorite.

That birthday had not been the last time his mother had given him gloves. Frequently, she added to his collection. After he was older and they had become lovers, the gloves were an integral part of their lovemaking routine.

He would be doing homework or watching TV when suddenly a gloved hand would reach around him, slide down his chest, and nestle in his groin. Sometimes it would be a soft kid leather, a white cotton, or a black silk. He remembered delirious encounters that had begun with gold lamé, or her personal favorite, elbow-length black lace. Soon he could identify the game she wanted to play by the gloves she chose. Sex was always better for him when she was wearing them. The first time they had both worn them, it had been ecstasy.

Sometimes the games turned nasty. One particular incident stood out in his mind. He had been in the attic, sorting through his gloves, enjoying their scent and texture, rubbing them over his bare chest when he heard her footsteps behind him. His sixteenth birthday had come and gone with no acknowledgment from his mother. He knew she hadn't forgotten the date; she was just waiting for him to ask her why she had chosen to ignore it.

"Dear boy, Mother has a surprise for you!"

He turned around. She was wearing her robe and holding a box and several lengths of cord.

"What is it?" He felt a little foolish at being caught fondling his collection. More and more he wanted to handle the gloves in private. They had become a wonderful

aphrodisiac for him, much more titillating than girlie magazines or the sex videos he had heard other guys discussing in the school locker room. Once he had gotten so
caught up in wearing the black net ones with the pearl buttons he had ejaculated. The experience had been exhila-
rating and he tried to repeat it often.

"Put away your playthings for now. I have a new toy
for us."

He put the shelves back into the trunk and stood up.
"What's in the box, Mother?"

"Oh no, first I have to get you in the proper mood. Lie
down on the bed."

Lenny obeyed and allowed her to tie his arms to the
bars of the headboard. Sometimes bondage was an important part of the game, and usually one he enjoyed. Then
she took off her robe and sat down beside him on the mattress. The low light from the oil lamp gleamed against her
white slip. He knew she wore nothing under it. For now
its cheap material hid her protruding belly and ample
breasts. Its hem, shifting slightly, revealed surprisingly
slender thighs and knees.

"I sent for something special for you, and it just arrived
in today's mail."

Lenny remained quiet, knowing from past experience
that it was better to let her do the talking.

"Don't you want to see what it is?"

Again, Lenny said nothing.

"You've chosen to give me the silent treatment. Why
do I deserve that, I wonder? Do you think you can get the
upper hand with me?"

"No, Mother, that's not what I think," he said at last.

"Well, I should hope not. This is my surprise and
you're ruining it. It's rude not to answer your mother. I'll
have to tell your Uncle Phil. He'll punish you if you're
mean to me. Besides, I may have something that you
really want!" She allowed her green eyes to wander down
his body, stopping at his crotch.

"Yes, Mother," came the instant reply.

"Much better, my dear."

She tore off the brown wrapping paper and showed him the white box beneath. In the dim light he was able to read the words, "latex," "examination," and the numeral "100."

"Look!" she said as she opened the box. "Something different from your feminine finery. Surgeon's gloves. Think of the possibilities!" Lifting a pair of gloves from the box, she pulled them onto her hands. He loved watching the stretchy material encase and squeeze the skin on her fingers, but he jumped when she snapped them against her wrists as she continued talking.

"And they're throwaways. You can do all sorts of things and you never have to wash them afterwards. I love them! Don't you?"

She leaned over him and moved her gloved hands within millimeters of his bare chest. He could feel their motion and imagine their heat, but they never touched his skin. After long moments, he saw the latex-covered fingers drop the straps of her slip, and slide them over her shoulders before edging them down over the slopes and ridges of her body. He felt his body responding to her striptease. He closed his eyes to shut her out, to beat her at her game, but her green eyes commanded him to watch. Suddenly, her fingers reached out and plucked at his zipper.

"Oh, yes, Mother, yes . . ." he murmured.

She smiled, ripped open his fly, and pushed down his jeans and underwear. They were tight. She slid them to his thighs but stopped where they held his legs immobile. Again she positioned her hands less than an inch from his skin. She slowly moved them back and forth below his waist, close, but never making contact.

He was on fire now, the ropes biting into his wrists as he fought for control. Finally, he could endure the torment no longer.

"Touch me, Mother. The gloves, let them touch me. Let them take me. Please! Oh, please!"

Even now as he watched her sleep, years after that rainy afternoon, he could hear her gruff laughter as she dressed and left him tied and churning on the bed. It had taken him two hours to calm himself and get free. When he got downstairs, she was gone.

She had left her box of gloves behind. He had kept them for a while, even ordering new ones when he feared they might have gone bad in the stifling heat of the Texas summers. He did not keep them with the rest of his collection, though. He stored them on the top shelf of his closet, not in remembrance, but awaiting revenge. Someday, he would get even.

# chapter
# 19

David Riley's clock radio flipped on promptly at six A.M., but he'd been awake since four-thirty. His bed looked as if a war had been fought between the sheets: The navy-striped fabric, pulled loose hours before, was twisted like rope. His blanket had slipped to the floor.

Usually, he looked forward to Fridays, his "catch-up" days at home when he'd breakfast with his son, Colin, before driving him to school. Then he'd take a long run on the nearby bike trails, enjoy a leisurely shower, and have the morning to spend as he wished. Today would be different.

Yesterday he thought he'd hit bottom after the conversation with Randy and John, but this morning he was raw nerves. Randy had asked some difficult questions last night on the way to the precinct. If Monica's absence was not one of choice, he wanted to know who might have it in for Monica or John Foyles?

"I can't imagine," David had replied.

"Is she a beautiful woman, one who invites men to notice her?"

"She's a lovely woman, but she has none of the qualities you're hinting at. She works at a school. You've seen her home, her kids. C'mon, Randy, She's not some tart."

"How about the husband? Know anything about the marriage?"

David paused. "I don't really know John, but I don't think he would harm her."

"Has he talked to all of her close friends? How about the ones back East?"

"Nancy called as many as she could find numbers for, but had no luck."

"How well do you know Monica, David? Where do you think she is?"

"I . . . I'd . . . give my right arm for the answer to that one. And Monica and I are good friends, that's all."

Randy stared at David for a moment, shrugged his shoulders and opened the door. David had been relieved when Randy exited the car and jogged up the steps to the police station.

Unlike John and Randy, David felt certain that something terrible had happened to Monica. When he'd last seen her in his examining room on Wednesday afternoon, she'd been talking and laughing, perfectly at ease and perfectly gorgeous in a soft, green sweater that matched her eyes. She'd said nothing that led him to believe she was upset.

Even as rushed as he had been when the emergency came in, he'd been aware of her, completely tuned into her mind. His heart had been tuned in, too. As many times as he had told himself he should not care so much about her, that their relationship could go nowhere, he knew he could not change how he felt about her.

As he lay in the early-morning dimness atop the tangled sheets and tried to relax, he had to face how deeply he cared for her. How did she feel about him? Were there genuine feelings, or was she just appreciative that he was sympathetic and there when she needed him? What did he need? A cold shower, some hot coffee? Neither option appealed to him, but he had to get his emotions under control before walking down the hall to awaken his son.

On his radio, the KCOW deejays, two Texas imports who called themselves the "Sooner Slick" and the

"Hoosier Hick," rattled through their early morning radio spiel of tasteless jokes and corny puns that were as bad as the music they chose to feature. David turned to this station only to get himself out of bed and moving, a tactic that was not working for him today.

Slick was teasing Hick for driving to work on Harry Hines Boulevard, a well-known Dallas street frequented by prostitutes.

"Hey, Hick!"

"Yeah, Slick?"

"What'd you say to that purty l'il chick in them tight white shorts on your way home last night?"

"Well, I wuz real nice to her. She's a special gal!"

"How so, Hick?"

"Fer one thing, she wuz blind."

"Man, that's amazin', Hick. Whoever heard of a blind hooker?"

"Yeah, you really had to hand it to her!"

Canned laughter and applause heralded the punch line, followed by ads for Dixie Darlin' Doughnuts and Weber's Resale Auto Parts. David groaned and rolled over in bed.

"Hey, Slick!"

"Yeah, Hick?"

"Must be time to catch up with Lowraine and the famous KCOW rusty red pickup."

"C'mon in, Lowraine. You got that cute l'il blue dress on I like so much?"

"Hey there, fellers. You guys are bad this mornin'."

"Who you kissin' and tellin' on today, Lowraine?" Hick asked, setting up the next segment which Lowraine called her "Cheatin' Heart Hunt."

"Since I'm right here on Mockingbird, I thought I'd check out a few parking lots. Two-timin' guys never think to hide their cars when they've gone off for the night with some chick they picked up in one of these places. Whoa! Here I am at the Gentleman's Playhouse."

"And?" Slick and Hick prodded together.

"And there's only two cars parked out back that I can see."

"Slo-o-o-w night. Why don't you cruise around and tell us if you see anything incriminatin'," Hick said.

"I'm going next door to Ponytails' Topless," she said. "There's a bunch of cars over there. I'm bound to find some cheatin' varmints in that crowd."

"Go get 'em, Lowraine," Slick said.

"Yes sir, from the looks of these cars, and we got some fancy ones, too, Ponytails is the place to go if you've got cheatin' on your mind today," she said.

"Write that down, Slick."

"I got it, Hick. Lowraine, read off them license plate numbers of those cheatin', low-down dogs. Then we'll open the phone lines to give the grievin' girlfriends and spouses equal time."

"Ah, here's a beaut! A bright red ragtop, tag number 34T GGF."

A chorus of canned ooh's and ahh's followed.

"Let's give those sweet gals one more to chew on. Pick us out a real choice one," Slick said.

"I got something real interestin' here, boys. This cheater's so worried about getting caught, he took his tags with him. Looks like he borrowed his wife's navy blue station wagon, too."

A tape with James Cagney's famous line, "You dirty rat!" played over and over, but David heard only the words "navy blue station wagon." He sat up in bed and turned up the radio volume. Monica's car was a station wagon, and it was navy blue. It was against all odds that the car was hers, but still, he leaned closer to the radio, straining to hear every word.

"How can you tell the car belongs to his wife?" Hick asked.

"Cause it's got one of them fancy bumper stickers on it," Lowraine said.

"Whad'ya mean? Men're allowed to have bumper

stickers, too. Slick, I think she's been eatin' too many of them cream doughnuts. The sugar's gone to her brain."

"Listen up, boy. Go on, Lowraine, tell us about the car," Slick said.

"Well, it's got one of those sticker things that moms love to put on their cars, and men hate. This one says 'My child is an honor student at Hyler Elementary.' "

It had to be Monica's car. Where was that radio woman? Mockingbird and what? Rosemont Drive? David had missed the phone number of the radio station. He rushed into the den and opened the bottom drawer of his desk. He grabbed the Yellow Pages, and rifled through them until he came to the section listing radio stations. Dropping the phone book, he dialed KCOW as quickly as he could get his shaking fingers to punch the numbers.

After several harried moments of trying to make himself understood, he got the information he wanted. He jotted down the club name on a piece of paper, even though he knew he would remember its name until the day he died.

John was just stepping out of the shower as the phone rang. He grabbed a towel from the rack, and wrapped it around his waist as he walked into the bedroom.

"Hello," he said. This had better be important. It was six-thirty in the morning and he was dripping water all over the carpet.

"John, this is David Riley. I think I know where Monica's car is."

"You what? Where?"

"It's a long story. I'll explain it to you on the way over there. How soon can you be ready?"

"Wait a minute. What are you talking about?"

"Trust me, John. Believe me, if I didn't think there was a good chance this could be it, I wouldn't have called so early."

John didn't feel like trusting anyone. "Should we call

the detective?" he asked. "Maybe he could meet us there."
And then Riley could look like a fool in front of his friend
when this turns out to be a wild goose chase.

"Let's take a look at the car first and then call him,"
David said. When John said nothing, he added, "Come on,
John. Can you be ready in, say, fifteen minutes? I'll pick
you up."

"I'll need someone to watch the kids."

"My housekeeper's here. If you want, I'll bring her and
Colin over to your house."

"No, that's not good," John said.

"Give Nancy a call! This could be the first big break
we've had. C'mon man, give it a chance!" David said.

"Well, I could do that, I guess. I'll work it out. See you
in a few minutes."

John hung up, oddly reluctant to call Nancy, and get
ready. Why was he in such a bad mood? He wanted to
dress in peace, eat his breakfast, and begin his day as he
had planned it. Monica's parents were arriving sometime
this afternoon. Before they came, he had to pick up the
flyers and organize their distribution. He had a carefully
planned agenda: time for home, children, office, and Beth
were all scheduled in his mind. He had no time for Riley's
harebrained long shot.

John knew that he had no choice but to go along on this
joy ride. But he could damn well make sure there
wouldn't be another, he thought as he picked up the phone
to call Nancy.

Fifteen minutes later, John listened without comment to
David's explanation as they traveled to Ponytails' Topless
Club on Mockingbird Lane.

"The people at the radio station only told me the club
name, not the location of the car," David said. He wanted
the station wagon to be Monica's, and a part of him
wanted to see the look on John's face when it was. What
an arrogant bastard! He wondered again how Monica
dealt with him.

David turned off the highway and drove to the front of a large, gray building. The only activity in the immediate area came from a Mexican fast-food place across the parking lot. People were eating inside, and a single car waited at the drive-in window. Both men glanced at the club, then studied the long red canopy that sheltered the dark entrance.

David drove slowly through the side parking lot, then drove around to the back of the building.

"Look, John! Over there, by that old Mercedes!"

"Where? Oh, my God. That looks like my car!"

"Let me park and we'll take a look." David's heart was racing.

He pulled his Jeep into a space and they got out. David stood by the rear bumper of the station wagon while John walked around the car. He checked the inspection sticker and leaned down to look in the windows.

"Son of a bitch," John said. "It's mine! How the hell did it get out here?"

"I recognize the bumper sticker!" David felt a jab at this positive indication that something awful had befallen Monica. Months ago, he had been at school on Pet Fair business, and had stopped by Monica's office to say hello when the twins had rushed in, each holding a bumper sticker and a report card.

"The license tags are gone. Why would anyone do that? They can be traced," John said as he circled the car again. "The police have to get involved now. This car's clearly been tampered with."

David watched John kneel down to look beneath the car, but all he could think about was Monica. He prayed this discovery might mean they still had a chance to find her unharmed, and he sent a silent entreaty to her. *Hang in there! Wherever you are, we'll find you, just please hang on!*

"It's definitely her car." Pulling a set of keys from his pocket, John moved as though to open the door.

"No," David said, "we shouldn't touch it, John. There could be fingerprints or something. We need to find a phone and call Randy."

Obviously miffed that he hadn't thought about the prints first, John nodded curtly. "Maybe we can find a passable cup of coffee, too." He pointed across the way to the Mexican place. "After we call, we can wait for him at the restaurant."

David led the way to the public phones they had seen by the club's front door. Although the air was cool, sweat broke out on his forehead. He dialed his friend's number, but handed John the phone so that he could talk to the detective.

"You two have been busy this morning," Randy said, after John had explained the reason for the early call. "You can positively identify the vehicle?"

"Yes, I'm certain it's our car. Monica always drove it. It appears to be in good shape; only the plates are missing."

"Fair enough. I'll send some of the lab boys out to go over it. I'll come, too. Just don't try to start it up or anything. We'll tow it into our shop to check it out."

"Does this mean the police are finally getting involved?" John asked.

"Up to our ears, and then some," Randy said. "You'll be sick of us before this is over. Now, where will you be? By the car?"

"Yeah, we're going to grab a cup of coffee, but we'll be around when you get here." John added a few terse directions on where to find them.

"Got it. Thanks. We'll do everything we can to locate your wife," Randy said.

John hung up the phone and looked at David. "They're on their way. I can't decide whether finding the car is good news or bad, but at least it's got the police moving."

David nodded and the men walked across the parking

lot. David barely recognized John's voice when he choked out the words, "Thanks. I guess I owe you one."

"Well, we wouldn't want to leave you in debt to me, would we? You can buy the coffee," he told John with a friendliness he didn't feel.

"I'll need your signature on some papers before we can officially begin, John." Randy Abbott rested his arm on the open passenger door of David's Jeep, and spoke with him and John, who sat inside. "I'll also send somebody out to your house to pick up a couple of pictures of your wife and dust some of her things to get her fingerprints. Yours, too."

"Of course," John said. "Just tell me when you'll be there."

"Not before lunch. We need to take a preliminary look at the car and get the paperwork started. I'll try to get it all together and save you a trip to the station."

"I'd appreciate that. Guess I'll have to give another statement?"

"Yeah, we'll want to get your story down in writing, plus we'll talk to the kids and to you, David, since Mrs. Foyles was in your office the day she disappeared."

"Yes. I'll do anything I can to help. You'll want to speak to Monica's friend, Nancy Crawford," said David. "I believe she visited with Monica just before she left the house on Wednesday."

"She's the woman I met the other night?" Randy asked John.

"Yes, she's my wife's best friend."

Randy pulled out a small spiral-bound notebook and jotted down a few notes. The brisk morning wind blew his blue-striped tie over his shoulder. He grabbed it and smoothed it down on his shirtfront. "I think it goes without saying that your wife doesn't frequent places like this." He jerked his thumb at the strip joint.

"I doubt if Monica is even aware of their existence. She would never have consented to meet anyone here."

Randy looked for David's nod of agreement before going on. "So, you're saying that you don't think your wife brought the car here?"

"Absolutely not. What would she be doing in a dump like this? Besides, the car was backed into the space. Detective, I've known my wife for over twenty years, and never in all that time has she ever backed into a parking place. I doubt she could even do it."

"Any ideas how it got here?" Randy asked, writing again.

"None."

"Okay. You guys can push off now. I'm going to have a look around. The sign says Ponytails' opens at eleven, but someone is watching us from behind that second-story window. I'll see if I can get him to talk to me."

John and David looked up at the window, but saw nothing.

"Think I'll check out the Taco Express, too," Randy said, rubbing his stomach and looking across the lot. "Never can tell when somebody might get hungry."

"Just don't order the coffee." David slapped his friend on the shoulder. "Thanks for coming."

"Randy's a smart man," David said to John as they drove back to the Foyles' house. "If anyone can unravel this mystery, he can. We're lucky to have him on the case."

"It's a relief that he at least pretends to agree with us that Monica didn't disappear voluntarily," John said. "There's no way she drove the car and parked it at that club. Which means that whoever took her, didn't want, or need the car. But why would anyone take the tags, and leave everything else?"

"Obviously, theft was not a motive. That's an expensive car, and it seemed virtually untouched." David waited for the light to change and continued east toward the expressway.

"When I looked in the window, I didn't see her handbag. She must have it with her," John said.

"Maybe," David answered. "When will you check her desk at school? Randy thinks it might be important."

"I'll try to get to it today, but I have a lot to do."

"The school will be closed tomorrow and Sunday. You'd better take a look before Monday."

"What could be there? A bunch of books and papers, some office stuff? She only works part-time; it's not like she handles anything out of the ordinary. Right now I've got to pick up the flyers because I have people coming in a couple of hours to distribute them. Monica's parents are due today, and I need to check on the kids and stay by the phone."

"Have you any help there?" David asked.

"A few women, friends of Monica's, have volunteered to field the calls today, but I want to be near in case something important comes in."

"So you'll be too busy to go to school?" David asked.

"Randy's getting paid to handle the detective work now," John said with an edge in his voice.

"How about if I check out the school? I have a hunch something will turn up there."

"Two hunches in one day? And it's not even nine o'clock!" John shrugged, and then gave in. "Go ahead. You could be right, I guess."

David realized this statement was the second time John had acknowledged the contribution David was making to the search. If he didn't watch out, the man was likely to become human.

"Thanks, John. Let me know if I can help with the phone calls."

# chapter
# 20

Mr. Himes, the janitor, met David at the front entrance of Hyler Elementary School. The elderly man was polishing the glass windows on the doors. He looked at David over the tops of his wire-rimmed glasses and smiled.

"Don't know why I spend the time spiffing up this glass. Come Monday lunch, it'll be all dirty again. What are you doing here, Dr. Riley? No pet shows today. All the kids have the day off."

"I'm here on official business. There's a rumor going around that you've been slacking off, and I was sent to check it out."

The man threw back his head and let out a hearty guffaw before slapping David with his cleaning cloth. "Now I know you're a much better vet than you are a liar, so maybe you should stick to vettin' and let me do the lyin' around here. Whatdaya say?"

"Sounds good to me, Mr. Himes. Say, you haven't seen Monica Foyles around, have you?"

"No, sir. She only worked two days this week. I helped her carry some things out to her car on Tuesday afternoon, but I haven't seen her since then."

"She must have had some heavy stuff, huh?"

"Naw, it was really only a small box of colored paper. She was making something for one of the teachers. She coulda hefted it herself, but I saw her comin' down the hall, and I offered to help her. Seemed the neighborly thing to do."

"I'm sure she was grateful."

"She thanked me a hundred times over. She's a real nice lady."

"Yes, she is. You take care now, Mr. Himes. I'll see you later." David patted the man on the shoulder and went into the school office. No one was in, but judging from the cup of steaming coffee on the secretary's desk, she was somewhere in the building. David headed down the hall and turned into a large, airy room that Monica shared with the traveling art teacher. David had been here a few times before.

He circled the room, touched the yellow bulky-knit cardigan that hung behind the door, and opened the middle drawer of Monica's desk. A divided tray held an assortment of pencils, paper clips, markers, and pens. He fingered her scissors, a Pink Pearl eraser with the initials "M.F." written on it, several rulers, a packet of springtime stickers, and an unopened cherry lollipop. Several handmade "I love you!" cards, one featuring a stick-figure lady in a yellow sweater and lots of fire-engine-red hair made him smile. He opened the only other drawer and saw class lists of children's names, some printed duty schedules, two empty legal tablets, a manual of Hyler rules, a pack of index cards, and a box of tissues. The desk top held a calendar, a stapler, and a small framed picture of her children.

David picked up the calendar and flipped through the months. Except for a few notations of porch duty and inservice days, the calendar pages were blank.

*There's nothing here. John was right. So much for my hunch.* He stood up and walked over to the other desk in the area, piled high with books, magazines, and art supplies. Paint brushes, paint, and easel paper cluttered the nearby table. Children's artwork covered the walls. Two child-sized tables with matching chairs were arranged in the center of the room.

Several times when David had stuck his head in to say hello to Monica, busy children had filled the room with activity. He had loved his brief glimpses of her at work, supervising a review lesson, or reading aloud from a storybook. Now the room was silent, giving no indication of the wonderful, vivacious woman who worked there. Closing his eyes he remembered the last time he had visited her here. . . .

Monica had been lining up twenty wiggling first graders when David stuck his head into her room.

"Jerrod, I'd love to see your hands at your sides instead of in Therese's hair. Morton, face me, please. Miss Thompson is coming and I want her to see how well you can walk down the hall to meet her."

Monica held a finger up to David, indicating that he should wait, and ushered the children out the door. She removed Jerrod's hands from Therese's ponytails one last time, patted Connie Brewster's shoulder for ignoring Nick Altland's nudge in the back, and the little band was gone.

"That's quite a group. I forgot how frenetic kids are at that age," David said.

"Never a dull moment, but they're so sweet."

David laughed, not entirely convinced about the last part of her statement. He followed Monica to her desk and propped himself on the edge of it. Her hair hung loosely and drifted over her left eye as she stacked some papers and slipped them into a blue folder.

"What brings you to Hyler?" she asked, her gaze moving across his wool sports jacket and tailored slacks.

"I was the featured speaker in the third grade area this morning. They're finishing up their animal unit."

"Ah, the culminating activity sits before me."

"The what?" he asked.

"That's teacherese for 'big finish,' " Monica said with a laugh.

David smiled and stood up. "Have you got a minute, or are you expecting another group in here?"

"I should be free for the next fifteen minutes," she said as she glanced at the clock. "What's up?"

"Female problems. I need some advice."

Monica rolled her eyes but said nothing.

"Colin has a girlfriend and her birthday is next week."

"Oh, my."

"Yeah, he wants to buy her a gift and take her to Arpeggio's for dinner."

"Wow! How old is she? Eighteen?"

David stuffed his hands in his pockets and rocked back on his heels. "Nope, worse than that. She's twelve."

Monica nodded, biting her lip to keep from laughing.

"I can probably talk him into MacDonald's, but he's determined to use a big chunk of his savings to buy her a gold bracelet."

"Must be true love."

"That's the problem. I just saw the fair maiden in the hall. She was telling her friends what a dweeb she thinks Colin is. Yelling it from the rooftops!"

"Oh, no!"

"Yeah, poor kid. So, do I tell him?"

"I wouldn't, but get him to hold off on the bracelet. Everything will work itself out." She walked over to him and patted him on the back. "Relax, Dad, it'll be okay."

"I don't remember it being this tough at thirteen."

"Maybe you never felt like you'd met the girl of your dreams."

"I was too wrapped up in baseball and snakes. Not a combination that attracts many dream girls." He leaned over and bumped her shoulder with his and asked, "How about you? How young were you?"

"When I first fell in love?"

"Yeah."

"Let's see, I was six, no, seven. His name was Lionel, and his hair was even redder than mine. I thought we were fated to be together forever. He kissed me on the steps of the post office right in front of Mrs. Sheetz, the town gossip."

"That sounds serious."

"Yes, I probably didn't beat him up for at least a week."

David looked at her, trying to imagine this slim, graceful woman at seven. "I thought you'd be dressed up in lace and ruffles, serving tea to your doll babies and teddy bears."

"No, you've got your images confused. I was the one climbing trees and calculating the timing and exact angle of my spit so that it would hit an unsuspecting bike rider below. Or, I was eating green apples and swapping dirty jokes in Billy Evans's hayloft."

"What an engaging child you must have been! When did you discover the finer, more genteel side of life?"

"Junior high school was a real eye-opener. Suddenly, all the guys I'd hung around with for years started paying genuine attention to Jill Starner's bustline."

"And you wanted them to notice yours?"

Monica laughed and tried a punch, which he neatly dodged. He caught her fist and pulled her close. Her face flushed beneath his gaze. After a moment, he released her.

"Eventually I did want them to notice, much to my mother's great relief," she said. "She harbored feelings of dread that her daughter would be the first girl to make the varsity football squad. Luckily, my size, if not my ambition, kept that from happening."

"We'd have been good friends back then. I was always in awe of girls who climbed trees and played sports. They made more sense to me than the ones who did all that silly giggling."

Monica's smile slid away. "I'm sure I did my share of giggling. I think I enjoyed just about every minute of my childhood, but I'm a different person today. I'm not so tough anymore." Or so happy, her voice implied.

"Well," said David, wondering what triggered the rapid change in her mood, "we're good friends now. It took us a few years to get together, but we finally made it."

She looked at him and the sadness in her eyes evaporated like mist in the wind. They stood there together, among the easels and paints, the picture books stacked on the shelf, the chalk dust on the floor, and something between them locked into place. Suddenly he knew with certainty that they would remember each other for as long as they lived. It was a simple thing, too ridiculously dramatic for either of them to mention aloud, but he knew they both felt it. Without understanding what part they would play in each other's lives, they treasured the extraordinary feeling it gave them.

David was the first to break away. He looked at his watch and was amazed to see that his hands were shaking. "I've really got to run. My patients will be tearing down the door." He put out his hand and she placed hers in it.

"Thanks for the advice to the lovelorn," he said.

"Any time." She emitted something close to a giggle and held his hand a moment longer.

As he had walked to his car, he had wondered how many men had lost themselves in the depths of her green eyes. . . .

Now sitting at her desk, he swung around and looked at her yellow sweater behind the door. Giving in to an urge he couldn't ignore, he pulled the sweater from the hook and held it to his face, closing his eyes and breathing in her scent, which clung to its folds.

A noise outside the door startled him and he returned the sweater to the hook. From his haste to put it back, two small pieces of paper fell from the pocket and fluttered across the floor. He stooped to pick them up. Without looking at them, he stuffed them into his pocket just as the principal opened the door.

# chapter
# 21

On Friday, Monica awoke at noon, barely able to remember the early morning hours when she had last seen Lenny. Tired, aching, and terrified of what he would do to her next, it had hurt even to think about moving her body. Lenny had dashed into the attic and uncuffed her. Mumbling something about being late to make corn, he hustled her into the bathroom and back upstairs before leaving her with fresh water, and some crackers.

She hadn't spoken much, nor had he, saying only that he'd see her for supper. When he recuffed her hand, he had asked if she needed one of her pills since she appeared to be uncomfortable. She shook her head and he left.

For a while, Monica had nodded in and out of sleep. The attic room warmed and her dress and the mattress beneath her grew damp with her perspiration. The long sleeves of the ill-fitting dress stuck to her arms and her back. Its smell of moth balls, cheap perfume, and stale body odor added to her misery.

She looked around the perimeter of the attic, noting in the dimness the outline of a chest, a rocking chair, an old-fashioned oil-burning lamp, a few pasteboard cartons, and stacks of magazines. The hours she had spent up here had made it no more familiar. It remained a prison.

High above her head, two small windows nestled in the

eaves. Someone had painted the panes black, but even so, she could tell it was daylight outside. If she got up there, then what? Could she break them open? After that, her only option would be to yell to someone on the street. She would never be able to squeeze through the small squares.

Earlier this morning she had heard the continuous sound of large airplanes taking off and landing. She had been too drugged to notice the sounds before, but in these past two days, she might have missed hearing a bomb drop in the next block.

Airports meant people. People meant help. How could she get out of this house? Focusing on regaining her freedom made her feel better. She knew the bathroom window was too small for her to fit through, as was the one over the kitchen sink. The living room had two windows, and the heavy drapes gave no inkling of what lay behind them.

The bedrooms? She had never seen beyond the two closed doors in the hall by the bathroom, but she assumed those rooms might have windows, perhaps even ones that opened easily. She eliminated the idea of getting out through the kitchen door. It was so heavily secured with double locks and chains that she knew she would never get it open. The unseen bedroom windows offered her the best escape route. But what if they had window air-conditioning units in them? She doubted this place had central air.

As quickly as it had appeared, her spurt of optimism dissolved. How could she expect to get away from her captor? The only times she wasn't handcuffed to the bed were when he was with her.

She plotted how she could earn Lenny's trust and thereby gain some freedom. Her mind pieced together parts of conversations, clues he had given her. She decided to stop worrying about why he called her "Mother," and accept the bizarre fact that to him, she was his mother.

If she could become this woman to some extent, maybe she could influence his tangled thinking. Was that the answer? Perhaps . . . She shifted on the bed to find a more comfortable spot. The sharp-edged springs beneath the thin mattress punched her body with each movement she made.

The attic grew dimmer and she heard rain falling on the roof. Sarah was afraid of thunderstorms. Monica hoped this was just a brief spring shower. How she wished she could be home watching the rain with her children. Maybe they would all be on the window seat in the kitchen, the twins snuggling close with her arms around them. Monica shut her eyes, and imagined the clean, fresh scent of their hair, the warm weight of their bodies against her. Jeb would be trying to coax Peach onto the padded seat with them, and everyone would be laughing.

She snapped back from her daydream and thought about what the house must be like without her. Someone, probably Nancy, would have called John home from Atlanta. How had he reacted to her disappearance? She knew the children would be desperate to see her; her parents, wild with worry. And David? Does he still have Peach? David might be more than concerned. A pang of guilt crept into her heart. She had no right to care about him as much as she did, but the thought of never seeing him again was intolerable. Did the thought of never seeing John again hurt as much? She wasn't sure.

Would John blame *her* for disappearing? For interrupting his well-ordered life? Would the children have to grow up without her?

How much was she willing to risk?

She wondered if she could go through with her plan to become Mother, knowing that Lenny wasn't looking for someone to darn his socks. He would rape her. And he wouldn't stop after one time. Was there no other choice? She curled into a ball and tried to find solace in sleep.

Monica dozed through most of the afternoon. Lenny

arrived a little after five, and hustled her downstairs for a quick dinner of soup and crackers. Monica was despondent. She ate little and refused to talk or even look at him. When she could no longer stand being at the table with him, she stood and for something to do, gathered her dishes and carried them to the sink. Lenny was beside her in seconds.

"Since you've decided you like housework better than keeping me company, you can do the dinner dishes, Mother," Lenny announced, as he inspected his nails. "Your hands are a mess anyhow. They match your hair. You really are a fright, Mother."

"Why did you do it, Lenny? Why did you cut my hair?" She hung her head and started to sob. "I liked my hair. Why did you cut it?"

"I don't give a damn what you like, Mother. What counts now is what I like!"

The pitch of his voice had changed. Its high squeaky tone scared her. He kicked at a chair, and sent it crashing to the floor. Startled, she bumped against the sink.

"Don't just stand there! Get busy and wash the dishes!" He yelled and began to pace the tiny kitchen. His foot caught the table leg and he gave it a vicious kick. Then he picked up a pile of newspapers that got in his way and threw them across the room. They smacked into a cupboard and scattered on the floor.

Monica reached across the drainboard. She tried to stack the small fruit bowls, but her hands felt as though they were suspended on wires that someone else controlled. They would not perform this simple task. She wiped her hands on her skirt and picked up the glasses, but the combination of terror and drugs took its toll. Halfway to the sink, they slid out of her fingers and crashed to the floor. Speechless, she stood clutching her dress, staring down at the broken glass.

"You bitch!" shrieked Lenny. He reached out and grabbed her shoulder. With his other hand, he slapped her across the face. The impact threw her against the stove. Her legs crumpled beneath her. She slumped to the floor, too dazed to do anything but groan and wrap her arms protectively around her legs.

He leapt to where she was huddled, the spiraling anger inside him swelling to a frenzied pitch. He gripped her neck and forced her head back. Her yelp of pain infuriated him. How dare she cry out, as if to win his pity!

"You can break every fucking dish in the place and I'll still find more for you to wash!"

"But, I-I . . ."

"Shut your mouth and get to work!" he said. "You make me sick! You can dish it out, but you sure can't take it, can you, Mother, dear?"

"Please stop hurting me," Monica gasped. She felt as if every muscle in her body had been torn from her bones.

"Stop hurting you? When did my tears ever stop you from hurting me?"

Unable to speak, she shook her head from side to side. He towered over her, cursing her tears, roughly pushing her with his foot to punctuate his threats. She bowed her head beneath the abuse, and covered her ears, but he thrust her hands away.

"Do as I say, bitch! Now!"

Monica tried to rise, but she could no longer contain the heaving sobs that racked her body. She pushed herself to her hands and knees to gather the pieces of glass. Twice she cut her fingers on the broken shards. Blinded by tears, she lifted her hands to wipe them away and smeared blood from her cut fingers onto her cheeks.

"Faster, bitch!" Lenny picked up a broom and swatted her, sending her off balance. She lurched forward, catching herself with her hands and screamed again when a piece of glass pierced her right palm.

"You dumb cunt! You worthless trash!" he yelled.

She lifted her hand and nearly fainted when she saw the

large piece of glass jutting from the skin. "Help me," she sobbed.

"I'm sick of your whining! Your stupid moods!" He grabbed her palm, pulled out the glass, and yanked her to him, his eyes inches from hers. "You owe me! You'll do exactly as I say!" Rage and madness spewed from his eyes. His words slurred and ran together.

"Tell me you're mine! Tell me!"

"Yes, yes," she whispered, astonished that she was still able to think and speak. She would have said anything to stop him.

"Then get to work!" He threw her back to the floor. She heard something rip, but never realized it was her dress.

Finally, she was able to sit up and she scraped some of the glass pieces together into a small pile. The effort took all her strength. Her hands felt on fire, the searing pain the only feeling that kept her moving. She raised her arm to touch the sticky blood on her face. Her mind went blank, the stark terror had blotted out all ability to think, reason, or fight back.

Vaguely, she heard a new sound, and automatically cowered, unable to think, only react. She lifted her head in time to see him throw something at her.

"I said, get to work, dammit!"

She tried to duck, but the rusty metal dustpan caught her in the cheek, just below her right eye. Its sharp edge gouged out a piece of her flesh. She screamed again and covered her head with the ratty sweater, feebly trying to shield herself from his next blow.

"No, no," she moaned. "God, no."

"Don't ever tell me no, you cunt! Whore! Bitch! I'm just making you do what you made me do!"

He reached under her armpits and she felt herself being lifted bodily, suspended in air. He threw her against the porcelain sink. A sickening flash of unbearable pain ripped into her arm just before she slid, unconscious, to the floor.

# chapter
# 22

"Hello?"

"John? Randy Abbott here. I've had an interesting morning. Thought you'd like an update."

"Sure. You coming over?" John checked his watch. It was shortly past two. He had just returned from the airport with Monica's parents, who were unpacking and settling in.

"I can't be there until after dinner. Will you be around?"

"Yes, two of your men were already here. I've never been fingerprinted before, nor have the children."

"Yes, well, sorry. A necessary inconvenience, I'm afraid. I do have some good news, though. I found the license tags for your wife's car. One of the kids who works at the Mexican place where you bought your coffee this morning pulled them out of the trash yesterday. He planned to sell them to his Uncle Carlos, but I persuaded him to let me have them."

"Great. So whoever removed the tags just ditched them. I wonder why?"

"I'm working on that. We have a bunch of prints from the plates and the interior of the car, and some of them match up. I doubt that your wife was messing with the tags, so the prints probably belong to the person we're after. We'll know more after we get the final report. The lab's still processing everything."

"What does that mean? Are we finally getting somewhere?"

"It means we're dealing with an amateur."

"How do you know?"

"Because he didn't cover his ass on some basic stuff that a pro knows to do."

"You mean like fingerprints?"

"Yeah, and other stuff." Randy picked up his coffee. It was cold, but he drank it anyway.

"Will you be able to nail him from the prints?" John doubted it could be that simple.

"Contrary to what TV shows might tell you, we do not have the fingerprints of every person in the United States on file. If our man's an amateur, he probably doesn't have a record. So we won't have his prints. But even if we did, without some other means of identifying him, it's virtually impossible to find a man when all we have are his fingerprints."

John rubbed his hand through his hair and shifted his weight. "Are you tellin' me the fact that you got all those prints from Monica's car doesn't mean jack shit?"

"At this moment they don't, but they can really help us out later when we have a suspect."

"And you're also tellin' me we'd be better off if a pro kidnapped her?"

"John," Randy said patiently, "I'm only telling you what I know. I'm not speculating. It looks like an amateur. I'm not sure if that's good or bad. When I am sure, or if I just have an inkling in my butt, I promise you'll be the first to know."

"When you checked the car, was anything missing?"

"They found an empty Kenny G cassette case. Is he a favorite of your wife's?"

"I guess. The kids are always complaining that it's the only tape she ever wants to listen to."

"Well, it's gone. The boys really tore the car apart. That missing tape was the one thing that seemed out of the ordinary." Randy checked his notes. "The two people who worked the morning shift at Taco Expresso weren't there when I stopped. We're trying to track them down."

"What about the strip joint? Find anyone there who saw the car being parked?" John asked.

"It's rare if anyone 'sees' anything at those places. They're very protective of their clientele, but I don't think the guy I talked to this morning knew about the car."

"Why was he so interested in what we were doing? You said you saw someone watching us."

"I think nervous curiosity is the best answer, but I'll check back at that place, too. How about you, John? Get any leads today?"

"Nope, nothing new."

"Keep the faith. I'll see you in a few hours."


Randy knocked on David's door just as the late-afternoon sun dropped behind a bank of clouds. Rain was imminent, and the darkening skies added to the somberness of the men's moods.

"Come on in, Randy. You want a beer, or are you on duty?" David asked.

"Thanks, but I'll have to settle for a big glass of ice water."

David's phone rang just as the men entered the house.

"I'd better grab that. Have a seat in the den, and I'll be right back with the drinks." David disappeared down the hall.

Randy had never been in David's house before. They were both divorced, but unlike his own cluttered apartment, which to Randy was just a place to sleep and change clothes, David's house was a real home. The den held a comfortable assortment of antique tables, large, overstuffed leather furniture, bookshelves filled to overflowing, and copper urns planted with Boston ferns.

Randy sat down in one of the armchairs and leaned back, noting the impressive stereo system emitting soft, symphonic music he could not identify. The pleasant room welcomed him, beckoning him to shed the day's cares and relax. He gave in to its temptation and was almost asleep by the time David returned with two glasses of water.

The men drank in silence for a few minutes before Randy put down his glass and pulled out his small note-book and pen.

"We found Monica's plates and dusted for prints," he told David.

"Doesn't sound like a professional job, does it?" David said after Randy had explained the particulars. "What do you think? Are we dealing with kids?"

"I can't say at this point, but it appears that the person who parked the car wasn't concerned about covering up much. It seems more like a prank than actual tampering, or an intent to do serious damage," Randy said.

"Think someone will be back for the car?" David asked.

"I wish we had the manpower on the force to put a man out there just in case, but it's possible the car and Monica's disappearance aren't related."

"What do you mean?" David asked.

"Maybe some kids took her station wagon for a joyride. Happens all the time. When the ride's over, they strip the car for parts, or they ditch it. They could have hot-wired the parked car, driven off, and it would have absolutely nothing to do with Monica's disappearance."

"Yeah, I guess, but do you really think . . ."

"I don't know what to think." Randy pulled at his mus-tache and lifted his shoulders in exasperation. "This whole situation is weird. When the men at the lab went over the car, they found no blood, just the usual stuff you'd expect in anyone's car who spends a large portion of their time hauling around kids and dogs. They found nothing that would indicate the car was used for anything unusual. Even had a full tank of gas."

"So, whoever took it didn't drive it far. Doesn't that rule out the joyride?" asked David. "I doubt kids would fill the tank after they drove it. Besides, kids don't usually go for station wagons." David leaned back against the leather chair. "You mentioned a tape was missing?"

"Yeah, we found an empty plastic container . . . Kenny G. Monica's husband said she listened to it all the time."

David knew the tape well. He remembered the night he'd given it to her.

Randy changed the subject. "I know we talked a little about this last night, but let's go through it again. Have you thought of anyone who'd want to hurt Monica?"

"No."

"Tell me about John."

"Great job, lots of money. He travels at least three or four days each week. Got a big promotion as an incentive to move to Texas. The family has been here about a year."

"Now that you've had a chance to think about it, have you got any more ideas about the marriage?" Randy looked intently at David. "Has Monica ever mentioned that she suspected there might be another woman in her husband's life?"

David rubbed his hands and shook his head. "Monica may have thought that, but we never talked about it."

"Does Monica have someone else in *her* life?"

David sat up straighter in his chair. "I . . . I suppose you mean me?"

Randy nodded. "It has crossed my mind."

"If the circumstances were different, I admit I'd be the first one in line. She's special. We're good friends, maybe best friends, but hell, things aren't different, and I have to respect that." David looked at Randy and shrugged. "You're not going to write all of this down in your damned book, are you?"

"No, I'm not."

Both men were silent for a few moments.

"So, you don't think John's behind this?" Randy asked at last.

"Behind what?" asked David. "Her disappearance? No."

"You really believe that?"

"Yeah, he's a jerk sometimes, but he's not crazy."

The doorbell rang and David excused himself to answer it.

When David returned to the den, Randy was looking out the window, deep in thought, ignoring the steady rain outside. "Sorry, UPS. Something Colin ordered," David said.

Randy swung around. David looked like a survivor of a plane crash—totally numb, yet somehow still functioning. In his job he'd seen that look on too many people's faces, and wondered how long it would be before David collapsed.

"The people at Monica's school told me you dropped by today," Randy said softly. "So did I. She seems well-liked, no skeletons in that closet. Her desk was so neat, I couldn't find a thing to help us."

"Me, either. There was something in her sweater. I stuck it in my . . ."

David had Randy's full attention. If ever the detective had seen a light bulb go on in someone's brain, one was shining brightly in David's as he plunged his hands into the pockets of his tan pants, dumping change, a few bills, keys, and finally, two small slips of paper onto the leather couch.

"I found these. They fell out of her sweater," David said as he smoothed out the small scraps and turned on a lamp. Both men bent over to peer at them as David laid them on the table.

"They're ticket stubs from a movie," he said. "She must have worn that sweater one time when they went to see a show."

"You mean *shows*." Randy held the tickets up to the

light. "These stubs are for two different films. Afternoon matinees. Get me a calendar."

"Thanks," Randy said as David handed him a small calendar he had picked up from the desk. Randy flipped the pages and ran a finger down the days while comparing them to the stubs. "Look at this. Both these tickets were for Wednesday matinees. She disappeared on a Wednesday. Do you suppose that after she left you, she went to a movie?"

"She never said anything about going, but it's certainly possible. I know Wednesday is her day off."

Randy checked the ticket stubs again. "Hmm-mm. One of these is from a Unity theater. The other is from a Circle Triplex Cinema."

David peered at the faded writing on the tiny piece of paper. "There're dozens of those theaters in the Dallas area. How do we know which one she went to?"

"I don't know. These numbers at the bottom must be some sort of code. First, I'll check the ones closest to her house, and if it wasn't one of them, somebody at the theaters should have a list of the different codes. Finding out where she went will be the easy part," said Randy.

The men walked to the door. Because of the steady downpour, they stood under David's porch roof for a few minutes.

"Call me tonight and let me know if you find anything out about the theaters. If that's where Monica was on Wednesday, somebody might have recognized her," David said. "This might be a real breakthrough. Do you have a picture of her to show them? I can give you a flyer."

"Yes, I already have one. If she's a regular Wednesday patron, our chances are even better."

"I'll be at my office tomorrow until two," said David. "If you need anyone to do some legwork after that, I'll be available."

"Thanks. I just have one question. It's been bugging me since I walked into your house."

"What?"

"How come you don't have a dog? All vets have dogs, and maybe a couple of cats. It's in the rules. You've got to have some pets."

David smiled for the first time in hours. How strange the sensation felt. "Our dog died five months ago, and we aren't ready to get another one yet. Colin's allergic to cats, but he has a huge fish tank and six hamsters in his room. Do they count?"

Randy grinned. "Yeah, they count. You know, sometimes things like that just bother me, and then I have to ask."

"No problem. You're supposed to ask questions. You're doing a good job."

Randy reached out to shake David's outstretched hand. "Thanks, pal. Tell that to the captain. He doesn't know it yet, but I'm after his job!"

Randy parked his car in a lot next to the Town Park Eight, just off the expressway, and watched the matinee crowd exit the theater. The group consisted of women of all ages, some together, others alone; retirement-age couples, and a few single men. Even in the rain, most were moving at a leisurely pace, although some of the younger women hurried as if they had someplace else they needed to be. He should have been at the Foyles', but since he had to pass by this place on his way, he decided to stop for a few minutes and ask some questions.

The woman at the ticket window looked at his badge and picked up a phone beneath her counter to call the assistant manager on duty. Within three minutes a tall, dark-haired man was waving Randy through the glass doors, past the young man tearing tickets.

"Hi, I'm Mark Gentry. How can I help you?"

"Detective Abbott. I'd like to ask you a few questions."

People filed through the doors en route to the five o'clock shows. After dodging several groups shaking wet umbrellas, Randy asked, "Is there someplace we could talk?"

"Certainly, we can use the office upstairs. It'll be much quieter up there."

Mark motioned for Randy to follow him. The men rounded the concession stand and stopped at a door about halfway up the sloped hallway that led to the theaters. Randy saw that the door was covered with the same fabric as the walls and wondered how many people passed by without ever realizing that a door was there. He waited while Mark punched in a code on a security pad that enabled him to unlatch the door.

"Who has the code to come up here?" Randy asked as they climbed the steep steps to the second level.

"All the employees do. We take our breaks up here." Randy followed his gesture and looked into the room at the top of the stairs. Metal lockers lined one wall, two long tables with a scattering of chairs stood in the middle. Two girls in maroon uniforms sprawled across an imitation-leather sofa beside a refrigerator, and soda and candy machines.

"The boss keeps the rest of the doors up here locked, and only he and his assistants have keys." Mark pointed to the doors at the end of the short hall. "Those two are supply rooms where we keep the salable items, like the extra candy and stuff. We also store all the operational items—the cups, napkins, popcorn boxes, straws—things like that here, too. This here's the office."

Mark unlocked the door and ushered Randy into a large, comfortable room with tinted windows overlooking the concession stand on the main floor.

"The manager likes to keep his eye on the profits. Guess not many people realize someone could be watching them buy their sodas and popcorn."

"This is quite a setup," Randy said, indicating the computer and fax machine on the credenza along the wall. He walked past a desk piled high with papers, catalogues, thick reams of printed paper in colored folders, and movie ads.

"Yeah, we need to send daily cash and attendance records to the district office. The computer helps us keep track of the inventory and the amount of money in the individual cash drawers. Why don't we have a seat over here?" Mark said, pointing to two small armchairs opposite the desk.

Randy looked over Mark's head and noted framed movie posters on the wall. Scenes from *Rocky*, *Star Trek*, *Xanadu*, and *Karate Kid* reminded him of how seldom he got to the movies. Of the four, he'd only seen *Rocky* and that had been on TV.

"How can I help you?" Mark asked.

"This place is fascinating. I've never been 'behind the scenes' before."

"Ah, yes, the magic of Hollywood. Gets 'em every time. You should see the film room. I don't have a key because I don't thread the reels yet, or I'd take you in." He looked at his watch. "Another assistant manager is due in an hour to set up the seven o'clock runs. If you can hang around, Lenny could show you the ropes in there. The film platters we use are really interesting."

"No, I'm on a tight schedule today. Maybe another time, but thanks. What I need is some information about this." Randy opened his notebook and handed one of the ticket stubs to Mark. "What do all those numbers mean?" Randy asked.

Mark looked at the stub. "This was for a two-fifty p.m. show on March seventh. The person who bought the ticket paid matinee prices to see *Deathstalk* in auditorium four. The numbers at the bottom tell which Unity theater the person attended. This is one of our stubs."

"I see. I have another one here from a Circle Triplex Cinema. I don't suppose you could tell me which of their theaters it's from," said Randy.

"No, sorry, in fact the only Unity code I recognize is ours. Guess you could call me the rookie on the team. I've only been in this position about three weeks."

"That's okay. You've been real helpful. We're trying to locate a missing woman. We know she sometimes comes to matinees. In fact, this is her stub. We think she may have attended a matinee on the day she disappeared."

Randy flipped to the back of his notebook and removed one of the small photographs of Monica. He handed it to Mark.

"This is her picture. Have you ever seen her before?"

"No, I don't think so. Let me have this photo and I'll pass it around. Someone might recognize her, but we can get up to fifty thousand people in here during a good week, so it's tough to remember faces."

"Yeah, okay, keep the photo. I have more. Here's my card, too. I hope you'll call me if you or anyone else can help."

"Be glad to. I'll tell the manager you were here." Mark smiled. "I'll put your business card and the woman's picture on the bulletin board in the hallway."

Randy stood up and walked to the door. "When's the best time to catch the manager?" he asked.

"He's here a lot. We have seven shifts a day that overlap, and he tries to touch base with all of them. He's real picky about the on-screen presentation, so he spends most of his time upstairs in the film room. I can have him call you if you like. His name is Phil Bruns."

"Yeah, ask him to give me a ring, say, tomorrow morning, if he's around. Do you have his home phone number by chance?"

Randy jotted down the man's name and number, then thanked Mark for his time. The unmistakable smell of popping corn followed him out of the theater. He should have made the connection earlier: Monica Foyles's favorite junk food was popcorn.

* * *

"Moth-er, Moth-er . . . wake up now. I must go back to work, but I want to talk to you first."

Monica cringed at the sound of his voice, terrified of what he might do to her. She kept her eyes closed, hoping he might think she was sleeping and leave her alone.

"Moth-er, don't be mad at me. We had a little disagreement. It's over now. Everything is fine. I think you finally understand that you have to listen to me and do things my way. Mother, open your eyes and look at me."

"I hurt. . . . My arm . . . Where am I?"

"You're on the couch in the living room. I brought you here when you fell in the kitchen. Your arm is just bruised, that's all. I wrapped it in a sling so you won't hurt it more. You must never make me that angry again."

"Could I have some water, please?" she whispered. Moving her lips hurt. She could feel a large bandage on her cheek and the palms of her hands were wrapped in gauze.

"One glass of water coming up. Easy on the ice, right?"

Even through her haze of pain, Monica recalled how he always asked her that question at the theater when she bought a soda before a matinee. If he remembered that, too, then why did he keep calling her "Mother?" It hurt to think. It was much easier to close her eyes and slip back into the darkness.

He returned with the water and gently pushed his arm under the pillow to lift her head so that she could drink. "Let me help you, Mother."

She tried to move away from him, but she was too weak. The water tasted good and she drank half the glassful.

"Thirsty, weren't you? I'll have to take better care of you. After all, you're the only mother I've got, and I love you." He kissed her mouth.

She worried he would hit her if she showed any negative response to his touch. She forced herself to remain calm as he caressed her cheek. Her stomach refused to cooperate. The combination of pain, terror, and an excess of water was too much for it. She turned her head to the side, and vomited on the floor.

Sick, weak, and crying, she lay back on the pillow. Her stomach roiled and she threw up again, this time soiling her dress and the scarf that held her arm. She tried to wipe her mouth and her eyes with the sleeve of her sweater, but he stopped her, picking up the washcloth that had slid to her chest and dabbing her face with it.

"Let me do it. Let me clean you up. Have you eaten something that didn't agree with you? Did you drink that water too fast? Poor Mother. You're really having a rough time, aren't you?"

Monica caught her breath, wishing she had the nerve and the strength to knock that sickly sweet smile from his face. But the fact that he was crazy enough to believe what he was saying stopped her from retaliating, even if she could have.

"Up you go, Mother," he said, lifting her off the couch. "I think the bathtub is the only place for you."

Monica cried out in pain when he jostled her arm. He carried her through the hall and sat her down on the commode seat, holding her upright until she was steady enough to sit without falling. Then he reached around her neck and removed the bandana.

"Hold your arm to your chest. I'll try not to hurt it when I take off your sweater and dress."

"No!" she sobbed, clutching the pink cardigan as if it were a life vest.

"Mother, you have to let me help you. You can't do this yourself and there's no one here but me. You'll feel so much better when you're washed and have a clean dress on."

"May I have my . . . my own clothes then?"

"We'll see. We'll see. Let's get you undressed and into the tub."

Monica relaxed her grip on the sweater and allowed him to remove it. Then she closed her eyes tightly while he unbuttoned the soiled blue crepe dress and slid it off her shoulders. He lifted her slightly to push the dress past her hips. She sat shivering in her bra and panties, her hand over her mouth in a feeble attempt to stop crying. Her only thought as she heard the water running in the tub was that at least he had allowed her to keep her own underwear.

Lenny had never seen a more pitiful sight. It was unlike Mother to give in this way, to look so defeated and sad. He had expected her to act like a raging she-cat after the way he had slapped her around in the kitchen. Her attempts to stay dressed in dirty clothes made no sense, either, but her blatant modesty baffled him most of all. He remembered a woman who never passed up an opportunity to shed her clothes.

"C'mon, Mother. I'm going to be late for work. This isn't too bad. It's just a bath. It'll feel good." He turned off the taps and removed her bra. Then he pulled her to her feet, pushed down her panties, and steered her to the edge of the big, claw-footed tub.

"You're so tiny, Mother. I don't think you can get in by yourself." He slid his hands up her arms, his fingertips touching the sides of her breasts as he pulled her back against his suddenly aroused body.

Monica yanked away from him and cried out at the pain from the hasty movement. She gritted her teeth. She would get herself into that tub or die trying. He was not going to touch her naked body one more time. She grabbed the side of the porcelain tub with the bandaged hand on her good arm, tried to climb over it and lower herself into the water. After three tries, she finally made it, hating that it had taken her so long to accomplish such a simple act, and that he stood there watching while she did it.

She sank down, holding her hands to her chest, wincing as the hot water licked at her battered flesh. Lowering her head to her upraised knees, she sat quietly in the tub. The smell of vomit emanating from her body made her sick. She flinched when a warm, wet washcloth glided down her back.

"This reminds me of the times we bathed together. Remember how we used to wash each other's backs? It always led to other things."

The thought of sharing a bath with this man made her gag. What else had he and the person he called Mother done? *Everything there is to do.* She gagged again.

Lenny moved the washcloth up and down her legs. "You're so beautiful. Even when you make me so angry that I have to hurt you, I love your body, your hair, yes, even now, and I especially love those green eyes of yours that drive me wild."

He washed her arms gently, then scrubbed the back of her neck. She kept her face hidden, her head resting on her knees. Her arm throbbed with pain, but she was too afraid to move. She flinched again when she felt warm water from a spray hose rinse the soap from her body and wet down her hair.

"Lean back, Mother, so that I can wash your hair. I don't have much time. We've got to hurry."

Monica did as he asked. If she cooperated, maybe this ordeal would end and she could sleep. She felt his hands rubbing shampoo into her hair and before long, he told her to get out of the tub. She slowly got to her feet and reached for the towel he held out for her. He shook his head and watched as she stood there, shivering in the ankle-deep water.

"Lenny, please ... the towel?" She felt his eyes caressing every curve, every crevice, every inch of her body. Refusing to play his game, she hung her head and waited.

Finally he snapped open the towel and wrapped it around her, taking great care with her broken arm before deftly tucking the end of it into the cleft between her breasts. He scooped her up out of the tub and set her on the floor. He pulled a second towel from a shelf and rubbed her head with it.

"I have to go to the bathroom," she said.

"Go ahead. I'll get you some clean clothes." He pulled the key from the inside lock, shut the door, and locked her in from the outside.

She gazed at the small bathroom window, afraid to touch it, wondering what it overlooked, and if she could fit through it.

Lenny returned with an armload of clothes. He threw her an old slip and told her to put it on.

"This isn't mine. I thought you'd let me have my own clothes."

He grabbed her chin and yanked her face to his. "You'll wear what I give you, or nothing at all. Is that clear?"

Monica nodded and stepped into the slip. Her arm and both hands ached, her torn cheek burned, but she continued, determined to dress herself. The huge garment swamped her, and she had barely settled its twisted straps on her shoulders when he threw a dress at her. She swayed like a drunk.

"You've lost too much weight for any of your stuff to look good on you," he told her.

She unzipped the long-sleeved knit dress and pulled it over her head as best she could using her good arm. She looked down at the garish orange flowers splashed across the dark green fabric and decided that even though the dress was hideous, it was better than being naked. She had no choice but to turn to him for help with the zipper. He jerked it angrily, ripping it up over her back. She tried to pull away, but he stopped her by tying a fresh bandana around her neck to support her arm.

Then he removed a small, shiny cylinder from his pocket and pulled off its top. He lifted her chin and hurriedly smeared some lipstick on her trembling mouth. "Now you're ready. It's time to go upstairs. Leave your hair alone. There's not enough to bother with," he told her when she reached for a towel to dry it. "You won't catch cold."

Monica slumped down on the commode, too weak to remain standing. "I need to sit a minute. I'm feeling sick again."

"There's nothing left in your stomach for you to throw up. You can lie down once you're in the attic. Now, c'mon. You're making me late for work."

He pulled her to her feet and out into the hall. The steps spun in front of her eyes and she stopped to regain her equilibrium.

"I said let's go, damn it." He half carried, half dragged her to the attic where he flung her onto the bed. "Give me your hand."

"Lenny, you always . . . lock the door. Why can't you . . . let me be?" She stopped to catch her breath. "I can't go anywhere. The handcuff hurts."

He snatched her hand from her lap and cuffed it to the bed. His rough handling caused the cut on her hand to bleed. "I don't think you've earned any special privileges today, Mother. I'll see you tonight." After checking the bottle of water he had left her, he locked the door behind him.

Monica lay on her back thinking about the mercurial changes she had seen in him today—the raging maniac, the tender nurse, and the cruel jailer who dragged her to the attic and chained her as though she were a wild dog.

Any hope that she could return to her former life was gone. The only steps she had taken were backward ones. She had gotten nothing from her captor: no freedom, not even in the attic, no clothes that were hers, no privacy, and worst of all, no answers as to why she was being held. The thought of what lay ahead for her in this place was so hideous that for the first time in her life, Monica sincerely wished she could die.

# chapter

# 23

William Herdman held the rounded handle of the big blue-and-white striped golf umbrella in one hand and his granddaughter's hand in his other.

"Why do you like to walk in the rain, Gramp?" Sarah asked.

"I like to walk in any kind of weather when I have my favorite girl for company."

"Oh, Gramp."

"I know. You think I'm too old for you. It won't be long until some young buck will be beating my time for a walk with you."

William looked down at his grandchild, happy to see a touch of color in her cheeks. He worried about Sarah, about all of them, so much that he could hardly put his thoughts together rationally, let alone voice his fears. But he forced himself to maintain a veneer of normalcy. His wife, Grace, had been able to set aside her grief and despair since their arrival a few hours ago to respond to the children, shop for groceries, and begin preparing the evening meal. Thank God for the mundane trivialities of life. Sometimes they were all that kept a person going in the tough times.

While Grace had Jeb and Mia involved in the kitchen, William had suggested a short walk with Sarah. Rain or no rain, he needed to remove this stricken child from the tension in the house, if only for a brief time.

"You're fortunate to have this lovely weather, Sarah."

Sarah looked up at him and tried to smile. "It's raining, Gramp."

"It's icy and cold in Connecticut. The daffodils are only up a few inches and they're blanketed with snow. Here it rains, but it's a soft, warm rain. You remember how nasty the spring storms can be up north?"

"I miss the snow. We didn't have any at all in Dallas this year."

"But I couldn't wear my short pants in February, and you had a weekend here in the eighties that month," William said.

"Did you bring them along?"

"My short pants? Of course, I did. Even if you and the rest laugh at my knobby knees, I won't pass up an opportunity to wear them."

Sarah squeezed his hand tighter, and pressed her body against him. William stopped walking and, still managing to hold the umbrella over them, knelt and hugged Sarah. "Scared, are you? I know, honey. I know."

"What if Mom never comes back? What if horrible people have her and they're hurting her? What if we never see her again?"

Tears spilled onto her cheeks and she wept against her grandfather's jacket. William had no more words to soothe her. He held her tightly, praying she would not realize that some of the tears were his own.

Bright lights in the Foyles' house dispelled the gloomy dusk as Randy parked by the front walk. He locked the car doors and ran through the rain to the porch. After ringing the doorbell, he turned, and saw two figures, a man and a little girl, coming up the sidewalk.

Randy wondered who the elderly man walking beside Sarah might be. He was roughly the same height and build as her father. Then he remembered that the grandparents were in town. This thought was confirmed when a petite woman with touches of gray in her auburn hair opened the door. She was dressed casually in gray slacks and a sapphire blue turtleneck sweater. Her face was dead white. With one brief glance at her eyes, Randy could see the tremendous toll this situation was exacting from her.

"Hello, ma'am. I'm Detective Randy Abbott. John is expecting me. I'm later than I thought I would be. I hope I'm not interfering with dinner." He had his I.D. in his hand, but she ignored it and opened the door wider.

"No, of course not. How do you do? I'm Grace Herdman. Please come in." She stepped inside and motioned him through the door. Scanning the street, she saw William and Sarah nearing the house and waited for them. She introduced the men, and studied Sarah before pulling the tearful child close.

"John is in the den. Would you like some coffee, Mr. Abbott? I've just made an apple cake. Perhaps we could tempt you with a piece?"

Randy nodded and smiled. "Coffee sounds great, and I won't ever say no to homemade anything." Lunch for him had consisted of one hurried glass of iced tea, and his prospects for dinner weren't much better.

William Herdman removed his jacket and hung it on the doorknob of the hall closet. He reached out and cupped Sarah's chin in his hand. "You go with Gran now, honey. I'll see you a little later." He tried unsuccessfully to clear the knot in his throat and whispered, "Mr. Abbott, I'll take you to John. Grace will get your coffee."

"Thank you, sir."

Randy followed the older man down the hall. The moment he'd stepped across the threshold, Randy had felt the fear, the barely restrained tension, and above all, the overwhelming sadness in the house. All the lights were on. That vain attempt at cheerfulness, added to the hushed tones of the Herdmans and the quiet sobs of the child he'd just seen, lent an unmistakable heaviness to the atmosphere. It reminded him of the all-too-familiar scene of a hospital lounge, where, after receiving news of an unexpected tragedy, families gathered to wait for news of a loved one who probably wouldn't survive the night.

As always in cases like this one, Randy had to fight to remain neutral, to turn off his feelings, knowing he couldn't do his best work if he was to become personally involved. He had to be compassionate, but he also needed to keep a tight rein on his emotions. Maintaining that balance was always a difficult challenge, one that didn't get easier with experience.

William knocked on the study door before entering. John was on the phone, talking to a local newspaper reporter. He waved the men into matching red-leather side chairs in front of his desk.

Randy sat down and listened to John, noting the man's haggard countenance. Although he was dressed impeccably in a light green sweater, buttoned-down striped shirt, and brown slacks, the lines that bracketed his mouth appeared deeper than yesterday. One shiny, tasseled loafer rested on his knee with an air of nonchalance, but as he spoke into the phone, John's shadowed eyes reflected the strain of the past two days.

The iceman was melting. . . .

"You'll carry the article in all the editions?" John asked. He waited for a reply, curtly thanked the reporter, and hung up the phone.

Grace entered the room carrying a tray with a carafe, mugs, and a large piece of cake. She set it on the small, round table next to Randy's chair. "Let me know if you need anything else. I'll keep the children with me while you talk."

John nodded and she turned away, catching her husband's hand for a quick squeeze before she left. William lowered his head and took several deep breaths.

Randy helped himself to the coffee before speaking.

"I've got a couple of things to report, John. First off, we found some ticket stubs in a sweater your wife left at school. One of them was for the Town Park Eight movie theater on Central."

"So?" John pushed himself back from the desk.

"Both the stubs were for matinees, Wednesday matinees."

"Matinees? Are you certain they were hers?" John asked, remembering she had asked him to take her, but that was months ago.

"No, not positively, but they were in her sweater."

"Monica wouldn't spend her time in afternoon movies, not during the week. Not without the children. She has better things to do," said John.

"Lots of people go to matinees. Are you sure she never mentioned going?" asked Randy.

"Never," replied John.

William leaned forward in his chair and smiled at John. "My wife and daughter often went to movies in the afternoon when Monica lived at home," he said quietly. "They both loved them. Grace still goes occasionally."

John lowered his foot and stood up. For a few minutes, the only sound in the room came from the rain spattering against the window.

"But wouldn't I know if my own wife had a habit of attending matinees alone?"

William sat back in his chair and said nothing. Finally John answered his own question. "Perhaps not. I guess I'm missing your point, Randy. What's the deal with the tickets?"

"The stubs were from two different Wednesday matinees. She disappeared this past Wednesday afternoon. Could she have gone to a matinee after leaving Dr. Riley's office? She had the time. That's her day off."

"But even so, what the hell could happen in a theater with all those people around?" John asked.

"Sometimes when we've been visiting in Dallas, and you folks were busy with other things, I've taken Grace to

some of those big movie places in the daytime, and it
always amazes me that the management will run the show
even if there's only one person to watch it," William said.
"It's kind of eerie being in those huge auditoriums with so
few people in them. I'd be half afraid to let Grace go by
herself."

"Aren't those theaters patrolled?" asked John.

"No, not really." Randy turned to include both men in
the conversation. "At Town Park Eight, the guys
threading the machines are so busy getting eight different
presentations up and running that I doubt that they ever
have time to check on the audience."

"So you . . . do you think somebody could have . . .
taken her when she went to the matinee?" asked William.

Randy watched the droplets of perspiration break out
on William's forehead as the older man reached into his
pocket for a handkerchief. Had John noticed how badly
William's hands shook?

"To answer your question honestly, Mr. Herdman, I
don't know. Before I came over here, I stopped by the
theater complex and talked to one of the managers. I
showed him Monica's picture, left him one in fact, and
he's going to check around to see if anyone remembers
seeing her. It's a long shot, but you never know." Randy
became more aware of the older man's building panic.

John noted William's agitation, but started talking.
"Monica loves the gory books and the flicks, too—the
bloodier, the better. I told you Stephen King was her
favorite author. Was the theater showing any of those?"

"John, I haven't had a chance to look. Do you have
Wednesday's paper? We'll check the listing," Randy said.

"I'll get it," said William, rising from his chair. "I think
it's in the garage."

"Are you sure your father-in-law can handle this?"
Randy asked as soon as William left the room. "He seems
a little shaky. Maybe we shouldn't include him in these
sessions."

"He's a lot tougher than he looks. He's scared. Hell, who isn't? But he'll be okay. He wants to help. I think he'd feel worse if he weren't included."

Randy drank his coffee. He flinched as the hot liquid hit his empty stomach. How many cups had he had today? He'd lost count.

"Any word from your men who are checking on the strip joint? Anybody come looking for the car?" John asked as they waited for William to return.

"Nope. I did get ahold of one of the guys who worked yesterday's early shift at the taco place. They had their normal morning crowd. The only unusual thing he remembered was that some kid made a ruckus when there wasn't any hand soap in the john. Came out complaining and waving his hands like they were made of glass or something."

"Probably some jerk on drugs," said John.

"Maybe. Nobody recognized him, but I got a description . . . just in case"

# chapter
# 24

Monica shifted in bed when she heard the kitchen door open and close. The monster was back. She had no idea what time it was. The attic was dark and she supposed she had slept for several hours. Every bone, every muscle in her body ached. Her arm in its makeshift sling throbbed whenever she moved it. She knew it was broken, or at least badly injured. Though she still had some movement in her fingers, she could feel that her wrist had swollen to double its normal size. Her hand and her face stung with pain from the cuts. Lenny had removed the mirror in the bathroom. She wondered why he had not forced her to endure the final indignity of seeing herself. Maybe he was saving that punishment for later.

How could she get through the hours to come? He would kill her. She knew that now. She would die here unless she killed him first. It had come to that. Never in her life had she even considered taking anyone's life, but she knew now she wanted to kill Lenny. She hated him enough to do it.

Her earlier plan entered her mind, and she focused on it with what concentration she could muster. Could she be Mother? He seemed afraid of her. Mother knew his weaknesses. Mother might be able to kill him.

"Hope you still like mustard and pickles on your

cheeseburger, Mother," Lenny said, tossing a greasy bag onto the bed. "No time to cook."

Monica lifted her head and tried to force a smile with no luck. He seemed almost rational. Where was the madman? What would Mother do? What would Mother say? "Uh . . . of . . . course, I do."

"Got you some fries, too."

She allowed Lenny to help her to a sitting position. His hands felt cool and smooth on her skin, gliding snakelike over her arm. It took everything she had not to recoil from his touch.

Placing their sodas on the table beside the bed, he spread a napkin on her lap and handed her a sandwich from the bag.

"Will you take the cuff off? I can't manage otherwise." She watched his face to see how he responded to her request.

"Sure thing." He laid the burger on her napkin. The smell of it nauseated her and she held her breath as she watched him pull a ring of keys from his pocket. He chose a small silver one and unlocked the cuff.

"That's better," she said, shaking her hand. She pulled the sleeve of her dress over the angry red welts left by the constant rubbing of the handcuff, relishing the small freedom, but unable to relax in his presence.

"Poor Mother." He leaned over her arm and kissed her sleeve. "You shouldn't struggle so."

She had never hated him more. "I know. You're right." She nearly choked on the words.

Lenny looked at her suspiciously. "Why are you being so nice all of a sudden? You planning something?"

What had she done? Oh, God! Please don't let the monster come back!

"Oh, no. I . . . I . . . guess I finally got caught up on my sleep. Maybe it's put me in a better mood." She took a bite of cheeseburger, wincing at the tartness of the pickle juice on her cut lip. She hated mustard, her stomach was roiling, but she forced herself to finish the cold, greasy sandwich.

Lenny devoured two burgers within minutes. The fries were lukewarm and gummy. When she saw that he'd finished his, she pushed her share over to him. "Go ahead and eat these, too. The sandwich is all I want tonight."

"Make sure you leave room for dessert. I brought you something from the theater I know you like." He pulled a packet of peanut butter cups from his pocket and looked at her expectantly.

She wanted to stuff them into his face, but taking the cue, she carefully exclaimed, "Ah, my favorites!" Were they? She forced a small smile. "I haven't had any for a long time. Thanks."

Pleased that she had acknowledged his thoughtfulness, Lenny beamed. "I wish I could stay with you, but I pulled the late shift again tonight."

Monica hid her relief. She asked him to take her to the bathroom. He complied immediately, leading her down the steps and even allowing her some privacy. The mirror over the sink was still missing. She wondered why he didn't want her to see herself. Was her appearance even more shocking than she imagined it would be? Her hard-won bravado slipped away, and she choked back tears as he led her back up the stairs to the dark attic.

"Since I'm going to be alone, may I have the oil lamp lit, just for company?"

"Yeah, I guess, Mother. I have to build a feature tonight at the theater so I'll be real late. It'll be after the midnight show before I even start. I'll turn the lamp off when I come in to say good night to you. Give me your hand."

When she hesitated a moment, he reached over and took it, then snapped the metal circle around her wrist.

"Thanks for the candy. You better hurry on now. You don't want to get into trouble." Why didn't he leave? She couldn't bear it if he touched her again.

"Kiss me good-bye, Mother."

She shrunk back. "I . . . I . . . can't . . ." She stifled a cry when suddenly he lifted her by the shoulders and flicked his tongue between her lips.

His laughter bellowed out and filled the room. "G'night, Mother. See you later."

"I'll be asleep when you get home."

"Yeah, I'll probably go right to bed, too. I didn't get much sleep last night. By the way, how do you like your nails? You never thanked me for doing them."

"What?" She peered at her fingers and looked at the rich rose color staining her short nails. She hadn't even noticed them before. The idea of him touching her without her knowing it infuriated her at first, and then made her skin crawl. The horror was compounding. When had he painted them? Because he stood waiting for her reply, she mustered a whispered "Thank you."

Lenny put the lamp on the table beside the bed and lifted her hand that was cuffed to the bed. "Don't you just love the shade? We don't often agree on a color, Mother, but this polish looks as good on me as it does on you. Although, since I'm working tonight, I skipped the color and just gave my nails a good buffing." He moved closer to her and nuzzled her neck.

Monica wanted to scream when she felt the small nibbles around her ear. Could she go through with this? Like a cornered animal she watched his fingers slither across her breast, stopping to twist and squeeze her left nipple through the dress. Finally he raised his head, but his hand stayed on her body.

"If you don't hurry, you really are going to be late," she said. If he didn't leave soon, she would be as mad as he was. How long could she keep from screaming out loud?

"Last night after you were asleep and my nails had dried, I tried on the white nylon gloves. You know, the ones you bought to go with that flowered summer dress of yours? God! It was a beautiful sight! Do you think I might have those for my collection?"

Monica stared at him, telling herself to breathe deeply and stay calm. He had to go to work. She would be all right. He didn't have time to do anything to her now. "Yes, yes." Anything. Just go!

"Oh, Mother, last night I wanted you so much. Touch me, Mother. Touch me so you'll know how much I want you now."

"I . . . I . . . shouldn't. You need to get to . . . the theater. I don't want you to drive too fast."

He sighed and stood up, turning away from her to collect himself. "You're right. The boss will blast me if I'm late again."

# chapter
# 25

Randy knew he was operating on pure hunch when he stopped again at the Town Park Eight after leaving the Foyles' house. When he read that one of the movies now showing was *Deathstalk,* a chilling little piece about a mass murderer, his antennae went up and were working double time.

He circled the packed lot several times before he found a parking place behind the theater, near the Dumpsters. The rear door was locked. Minutes later, he entered the theater through the front door. He assumed it was between shows, since no one was taking tickets, and the girl at the box office was touching up her lipstick. At the concession stand, a young man stood with his back to the counter, loading the popcorn machine. A girl with long dark hair smiled at Randy and playfully offered him a box of chocolates as she restocked the candy shelves. He declined with a nod and moved on. He'd sworn off women, at least temporarily, after his divorce. Being a full-time detective rained hell on personal relationships.

Walking down one of the red carpeted hallways that led to the auditoriums, he was puzzled that no one tried to stop him. Security was certainly loose. He wandered in and out of several auditoriums, scanning the crowds. Some of the large rooms were full, but in others, like the one showing *Deathstalk,* fewer than a fourth of the seats were filled. He returned to the concession stand. The girl was alone.

"Excuse me. Is Mr. Bruns in the building?" he asked her.

The girl cocked her head and looked him over. "He's probably in the film room," she said. "I could page him if you like."

"Thanks."

She lifted a phone beneath the counter, spoke into it softly, and replaced it. "He'll be down in a few minutes. You look familiar. Are you one of the bookers?" she asked Randy, referring to the men from the central office who scheduled the films.

"No, 'fraid not."

"Last I heard, all the shows were up and running, and you don't have a tool box so you can't be an engineer. Mr. Bruns always makes such a fuss if someone messes up— the whole place knows if he's had to call for outside help," she continued, as she leaned across the counter, her full breasts teasing its glass top.

Randy, amused at her obvious come-on, looked at the girl's name tag and asked, "How long have you worked here, Susan?"

"Oh, about eight or nine weeks. I usually sell tickets."

"Ever work the matinees?"

"Yeah, but our shifts change all the time. I worked the afternoon box office when I first started. Now that I'm more experienced, I work the heavier crowds in the evenings and on weekends."

"Remember any regulars? People that seem to show up for the same time slot a lot, especially in the daytime?"

Susan looked at the ceiling and then at him. "Sometimes. Who are you anyway? You're beginning to sound like a cop."

Randy gave her extra points for intuition. He pulled out his wallet and showed her his I.D. "I am a cop," he said quietly.

Susan's eyes widened. "You the one who was here earlier? Mark was talking about some detective he showed around. You're looking for a missing woman. Her picture's on the bulletin board upstairs."

"Have you ever seen her?"

"Maybe, I'm not sure. We get a lot of suburban mom types in here, especially for the matinees. Now if it were a guy who was missing, I'd be much more helpful. I remember all the good-looking men." She studied him and smiled in a way that left no question about her motives.

*Dead end.* Randy stepped back from the counter. "You've been real helpful, Susan. Mark has my card. If you do remember something, will you have him give me a call?"

*Dead end.* Susan returned to her candy. She must be slipping. Two putdowns in three days. This one was probably out of her league, but she wasn't about to give up on Lenny. "Sure thing," she told Randy. "There's Mr. Bruns. I gotta get back to work."

Randy turned to watch a fiftyish man with pale skin and thinning gray hair hurrying toward him. Phil Bruns looked more like the kind of guy who would run a sleazy bar or a strip joint than a movie complex. There was nothing remotely wholesome about him. He probably surrounded himself with friendly, talkative types like Mark, the assistant manager Randy had met earlier, so that he could spend the bulk of his time behind the scenes, threading the platters and counting the money.

Randy stepped forward and flashed his I.D. in one smooth motion. "Thank you for seeing me. I'm Detective Abbott, Dallas P.D. I'd like to ask you a few questions."

"I got no trouble here. Mark told me about the missing woman. We posted her picture, but so far no one has recognized her. Thousands of people move through here, and my employees are too busy to remember one face."

"Do you have a list of people who worked the matinee shift this past Wednesday?" asked Randy. "We think she might have come to see the three o'clock showing of *Deathstalk*."

"You think something happened to her here? You're crazy!"

The man's insolence aroused Randy's suspicions. Why was he so hostile? He made a mental note to check whether Phil Bruns's fingerprints were on file.

"I'm not sure of anything at this point. I'm just following some leads. A woman has disappeared and I'm trying to find her. You can answer my questions here, or you can answer them at the station. It's up to you."

Bruns looked at him sullenly. "I'll get you the list. You want to know how many tickets we sold for that showing on Wednesday? It won't be many. Film's too violent for most folks." He turned to the door in the wall, leaving Randy to walk behind him, uninvited.

Randy followed Bruns to his second floor office. A tall, fair-haired teenager passed them on the stairs. Phil reached out and stopped him in midstep.

"You're late again, kid. That assistant manager's title isn't carved in stone, you know. I can yank it out from under your ass anytime I feel like it."

The boy snatched his arm away from Phil's hand and lifted his heavily lashed blue eyes to look at the older man. Randy was too surprised by the open hatred reflected on both their faces to address the fleeting feeling that he had seen the boy somewhere before.

Phil continued up to the second floor. The kid ran down the steps, slamming the door at the bottom.

Lenny replaced a malfunctioning hose on one of the charged soda tanks in the kitchen, then shouldered his way through the ten o'clock movie throng, amazed at all the people. Usually the earlier shows pulled the heaviest crowds. At this rate, he wouldn't get started on the Costner film until midnight, or later. Uncle Phil insisted that the theaters had to be spotless before the previews began, and part of Lenny's job was to oversee the kids on cleanup.

*Dammit, there'll be no time with Mother tonight.*

At the earliest, he'd be home at three-thirty A.M. Before Mother came back, he never minded the late hours, but now things were different and he resented every minute away from her. To make matters worse, he was stuck in concessions with Susan Malone. Lenny supposed he should be flattered by her interest in him, but he considered her a dimwitted nuisance. Couldn't she see how cheap she appeared with her cotton-candy hairdo and her six pounds of makeup, to say nothing of her nails? Fifteen minutes with a good magazine article on nail care would change her life, but obviously she wasn't interested. Her cuticles were rough and uneven and her nail color was all wrong. Who would wear orange polish with a burgundy uniform? It made him sick just to look at her.

"Lenny, I'm so glad you're back," Susan gushed. "Kyle and I've been swamped!"

Lenny glanced at the other person behind the counter. Kyle was pulling sodas and scooping corn with ease. Even though he was now doing Susan's job as well, the lines moved quickly and everything was under control. As usual, Susan had exaggerated the situation. Lenny ignored her and turned to a customer.

Twice during the next fifteen minutes, Susan found excuses to talk to Lenny. Receiving only the barest of replies, she became more determined. After the rush of people abated, she sidled up to him and propped her sizable breasts on his outstretched arm as he cleaned the counter, stopping his hand in midstroke.

"Going to the preview tonight, Lenny?"

"I'm building it." He slid his arm out from under her, repulsed by her advances.

"Thought Mark had that job."

"Nope, the old man gave it to me."

"How about after? Wanna come over to my place for a

few beers?" Moving closer to him, she twisted a long curl and drew the end of it across his cheek.

"It'll be too late." Lenny stepped back, mortified by how his body was responding to her.

"Didn't your mother ever tell you it's never too late?" She slid her finger between her teeth, then pulled it out to tug at her lower lip before she sucked it back into her mouth.

Lenny shook his head and finished wiping the counter. How dare this slut make a reference to Mother!

"Hey, you two, I could use a little help down here." Kyle loaded the fifth soda onto a cardboard tray and changed the woman's twenty.

"Cool it, Kyle. I'm coming." Susan looked back at Lenny. "Well, how about we keep the offer open, huh?" Reaching over, she ran her wet finger down his arm.

Lenny grabbed her upper arms and roughly bent her backward over the counter, forcing three teenagers to step back and holler encouraging words until they realized that this was no lighthearted tussle. Kyle quickly closed the cash drawer and moved toward them.

"Lenny, what the hell are you doing? For God's sakes let her up before you get us all fired."

"Yeah, big guy. Let's take this up in private." Susan tried to move out from under his hold, but could not budge him.

Lenny ignored them both and kept Susan pinned to the counter. "Here's my answer to your damned offer. My mother's worth three of you." He kissed her hard on the mouth and then let her go, just as one of the teenagers started to applaud. Kyle grabbed Lenny's arm as he picked up a box of popcorn to throw at the kid.

Lenny shrugged off Kyle's arm and turned to an elderly couple to his right. "How can I help you?" he asked. "Popcorn? Soda? Have you ever tried our hot dogs?"

Kyle slowly shook his head and moved to his station behind the cash drawer, thinking that if he couldn't get off

Lenny's shift, he needed to quit this job. Working crazy hours was one thing. Working with crazy people was another thing entirely. Maybe this time he really should report Lenny to the boss.

# chapter
# 26

"Let's go, kid. It's twelve-thirty. The place looks good. I want to get started on the film."

Lenny watched two teenagers wheel the last of the trash toward the back exit before he followed his uncle to the door that led upstairs. A few lost-and-found items were stacked on the steps. Out of habit, Lenny quickly perused the pile to see if there was anything he wanted.

"Pisser of a day, huh, kid?"

"It was okay, I guess."

"That's 'cause you didn't have cops sniffin' around your ass."

Lenny stiffened. "What do you mean?"

"Some cunt turned up missin' and the cops think she mighta been at one of our matinees just before she took a hike. God, that's all I need. My numbers were down last month, and central's gettin' nervous. This gets around, we'll have to shell out for a rent-a-cop, and the numbers'll be even worse."

"Why did they think she was here?" White rage pumped through Lenny's veins. How could she have gotten to the police? That bitch! Just a few hours ago, butter wouldn't melt in her mouth, and now this!

"Who knows what those bastards think? They even left a picture of her. Mark said he'd posted it on the board. I haven't seen it yet."

Phil climbed the last of the steps and turned toward his office. Out of the corner of his eye, he saw Monica's picture on the bulletin board.

"Well, lookie there. That's some cunt, wouldn't you say?" Phil said, licking his lips and grinning.

Lenny didn't stop to hear any more, Suddenly, everything was crystal clear. Mother wanted to see Phil. All of this was only a ploy to let his uncle know that she was back. How could he have underestimated her so badly? As clearly as if he'd been flipping through a photo album, pictures of Mother with Phil eating from the same fork, necking on the sofa, sitting in the tub, and fondling each other under the table smacked him in the face. He raced past his uncle and threw open the door to the film room so hard that it snapped back on its hinges.

Phil grabbed him before he could kick the first projector. He slapped Lenny and threw him to the floor.

"What's got into you? Don't you dare touch my equipment when you're in one of your moods! What do you want, kid? Some of my special attention?" This time he caught Lenny before he regained his feet and shoved the boy back down to the floor.

Dazed for a moment from the unexpected hit, Lenny caught his breath and reared up again just as Phil planted his foot firmly on Lenny's fingers.

"If I didn't need you so much tonight I'd throw your miserable little ass outta here so fast you wouldn't know if you were comin' or goin'. But the fact is, I do need you, so you're gonna park whatever shit is botherin' you on the shelf for a while, or I'm gonna break every one of your fuckin' knuckles on your fuckin', lily-white hand. Do you understand me, kid, or do you need a demonstration?" Phil pressed harder until Lenny cried out in pain.

"Please, please . . . I'm okay. I'm okay now," panted Lenny.

Satisfied, Phil lifted his foot and gave Lenny's leg a

hard kick. He smiled as the boy grabbed his knee and grunted.

"Time to work, kid. Hand me those reels."

Lenny locked the rear door of the theater and pushed it shut behind him. Long hours on his feet and the added emotional upheavals of the day had exhausted him. He would get to the bottom of Mother's little caper, but not tonight. Even the virulent hatred he felt for his uncle had tightened into a manageable knot. That, too, could be dealt with later.

He was approaching his car when he saw the sheet of paper sticking to his windshield. Wondering what somebody was selling at three o'clock in the morning, he lifted the wiper blade and retrieved the paper, holding it toward the light in the parking lot to read it. Mother's face stared back at him. The words blurred and faded away until the only things on the paper were her green eyes. They grew larger and larger as he looked at them.

Outraged by her trickery, he shredded the paper, threw it on the ground, and stomped on it, but her eyes continued to glare at him, their green fire burning him until he cried out. How had she done it? First the police and the picture on the board. And now this flyer.

He knew she was waiting at home to revel in his defeat, to lord it over him that she had returned to him with powers that he could never match. Even as he stood there in the parking lot, he could hear her shrill laughter. She had reduced him to less than nothing. She had put him back into his old role as her pawn, her plaything, unable to think or act for himself. His ego shattered, he opened the door and crawled into his car.

"Sugar, whatever it is, it can't be that bad," Susan said, leaning across the seat and patting his knee. "Why don't you just tell me all about it?"

Lenny's head swung around so fast she had to laugh.

"You don't mind if we take up where we left off earlier

tonight, do you? Can't tell you how exciting it was to have you on top of me. You're quite a stud, know that?"

"You can't get to me. I'm not interested."

She unbuttoned her shirt and freed one breast from her lacy push-up bra. Its aroused nipple pointed straight at Lenny.

"Wanna bet?"

"How the hell did you get in here?" Lenny growled, as soon as his heart began beating again.

"Easy. The door was unlocked. Aren't you glad to see me?" She moved her hand up his leg and was elated to find him hard. "You don't have to get home to Mother or anything, do you?"

"No, goddammit, I don't." In one motion he dragged her to him and ground his mouth against hers, forcing her down on the seat. Suddenly, his hands were everywhere. He tore open her bra and slacks before their first kiss ended.

"Hey, let me go a minute, sugar. I need some air." Susan pulled back and wound her fingers through his hair. "I knew it could be like this between us, Lenny. I knew it." She massaged his scalp and kissed him again, delighting in his passion, his eagerness to have her.

Lenny stopped kissing her and buried his face in her naked breasts. Her flesh surrounded him, hiding him from Mother's eyes. He felt Susan fumble with his belt and unzip his pants, and then he was free, free to soar without Mother, without Phil.

Susan pushed him back and took him into her mouth. He was bursting open, he'd never been higher, longer, or harder. He felt her leave him and shift around to take him again, this time into her slippery warmth.

"C'mon, baby," he heard her say, as she rocked back and forth on top of him. "C'mon to mama!"

"Look at me! Oh, Mother! Look at me!" he cried out, as his body emptied and he shuddered in its final release.

*She knows.* . . . That was his only thought as he locked the attic door and started down the steps toward his room. *She knows.*

Mother had ignored him deliberately. She had even refused to acknowledge his whispered "good night."

She had seen him with Susan. She had watched his entire performance and probably laughed when he had come so soon. What would she do to him? How could he possibly make it up to her? He had been pure in spirit; she had been his only woman until two hours ago. She couldn't hate him any more than he already hated himself. He had broken a solemn promise. She would make him pay, and the price would be high.

His darkened bedroom offered no solace. He threw himself onto the bed, too upset to remove his jacket, and buried his face in his arms. His sobs echoed through the house long past sunrise.

# chapter
# 27

"Hello, Grace. I'm Nancy Crawford, Monica's friend. I met you last Thanksgiving at a little open house we gave. You and your husband came with John and Monica."

"Of course. Hello, Nancy. Please come in. Peach Pie, move back. He won't hurt you, dear." Grace slipped her hand under the dog's collar.

"I know he won't. Hi ya, Peach!" Nancy said, leaning down to rub his ears. "We're old friends, aren't we, boy?" Looking up, she solemnly addressed Grace, "I'm here to help with the phone calls this morning. I won't ask how you are. I still can't believe this is happening."

Grace bit her lip. "It's a nightmare. I keep hoping I'll wake up and everything will be fine, but, well . . . forgive me." She turned away and reached for a handkerchief to dab at her eyes.

Nancy put her arm around the older woman. "Please don't apologize. I understand completely. How are Jeb and the twins this morning?"

"Terrified. My husband took Jeb off to the hardware store. A friend asked the girls to come over for the morning and stay for lunch, but only Mia would go. Sarah is in her room. A television reporter tried to interview her when she and Peach went out to get the paper today and he scared her to death."

"Oh, dear. Why did it have to be Sarah?"

"I know. I worry about her the most. She hardly speaks—"

The jarring sound of the phone interrupted them. The women looked at each other with fear, hope, and uncertainty colliding in their eyes.

"I'll get it," Nancy said.

"I'll check on Sarah," Grace replied as Nancy picked up the phone.

"Foyles' residence."

"Ah seen her," a female voice said.

"What?" Nancy scrambled for a pencil and noted the time on the tablet by the phone.

"Ah seen her. Dat lady dat's been missin' "

"Where?" Nancy was breathless.

"She in my neighborhood. In the crazy boy's house."

Could this call be on the level? Nancy squeezed her eyes shut and hoped.

"Ah gotta go now, but ah seen her."

"Wait! Please! Who are you? Tell me where you live! Hello? Hello?" Nancy continued to hold the phone, even after the dial tone buzzed in her ear.

"They hung up on you, didn't they?" Grace asked as she entered the kitchen.

"Yes! Why wouldn't she talk to me?"

"Oh, Nancy, I'm afraid it's because she had nothing more to say. We've had dozens of these calls. They're the worst, the cruelest. They tell you they've seen her, give you a tiny scrap of information, and then hang up."

"But, but, this one sounded so real."

"I know, dear. They all do. Just make note of what was said and the detective will check it out." She picked up the teapot and poured the fragrant liquid into cups.

They moved in unison to sit at the table. Nancy sipped her tea and reached to cover Grace's hand with hers. Except for the sparrows chirping on the Carolina jasmine vines outside the window, all else was silent. The phone rang again and Nancy answered it.

"That was Mrs. Chester, the principal at the elementary school," she told Grace after she hung up the phone. As Nancy further related the details of the conversation, her mind kept darting back to the first call. "A crazy boy's house." What did that mean?

"Baby, it's been days since I've seen you." Beth Mc-Kinnon closed the door to John's office, and crossed the room to throw herself in his arms. She kissed him passionately. John returned her kiss and then gently pushed her away.

"That was some greeting! I missed you, too. You're not usually like this at the office." John stepped away and moved behind his desk that was piled high with memos, reports, printouts, and file folders. "What a mess. I feel like I've been out of step here for weeks instead of days."

Beth joined him behind the desk and put her arms around his waist. "Hey, it's okay. You've had an incredible time. What's the news on your wife?"

"Nothing. The police are working on it. The guy they've assigned to the case seems sharp enough, but, so far . . ." John lifted his hands and then dropped them. "So far, nothing!"

"You'd think with all the available technology, finding one person would not be a big deal." Beth tightened her arms and tried to engage him in another kiss.

"My kids are wild. And her parents? I die a little every time I see them. I ask myself how long any of us is going to be able to handle this, and I just don't know." He broke free of her arms and walked to the window. He had always been so proud of his corner office with its magnificent view of downtown Dallas, but now he hardly noticed where he was.

Beth followed him. She put her hand on his face and turned it toward her. "Baby, I can't stand to see you hurting this way. You've got to let some of this go. These people will find your wife. I'm worried about you." She kissed his mouth. "Just for a few hours, baby, let it go. Why don't we grab an early lunch? We could have a picnic at my place." She kissed him again.

"You know, I think that's the best offer I've had in days. You go on and I'll meet you there in about twenty minutes."

They kissed again.

"Don't be late," she said as she crossed the room and let herself out the door.

"David, I'm sorry I'm late," Randy said as he slid into the booth.

"No problem. You're doing me a favor just by being here."

"I told you I'd try to keep you posted," Randy said, nodding to the waitress who appeared to take their order. He felt a bit odd talking about finding Monica not with her husband, but with a man he suspected might love her more.

While they waited for their lunch, Randy filled David in on his visit to Town Park Eight and his confrontation with Phil Bruns, the manager.

"What a sweetheart that guy is! Belligerent as hell and practically no help. The place is so big that fifteen to twenty kids do the day shifts, sometimes twice that many at night and on weekends. They all work odd hours and half the time they can't remember who worked which shift. The records that guy keeps, or at least the ones he showed to me, are worthless."

"Did anyone recognize her picture?" asked David, lifting his arms from the table as their food arrived.

"Not a soul, but like I said, it's a big place with a lot of people. We'd have to be damned lucky to get a positive I.D." Randy shook the ketchup bottle as if it were somebody's neck and doused his french fries.

"Doesn't the manager have a list of the people who worked last Wednesday afternoon?"

"He hauled me up to his office and with great reluctance gave me a list of the people who were supposed to work that day. He didn't have a shift breakdown, and according to him, the kids swap times so often that it's tough to get an accurate account of who's on duty at any one time."

David's food remained untouched. He took a swallow of tea and nearly gagged. Damn! He'd sugared it twice again. "Do you really think he runs that loose a ship?" he asked.

"Hell, no! I'd bet the guy's a goddamned tyrant. He runs seven shifts a day. He probably has his fingers on every kid and every dime that passes through the place."

"Why isn't he being more helpful then?" David asked as he poured ketchup on his fries. Then, staring at his plate, he shook his head in disgust. He hated ketchup, never ate it on anything. He pushed the plate away.

"Good question, and one I can't answer. I checked him out. He's clean, so he's either cop-shy, hiding something, or just an asshole." Randy picked up his milk shake and downed it in three gulps.

"Has John heard anything? How're the calls coming?" asked David.

"Nothing really. I stopped by his place last night between visits to the theater. His wife's parents are in town. Nice people."

"I've never met them."

"They're great with the kids. John's handling the press, and friends are around to man the phone, but you can tell the old people are ripped up as hell inside."

Randy saw the same naked anguish on David's face that he had seen on the faces of Monica's parents. "You okay?" he asked. "Something the matter with your lunch?"

"I'm just wishing, like everyone else, this nightmare was over."

"I got a possible lead this morning at Circle Triplex

Theater," Randy said. He had to give his friend some hope. "That's the other ticket stub you found in her pocket."

David nodded. "I remember."

"I went over there this morning. Looked around, thinking, another dead end. Then the eleven o'clock shift comes on and I show them Monica's picture. Suddenly, one girl recognizes her and says she's sure Monica was there last Wednesday. The girl remembered her being there at other times, too. Says she loves Monica's hair . . . yeah, I know it sounds fishy," he said in answer to David's questioning look, "but she was so sure. Said she also remembers her eyes. They must be a memorable shade of green."

"Yes, they are," David replied quietly.

"No one else recognized her, but we've got two things in our favor."

"What are they?"

"First, they're showing a murder flick, plenty of blood and bodies, and second, Wednesday afternoon's showing of that movie was a disaster."

"How so?" David picked up the check and the men walked to the cash register.

"There were an unusually large number of kids at the show. Gang members or something, the theater people said. Whoever put the show together had one reel upside down. Evidently they hadn't previewed it. The girl I talked to said all hell broke loose when it wasn't fixed immediately. The kids threw cups of popcorn and soda at the screen. When that started, a few people got up and left. Some demanded their money back and others just disappeared."

"So anything could have happened during the fracas?"

"The assistant manager called the police to clear the theater. Must have been some matinee."

"If somebody wanted to grab her, he couldn't have asked for a better smoke screen," David said.

"That's right. The police booked eight of the hoodlums. Three are still in jail. I spoke briefly with them this morning. That's why I was late meeting you."

"Any leads?" David asked as they stepped outside. "Maybe one of them knows where she is?" His anger soared. "If some punk has his hands on her . . ."

"I don't know, David. I'm going back after lunch to talk to them again, maybe set up a lie detector test. These guys are real pros, though. Not much shakes them up."

"How old are they?" David wanted to know.

"One's seventeen, one's nineteen, and the other's being held in Juvenile. He's fourteen." Randy shielded his eyes with sunglasses and tossed his keys up and down, catching them in his palm.

"Pros at fourteen?" David asked.

"Sometimes the world just plain sucks, my friend." Randy gave David a quick slap on the arm and got into his car. "I'll be in touch."


An hour passed, and then another. Nancy answered the phone calls and Grace cleaned the pantry to pass the time. Mrs. Chester had delivered a mountain of food and had stayed to visit for a while. After she left, Sarah helped her grandmother and Nancy sort out and put away the food.

"I know whose tin that is," Sarah said, tapping the lid of a bright, hand-painted can. "It's Mrs. Edwards. She's my reading teacher."

"What did she make for you?" asked Nancy.

Sarah removed the lid and lifted the waxed paper to reveal large sugar cookies dotted with candies. A note with Sarah's name on it was tucked in the paper.

"Mrs. Edwards wants to take me with her when she goes to the mall today. I'm supposed to call her."

"How special, Sarah! Would you like to go with her?" asked Grace.

"I can't! I can't ever leave here!" Sarah exclaimed and ran out of the room.

Both women started after her, but stopped when the door opened and Jeb and William came into the kitchen.

Jeb greeted them and sat down to pet Peach. William took one look at Grace's face and went to her.

"What's happened?"

"It's Sarah." She introduced him to Nancy and together they told him what had just occurred.

"I'll go talk to her," he replied quietly. "Guess John's not home yet." He didn't wait for an answer.

Halfway to the staircase, he heard the phone ring. He retraced his steps to the kitchen in time to hear Nancy say, "Yes, this is the Foyles' residence." He waited as she verified the caller's name, address, and phone number, assuming it was one more of the numerous, useless calls they'd already received.

Then he looked at her face. She was grinning from ear to ear.

# chapter
# 28

A bit of mottled daylight filtered through the skylights, allowing Monica to see around the attic. Was he still home? Her bedside oil lamp had been turned off, but she hadn't seen him since he took her to the bathroom what seemed like several hours ago. Was he planning to starve her, or let her die from thirst? She hadn't had anything to drink since yesterday and her empty stomach ached.

She called his name. There was no answer. She rattled her handcuff against the metal frame, and rolled back and forth on the mattress so that the bed springs screeched and the bed scraped and thumped on the floor. Where could he be?

Airplanes flew over the house. Monica counted seven in a row. She listened for the sounds of birdsong or children playing, but heard nothing except the planes. The rain had stopped. At this moment, her children might be outside riding bikes or roller blading. Or were they inside, sitting quietly, their lives on hold until her return? Did they think she had abandoned them? Might they be more hurt or angry at her absence than worried? What she would give to see them, to hold them, if only for a few moments! She pulled at her handcuff, rattling it back and forth along the metal post. Tears stung her eyes and ran down her face.

"Oh, why? Why has this happened to me?" she sobbed

over and over until the mattress beneath that side of her face was soaked and she dozed off from exhaustion.

"Daddy?" she whimpered in her sleep. "Have you come to take care of my children? You have to, Daddy. John can't do it alone." She awoke and began to cry again, as she imagined her children might be crying for her.

Would her dad be holding up? After his heart attack last summer, he had seemed so frail at Christmas. Her mother was getting older, too. She loved them both. Her disappearance would ruin their lives. She rubbed away another flood of tears that came to her eyes.

"Stop it!" she told herself. "Concentrate! Concentrate on the immediate problem. That's the only thing that will help. You've got to outwit Lenny."

Finally, she heard him on the steps and turned her head toward the door. Despite her need for sustenance, now that he was coming to her, she was suddenly terrified. How would he behave? Would he hurt her again?

When he appeared in front of her, he seemed strangely subdued. His hair needed combing and his work clothes looked as though he had slept in them. Obviously, he had just gotten out of bed.

"Good morning, Mother," he whispered. "I overslept. I'll take you right to the bathroom and get you something to eat." He uncuffed her and helped her sit up, but refused to meet her eyes.

"I thought you'd forgotten me."

"Never, Mother. Let's go now."

He led her down the steps and allowed her to close the bathroom door while he waited in the hall. As she splashed water on her face, he called out, "There's a new toothbrush in the medicine cabinet for you. The toothpaste is beside it."

She didn't know why he was being so nice to her, but she knew from experience his mood could change without warning. She quickly cleaned her teeth. Then she used a dingy rag to scrub her hands and face, moving carefully around the bandage on her cheek. The gauze circling her palm was wet and so she pulled it off. Her hand ached, but the bleeding had stopped.

When she returned to the hallway, it was empty. She peered in the direction of the living room. Nobody. She thought she heard him in the kitchen. Stepping down the hall, she stopped between the two closed doors.

She chose the door on the left and opened it. Lenny's room. The double bed was unmade. One of the bed pillows and a faded patchwork quilt lay scrambled together on the bare, wooden floor. Piles of dirty laundry stood in the corners and a musty odor met her nostrils. Beneath a dark, shaded window, she saw a small table covered with a white towel. Several colors of nail lacquer, a bottle of polish remover, jars of cream, scissors, files, and other manicure paraphernalia lay on top of the towel.

Her eyes lingered on the scissors. Could she use them to kill him? No, they would only injure him. When she made her move, she needed something that would kill. Once again the thought that she could end someone's life amazed her. Was she as crazy as he was? Perhaps, she decided as she looked around his room.

The rest of the room was a mess, but everything on the table was in perfect order. A collage of crudely cut magazine pictures featuring hands and gloves covered the wall in front of the bed. Monica shivered and backed out of the room, looking toward the kitchen to see if Lenny was still there.

She opened the other door. At first she thought it might be a young girl's room, given the youthful appearance of white furniture covered with flounces and frills. Then she peeked behind the closet door and saw a motley assortment of women's clothing and shoes that reminded her of the castoffs her great aunt had once given her to play dress up. The clothes were anything but childish. The dresses Monica wore and the clothes in this closet had been chosen by the same person.

A pale pink organdy counterpane covered a bed heaped with faded pink and green ruffled pillows. The room, like the clothes in the closet, had a distinctive odor: a combination of cloying sweetness and mildew. The dressing table and stool were covered in ruffles matching those of the bedspread and pillows. All the fabrics in the room looked tired and badly in need of a wash.

On the tabletop was a vase of long-dead roses, bottles and jars, cannisters of face powder and makeup, hairbrushes, combs, and two hand mirrors clustered around an old cedar box with the faintly legible words OZARK MOUNTAINS painted on its top. Monica lifted the lid and saw a garish collection of tarnished costume jewelry and several photographs. She reached out to pick one up—

"Do you miss your old room?" Lenny pushed himself away from the door frame where he had watched her reacquaint herself with her bedroom. He ran his hands through his hair, nervously smoothing it down, and then plunged them into his jacket pockets.

Monica jumped. "I-I-I . . . uh, you scared me!"

Now she was in real trouble. She should have waited for him in the hall instead of snooping around. Before he could throw her out, she scanned the walls and found a midsized window, large enough for her to fit through, curtained in pale pink fabric with flounced edges. She pushed aside the ratty pink sheers, and pulled on the sash. The blind rattled up and spun around its top rod. She could see into an ill-kept yard bordered by a chain-link fence.

For the first time she realized that they were on the second floor. Did anyone live beneath him? She saw another house behind the fence and got a quick glimpse of a street. As she memorized the scene, Lenny crossed the room, reached under the top ruffle framing the window and yanked the dirty white shade down to the sill.

"Too much sunlight is bad for the complexion. Isn't that what you always said, Mother?"

"Well, uh, yes, I guess." Monica turned away in anguish. For a moment, she had been close to the world outside. She bowed her head and cradled her broken arm.

"Oh, please, Mother, please don't be sad." Lenny started toward her, but stopped when he saw her flinch and pull away, her eyes awash with pain.

"I'm sorry. I know you can never understand why I did it. I can't explain it, either. It just happened." Lenny reached out his arms to her. "Please, forgive me!"

Monica refused to look at him. "H-how can you ask me that after what you've done to me?"

"I know I have no right to ask you for anything, but in a way you do owe me. I brought you back here. Be grateful for that."

"Grateful, Lenny? Grateful that you've chained me in the attic? That you've beaten me, cut my hair off, and made my life a living hell?"

"All right! You win! I promise I'll never look at Susan again!" He circled the room several times like a caged tiger, then kicked over the dressing table stool, and threw himself on the daybed in the corner. Monica shrank from him. The motion was not lost on Lenny. He lowered his voice, sat up and leaned forward.

"To show you how much I want you to forget last night ever happened between me and Susan, I'll let you back into your old room. You can choose your own clothes, wear your own jewelry, and be free to move about as long as I'm in the house."

Monica said nothing. Lenny looked at her face and saw her eyes considering his penance. This was going to work out better than he had hoped. Mother had been hurt and humiliated, naturally, but she wasn't going to be vengeful. It felt good to see how jealous Mother was over the incident. He stood up and slowly removed his jacket and unbuttoned his shirt to expose his naked chest. Lifting his hands, he crossed them and allowed them to lie flat on his skin so that she could remember their beauty.

"I'm still here for you. No matter what you might imagine, Mother, everything you see is yours," he said.

"You mean it? I can stay in this . . . my room?" Was this perhaps the first ray of light at the end of her tunnel?

Lenny snorted and checked his nails. She hadn't acknowledged his exceptional hands or given him the adoration he craved, but he would let it go. He dared not press his luck after what he had done with Susan.

"If that's what you want. I was going to move you down here soon, anyway." He pulled off his shirt and walked toward her.

Monica steeled herself not to flinch when he touched her. When his hands settled lightly on her shoulders, she swayed, but forced herself to concentrate and count the heartbeats she saw in his neck. She felt his left hand leave her shoulder and glide across her scalp.

"Even without all your hair, you are still beautiful to me, Mother. You think I only care about your outward appearance." His other hand left her shoulder and crawled up to circle the contours of her face. "No, I love all of you. Do you want to see what I see when I look at you?" When she said nothing, the hands on her face and scalp tightened. "Answer me, Mother. Tell me you want to see yourself as I see you."

"No, I . . . don't. Please. You're hurting me again." Was this the time? Would he kill her?

"Oh, yes. You have no choice now." He turned her toward the large cheval glass that hung above the vanity. How had she missed the mirror when she was first alone in the room?

At the first sight of herself, her hair shorn, her face bruised and cut, her body swathed in a dress three sizes too large, she felt the wind leave her lungs in a rush. Sickened and defenseless, she closed her eyes and gasped for air, faintly aware that his arms were all that kept her upright.

"Open your green eyes, Mother." He slipped an arm

beneath her breasts and pulled her tightly against him. "Now you know how it feels to be ugly. I've been ugly all my life."

He rocked back and forth, holding her with one arm, caressing her head with his other hand. She saw through the haze of her pain that his eyes were closed and that his lips moved, though she could hear no sounds. They stayed in that eerie position for several moments until he stopped rocking and abruptly let her go.

"We need to eat, Mother. You must be starved. I'll go see what I can find." He headed toward the door. "Maybe sloppy joes. I haven't had a sloppy joe in a very long time."

# chapter
# 29

"John, this is Randy. What's up?"

"Nancy Crawford just called. She's been manning the home phones this morning. I think it's probably another crank, but she just got a call from a woman she's convinced is legit."

Randy, shifted some papers on his desk and pulled out his notebook and pen. "Tell me about it."

"A woman called. Said her son recognized Monica's picture from a flyer. The boy says he saw her at the Town Park Eight last Wednesday."

"Anything else?"

"Says she was sick, all bent over and moaning. She asked him and his friend to get her some help."

Randy kept writing. "You got a name?"

"Yeah, Allyson Farrell. Lives on University."

"Hang on a minute." Randy double-checked her phone and house numbers before allowing John to continue.

"Where'd the kids say they found her?"

"They sneaked into *Deathstalk*."

"Who'd they get to help her?"

"Some kid at the popcorn counter. He gave them hell for switching theaters. Rubbed them hard. The kids really remember him."

"John, this could be a dead end or the break we've been

waiting for." Despite himself, Randy's excitement was building.

"Guess you're on your way to check it out?"

"I'll call you when I know something."

"Thanks."

"Sure, John." He disconnected John and punched the number on University. A woman answered on the first ring.

"Mrs. Farrell?"

"Yes?"

"This is Randy Abbott. I'm the detective investigating Monica Foyles's disappearance. May I stop by in a few minutes?"

"Certainly. My son and I will be home all day."

"Mr. Bruns?"

"Yeah, Mark? Make it fast. I'm busy."

"Can we talk a minute?"

Phil looked at his newest assistant manager. The boy looked rattled and he was usually Mr. Cool. His low-key demeanor and his ability to think on his feet were the major reasons Phil had promoted him.

"Help me finish unloading these reels I brought this morning," Phil ordered. Since he lived near the central distribution center, Phil often stopped by there on his way to work and picked up films. He continued out the rear door, assuming Mark would follow him.

"Uh, this is pretty important, Mr. Bruns." Mark stood at the back of Phil's station wagon, but made no move to heft the cases from the car.

"Help me with the reels, goddammit, and then we'll talk."

"Yes, sir."

When the last case was on the film room floor, Phil pulled off his jacket and scanned the clipboards hanging from the projectors. He double-checked that Lenny had accurately recorded the start and finish times from the previous night.

Satisfied that the kid had, for once, done his job correctly, he turned to Mark. "So, what's on your mind?"

"That police detective was here again about twenty minutes ago. He talked to Susan and me, but he really wanted to see you."

"What the hell did he want this time?"

"It's about that woman who disappeared, you know the one whose picture is on the bulletin board?"

"Yeah, yeah, what about her?" Phil put his hands on his hips. "Jesus Christ! Doesn't he have anything better to do than come around bothering us? People are dying in the streets and he's here checking out Susan's tits."

"He had a description of somebody who helped this lady at our theater, on the day she disappeared." Mark could feel the sweat trickle down his back. He had heard about the boss's temper, but had never experienced it firsthand.

"The hell you say! One of my people?" He walked over and kicked one of the film cases. The latches held, but the case toppled over and smacked onto the floor.

"Yes, sir," answered Mark, taking a step toward the door.

Phil followed him and stuck his fist into the air. "Who'd he finger? The new kid?"

"N-no, sir, I'm pretty sure it was, it was Lenny he described."

"Lenny!" he yelled. "Where is that son of a bitch? Find him and get him in here, right now!" Phil paced the floor between the cases and the door. "If he's done anything to hurt the reputation of my place, I'll kill him!"

"He's not here. He doesn't come in 'til five," Mark edged closer to the door until his back was against it and he could feel the knob punching his backside.

"Dammit! What'd you tell the fuzz?"

"Nothing really. Susan and I just listened. We didn't know what to say." Mark related the details to Phil, who was growing more infuriated by the second.

"I'll kill that little shit! I swear I'll kill him for putting the cops on us!"

Mark watched the man storming around the room, hating that he had been the one to bring the news. "There's more, Mr. Bruns."

"What?" This time Phil spoke in a whisper, even more intimidating than his shouting had been.

"The newspaper. They sent a reporter who asked a lot of questions. Evidently the woman's husband told them about the ticket stub they found in some of her things."

"And what did you tell him?" The whisper continued.

"N-Nothing, sir. I told him he'd have to talk to you. He left his number. He wants you to call him."

"Fuck it! The cops and the press, too! Killing is too good for that shit-assed kid!"

The roar was back. Mark was sure everyone on the second floor could hear Phil.

"So," Mark said, trying to keep the tremor out of his voice, "you'll need to call the detective and the reporter ASAP. Their cards are on your desk. The detective was insistent that you call him the minute you came in." Mark opened the door. "Joe's waiting on me," he said, referring to the third assistant manager besides Lenny and himself. "I better get back to work."

Phil did not even hear him leave. He was pulling the pockets out of his jacket, looking for his keys and cursing Lenny. Finding his key ring, he slammed across the hall and into his office, nearly knocking Susan down in his rush.

"That damned little shit! I'm gonna teach his hide a lesson it'll never forget." Phil threw his coat on his desktop and unlocked the lower drawer on the left. He rummaged beneath some papers and withdrew a revolver and a small cardboard box. The box top stuck and he swore again as he ripped the lid off the box and threw it against the wall.

"Mr. Bruns," Mark said, moving next to Susan at the doorway, "there's another reporter down—" He stopped and pushed Susan behind him when he saw the gun in Phil's hands.

"Get rid of him!" Phil snarled. He shoved the gun into his jacket pocket and pushed by them to get to the stairs.

# chapter
# 30

"It's time now, Mother. You've kept me waiting long enough." Lenny and Monica had just finished lunch.

"Don't you have to work on Saturday?"

"Yeah, but not until five. I got the late shift again tonight. We have all afternoon together."

Lenny threw his fork on the table and stood up. When he had approached her before in her room, she'd pleaded hunger. Though his appetite for her body was far greater than any he had for food, he had allowed her to eat first. He grilled two cheese sandwiches and opened a can of corn. She nibbled at her corn and he ate both of the sandwiches.

As the meal ended, fear splintered down her spine. She shredded the paper napkin in her lap with one hand.

"Lenny, no. Oh, please, no. Don't do this to me!" she cried, as he pulled her from her chair to stand beside him. He had left his shirt in the other room. A light film of sweat covered his chest.

"What's wrong?" he asked her, perplexed by her hesitancy. "You've never acted like this before. You're usually the one who can't wait." He pulled her close and pressed the side of her face against his chest and rocked back and forth with her in his arms. He was so much taller than her that her forehead rubbed on the sharps ridge of his collar bone.

She watched three droplets of perspiration start at the base of his throat and meander down his body to catch in the hair between his nipples. She tried to think of something to say, something that would stop him, but his hold tightened into a death grip until she could barely breathe.

"Len-ny, my arm. You're h-hurting m-me—"

"God, I want you so much. I've waited a long time to hold you like this. Tell me you want me. Tell me!" He pulled the knot loose in the scarf that held her arm and whipped it off her neck.

"I can't. I don't. Lenny, I'm not who you think I am. My name is Mon—"

His mouth covered hers. She struggled, and with one good arm, tried to fight him, but got nowhere. When she felt her dress being ripped down her back, she opened her mouth to cry out. He quickly thrust his tongue between her lips.

She gagged at its intrusion, her body bucked, and she thought surely she would vomit. Lenny felt her response and lifted his head, his breath coming in short gasps that made it difficult for him to talk.

"What the hell's the matter with you?"

"No, no!" She coughed and heaved between sobs. "Please don't hurt me."

Frustrated and angry, Lenny yanked the dress and slip from her body. He lifted her into his arms and carried her, kicking and flailing through the house to her faded pink room. Why was she struggling? She was acting as if this were her first time. In the past, she had always liked it rough; she liked being the aggressor, too. Was that it? Did she want to call the shots? Fuck it, he decided. She was going to get it his way for once. He had earned it.

Monica hit the bed with a scream. He followed her down and covered her small body with his. She felt his erection, his hands on her naked body, and pulled her knees together.

"Touch me, Mother. Touch me, touch me," he moaned.

Monica worked a hand free and tried to push him off, but he grabbed her hand and ground it against his fly. The metal teeth of the zipper caught the already injured flesh of her palm and she cried out.

Lenny mistook her cry of pain for one of delight and sank into a realm of pleasure. She was truly his at last. He raised up and pulled his belt loose and tried to undo his pants.

"Oh, God, oh, God, I'm coming, Mother. Help me!"

With her last ounce of strength, Monica grabbed the top of his fly and held it closed. He bucked and squirmed under her hold. He was losing control and she pulled her knee between his legs and rubbed him hard. In moments, it was over. Semen soaked the front of his pants. She jerked her hand away and started to cry. He slumped into her neck and gasped, his body jerking in spasms.

"Sorry," he panted. "The first one always comes fast. Let me rest a minute and I'll be ready to go again." He rolled off her and yawned. "Maybe next time I'll use the gloves. Or the ropes . . ." He yawned and pulled her tightly against him, anchoring her with his arm. To ensure her closeness, he threw his large leg over hers, pinning her body to the bed.

Monica lay motionless, afraid to move lest she get him started again, torn between miserable relief and terror that this episode could be the first of many to come. Moving only her eyes, she searched the room, trying to find something she could use as a weapon. Would "Mother" have a long, sharp hat pin? A letter opener? Maybe she had a knife, or even better, a revolver. Monica imagined holding Lenny at gunpoint or sticking a knife through his heart. Could she kill him if it came to that? Absolutely, she decided.

Moments passed. She tried to work herself free of him, but when she shifted, he awakened and pulled her closer. His fingers caressed her forehead, and cheeks.

"Your eyes kept you alive for me, Mother," he whispered.

"Even after you went away, after we put you into the ground, your eyes never left me. They watched me constantly. But sometimes," he paused and closed his hand around her neck, "I hated them. They taunted me during the bad times, watched me."

Monica lay quietly, praying his hand would stop tightening on her throat. Little by little he was cutting off her wind.

"I should hate you for the misery you brought me before and after you left. How was it in hell, Mother? Surely, that's where you've been all this time until you turned up at the theater." The pitch of his voice grew higher, his tone accentuated with an eerie breathiness. "You enjoyed teasing me on Wednesday afternoons, didn't you? Pretending you didn't know me, when you were just waiting for me to bring you home." His eyes glowed with a strange light, and his hand slipped away from her neck and dropped to her breast. "You always were a flirt, weren't you?"

"The theater? I only go to the matinees on my day off, when my kids are in school," she whispered.

Monica tried to shift away from him. He was changing before her eyes. His muscles bulged and his arms became like bands of steel around her body, cutting off her circulation. Her flesh burned where his fingers touched her.

"Don't lie to me, bitch! I know dammed well why you were at the theater each week. You wanted me to beg, to grovel at your feet. You wanted me to lust after your body until I ached." He sat up and pulled her up with him, shaking her hard. "Never again. I'll never ache again."

He laughed then, a high-pitched screech that scared her almost as much as his hand leaving her body to rip open his pants and pull them off his legs.

"Now, Mother, time for the second round . . ." And he slammed his mouth over hers, forcing her back across the bed.

Monica tightened her lips and tried to pull away. He

easily caught her and fastened his mouth to her nipple. She screamed and bit his hand when he clapped it over her mouth. Simultaneously, they heard the loud knocking at the door.

"Lenny! Lenny! I know you're in there, kid. Let me in. I want to talk to you!"

The pounding increased. Lenny tensed on top of her. As the hammering continued, she felt the strength seeping out of him. He jumped off the bed and awkwardly pulled on his clothes, like a child covering up a misdeed. When he was dressed, he turned to her and grabbed her throat. The madman was back.

"You make one sound and I promise I'll kill you. Stay in this bed and go to sleep. You can't get away. The window is nailed shut and the door will be locked. Disobey and you're dead." He yanked back her hair. The pounding continued.

"Let me in, kid. I'm tellin' you, let me in!"

"Hang on a minute. I'm gettin' some clothes on," Lenny yelled back. He stuffed one of his socks into Monica's mouth and gaged her with the scarf he pulled from the lamp shade. Opening a drawer in the nightstand beside the bed, he lifted out three lengths of white rope. In one motion he grabbed her legs and bound them together and used a second piece of rope to tie her feet to the bed post. He left her broken arm free, but fastened the other hand to the bed before he pulled the bed clothing out from under her.

"You never left *me* a blanket, Mother. While I'm gone, maybe you can think of a way to earn it back."

Monica lay sprawled on the mattress, naked and tied fast to the bed. He looked at her and grinned before running out the door. She heard the key turn in the lock just before the pounding started again.

"Took you long enough, kid. Where the hell were you? Doin' your nails?" Phil's sneer turned nasty when he saw the slip and torn dress on the floor. "What's your mother's stuff doin' out here? Didn't I tell you to get rid of 'em? Or are you still wearing them?" He moved closer to Lenny until their bodies touched. "Are you missing me?" Phil rubbed the boy's crotch, feeling the slight stiffening of the boy's penis at his touch. "Hoping I might come back? Huh? Maybe it's my turn to wear the dress."

Lenny quickly stooped and picked up the clothing. He wadded them up and stuffed them into a kitchen drawer before Phil could see that the dress had been ripped down the back. "I needed some rags last night. Spilled a bottle of soda."

"Oh, so rather than give her things away to someone who could wear 'em, you're usin' 'em to mop up the goddamned floor. Real smart." He cuffed Lenny on the back of the head, then looked around the kitchen. "God, this place is a mess. You live like a pig."

Lenny turned to the table and shoved the plates and glasses together, hoping that Phil wouldn't notice that there were two place settings. He picked up the dishes and carried them to the sink while Phil stormed around the room.

"Whatcha been up to, kid? You've been on your own a year now. I've kept my part of the bargain and stayed away, but every time I turn my head, you get into trouble." Phil moved closer to Lenny.

Lenny stopped stacking the dishes and looked at his uncle. "I don't follow you."

"You don't follow me," Phil mimicked in a high falsetto voice. "You and that damned fancy language you always spit out. Your mother's responsible for it. I warned her a hundred times that teaching you to talk that way would only make you think you were better than everybody else. Well, you ain't, kid. You're trash, just like your old man was."

"Why're you here?" Lenny asked.

"I needed to ask you a few questions, and seein' you ain't got a phone, here I am."

"What questions? I'm already working late tonight." Lenny heard a thump from the back of the house and wondered what Mother was doing. He checked to see if Phil had heard it, too, but the man was helping himself to a can of soda from the refrigerator.

"The cops were back this morning, kid." Phil licked his lips and popped the top on his cola.

"So?"

"Seems they got a call from a lady who says her son saw that missing woman. You know, we got her picture on the board, at the theater. Recognized her from a flyer his mom found on her car yesterday. He remembered seein' her 'cause she was sick or something. She asked the kid and his friend to get some help."

Lenny watched his uncle's tongue circle his mouth and said, "What do dumb kids know about anything?"

"Well"—Phil's tongue made two more laps—"This dumb kid put the finger on you. Said you're the one they went to for help."

"I don't remember helping any sick woman. Musta been Mark or Jeff."

"Happened this past Wednesday. I checked the work schedules. Mark was inventoryin' the cups and candy with me, and Jeff didn't come on until six. Puts the finger on you, smart ass. The kid described you right down to your sissy hands. Now you want to tell me what's going on, or should I just turn you over to the cops? They'll get you talkin'. "

"Okay, so I helped a woman to her car. Big deal!"

Phil swore and grabbed the front of Lenny's shirt. "You're damned right it's a big deal. A customer gets sick in my place and I'm not told about it? Now the police are crawlin' all over my face. Shit! Even a dumb ass like you knows to report stuff like that!"

His uncle was so close that Lenny could count the

white patches on the underside of his tongue as it made another turn around his narrow lips. "I thought she was better. I just forgot to tell you about it." He stepped back and shrugged Phil's hand off him.

"So where do you think she is now? Good-looking cunt like that? Far as the police go, you were the last person to see her before she disappeared." Phil followed Lenny back a step and punched him in the shoulder. "You'd like to bring trouble down on me and my theater, wouldn't you, kid?" He gave Lenny another punch, this time to the stomach. "What'd you do to her? Take her out for a quick piece, huh? You tired of beatin' off in the storage room?"

Lenny's eyes widened. Phil laughed and hit him again. "Think I didn't know about that? Geez, kid, the whole place knows you're jackin' off in the corn. If I thought I could make any money, I'd sell tickets. Only I doubt anyone would be interested in such a disappointin' performance." Another punch to the stomach, and another lap around the lips.

Lenny groaned as the last punch knocked the wind out of him. He slumped to the floor, trying to catch his breath. Phil's grinning face loomed over him, his eyes spewing hatred.

"How was she, huh, kid? Did she come fast and hard like your mama used to? Did she?"

Phil pulled back to kick Lenny, but the younger man caught the foot before it connected. Lenny twisted it around and pushed his weight against his uncle's leg. Phil lost his balance. Lenny jumped up and kicked him in the groin. Phil yelled and fell to his knees. Before he could grab his crotch, Lenny pushed him to the floor and straddled him. He snatched Phil's hands and pinned them above the man's head.

"You filthy sonofabitch. Don't you ever talk about my mother like that!"

"Kid," wheezed Phil, "you got two seconds to get off me or you're dead."

"I'm real worried, old man." Lenny squeezed his fingernails into his uncle's wrists until blood oozed out and ran down into the sleeves of his jacket.

"Get off me and don't tell me what I can say about your fucking mother! I've had her, too, so I'm the expert here."

Suddenly, a woman's scream echoed from beyond the hallway. "Help me! Please help me! Help me!"

Phil used the break in Lenny's concentration to work one of his hands free. He pulled the gun from his pocket and shoved it into Lenny's side. The boy fell back and Phil rolled out from under him. Lenny sat up, but not in time to avoid Phil's uppercut to his chin with the butt of the gun. Lenny slumped to the floor.

"Who's back there in that room?" Phil yelled. "You got her, don't you?"

"You heard somebody outside," Lenny said, shaking his head.

Monica screamed again and again. The men struggled over the gun. Phil grabbed Lenny's hand and slammed it to the floor. Lenny cried out and reached for Phil's face. Phil ducked, kneed Lenny in the stomach, and stood up. Lenny doubled over and lay on the floor.

"I'm gettin' her, you hear! She's comin' with me! You're going to jail where you belong, you worthless piece of shit."

Phil kicked Lenny in the ribs. "I'd like to kill you right now, but I know how much the boys in prison'll love your tight little ass. My loss is their gain!" Another kick. "Now I'm gettin' her. She's mine, kid." Phil turned and pocketed the gun.

Lenny rolled to his feet. In a flash, all pain and the last of his sanity fled. He crouched like an animal, growling and shrieking, and circled his uncle. As Phil looked around, Lenny seized his uncle's shoulders and threw him to the floor.

On the way down, the man's forehead smashed against the corner of the table. Blood gushed through his hair. He moaned and reached for his head, but Lenny jumped on him, twisting his hands away and pummeling his face until his uncle's features disappeared under a deluge of blood. Phil cried out and reached for his gun. Lenny pulled the weapon out of his fingers and threw it across the floor. Phil's hands tried to ward off the blows that landed on his ribs and stomach, but he was no match for the younger man.

Lenny continued his relentless, methodical beating long after Phil stopped resisting. "She'll never be yours! We're safe from you now. Tell me you'll never touch her again! Never touch me again, either! Tell me, you bastard! Tell me!"

Phil remained silent. Lenny beat him harder, pulling the bloody head up and smashing it against the floor, over and over again, until the back of the head split open and the man's life emptied onto the floor.

# chapter
# 31

Monica sat up and despite intense pain, used her broken arm to pull off her gag as soon as he left. Releasing her other arm was harder than anything she had ever done. The swollen fingers on her right hand refused to work quickly, and precious minutes went by before she was able to pick the knot.

The voices in the kitchen got louder. Were they threatening to take turns with her?

Her body's defenses kicked into high gear and she bent to untie her feet, then jumped off the bed and opened the closet door. Pulling out the first thing she touched, she slipped a sleeveless red tent dress over her head. Again, pain shot through her arm as she hurriedly buttoned the bodice.

She eyed the window and the door. Someone screamed in the kitchen. She pushed aside the sheers and opened the window shade. Sunlight jumped into the room, and just the sight of it shining on the grass below and bouncing off the tin rooftop of a shed refueled her.

Frantically, she pulled to open the window. Decorative iron grillwork covered the window on the outside. It wouldn't budge. She cursed the rusted nails sealing it shut. Could she break the glass?

Scuffling in the kitchen shook the walls. She ran to the door and listened. She could hear the men's hoarse, angry shouts but could not make out what they were saying. She rattled the door, even though she knew it was locked.

Terrified that they would come to her next, she ran back to the window and leaned on the sill. Suddenly a woman appeared in the backyard of the house beyond Lenny's fence. She had a basket of laundry under her arm and proceeded to hang it on the wash line.

Monica screamed, "Help me! Please help me! Help me!" and rapped on the window. The woman glanced her way, threw a shirt over the line and pinned it fast. Monica shouted and rapped on the window again. This time the woman didn't even look up.

In the distance a plane climbed into the sky. Monica recognized its identifying color and logo. Southwest Airlines flew from Dallas's Love Field. She was only ten miles from her home.

Loud thumping noises, punctuated with intermittent screams, continued in the other part of the apartment. Monica felt the walls and floors vibrate with the struggle. She backed away from the window and circled the room looking for a hiding place. Like a crazed animal, she ran back to the door, and tried it again. Suddenly, the thumping noise stopped. What was going on? Was he coming back? What would he do when he saw that she'd untied herself? She was sure he had heard her cries for help.

Desperately, she rifled through the drawers of the night stand, the dressing table, and the small chest behind the daybed for something . . . anything she might use to defend herself. Underwear, stockings, belts, and scarves, knit tops, and sweaters fell through her fingers. Two large drawers held nothing but gloves. A chest under the bed housed old letters, magazines, and a few, well-read, paperback romances. Time passed and still Lenny did not return, nor did she find a weapon. She returned to the door and placed her ear on the door panel, but heard nothing. Had the men left the house? She hadn't heard a door close.

Monica moved to the dressing table and flipped open the wooden jewelry box to look for a hat pin. There were none. As she had earlier, she picked up the small stack of photographs and saw that the top one pictured a much younger Lenny standing in a yard, holding a woman's hand.

She threw the photos onto the dressing table and then, in spite of her need for haste, bent and peered at the woman, thinking it might be "Mother." The old black-and-white photo gave no clues.

Suddenly she heard footsteps in the hall. She dashed to the closet to pick up a high-heeled shoe from the floor. Her shaking knees made standing any longer impossible and she sunk to the bed. She clenched the shoe behind her with her good hand. If they came through the door, she would use it.

The footsteps passed by her door without stopping. Shuffling noises continued toward the attic stairs. A door opened and closed. Silence.

Several minutes passed. Rapid footsteps retraced their path to her door. They paused. She held her breath and listened, breathing only when she heard them move down the hall. There were sounds of water running, and a door slamming. Was the other man leaving now? Had the visitor come only to yell and scream, and then leave?

She ran to the window to check on the woman hanging the wash. A line full of colored shirts danced in the breeze, but no one was around. Monica tried the window again, hoping for a miracle. Nothing happened. She pushed the vanity stool toward the window. Maybe she could use it to break the glass? But, then what?

"Dammit!" she cried. *The bars. I still can't get through the bars!*

In a few minutes, she heard swishing noises. Someone

was washing the floor. Was Lenny catching up on house-work? Hysterical laughter bubbled up in her throat.

The mopping passed by her doorway and paused at the attic steps. A door opened, and moments later, closed. The footsteps returned to the kitchen. Later, she heard running water in the bathroom. She was certain that he was alone.

Monica found the sheets and bedspread Lenny had torn from the bed. She lay across the bed to rest a moment, pulling the ragged spread around her body. She rubbed her fingers back and forth on her broken arm. The quiet was as terrifying as the shouting and brawling had been. When would he return? Exhaustion overcame her. Her mind and her body shut down, ignoring her pleas to stay alert.

The room was dark when she opened her eyes again. She sat up on the bed and listened for Lenny. The house was still quiet. Amazed that she had slept, she leaned over and turned on the bedside lamp.

She glanced around the bedroom and froze. A tray of food sat on the floor. He must have come and gone while she'd slept. Why hadn't he retied her to the bed? As she lifted the peanut butter sandwich and the cookies from the tray, she couldn't decide. Had she taken a step forward or backward?

Monica heard water running and thought John must have an early meeting. Either that or he wanted to be out of their bed before she awoke, knowing that no demands for intimacy could be made if he wasn't there. She resolved to force the issue today. If he wanted to end their marriage, then it was time to make some plans. Life was too short and too precious to waste on "if only" or "maybe one day."

She rolled over in bed and reached for her clock. Opening her eyes, she saw a faded pink coverlet. Her eyes closed and her hand stifled a cry. It was Sunday morning, and she was still in hell.

John was at home with the children. Was he moving Heaven and Earth to find her, not necessarily because he cared so much, but because he would feel it was expected of him? Just how far would he go, how much would he pay to have her back? He would make all the proper gestures for the children's sakes.

For years she had rationalized his selfish, often demeaning behavior toward her, making excuses for him, both to herself and to her friends and family. Now, everything seemed so simple. If she ever got out of here. . . .

Lenny opened the door. She yanked the cover to her chin and stared at him. His slick, wet hair changed his appearance. Standing there in the doorway, dressed in his work clothes, he looked older. Why had she ever thought he was a kid?

"Good morning, Mother. Did you sleep well in your old bedroom?"

"I need to use the bathroom."

"Of course. I'll be in the kitchen when you finish." Without another word he left her.

She slipped out of bed and went to the closet. The red dress she'd slept in was wrinkled and dirty. She pulled an elastic-waist blue-flowered skirt from a rusted hanger and closed the door. In one of the drawers she found a white, short-sleeved sweater and a plain cotton slip she thought might come close to fitting. She fingered through the underwear, but couldn't bring herself to wear any of it, even if it had been the right size.

She picked up the clothes and stood in the doorway, eying the lock. This was too easy. Something was up. Why wasn't he dogging her every move?

The bathroom door was minus the key, but she closed it to escape Lenny's prying eyes. She stripped off the red dress, took a quick bath, and dressed in the skirt and sweater. Her hand had swollen to twice its size, but she had grown used to its constant throbbing. Maybe Lenny would allow her to see a doctor. *When hell freezes over.* Perhaps "Mother" could insist.

Back in the pink bedroom, she ran a brush through her short hair. She went to the window. Since yesterday the panes of glass had been spray-painted white. She scratched her fingernail across the surface, hoping to scrape enough away so that she could see out, but it had been painted on the outside. When had he done this?

Walking down the hallway without him felt strange. She passed through the cluttered living room and found him in the kitchen, making pancakes. The griddle was ancient and he had made an unsavory mess. She thought about the last time she'd eaten pancakes with her children and lost her appetite.

"Thought we'd have something different before I go to work," Lenny said. He laid the spatula down and came to her. "I see you found something to wear. You always liked that skirt." He leaned over, nuzzled her neck, and pulled away laughing when he felt her flinch. "What? No perfume? Mother, I can't believe you forgot it. You used to bathe in it."

Monica forced herself to look at him. He seemed physically larger to her and more in charge than ever before. For a moment he reminded her a little of John, but then he leered at her and the similarity ended. When he finished his perusal of her body, their eyes met and held. She looked away first. Her skin felt clammy and soiled.

She sat down at the table. "What time is it?"

"Almost half past nine. I'm working the eleven to four shift today. It's my short day, and I have tomorrow off."

Lenny set a steaming plate of pancakes in front of her. When she looked up, he handed her the bottle of syrup and kissed her cheek.

"Mother, I want us to have a special dinner tonight. Can you think of anything you'd especially like?"

*Your head on a platter.*

She shook her head.

"Nothing? That's not like you. You were always full of suggestions when it came to food."

"I just want to go home."

"You are home." Lenny sat opposite her and doused his pancakes with syrup. "Let's change the subject."

"How about my arm? Can I see a doctor?"

"Your arm's a little bruised, nothing that won't heal on its own. There's some aspirin in the bathroom. You can take a couple of those."

"But Lenny, I—"

"Eat your breakfast and shut up about your arm. I got enough on my mind."

Monica picked at her food. The respite was over. She forced herself to eat, knowing she needed the food for strength. Terror squeezed her chest and darted to her stomach. So many questions ran through her mind. Why hadn't he punished her for untying herself and screaming out the window? Certainly the man who had come to the house yesterday had heard her cries. Is that why he and Lenny fought? What would Lenny do with her today? More time in the attic?

He stood up and carried his plate to the sink. Making no attempt to clean up the kitchen, he grabbed his jacket and pulled her out of the chair.

"Since you're not eating, we might as well get you set for the day."

He hustled her in and out of the bathroom and then threw her on the bed. "Move up so that your head is on the pillow and give me your hand." He pulled the handcuffs from his pocket and clipped them to her wrist and the tall bed post. Monica looked up and saw that the ball at the top of the post would keep the cuff in place.

"Why must I wear this?" she asked. "I can't go anywhere."

"Just making sure, Mother. Let's call it a compromise. You get to stay in your room."

"But, I—"

"Forget it. I'll see you at five. Think about what dress you'll wear for me tonight. Make it something sexy. I promise you a night you'll never forget." Leaning down he caught her chin in a firm grasp. His erotic kiss left nothing to her imagination.

Monica yanked at the cuff as he left. Her time was running short. Whether or not she was ready, she had to play her final card. *Yes, Lenny,* she said to herself, *"Mother" will be waiting for you all right. And eagerly. She's going to give you a very special night, indeed; more "Mother" than you ever dreamed of or will ever want or need again.* She smiled bitterly, feeling at last she had found a way out of her hell.

# chapter
# 32

Lenny's heartbeat quickened as he drove past Gaither Park on his way to the theater to see if Uncle Phil's car was still where he had ditched it last night. He was surprised to see it there at all. The neighborhood thugs were slipping. He looked around. The streets seemed empty. He stopped at a light and checked his rearview mirror. A police cruiser pulled up behind him.

He reached under the front seat of his car, and felt the sharp edges of the license plates he'd removed from Phil's car. He needed to get rid of them as soon as he could. What if the cop stopped him and wanted to search the car? The light changed to green. In his rush to get away, he pressed too hard on the gas pedal. The car stalled and then died. Frantically, he checked his mirror. The cop was waiting. Would he get out of his car? Lenny turned the ignition key. Nothing. He tried again. This time the engine caught. He shifted into drive and pulled away from the light. Halfway down the next block, he carefully signaled and turned into a convenience store parking lot. The cruiser continued down the street. Lenny wasted no time finding a Dumpster to trash the plates.

When he got to the theater, he saw Susan's car in the back lot. Had she read the duty schedule to see that he was on the early shift today? In spite of himself, he became aroused thinking of her. He parked his car and headed for the rear door of the theater, refusing to be tempted; everything he needed in a woman was waiting for him at home.

Susan met him at the door. He assumed her flushed cheeks and breathless voice indicated her excitement at seeing him. Her hands were shaking and she quickly pulled him inside and locked the door.

"What the hell are you doing? Let go of me." Lenny pulled his arm away, wondering if her libido ever took a break. "We can't—"

"Did you see him?"

"Who?"

"Mr. Bruns."

"Why? What's this about?" He realized that Susan wasn't hot, she was afraid, terrified, in fact. He struggled for composure. He kept telling himself to stay calm. No one knows anything. No one can know anything. Unless . . . had Mother gotten loose and found Phil? The thought almost paralyzed him.

"He's got a gun, and he's looking for you. Oh, Lenny, he was crazy when he left here yesterday. I begged Mark to give me a key so that I could be here when you came in this morning. I'd have gone to your house, but no one knows where you live."

"I'm okay. He never found me. Maybe he cooled off and changed his mind." Lenny looked at her. "You saw the gun?"

"Yes! We were so scared!" She snuggled closer to him and rested her head on his chest.

Lenny doubted the sincerity of her concern. He remembered she had forced him to be unfaithful to Mother and had nearly made him lose everything.

"And then when the police came, asking to see you . . . Lenny, what have you done?"

"The police? I haven't done anything! Go start the corn and leave me alone!"

He shouldered his way past her and ran down the hall.

Upstairs, he opened the office and went to Phil's desk. Working quickly but methodically, he opened every drawer and sorted through the man's papers. He knew his uncle always kept three or four hundred dollars around for emergencies. He found it and stuffed the thick roll of cash into his pocket.

Lenny looked for records listing his address but he found none. For the first time, he was glad Phil had always paid him separately in cash, unlike the others who received weekly checks. Lenny knew he was paid less than the rest of the kids even though he had worked here longer than anyone. The lousy money he'd gotten for busting his tail at the theater all these years was another score he had settled yesterday.

Lenny was in the film room when the interoffice phone rang. He wondered who had a problem. He assumed the kids were in place for the eleven-forty-five and twelve o'clock showings, and the doors were open. Again, Lenny thought how smoothly the place ran without his uncle.

"Yeah?" he answered.

"It's Susan. The cop's back and he's not alone. He wants Mr. Bruns or the assistant on duty. He just walked over to the box office."

"You haven't seen me. I'm not in the building. Mr. Bruns is away for the weekend."

"But, he's real—"

"Get rid of him!" he screamed into the phone.

"It's probably about that missing woman. They think you saw her last. Lenny, he wants to talk to you. I don't think he'll give up."

"Susan, if you care about me, get rid of him!"

"But—"

"You won't have a job here if you don't. The boss will have both our hides if we talk to this guy without his say-so. Understand?"

"Okay, I'll try."

Lenny raced across the hall and peered down into the concession area through the one-way windows in Phil's office. He saw Susan and Jeff talking to a tall man in a dark suit. Behind the man stood two officers in uniform. Red and blue lights of a squad car flashed through the box office window.

This could only be another trick of Mother's. How had she done it? Did she know about Phil? Was sending the police here a warning . . . or retaliation?

He watched the scene below. Evidently, Susan convinced the cops. They were leaving. Lenny stayed by the window until the flashing lights disappeared. Mother hadn't won yet. His legs felt shaky as relief surged through him.

Someone pounded on the office door. Lenny unlocked it and Susan rushed inside. Seeing the agitation on her face, he closed the door and leaned against it. Her breasts heaved beneath her uniform. He couldn't take his eyes off them.

"You did it," he said at last.

"They've gone, but they'll be back. The detective said he'd get a court order to search the premises. They've already been to Mr. Bruns's house and no one was there."

"How soon will they be back?"

"What? I don't know. They want information on all of us, where we live, what kind of cars we drive, stuff like that. They're especially interested in finding you."

"Did you tell them anything?"

"You said not to. What's going on, Lenny? Jeff said we could be arrested for withholding information and that we had to cooperate the next time they came back, whether Mr. Bruns was here or not." She moved toward Lenny. "Please hold me. I'm so scared."

Lenny had no choice but to put his arms around her. She was much taller than Mother and their bodies meshed at thigh, groin, and chest. Lenny had not noticed before how well they fit together. He commanded his body to relax, only to find it doing exactly the opposite. Before he could push her away, she had his face in her hands and was kissing him. Her tongue felt like cool rain as it washed over his fevered mouth. Mother had never kissed him like this; nor had she ever offered herself so freely.

Suddenly, he realized what this was about. This was a test. Mother had sent Susan to test him and at the worst possible time; the theaters were filling with matinee crowds and both he and Susan would be missed. How could he allow his weakness to overtake him? Mother would have the upper hand again. Or, would she? He'd show her he was man enough to satisfy them both.

"Watch this, Mother," he whispered, as he shifted around Susan to lock the door. "Watch this!"

# chapter
# 33

Lenny fondled the green-sequin dress. What more could he do to make it up to her? He'd bought her a new dress for tonight and a present. He would prepare her favorite food, just as he had in the old days. Mother could never resist a good meal. When she opened the special gift he had bought her, she would be all his, regardless of his behavior with Susan today. She would be in awe of his prowess and virility. It would be a night to remember. . . .

He glanced at his watch. It was almost four o'clock. The police had returned at three, but he had seen them from Phil's window and slipped down the fire escape before they parked their car. They didn't frighten him. They would find no record of where he lived. Perhaps Jeff could describe his car, but that was all the information the cops would get on him. Susan would say nothing. Susan was in love. The thought amused him. She was so easy to dupe, unlike Mother.

He hurried through the Sunday afternoon traffic, but he knew Mother would forgive him for being late when he gave her the new dress and her welcome home gift. The dress had been easy to choose, but he had spent at least thirty minutes mulling over his special surprise.

His breath quickened when he saw the house, knowing that she was waiting for him, wanting him. Phil was gone. After tonight, she would be his alone. . . .

He parked the car and raced up the steps. The door opened on his first try with the key, and Lenny sailed inside to deposit his gifts on the living room sofa.

"Mother," he called cheerily, "are you awake?"

Only silence greeted him. He unlocked her door and peeked inside at her. He walked to the bed and leaned over to caress her cheek. Her eyes opened and she glared at him. Hatred splashed over her eyelashes and ran down her face, pinching harsh creases around her mouth.

"Where have you been?" she screamed. "You're an hour late! How dare you allow me to lie here in chains while you're off enjoying yourself."

"But, Mother, I . . . I . . ." Lenny fumbled in his pocket for the key to the cuffs.

"Hurry up! I have to use the toilet. You ungrateful child! What were you thinking of, leaving me alone for hours, unable to move?"

"I'm sorry, Mother. I'll make it up to you." He unlocked the cuffs and slid them off. He started to rub her wrist where the cuff had bitten into it, but she slapped him and snatched back her hand.

"Get away from me!" She stood up and marched to the door. "I'm going to take a bath. What did you bring me for dinner? It better not be any of that fast food swill or you can take it right back!"

"No, no, Mother. I'm cooking! One of your favorite meals—pasta—just the way you like it."

"With the red sauce?"

"Of course."

"And the bread?"

"Yes, yes. Garlic bread, with extra salt, just for you!" Lenny followed her to the bathroom door. All at once he remembered the dress. "Wait here, Mother. Wait! I have a surprise for you!" He dashed to the living room and returned with a bag.

She tapped her hand against the door frame, frowning. "Well, what is it?"

He opened the bag and lifted out the glittery, green minidress. "Isn't it beautiful? I chose it for you."

"My God! I'll look like a tart! Is that how you want your mother to look? Lenny, you know better!"

Lenny's shoulders drooped and tears stung his eyes. "But all your things are so big, and I thought this would match your eyes and—"

"Stop sniveling. I'll wear the dress. Now, go get the sauce started while I have a bath. I don't suppose you thought to buy me any shoes to go with this whore's dress, did you?" At Lenny's downcast sigh, she answered, "Of course not. Why do I even bother with you? You're completely irresponsible."

"I'm sorry, Mother. I did try."

Mother's only answer was the slamming of the bathroom door.


"Detective?"

"Yes, Randy Abbott. Mark, isn't it?"

"Yes, sir. How can I help you?" Mark moved aside to let a group of teenagers get in the concession line. Sunday matinees were busy times at the theater and today was no different.

"Perhaps we could talk upstairs in the office?" Randy and the two policemen he had brought along were attracting a lot of attention from the movie crowd.

"Okay. Please follow me." Mark led the way up the stairs and unlocked Phil's office. Randy walked inside with Mark, but the policemen waited at the door.

"Mr. Bruns around?" Randy asked.

"No, sir. I haven't seen him today."

"When was the last time you saw him?" Randy was getting impatient with this cat-and-mouse game with Phil.

"Well, I . . . I guess it was yesterday about this time."

"Is that unusual? I would think he'd want to be here for the weekend."

"Yes, he usually is." Mark fidgeted, remembering Mr.

Brun's hasty exit yesterday. No one had seen him since. "Maybe he decided to take the weekend off," Mark added. "Maybe he's at home. He doesn't check in with us."

"We've been to his home and he's not there."

"I'm sorry, but I honestly don't know where he is. Like I said, he doesn't check in with us." Mark could feel a line of perspiration forming on his top lip. He was sure the detective could see it. He shifted toward the desk and picked up a file folder for something to do with his hands.

"How about the young man I told you about yesterday?"

Mark squirmed a bit and concentrated on the space above Randy's head.

Randy moved closer. The boy backed up, but Randy moved in tighter until he had Mark cornered between the credenza and the wall. "Like I told your boss, we can talk about it here, or we can talk about it at the station." He indicated the policemen who stood outside the room. "It's up to you."

"I want to cooperate." Mark was openly perspiring now. He rubbed the droplets from his upper lip and looked at Randy.

"Okay. Let's try this again. Where can I find the big man with the unusually feminine hands?"

"I'm not sure where Len—Where he might be."

"What did you call him, Mark?"

"I . . . I believe they must have meant Lenny, Lenny Bruns, sir. He's one of the assistant managers. H-he should be around, though you may have missed him. His shift really ends at four, but maybe he left early." Mark wiped his hands down over his pants and waited.

Randy backed off and removed his pen and notebook from his inside jacket pocket. "Where does Lenny live?"

"I don't know. He keeps to himself. No one knows him."

Randy pulled out a packet of papers and handed them to Mark. "Since you're the one in charge here, these are for you. We have a search warrant for these premises.

You can check it, but you'll find it in order. We want to access the files and personnel records in this office. We will not, at this time, disturb the operation of the theatre in any way. No one needs to know we're here."

"Jesus Christ!" Mark muttered. His hands shook as he read the warrant. "How'd you get one of these on a Sunday?" It looked too official not to be the real thing, and he wasn't about to argue with the steely-eyed detective standing before him.

"I think I should call someone from the central office. Don't y-you think?" he asked no one in particular.

"As you wish," Randy replied. He opened the top drawer of the filing cabinet and flipped through the folders. Then he turned to the policemen. "Pete, check out the theater. See if a Mr. Lenny Bruns is in the building. Bill, call Records. Get them to run a make on him."

Two hours later, Randy felt as though he could manage a movie complex single-handedly if he ever grew tired of law enforcement. Contrary to their first meeting when Phil had seemed so scattered, and his records impossible to decipher, Randy knew now that Bruns was an astute businessman. His accounts and records were in perfect order with one exception. Nowhere in any of his papers was there a scrap of information about Lenny Bruns.

The only thing of real interest to Randy was that Phil was a man of property. Not only did he have his own home, the one Randy had visited earlier, but he owned two other places, both residential. Randy rechecked the addresses. He didn't recognize either street, but finding them would be easy. A phone call to the precinct told him one was in Lancaster, a town twenty miles south of Dallas, and the other was in the Love Field area.

Before he left the theater office, he called John Foyles. "John, do you know a guy named Lenny Bruns?"

"I don't think so."

"A kid, twenty or so."

"How would I know him?"

"Just asking. How about a Phil Bruns?"

"Don't think so. What's going on?"

"They both work at Town Park Eight, and they may have been the last people to see your wife before she disappeared. Wondered if the names meant anything to you. Did Monica ever mention either of them?"

"Detective, I wasn't even aware she attended the damned movies, so, no, she never mentioned either of these guys to me."

"Okay, John. Thanks for your time. I'll be in touch." Randy was getting used to John's brusque behavior that stopped just short of rudeness, but it puzzled him.

He stood up and put the last of the files away. The two policemen had left earlier. Neither had found anything on Lenny. Randy walked to the window overlooking the concession stand and watched the busy scene below.

"Detective Abbott?"

Randy swung around. A huge bear of a man, well over six feet tall, and carrying at least three hundred pounds on his frame, entered the office.

"I'm Jim Levering, District Manager for Unity Films, the corporation that owns Town Park. I hear we have a problem." Jim joined Randy at the window. "Mark Gentry called me. It's not like Phil Bruns to disappear. You think there's a connection between him and the missing woman?"

"We have two eyewitnesses that put her here the day she disappeared. How long have you known Mr. Bruns?" Randy asked.

Jim pulled a bag of candy from his pocket. "Got a sweet tooth. Never could keep my hands off the candy counter at the theaters. Probably the reason why they kicked me upstairs." He grinned at Randy and then answered his question. "I've worked with Phil Bruns for over twenty years. He's a son of a bitch, but he runs the tightest ship in the company. His profits are always among the highest. Not like him to just disappear. Not like him at all."

"Does he have any family, any close friends?"

"Not to my knowledge, but then Phil was never the type to encourage anybody, at least in his business life, to get too chummy."

"Does he have a favorite place he likes to go, or something that he likes to do? You know, fish, play pool, or gamble maybe?" Randy backed away from the window and circled the room.

Again Jim shook his head. " 'Fraid I don't know that, either. He never attends any of the recreational things the company puts together from time to time. He's won several company incentive trips for his outstanding attendance records and high profits, but he never took them. As far as I know, this theater is his whole life."

"Would you say he's a man who could collect a few enemies?"

"His share and more, probably. Nobody ever wants to tangle with him. He's got a nasty temper."

The men talked for a few minutes more before leaving the office together.

"Detective, you have my card. I hope you'll call me immediately if you get any information about Phil Bruns."

"Thanks, you've been real helpful." Randy shook the man's outstretched hand.

"Keep me posted."

"Will do." Randy took a last look around the second floor and went down the steps. Jim stopped to say hello to three young people in the break room.

Downstairs, Randy saw Mark talking with the young woman he'd spoken with earlier, the one who couldn't, or wouldn't, identify Lenny. She was out of uniform, dressed casually in jeans and a tight red sweater. Just as he started to approach her, she whispered something to Mark and fled to the ladies' room. Randy glanced at his watch and decided not to wait for her. He needed to check out Phil Bruns's other properties before it got much later.

# chapter
# 34

Mother sat at her vanity table making liberal use of the contents of the various paints and powders there. She had washed her hair as best she could, and while it was wet, had combed it straight back from her forehead and sprayed it. The severe style accented her thin face and heavily madeup eyes. The new green dress fit tightly. Even with its front closure, she had struggled to get it on. It rode high on her shapely thighs and the neckline revealed more than a hint of cleavage above its sequined edge.

She clipped long rhinestone earrings to her ears and slid several multicolored, beaded necklaces over her head. Next she added three tarnished bangle bracelets to her wrist, and as a final touch, drenched herself in rancid rosewater perfume she found in a gold atomizer on her dresser. Her feet were bare and would remain that way. None of the shoes in the closet would do.

Refusing to exhibit any sign of weakness, she'd abandoned the sling, but kept her left arm bent at the elbow. If she remembered to hold it close to her body, she might make it, at least for an hour or so. After a final coat of cakey mascara on her long lashes and a last slap of color on her trembling mouth, she left the room.

Lenny, freshly showered and dressed in a flowing, white silk shirt and tailored slacks, lifted the boiling kettle of pasta from the stove as she entered the kitchen. A lock of his still-wet hair separated from the rest and curled down over his brow, giving him the appearance of an innocent schoolboy.

"Watch out! You're slopping the water all over the counter!" Mother rushed to grab a cloth that was thrown in the sink and began mopping up the starchy water. "You have to drain the water off first, then put it in the plates."

"I'm sorry, Mother. I just didn't think." He looked to her for some sign of forgiveness, and for the first time, noticed her dress, styled hair, jewelry, and makeup.

"Mother, you're beautiful!" The dinner forgotten, he worshipped her with his eyes. He had never seen her so alluring. This fantastic creature was his, all his. He nearly fell to his knees to kiss her bare feet. Mother had truly come home. He would never be lonely again.

"I'll tell you what I am and that is hungry! Get the food on the table!" She threw the sodden cloth into the sink and flounced to the table, seating herself in the chair nearest the door.

Lenny unearthed a strainer from the cupboard and drained the pasta. He divided it between the plates and slathered sauce onto it. After carefully placing the brimming plates on the table, he handed Mother a napkin.

"Where's the bread?" she demanded.

"It's ready. I put it into the oven to keep it warm." He grabbed a bowl and opened the oven door. A cloud of gray smoke streamed from the oven. He batted it away and pulled out the bread.

"You imbecile! Now look at what you've done! My garlic bread is ruined." The timbre of her voice rose with each word.

Lenny was sure the whole neighborhood could hear her scolding him, not that it was anything they hadn't heard before. Mother's tantrums were never quiet. He dumped the ruined bread into the trash can. Maybe dessert would make up for burning the bread.

He lit two candles on the table and turned out the kitchen light. The glow softened her features, and her eyes smoldered. Even in the best of the old days, she had never looked this good. He had never loved nor needed her more.

"You're not eating. Didn't I always teach you it is bad to waste food?" Mother picked up her water. "This glass is chipped! Get me another one!" she ordered loudly.

Lenny jumped up to get a clean tumbler from the dish drainer in the sink. He filled it with water and added three ice cubes, exactly as she liked it, and carried it to the table. She snatched it out of his fingers and told him to sit down and eat.

"Oh, I forgot! I have a surprise for you. I hope you'll like it." He hurried to his room, and returned in a moment with a small, inexpensive tape player. He pushed the on button but nothing happened. Lenny shook the machine, ejected the tape, flipped it over and reinserted it.

"Some surprise." She picked up her fork. "Lenny! For heaven's sakes, stop playing with that blasted machine and eat—"

The soft, jazzy sounds of Kenny G.'s sax filled the room. Mother's mouth dropped open and her fork slipped from her fingers and fell to the floor.

"You like it! You like my surprise!" Lenny was shocked. Finally, he had done something right. Mother was speechless with joy. Were those tears forming in her eyes?

"Wh-where did you get that?" she whispered.

"It's a special treat, and you're not supposed to ask where it came from. You're just supposed to enjoy it." He got her another fork and sat down to eat.

Mother played with the rest of her spaghetti, but didn't take another bite. *David, I remember when you gave that to me. How can I go through with this? Help me, David . . . Help me.*

Lenny's anticipation grew. Dinner couldn't be over fast

enough. He could see how moved she was by the music. She was nearly in a daze. He cleaned his plate and took the dinnerware to the sink.

"Are you ready for another surprise?" Lenny pulled a gaily wrapped package from behind the toaster and laid it in front of her. "Open it! Open it!" he cried.

Mother lifted her hand and fingered the red bow on the top of the package. Kenny G. still played and she seemed lost in the moody sound, a million miles away. She wasn't aware of anything else until Lenny's insistent voice interrupted her reverie and brought her crashing back to reality.

"Open it! Open it!"

"All right, Lenny. Just give me a moment's peace, won't you? My God, you can be so exasperating sometimes!"

Lenny jolted back in his seat as if she had struck him. "I'm sorry, Mother. Please don't be mad at me."

"Oh, stop whining, and let me open this. I hope you didn't spend all your money on some frivolous piece of junk." With her good hand she tore off the ribbon and threw it on the floor. The wrapping paper joined it, followed by the lid of the small, rectangular box. She folded back the tissue paper and lifted out a pair of daintily made, very fragile, ecru lace gloves.

"They're called demi-gloves, Mother. They're very old. The woman who sold them to me said they were the height of fashion years ago. You see, they stop midjoint on the fingers. That way your hands are covered, but your fingertips are free! Aren't they wonderful? We don't have anything like them in our collection. They're much too small for me, but they will look beautiful on you."

The thought of them on her tiny, feminine hands made his body leap. It took every ounce of strength he had to remain in the chair. He wanted to reach across the table and crush her in his arms until she cried out with delight and passion.

"You're not saying anything, Mother. Don't you like them?"

"They're . . . they're very nice."

"I want you to wear them later tonight, when we're in bed. Promise you'll do that for me, Mother. Promise me?"

She had to clear her throat several times before she could speak. "What do I get in return?" *Help me, David!*

"Since we're celebrating your coming home, I'll let you choose the first part!"

"I should hope so," she said. "What are you going to do about the dishes?"

"Dessert, first," he announced. The candle flames bobbed and swayed from his movements as he gathered the glasses and the extra silverware from the table.

She watched his shadow on the wall. It grew larger and appeared to leap off the filthy cabinets and cavort around the room as he opened the refrigerator and pulled two dishes from the metal shelves.

"What is this? It looks awful!" She reared back as he set a cereal bowl filled with a dark, gelatinous liquid in front of her.

"Wait, it's not ready yet." He took a can of whipped cream from the refrigerator and squirted a foamy mound in the center of her bowl. The force of pressure from the can splashed some of the liquid out of the bowl. She jumped back.

"It's called 'Floating Cloud.' I saw it in a magazine. I used green gelatin just for you because I know it's your favorite."

He looked at the dollop of whipped cream, slowly sinking in her dish. "Guess I didn't let it set long enough to get thick. I made it while you were getting dressed."

"Remove this disgusting mess from my sight! You've killed my appetite!" Mother tossed her napkin on the table.

"We-we can eat it later, after it sets up." His fingers shook and he spilled some of the liquid as he put the dessert into the refrigerator. Then he turned the tape over. Taking her completely by surprise, he grabbed her shoulders and lifted her out of her chair and into his arms.

"You promised me a dance, Mother."

The jazzy sax was back and she felt him moving clumsily to the rhythm. "We never dance! You have two left feet. Let me go!"

"No, Mother. If I'm willing to let you choose later on, you have to do what I want now."

"Then don't step on me!" They moved around the dim kitchen, the candlelight flickering off the green sequins on her dress like sparkling fireflies on a summer evening.

She tried to pull away when the music stopped. "No," he said. "Since they are your favorites, I know you'll choose the black lace and ropes. For that, I get another dance."

"Black lace and ropes?" *I can't do this. I'll kill myself first.*

"Yes, but not in the attic. We'll do it in your room." He pulled her close until she was certain that the impression of the beads she wore would be permanently imprinted on her body.

Around and around they circled the small room. She was growing dizzy until he changed direction. Abruptly, he picked up the tape machine, pulled her through the living room and down the hall to her room.

The door remained open. They did not need the extra privacy of a closed door. He would take her in the street if need be, in the middle of a crowded store. It didn't matter. He was so proud of her he wanted the world to know that she was his at last.

She felt him open the buttons on her dress and soon she was naked except for her own pair of silky, bikini panties, which she'd found in a pile of laundry in the bathroom. He wanted the necklaces, bracelets, and earrings to remain. He had often dreamed of making love to her in her jewelry. From the drawer in her bedside table, he withdrew four lengths of white rope and two pairs of gloves. He threw the rope onto the bed.

"We'll use these now and save the new ecru ones for later," he said, handing her the gloves.

She took the gloves, but said nothing.

"Have you forgotten, Mother?" He pulled off his shoes. He had not bothered with socks. "Undress me now and put on the gloves. You know which ones are yours."

"It's t-too dark. I can't see to unbutton your sh-shirt." *I've got to go through with this. I've come too far to stop now.*

He bent to turn on the small lamp by the bed. He walked over and picked up the scarf lying on her dresser, snapping it out and letting it float down over the shade.

"Did you think I forgot how you like it? Oh, Mother, I haven't forgotten anything."

Ignoring the pain, she lifted her hands to his chest. The buttons slipped easily through their openings and the shirt slid from his body. Another button, a zipper, and he added his slacks to her dress and his shirt on the floor.

"You're shaking, Mother. Are you cold?" He pulled her close to warm her. She felt his erection and jumped involuntarily.

"Ah, not cold, I see. Definitely not cold. I'm glad you're ready. I can't wait either." He leaned down and pulled off the last bit of lace that covered her, and then removed his briefs.

She concentrated on the gloves in her hands, turning them over and over, finally pulling the smaller pair made of black lace over her fingers. He was swaying again, this time to music only he could hear.

"Yes, Mother, yes!"

He lifted his beautifully manicured hands and she slipped the gloves down over them. He flexed his fingers and the soft black leather that encased them sprang to life. It undulated over his body and then leapt to hers. She cried out, but her cries were stifled by his bruising mouth.

He lifted his lips from hers and licked her closed eyelids, trailing his tongue across the base of her lashes. He captured her hand with his and jammed her fingers into his mouth, sucking each one in turn.

"These eyes adore me and these hands I will obey. Tell me what they want me to do."

Lenny's face was inches from hers. She could feel him rubbing himself against her. He was growing larger again, much larger than the shadow on the wall.

"Lie down," she whispered. "Lie down on the bed."

He obeyed. When he lay on the pale pink satin of the counterpane, he spread his arms and legs wide so that they almost touched the four corner posts of the bed.

She snatched up the ropes and moved to the head of the bed. The rope was barely against his wrist when he reared up and pulled her to him for a passionate kiss.

"I know. I'm cheating." He released her at last and lay back quietly while she tied first his wrists and then his ankles to the bed.

"Test them, Lenny. Try to break free. I want to get everything right tonight." She moved back and watched him rail and heave against the rope. The knots held.

"Oh, yes, Mother. You've done well. Touch me, Mother. Look at me! I'm ready for you."

"Yes, I can see you are. Now shut your eyes so that I may begin." She leaned over him and blew a soft stream of air onto his chest.

He closed his eyes and panted. It was sweet agony lying here beneath her hands. He had to concentrate. He mustn't come too soon. Mother would be disappointed if she couldn't tease him . . . if it were over too quickly.

Hold back, hold back, he told himself. He couldn't wait. He must open his eyes to look at her, to tell her to untie him. He had to have her immediately!

He opened his eyes, but she was gone. . . .

# chapter
# 35

She stopped for nothing, not even a coat or his shirt to cover herself. The bolts on the kitchen door flew open beneath her fingers and the steps as she descended them, melted under her feet. She was free! She was whole! Her heart was beating so fast she thought it might work its way out of her chest, up through her throat and pop out her open, panting mouth. Somewhere behind her she heard him scream and she ran faster, down a street she had never seen before, toward bright lights she imagined in the distance. The airport! She could hear the planes rumbling overhead and she knew that she would soon be safe.

The beaded necklaces whipped up and slapped her face. She tore them over her head and threw them aside but kept running. Stones and pieces of glass cut into her feet but she didn't slow down. She could see the airport in front of her. The bright lights confused her. She stumbled and fell, scraping her knees and hitting her injured arm. Pain ripped through her. She tried to get up, to get to the lights. . . . There were voices now. Someone was running toward her.

She crawled to her knees and the voices grew louder.

"My God! Someone get her a blanket, a towel, anything! Kent, call 911! We need an ambulance here on the double."

A voice came closer. "Hey there, you're okay. Take it easy. You're gonna be okay."

The scratchy warmth of a blanket surrounded her. A woman's voice replaced the man's. "Honey, don't try to talk. Just relax. We're getting you some help."

She managed to push herself up to look at the woman who was kneeling beside her. A brief smile flitted across her mouth as she clutched the woman's hand.

"My name is Monica," she gasped. "Monica Foyles."

She looked down. She was still wearing the black lace gloves.


"Hello, this is Randy Abbott calling."

"Yes?" John listened carefully. "Oh, my God! Where?"

Just then William came in the kitchen. One look at his wife, who was standing behind John, told him something had happened. John was shouting into the phone. Grace and William had never seen him this excited.

"You're sure? . . . Why not? . . . When will you know? . . . Yes, yes, I'll meet you there." John slammed down the phone.

"What is it?" William asked.

"They think they've found her! She's alive!"

"Oh, my God! Oh, my God!" cried Grace. She grabbed her husband in a hug so fierce, she knocked him off balance. William took a deep breath as he held Grace. John reached out to steady them both.

"They've taken her to Parkland Hospital."

"Has Detective Abbott seen her?" Grace whispered.

"No, he just got the call from the policeman who was on the scene when she was picked up."

William nodded, unable to speak.

"Randy isn't sure it's Monica," John cautioned.

"It's got to be her. I know it's her," Grace said. She was squeezing William's fingers in one hand and a sodden handkerchief in the other.

"Randy's meeting me at the hospital." John fastened

the top button on his shirt and pushed up his tie. Then he pulled on his jacket.

"I'll go, too," William offered.

John thought about the heartbreak the man would face if it turned out to be a false call. He didn't want to deal with the extra emotion.

"Thanks, but I think you should wait here with Grace and the children. It might be hours before we know anything. You'll be more comfortable here." Sensing William's agitation, he added, "I'd really feel better knowing you're here, in case something else comes up."

"All right, John. If that's what you want." William met his wife's eyes in silence, but said nothing further. Together Monica's parents followed John to the garage.

"I'll call you as soon as I know," he told them as he slid behind the wheel. "Let's not tell the kids until we know something definite." He started the car and backed out into the alley.

Inside the house, William pulled Grace close and they shared a long hug, their tears mingling together as they held each other.

"I'll make some coffee," she whispered at last.

William nodded, knowing the hours ahead would be more difficult than the last four days had been.

# chapter
# 36

She must have forgotten how good he was at untying the ropes with his teeth. Once Lenny had maneuvered his body so that he could reach his wrist with his mouth, he had one knot loose in a few minutes. The second wrist was easier. His frantic fingers tore at the knots, gouging out some of the flesh on his arm in his haste.

"Mother! Mother!" he screamed over and over.

He freed his legs and ran out of the room. His bedroom and the living room were empty. The kitchen door stood ajar. He looked out on the street and saw no traces of her. She was gone! She had left him alone again. He sank to his knees and beat his head against the floor, crying out his anguish into the dirty mat by the door, knowing that he would never find her again. His last chance for happiness was gone.

A voice was calling him. He heard it whispering, commanding him from inside his head. He listened and knew he had to obey. *"How could you think that woman was me?"* it asked.

"Mother?"

*"You fool! She tried to tell you her name was Monica. She wasn't your mother. How could you have made such a stupid mistake?"*

"Her eyes. She had your eyes."

Suddenly those green eyes swam before him. *"You were wrong, Lenny. She was a fake. Someone you conjured up to avoid your duty. It almost worked, didn't it? You were almost free of your promise to me."*

"Mother, it was you. You even wore the locket I gave you. You came back to me. Why have you left me again?"

Her voice became angry. The eyes burned his face and he flinched at their scalding touch. His nude body trembled.

*"Get dressed!"* the voice screamed.

Lenny pushed himself up off the floor and stumbled to his room where piles of laundry lay on the floor. He grabbed the first thing he saw and threw it over his shoulders.

*"No! No!"* the voice screamed. *"You know what I want you to wear!"*

Sobbing now, Lenny pulled off the shirt and stumbled out in the hall and into his mother's room. He went to her closet and pulled open the door.

*"Yes, much better now,"* the voice purred. *"Run your fingers across the dresses. I'll tell you when to stop."*

Lenny did as he was told. His fingers stopped at a pink-flowered day dress that buttoned in front to the hem line. It was one of his mother's oldest dresses.

*"Put it on!"* the voice commanded. Lenny wrapped it around his body and started on the buttons. He knew from wearing the dress on other occasions that he would have to pin the belt because the buckle was broken.

*"The beads. Wear the pink ones."*

Lenny closed the closet door and seated himself at the vanity. He lifted the lid on her jewelry box and found the necklace. He pulled it over his head, not bothering with its complicated clasp.

*"Skip the bracelets. You let that woman take the best ones. But don't forget the perfume. Lots and lots of perfume."*

Lenny sprayed on Attar of Roses until he reeked of it. Then he stood up and went to the bed. The ropes were where he had left them, but all signs of the other woman were gone. Had he only imagined her? She had been an enchanting dream.

*"Lenny!"* The strident tone hurt. He lifted his hands to cover his ears.

"I'm sorry. I'm sorry!" he wailed. "What I did was awful! She meant nothing to me. She was just so beautiful. I wanted her, Mother, but not like I always wanted you."

*"Get the gun."*

"No, no, please, no!" Lenny yelled.

*"You have a promise to fulfill,"* the voice said in a whispery tone he had to obey. *"Get the gun!"*

He went to his room and pushed the nail polish bottles aside on his manicure table. Lifting the cover, he reached into the secret compartment beneath. The revolver was there, ready to fire. Mother had insisted he keep it that way.

*"Come to me."*

"No, no, please."

*"You're ready now. Come to me! I want you!"*

Lenny left the room. In the hall he turned and went to the attic steps. He laid his hand on the railing and hesitated. If only he could turn and run, hide where no one would ever find him.

*"Come on! Don't make me wait any longer!"* The voice had a rough, masculine edge to it. *"Come on, kid!"* Uncle Phil said. *"Pull up your pretty dress and assume the position. I'm ready for you. It's going to be like old times!"*

"Nancy? It's David. Randy Abbott just called me. They've found her!" David's hand that held the phone was still shaking. "My God, Nancy, she's alive!"

"Oh, David. I'm so glad. I just can't tell you how . . ." Tears choked her and she was unable to speak for a moment.

"I know, I know, Nancy. Believe me, I feel the same way."

"Is she at home? Can we see her?"

"No, she's at Parkland. She was in pretty bad shape when they found her, but she's holding her own now,

Randy says." Just the thought of what Monica must have been through made David physically ill.

"What happened to her, David? Where has she been?"

"Some kid had her. Randy said he was a real psycho."

"And he let her go?" Nancy asked.

"No, she fooled him somehow, and got away! She made it to a gas station on Mockingbird near Love Field and someone called an ambulance."

"Good for Monica! She's a real fighter! David, I'm so glad she's free. Did they get the guy?"

"No, but Monica was able to help Randy with the location. He's on his way there now."

"Thank God. I hope this is all over soon." Relief poured through Nancy. Her prayers had been answered. Her friend was safe.

"Yeah, me, too." David hung up the phone. He closed the bedroom door and sank down on the bed, needing a few moments alone before he returned to his son. The nightmare had ended and Monica was alive. It was enough.


Sobbing, Lenny climbed the steps to the attic. He couldn't let it happen. Not now, not after his beautiful dream had been shattered. He couldn't let Uncle Phil touch him.

"Oh, please, not tonight," he begged. "Protect me, Mother! Don't let him hurt me again! He can't have us both!"

The whispery voice returned. *"Come to me, Lenny. Mother will keep you safe. He won't hurt you if you're with me."*

The attic was dark as he knew it would be and he hurried to light the lamp. He noticed his gloves. They were the same ones the other woman had put on his hands. He had not changed them. A smile skipped across his face. She had been lovely. He had been so happy with her.

*"Get your tight little ass over here!"* screamed the man's voice.

Lenny crossed to the bed. Mother was gone. He had to obey Uncle Phil. He was all Lenny had left in the world. After his uncle finished with him, he wasn't good enough for anyone else to bother with. Phil had told him that many times.

Pockets of dried blood added to the grotesqueness of the mutilated features on the body lying on the mattress. Stooping low, Lenny could just discern the outline of the man's lips. They became Mother's lips. Lenny smiled. She was back. He touched her dress. It was another of her favorites. She would protect him now. He just needed to obey.

*"Kiss me!"* she demanded.

Lenny did.

*"Hold me!"*

Lenny did.

*"Join me!"*

Lenny did.

# chapter
# 37

William and Grace stood beside their sleeping daughter's hospital bed, thinking about how small and helpless she looked. A large gauze patch covered her cheek. A gray sling supported a navy-blue cast on her left arm and her right hand was bandaged. They wondered how she had ever managed to get away from that deranged man.

Grace noted the dark shadows beneath Monica's eyes and the gauntness in her face indicating she had lost weight. She leaned over and smoothed the uneven clumps of hair above Monica's forehead. She was not sure she could handle the truth about what had happened to her daughter. Not right now. My God, what had he done to her hair? She kissed Monica's brow. *Welcome back, my darling. May the rest of your life make up for the horror you've been through.*

William's eyes began to water as he bent to touch his daughter's hand. His tears were the first thing Monica saw when she awoke a moment later.

"Daddy," she whispered, "please don't cry. I'm fine. I really, really am." She rolled over and hugged him, and then reached for Grace. "Momma, I love you. I'm so glad you're here." Tears blurred her eyes and Monica thought of all the tears she had shed the past few days. How different it felt to cry now.

"We're just so happy to have you back," William said.

"I'm glad to have me back, too," whispered Monica, giving her dad another hug before resting back on her pillows. "Did you bring the children?"

Grace nodded and smiled, "Oh, yes. We're probably breaking all the hospital rules, but wild horses couldn't have kept them away."

John stepped to the other side of her bed. Monica had not realized he was in the room. She remembered seeing him before they set her arm, and he had been with her when she answered questions for the policeman, but they hadn't had any time alone.

"Nancy is with the kids. They're waiting in the hallway," he told her. "Do you feel up to seeing them?"

"Oh, yes, please, John," Monica said. "Let them come in."

John left the room. Moments later, he was back with Nancy and the children.

The hushed seriousness of the hospital and the enormity of the situation dampened the children's earlier jubilation at learning their mother had been found. They crept into the dimly lit room, and stood at the foot of the bed, looking at her. They didn't recognize what she was wearing. The plain blue gown wasn't like anything she usually wore to bed.

"Hi, you three," Monica said quietly. "I've missed you."

Mia and Sarah walked around and peered over the side of the bed.

"Mom, are you okay?" Mia asked. "What happened to your hair?"

"I will be fine now that you're here with me." Monica motioned them closer. "And my hair will grow back. But what I really need is a hug."

Sarah eyes shone as she reached out to Monica. "Mommy, Mommy. It was awful without you. We were really scared."

"I know, darling. I am sorry you were upset, but everything will soon be back to normal."

"Oh, Mom, don't ever leave us again like that." Mia hugged Monica and then touched the cast on her arm. "Does that hurt?"

"A little, but it'll be okay. I promise. Hey, Jeb. How're you doing?" Monica felt her eyes fill with tears as she looked at him.

"Much better now, Mom," he whispered.

"I sure love you three. Have you made any pancakes lately?"

"Naw, we wouldn't do that without you, Mom," Jeb said as he leaned over to give her a big hug.

Monica clung to him, and losing the last shred of bravado, wept in his young arms.

From the side of the room, Nancy watched the reunion, and rummaged in her handbag for a tissue. A nurse came by to check on her patient.

John shook his head. "Not now," he said.

The nurse nodded. "I'll come back later," she said with a smile.

Monica lifted her head and gave Jeb a weak smile. William stepped in and tousled the boy's hair. "Best get used to it, son. Chances are she won't be the last beautiful woman to cry in your arms."

Jeb ducked his head and grinned. Monica hugged him again and laughed. Suddenly, everyone was laughing with her.

Monica and Nancy shared a gentle, teary hug. "You helped keep my family together, my friend. I'll never be able to repay . . ." Monica bit her lip, unable to continue.

"You know what you've always told me," Nancy whispered. "Friends don't keep score."

Monica nodded her head and wiped her eyes. The tears stung the sutures in her cheek and her arm throbbed, but she wouldn't have traded this moment for anything. Her world was coming together again. She reached out to hug Nancy once more.

"Mrs. Crawford helped us with the flyer, too," said

Mia. "Have you seen one?" At her mother's negative response, Mia continued, her usual exuberance restored. "They're awesome, Mom! Totally together! We picked out a border for it, and it even has your picture on it. They're all over town."

With Jeb's help, Mia filled Monica in on the search. Sarah said little, content to snuggle in the circle of her mother's arm. Monica kept touching her children, as if she couldn't believe they were really here and her nightmare was over.

John watched her with the children. His own reunion with Monica had been quite different. She had been downstairs in the emergency room. Hordes of people had been moaning, screaming and crying in the hallways and rooms. He had never seen anything as shocking. A harried doctor was examining her, and at first the staff refused to allow him or Randy near her.

She had been a bloody, filthy mess. Her hair was unsightly, and the heavy makeup and mascara that smeared her face gave her a ghoulish look that repelled him. He was reluctant to touch her.

Only after Randy's measured glance had he forced himself to hug her in that sorry state. The embrace had been brief. She was too wrought up to relax in his arms. She felt like a stranger to him. When the detective took her hand and spoke quietly to her, he was able to elicit more of a response from her than John had.

He had worried that his Monica, the refined woman he relied on to rear his children and tend his home was gone, leaving in her place a wild-looking, terrified creature. In conversation with one of the attendants, he learned that except for some jewelry and a pair of gloves, she had been naked when they picked her up. That information bothered him more than anything. He was embarrassed to have Randy hear about her state of undress.

John looked at her now, surrounded by her family, and marveled at the difference in her. She was clean and fresh.

He couldn't recall when she had looked so happy. Despite the broken arm and assorted bandages, with her hair brushed and her tender smile, she reminded him of the girl he had fallen in love with. What a transformation she had undergone! A few hours ago she had escaped from a madman. He could only guess at what she must have endured in the past five days. It pleased him that she wasn't burdening any of them with the horror of her experience.

As he stood by her bed, his life came sharply into focus. He was a husband and a father as well as a successful businessman. Monica needed him more now than she ever had. He had been relieved to find out that despite her nakedness, she had not been raped. He could stand by her; she was practically a celebrity. Already he'd been approached by the media for further details of her life. It was time to close the gap that had widened between them. He was ready to devote himself one hundred percent to the marriage. Beth would have to go. . . .

"Mr. Foyles?"

John looked toward the door. The nurse was back.

"We really need to settle Mrs. Foyles for the night," she said. "It's past midnight. She may be able to go home tomorrow, but only if she gets some rest."

"Yes, of course. You hear that, group? It's time for us to clear out!"

Everyone needed to hug Monica again, to say a few last words, to assure themselves that she was really safe. Ten minutes later, John finally ushered Nancy, Monica's parents, and the children toward the elevator.

When they were gone, he returned to her room. She was lying back against her pillows, but her eyes followed him as he came near and sat on the edge of her bed.

"You can't imagine how good it was for me to see everyone tonight. Thank you so much for arranging it," she said.

John shrugged off her thanks. He wanted to take her

hand but it was cradling her broken arm, so he kept his hands folded in his lap.

"Are you hurting? Will you need something to help you sleep?" She seemed a little restless.

Monica looked around the room and slid farther down into the bed. She couldn't find the words to tell him how wonderful this bed felt; how grateful she was to be safe, to be free, to be able to hold her children again.

"I'll sleep," she said finally. "My arm hurts, but not that badly."

"Guess you're tired." He almost reached out and traced the dark shadows beneath her eyes.

"A little."

"Well, I . . . I'm glad you're back."

She sat up and reached for the glass of juice the nurse had left. John pulled back, feeling out of sync with her. They would be fine together, once she was home and back in her old routine. And, he'd see to it that there would be no more of those damned matinees.

"Anything else you need, Monica?"

"No, nothing." She frowned and looked beyond him. John felt her sliding away. He wondered if she was thinking about her experience. He supposed he should expect that sort of thing from her. She'd have to find a way to deal with all that.

"I'd better let you get some sleep."

"I'll call you in the morning if they're going to release me."

"They said they might. I'll be here about ten either way." John stood up and straightened his tie. "Good night, then." He kissed her lightly on the mouth. "Welcome home."

Monica nodded and watched him leave. Suddenly, she was crying again. She was still wiping away her tears when a pretty, gray-haired nurse came into her room.

"Company all gone?"

"Thanks for letting them stay so late." Monica reached

for a tissue, but the nurse intercepted and offered her the box.

"We're happy to make exceptions in special cases. I don't know anyone in this hospital or this city, for that matter, who deserves a treat more than you do tonight."

"Thanks . . . I guess."

"No, really. They've been talking about you all over the hospital. The nurses on the station here who got you settled say they've never seen anyone handle the after-shock as well as you are."

"I'm thankful to be here. Everyone has been wonderful to me."

"I'm real glad you got away!" She reached out and squeezed Monica's hand.

Monica smiled her thanks and lay quietly while the R.N. took her pulse, blood pressure, and temperature. After she left, Monica fiddled with her new plaster cast and drank the last of her juice. There was one more thing she needed to do before she tried to sleep.

Randy heard the single gunshot as he crossed the front yard. He ran to his car and radioed for backup. No one was on the street. All was quiet.

Five minutes later, he heard the sirens. One squad car blocked the gravel driveway, the other parked in front of Randy's car. The officers turned off the sirens, but left the roof lights flashing. They joined Randy behind his car.

"What's up, Detective?" asked one of the four policeman.

"One gunshot from the house. Nothing else."

"Shooting at you?" asked another.

"Nope, don't think so. Inside."

"We going in?" asked the oldest of the four.

"Yep. Send two men around the side of the house. You cover me 'til I get to the house."

"Gotcha."

Randy kept low and ran to the front door of the first

floor. He peered through the window. The room was
empty. Stepping back, he could see a fringe of light from
the edge of an upstairs window. He motioned to the
man covering him that he was going upstairs. Within
moments, another officer joined him. Together, they went
up the wide, planked steps that ran along the side of the
house and led to a covered porch. Inside, the door to the
house was open. They entered the dark kitchen with guns
positioned to fire. Randy scanned the room and saw dirty
dishes, piles of clutter, and garbage.

The men moved through the living room and down the
hall. They checked the bedrooms, the bath, and the
closets, but found no one. The cloying aroma of rancid
perfume hung in the air. Randy remembered the scent.
Less than an hour ago he had smelled it on Monica
Foyles. This had to be the place she had described. She
thought it was near Love Field, and he had taken a chance
that the address he'd found in Phil Bruns's desk at the
theater and the house where Monica had been held were
one and the same.

Randy and the officer stopped at the stairway leading to
a third floor. The door at the top was ajar. A faint light
shone through the opening.

The officer behind him yelled, "Police! We have the
house surrounded! Throw down your weapons and show
yourself!"

Silence. Randy looked at the man behind him. He figured the kid was maybe three months away from his
police training.

"They teach you that at the Academy?"

"Yes, sir!"

Randy nodded and climbed the steps. At the top, he
nudged the open door wider and smelled death. A woman
lay facedown over an old iron bedstead. The rest of the
attic was empty. Randy put his hands in his pockets and
walked closer. Another body lay beneath her. He slid his
finger along the woman's throat to check for a pulse.

"Oh my God!" said the rookie, as he joined Randy by the bed. "It's two women."

"No," Randy said. "Two men. Two dead men."

"But the dresses!"

"Two men, Officer. Get downstairs and radio head-quarters. Looks like a murder-suicide." *And a kidnapper.*

The rookie turned a pale shade of green and left. Randy heard him clattering down the steps. He'd probably stop to puke in the bushes. Randy remembered that he had after seeing his first dead body.

Alone now, Randy stepped closer to the bodies. The man on top was just a kid. He had died a short time ago from a direct shot to the heart. He was still clutching the gun with one hand and the dead man beneath him with the other. There were dark, sticky-looking red splotches on the boy's mouth. Randy figured it matched the blood on the old guy's face.

No doubt a tender kiss good-bye. . . .


"David? It's Monica. I'm safe."

Silence.

"David?"

"Do you have any idea how good it is to hear your voice?"

"It's good to hear yours, too. I had a few hours these last couple of days when I didn't think I ever would."

"Monica, I . . . ever since Randy called tonight to tell me you'd been found, I've been sitting here, waiting, hoping that you would call me. He said you're okay. Are you?"

"Yeah. I'm banged up a little. Probably won't sleep real soundly for a while, but there's no permanent damage."

"Where is the son of a bitch who kidnapped you?"

"I don't know. He's sick, David. Really sick."

David tucked the phone closer to his ear. He had waited so long to hear from her and now that he had, it wasn't enough. He wanted to hold her, to touch her face, to see for himself that she had survived. She was talking again and he forced himself to concentrate on her words.

"He was so scary. I never knew how he would act. One minute he was kind to me, the next minute he nearly killed me. Sometimes he was a raging maniac, and then he'd become a helpless, little boy. It was weird, David. He thought I was his mother. He wanted to have sex with his mother, with me!"

"Ohmigod! Are you all right?"

"Yeah, I'm okay. I got real lucky."

"Did he touch you? I mean did he . . . hurt you?"

"He slapped me around and I had some close calls, but he never raped me."

David released his breath. At least the bastard hadn't harmed her that way.

"He cut off my hair. David, I look awful."

"Never. Never in a million years could you look anything but terrific."

"Thanks," she whispered.

David heard the tears in her voice. "Where were you all this time?" he asked gently.

"At his place. It was near Love Field. I could hear the planes. He kept me drugged and tied in the attic for a couple of days. Then he moved me down to his mother's old room."

She needed to talk, to tell him everything. As much as it ripped him apart to listen, he did, knowing it was what she needed. She talked for almost two hours. She told him about the beating when Lenny had broken her arm, the gloves, the meals they had shared, the conversations they'd had, the clothes he'd forced her to wear, the agony of not knowing if she'd ever see her children again, the sexual confrontations—everything. Several times she broke down and wept. He wanted her to stop, but he listened to each word.

After she had shared every terrifying moment, she

stopped at last. Laughing softly, she said, "How's that for a bedtime story, David? Should we sell it to Hollywood?"

"Just as long as you don't play the lead, Monica. I can't go through this again."

"I know and I'm sorry. I wish I'd been able to let you know where I was, or that I was alive, at least."

"Please, Monica, don't—"

"David?"

"Yes?"

"I missed you. Have you been to Harry's lately? When I'm better I want you to meet me there. I thought about us, in that booth we sat in, talking and laughing, and it got me through some pretty rough moments."

"Monica?"

"Yes?"

"I don't expect you to respond . . . I just need to say this. Now. Tonight." He took a deep breath and let it out slowly. "I love you, Monica."

"David?" She sat up in bed.

"You don't have to say anything. I'm sorry if telling you makes you sad, or uncomfortable. I probably shouldn't have said it tonight. It's just that when you were gone, I made myself a promise that if you came back, I would tell you how I felt about you the first moment I had the chance."

"David, what a wonderful thing to say. I—"

"Hey, you've had several harrowing days. Put what I said in a corner of your mind, and concentrate on getting your strength back. And besides . . ."

It may have been his imagination, but he could feel her relax, and happily anticipate his next words, as she often did when they were together. Their solid line of communication was back. He envisioned her smile, the sparkle in her incredible eyes when she reacted to his bantering. He had missed her so much.

Fighting to play it straight, he said, "I'm warning you up front, though. This experience will not cut you any slack on the parent committee. I'll expect to see you this coming Thursday at four o'clock sharp!"

"And not before?"

His smart retort died on his lips. He could only speak the truth. "God, I hope so!"

# chapter
# 38

"What are you offering me, John?" Monica asked.

It was the following Wednesday afternoon. They had just returned from taking Monica's parents to the airport. The children were in school.

"What?" John looked up from the papers he had been gathering from his desk in the den.

"I was just thinking about our conversation on the way back from the airport. Could you elaborate a bit?"

"Does it have to be now? I'm due back at the office. The trip to the airport has already put me behind. Can't we talk tonight?"

He thought she was doing fine. Except for her arm and the cut on her face, no one would even guess what she had been through. Her hair looked different, but almost cute after a trip to the hairdresser's. Perhaps her experience hadn't been as bad as he thought at first. At any rate, she no longer needed extra coddling: She was certainly well enough that he could resume his normal routine.

Monica fingered the gray paisley scarf that supported her broken arm. It was now or never, she decided. "John, with the children, my parents, the police, the media, and all the people that have stopped by, we haven't had a minute to ourselves these past few days. You started something in the car, and I'd like to discuss it with you now."

"I just said you should think twice about some of the choices you're making in your life. Attending matinees behind my back was pretty stupid. You have too many responsibilities to waste your time like that."

"And what was it you said about the children?"

"I think you dote on them too much. Maybe you should look into a full-time job, or better yet, join some of those society women's clubs. Associations with the right people could bring me some great clients. But you can't ask the kids to fill your life. It's not fair to them."

"And?" She wondered if he was ever going to look at her. Since she had come into the den, he hadn't once lifted his eyes from his desktop.

"And I think our lives need to get back on track now. I've got my job and you've got your duties. I'm ready for some normalcy. We've had enough excitement. Now, may I return to this?" he asked, indicating the work on his desk.

"We need to talk, John. Now."

The determination in her voice finally penetrated his thoughts. He threw down his papers and looked at her. "All right, Monica. You want to talk here or in the living room?"

"In the living room."

When they were seated, she on the sofa, he on a nearby chair, he asked what was so important it couldn't wait until tonight.

"I want a clarification of your plans for the rest of our marriage. Are you offering me something different? Or more of what we've had for the past few years?"

"What do you mean?"

"I want to know what you're offering me."

"Monica, you're my wife. What's this about?" He shifted in his chair and rested his ankle on his opposite knee. His slacks had a small smudge near the cuff. He rubbed it and made a mental note to have her take them to the cleaners.

"It's about commitment, and love, and wanting to be together; to spend quality time, to be more than just a convenience to each other. I want a greater share of your life, John. I need more than the few crumbs you've set aside for me."

"A few crumbs? Lady, I busted my ass to find you these past few days. How about some credit for that? I put my entire life on hold!"

John stood up and paced the room. He had decided to stop seeing Beth. It was probably for the best. A relationship like theirs, so closely tied to his business life could cause problems eventually. Still, it would be tough to let Beth go. He couldn't expect Monica to know about that sacrifice, but it was one that counted with him. He turned away from the window and was unnerved to find his wife behind him.

"I know you did everything you could do to find me, John, and I'm grateful. I'll never be able to thank you for what you did, but that's over now, and we're back to leading separate lives."

She could feel his anger building. He glared at her and explained his point very slowly, as if she spoke another language. "I think I've given you a great life here. We have the kids, you've got the house—it's the nicest one you've ever lived in, and you've got plenty of money. I gave you all that! Me!"

"I appreciate everything you've done, John. You're a tremendous provider."

"What is it then? The kids? I spend whatever time I can with them. They know they can count on me. I may be gone a lot, but I try to be a good father."

Monica shook her head. "You're a great father! The kids adore you!"

John returned to his chair. "So . . . it must be *us,* then? You're worried about us. I'm working on that, too. I know I've been out of touch, but I've been honest about that. I told you I was having a rough time, trying to sort out my life, deciding what it was I needed. I get mixed up about that stuff sometimes."

"Are you mixed up about us?"

"We're married. We have kids. We share a home. I tell myself that's enough."

Now it was Monica's turn to walk around the room. The sun streamed through the bay window. Her geraniums and tulips had never looked prettier. She watched them nod in the breeze as she spoke.

"For a long time I've told myself that what we have is enough, but my experience, my . . ." She shivered when she thought about the attic, the ropes, Lenny's face when he beat her. "But now I know it's not enough."

"What's that supposed to mean?"

"It means that I'm not going to be content with just 'getting by,' ever again in my life. I've just survived a hellish time." She turned to him. "I almost died, John. He could have killed me at any minute."

John joined her at the window. "I know that, Monica." He ran his hand down her cheek and across the cast on her arm. "I know I nearly lost you. I'd kill that guy if he weren't already dead. When I think that he had his hands all over you and what he might have done to you, I want to beat the crap out of him and then kill him."

"I understand. It was horrible for you, too, but it's over, and I'll be fine. Can you tell me why it took something like this to make you realize that I'm more than a housekeeper and mother to your children? I can't help wondering how long this appreciation will last." She touched his face and managed to hide the slap of pain she felt when he stepped away from her. "John, is this marriage enough for you? Don't you want more?"

He looked at her. The anger was back in his eyes. "What do you want from me?"

"I'm not sure anymore. Whatever it is, I doubt you'll be able to furnish it." She forced herself to remain calm, to look him squarely in the eye.

John studied her. "Sounds like there's somebody else in your life."

"There might be."

"Christ, Monica!"

"There might be," she continued. "I'm not sure that I've met him yet, but there might be someone out there who could honestly care about me—not just as a convenience or for what I can do to make his life easier, but someone who really wants to share his life with me. I'm tired of being the fifth person you call in an emergency or the one you come to when you have nowhere else to go."

She moved so close to him that she could see the pulse beating in his temple. She was determined that this time he would not turn away. This time he would hear her out.

"I need someone who cares what *I* think and feel, who, more than once in a while, will put me first. I deserve that consideration. For a long time I thought that if I loved you, it really didn't matter how you felt about me as long as you stayed in the marriage. But now I know I can't settle for that, ever again."

What had happened to her? Who was this person? "Are you telling me you want a divorce? I don't understand you at all, Monica," he said.

Monica sighed and looked out the window. "I know you don't. I didn't expect you to. And yes, maybe it's time we think about some changes."

"Shit! Your timing is impeccable! How can I deal with one more thing today?" He looked at her, but got no response. "I think I need a beer." He headed toward the kitchen, then turned back and looked at her. "You want anything?"

"No, nothing, John." Nothing at all.

# chapter
# 39

"Randy? It's David. They make you captain yet?"

"Close. I'm just now picking out my new office furniture."

"Sure! You wouldn't give up that battered piece of junk you call a desk even if they did promote you."

"Damn, you know all my secrets," Randy said.

"Only the ones that'll get you in trouble."

"We both know there's plenty of them. It's nice of you to return my call just to hassle me." Randy picked up his cup of coffee and took a sip.

"Yeah, well, what are friends for? What's on your mind?"

"I have some interesting news. Ran across it today as I was doing some research for my final report on the case."

For no reason that he could put his finger on, David felt his heart rate quicken to a thousand. How long would it be before he could talk about anything concerning Monica's ordeal without a gut-wrenching reaction?

"What'd you find?" he asked.

"You know what Monica assumed about the kid's mother?"

"That she died maybe a couple of months ago and the kid went ballistic with grief?"

"Yeah."

"So?"

"So that was way off the mark. I checked the records. The kid's mother died in 1992."

"Three years ago?"

"When Lenny was sixteen. His uncle took care of him. Up until a year ago, they lived together in the place over by Love Field."

"Then all that crap about his mother?"

"I'm not totally sure, but we found some papers, a diary of sorts, and some other stuff in the house. Seems Mom was gone a lot. Often for months at a time. The uncle stayed with the kid, and evidently sexually and physically abused him."

"Geez, Randy. Do you think his mother—"

"Screwed him too? Again, I can't say, but she did slap him around and lock him in the attic. That's in her diary. So take your choice: Either Lenny fantasized that he was his mother's lover while Phil was abusing him, or Lenny *really* allowed himself to be used by her to 'prove his manhood,' so he wouldn't have to think of himself as entirely homosexual."

"What a choice! Either scenario would explain his madness," David said.

He could almost feel sorry for the kid. Monica did. Even after what he did to her.

Her Nolan Ryan T-shirt was soaked when Monica slid off her bike and smiled at Peach. He was dozing in his customary place beneath her built-in vanity in the bathroom. Since her abduction and subsequent return a month ago, he had rarely let her out of his sight. More than ever, Monica appreciated his vigilance. For several reasons, the past weeks had been an emotional roller coaster for her; at times, a terrifying ride that woke her in the middle of the night.

By mutual agreement, John had all but removed himself from her life. He had increased his travel schedule to five days a week, and often allowed his time away to overflow into the weekends. He still made some of the children's games and activities, and he phoned them a couple of times a week, but Jeb and the girls were getting used to his prolonged absences. John had urged them to continue with their lives as if nothing had changed. Monica wondered if they would be surprised when he stopped coming home at all.

She had seen David on several occasions. Each time, he had seemed glad to see her, but had suggested no further visits between the two of them. The phone conversation that night in the hospital when he told her he loved her might never have happened. His manner indicated nothing beyond friendship.

Monica couldn't believe how much she missed him, or how often he was in her thoughts. It had become an ache inside her that could no longer be satisfied with occasional glimpses at school or casual meetings in town. Right or wrong, she needed him in her life. Ironically, Peach had had his healthiest month in years, and so she couldn't even use the excuse of an ailing dog to see him.

The phone interrupted her thoughts. She caught it on the first ring and grinned when she recognized the voice. She felt like a school girl hoping for a date, and said the first thing that popped into her head.

"David, are you calling to badger me about today's meeting?" She had missed two of his parent meetings.

"Nope. It's been canceled. The superintendent is putting on a command performance at Central Office, and the principal and teachers must attend."

This was easier than she thought. "Gee, now what am I going to do with all the free time I'd set aside this afternoon?"

"Go to a matinee?"

"Funny, David. Very funny."

"How about some dessert and coffee at Harry's? I hear the lemon meringue is tremendous."

"About two o'clock?" Was that her heart pounding?

"Make it one. You can buy."

"Me? Why should I buy?" she asked.

"For the best of reasons. You have a rich husband."

"Uh, not for long, David."

Silence, then mumbling.

"What did you say?" she asked.

"Something along the lines of 'dreams really do come true.' Say, Monica?"

"Yes?"

"Let's make it twelve-thirty."

"And?" she asked.

"And I'm buying."

"David?"

"Yes?'

"I love you."

"I know. I'll be right over. . . ."

# FEAR IS ONLY THE BEGINNING